D0090177

HOMEROOMS &HALL PASSES

HEROES LEVEL UP

HOMEROOMS & HALL PASSES

HEROES LEVEL UP

By TOM O'DONNELL

Balzer + Bray
An Imprint of HarperCollins*Publishers*

Balzer + Bray is an imprint of HarperCollins Publishers.

Homerooms & Hall Passes: Heroes Level Up
Text copyright © 2020 by Tom O'Donnell
Illustrations copyright © 2020 by Stephen Gilpin
Map art copyright © 2020 by Jordan Saia
All rights reseverd. Manufactured in Germany.

ISBN 978-0-06-287217-3

Typography by Dana Fritts
20 21 22 23 24   CPIG   10 9 8 7 6 5 4 3 2 1
❖
First Edition

For Kieran, Ronan, Amelia, and Duke

STINKY SMITH

LEVEL: 9

PLAYER NAME: Devis

CLASS: Class Clown

ATTRIBUTES: Cunning: 18, Intelligence: 10, Likability: 14, Willpower: 10, Fitness: 12

SKILLS: Apple Polishing –8, Computer +4, Deception +8, Note Passing +7, Stealth +6, Persuasion +7, Practical Jokes +9, Standardized Testing –1, Trivia (British Sketch Comedy) +9

EQUIPMENT: Whoopee cushion, thermos of minestrone, new smartphone x 100

CLASS CLOWN

VALERIE STUMPF-TURNER

LEVEL: 9

PLAYER NAME: Vela the Valiant

CLASS: Overachiever

ATTRIBUTES: Cunning: 12, Intelligence: 16, Likability: 16, Willpower: 18, Fitness: 15

SKILLS: Academic Subject (English) +5, Academic Subject (Science) +5, Academic Subject (Social Studies) +5, Academic Subject (Math) +5, Apple Polishing +3, Athletics +5, Computer +5, Musical Instrument (Flute) +5, Standardized Testing +7

EQUIPMENT: Class schedule (erroneous), hand sanitizer, the Axe of Destiny

OVERACHIEVER

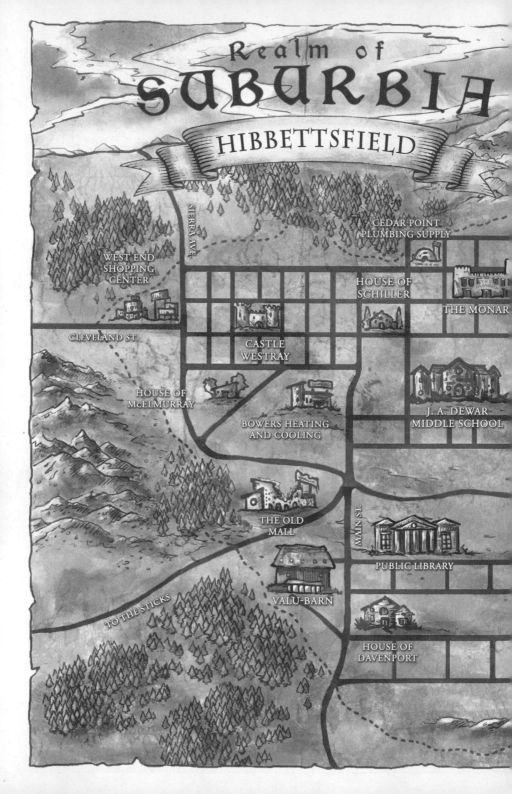

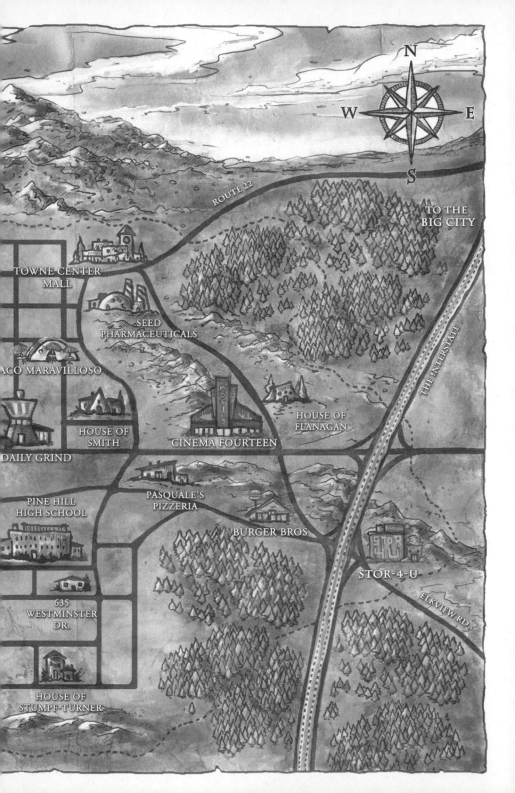

Chapter 1

So you think you know Homerooms & Hall Passes, huh? Well, think again, pal, because you don't know diddly-squat about the new and improved Advanced Homerooms & Hall Passes! Think you're ready to kick the greatest fantasy nonadventure game of all time up a notch? Welcome to high school.

—Excerpt from The Advanced Hall Master's Guide

FOUR YOUNG ADVENTURERS TRUDGED across a torrid wasteland. The scorching sun seemed to fill the sky above them. All around, shimmering dunes stretched out as far as the eye could see. The only landmarks here were the quickly fading tracks they left in the sand behind them.

"Onward, comrades," said Vela the Valiant, paladin and leader of the band. "We must not lose hope."

"Can't lose what you don't have," said Sorrowshade, the

gloom elf assassin, mopping her brow with a corner of her cloak. "I can admit wearing all black on this quest was a mistake, but Vela, how can you can have on armor in this heat?"

"It is not for a Knight of the Golden Sun to complain," said Vela. "But I will admit, there are some, ah, chafing issues."

"I just sneezed and nothing but dust came out," said Devis, the party's wily thief. "We better find this dungeon soon, because we're completely out of water." He dangled an empty waterskin upside down.

"Bah!" said Thromdurr, the mighty barbarian. "Water is for the weak! If I grow thirsty, I shall slurp the blood of my enemies!"

"Gross," said Sorrowshade as she surveyed the empty horizon. "Also, what enemies? There's nobody here. There's nothing but sand, sand, and more sand."

"We are not lost," said Vela, perhaps a tad too quickly. "Though it took us many months of adventuring, we collected all of the nine Sacred Keys, and we have journeyed to the very heart of the Blazing Barrens. The Sanctum of the Shifting Sands shall reveal itself soon."

"Before or after we die of thirst?" said Devis, plopping down on the hot ground to rest or possibly expire.

"You shall not perish, little friend!" cried Thromdurr.

"For I see an enemy full of thirst-quenching blood out yonder!"

"Nope," said Sorrowshade, whose eyes were far keener than those of her human companions. "That's just a pile of sand."

"Ah," said Thromdurr, continuing to search the landscape. "Well, is *that* a fearsome foe, mayhap?"

"No," said Sorrowshade. "That's different sand."

"Curses!" said Thromdurr. "But, wait, surely that dark speck, there, must be an adversary."

"Just a rock," said Sorrowshade. "I truly cannot imagine what it must be like to barely be able to see what's a mile in front of your face—"

"Did you say a rock?" asked Vela. "Legend tells of a rock, average in size and ordinary in appearance, that marks the hidden entrance to the sanctum!"

The paladin began to stride, then run, toward the distant speck, and the rest of the party quickly followed. Once Vela reached it—truly as unremarkable a rock as any the adventurers had ever encountered—she counted out forty steps due west and plunged her hand into a tall dune. At first she found nothing. Then a smile spread across her face as she brushed away the sand to reveal a heavy door made of bronze. Sure enough, it had nine keyholes.

"Behold," said Vela. "The Sanctum of the Shifting Sands."

"Well done, paladin!" said Thromdurr, cuffing her on the back. "You have truly—"

"Hold that thought," said Vela. "I just need to jot this down in my Journal of Deeds before I forget." Vela produced a small leather-bound book and a quill pen from her pack. "Located . . . long-lost . . . mythical . . . dungeon," she said as she wrote. Then she signed and dated the entry and got a witness (Sorrowshade) to initial beside it.

"Now then," said Vela. "What were you about to say, Thromdurr?"

"—outdone yourself this time!" said Thromdurr.

"Thank you, comrade," said Vela. "I only hope the Order of the Golden Sun is as impressed."

"Didn't you just earn a new rank from them?" said Sorrowshade. "Do you think another meaningless promotion will somehow distract you from the long, boring slog toward the grave?"

"Hopefully!" said Vela. "And I didn't *just* earn the rank. It's been nine whole weeks since I made Justiciar of Honor and Virtue. I cannot rest on my laurels."

"Bah!" said Thromdurr. "Climbing some imaginary ladder does not a hero make. 'Tis the glory of your exploits themselves that make them worth doing!"

"Personally, I prefer monetary compensation," said Devis. "Speaking of which, let's hit this temple that's supposedly filled with treasure beyond all imagining?" Despite his advanced dehydration, the thief was somehow drooling at the thought of so much gold. "I need to get my hands on that sweet, sweet loot. I hereby officially call dibs on any enchanted daggers, flasks of fleetness, cloaks of covertness, sandals of levitation, rat-summoning flutes, magic war hammers, and/or genie lamps we find."

"Wait," said Thromdurr. "Why should *you* get magic war hammers?"

Devis shrugged. "I dunno. I'm thinking using a war hammer could be my new thing."

"But it is already my old thing!" said Thromdurr. "None can deny that I am the war hammerer of this group!"

"Look," said Devis, "as the bard in my old party always used to say, 'There are no original ideas—'"

"Fine, then!" roared Thromdurr. "I hereby call dibs on all gold we find herein. How does that sound, thief?"

"You can't call dibs on gold," said Devis, shaking his head. "That's absurd. Totally against the spirit of dibs."

"You are inventing the rules of dibs as you go along!" said Thromdurr. "'Tis trickery meant to deceive a simple warrior like me!"

"You're so right," said Devis. "You *are* simple."

"Foolish mortals," said Sorrowshade, "arguing over riches you don't yet possess. Money can't buy happiness. Though, if this dungeon is as loaded as they say, I have always wanted to own my own castle. Somewhere dark, crumbling, preferably haunted. A nice, quiet place to just *brood*."

"I am sure we will find rewards aplenty," said Vela, "But do not forget the true reason we came here: to destroy the ancient evil that resides within."

"Sure, yep, uh-huh, the evil. Hate the evil," said Devis, still daydreaming about mounds of loot. "Ooh, just remembered I also need a cap of invisibility. Somebody write that down."

No one did. Instead, the heroes made their final preparations for the adventure ahead.

"Are we ready, comrades?" said Vela. "Torches?"

"Obviously," said Sorrowshade.

"Rations?" said Vela.

"We're really counting rations?" said Devis, rolling his eyes as he checked his pack. "Ugh. Okay, fine. Yes, we have enough rations."

"And is anyone currently afflicted with any persistent conditions such as temporary blindness, petrification, or magically induced fear?" said Vela.

The others shook their heads.

"Well then," said Vela, "may the Powers of Light guide our way." The paladin turned toward the dungeon entrance.

"Wait," said Thromdurr. "Before we enter in, can you

tell us anything of the evil we will face? The elders of the Sky Bear clan have a saying: 'Knowledge is the deadliest weapon (apart from swords, war hammers, axes, spears, morning stars, and ballistae).'"

Vela shrugged. "No one knows for sure the nature of that which haunts this dungeon. Only that it guards an item of immense power."

"Cha-ching," said Devis.

Sorrowshade dramatically threw up the hood of her cloak. "Perhaps the true evil is the greed that lurks within each of our hearts."

The heroes all looked at one another.

Vela cleared her throat. "No, I suspect it is more likely some sort of extra-large monster that will be difficult for us to defeat."

"Well, we will either vanquish the beast and emerge victorious or die the death of heroes and our names will live on in legend," said Thromdurr. "So I call it a win-win!"

"Into darkness then?" said Sorrowshade.

And so the party of adventurers inserted the Nine Sacred Keys into their Nine Sacred Keyholes to open the great bronze door. And they descended into the fabled Sanctum of the Shifting Sands, a labyrinthine temple of sandstone and glittering lapis lazuli. And there they did face many dangers. They were ambushed by a pack of magically animated jackal-headed statues, and they triggered a devilish trap that filled the room with sand, which was quite thematic. To disarm it, they were forced to decode a tile puzzle written in the hieroglyphics of a long-lost civilization (the solution was "Owl," "Owl," "Viper," "Eyeball," "Owl"). And indeed, they did accumulate much treasure along the way, filling their packs and pockets with coins and gemstones and fine jewelry.

Yet still they pressed on, till they came to a great stone doorway that was guarded by an evil sphinx, who posed a fiendish riddle to any who would pass. And when the party could not solve the riddle (the answer was "Sand"), they were at a bit of an impasse and it was slightly awkward. Even the sphinx seemed a little annoyed with them and gave them a few extra hints, to no avail. So at last they shrugged and simply attacked the creature (who, again, was quite evil!) and defeated it after a harrowing fight.

And here on the threshold, the heroes took a short rest to recuperate from their injuries before exploring further. While Devis power napped and Thromdurr quietly sang an ode to the great Sky Bear while he slathered on more muscle oil, Sorrowshade silently crept toward Vela as the paladin prayed to the Powers of Light.

"Look at this," said Sorrowshade, holding out a scrap of parchment.

"What is it?" said Vela. "A map?"

"No," said Sorrowshade, nodding toward the other two, "and keep your voice down."

Vela held the parchment close to the light of her sputtering torch. It read:

Warm and soft; they love to bound.
Puppies make the world go round.
Little noses, cold and wet—
Puppies are my favorite pet.

"What is this?" said Vela.

"A poem. Some pathetic, starry-eyed naïf must have written it," said Sorrowshade. "It sickens me. Do you like it?"

"I cannot lie," said Vela. "It is a *tad* saccharine. Even for me—"

"I wrote it!" hissed Sorrowshade.

The paladin was shocked. "Sorrowshade, I had no idea you had poetical aspirations. Nor a favorite pet. If you had pressed me, I suppose I would have guessed some sort of blind, venomous eel."

"I know," said Sorrowshade. "It's not like me at all. I've been feeling strange lately. Like I don't totally *hate* everything? It's awful."

"Perhaps," said Vela, "you are feeling . . . happy?"

"Ugh," said Sorrowshade. "Like you?"

Vela nodded.

"Is there a way to get rid of it?" said Sorrowshade.

"We cannot always control our feelings," said Vela. "Sometimes the best we can do is try to understand them."

"Okay, what you said did irritate me a little," said Sorrowshade. "It's a start."

And the gloom elf spoke no more of the matter. Though Vela did catch her out of the corner of her eye setting the scrap of parchment alight with her torch.

Rested and re-oiled, the adventuring party continued through the great stone doorway to the very heart of the subterranean complex. They came to a sheer ledge with a perilous rope bridge crossing a fathomless pit. Carefully they traversed the chasm, and on the other side they found a semicircular chamber lined with hundreds of sarcophagi— the final resting place of the forgotten pharaohs and queens who had built the place.

And there, upon a stone pedestal ahead, stood the prize of the Sanctum of the Shifting Sands: a splendid battle axe, illuminated by a slanting shaft of sunlight from somewhere far above.

Vela's eyes widened. "I *know* this weapon," said the paladin. "It is the Axe of Destiny!"

"Pure mithril with gold inlay and an emerald the size of

a goose egg stuck in the pommel," said Devis. "I'd have to consult my magic item price guide, but I'd say it's the Axe of Early Retirement."

"I call dibs on axes!" cried Thromdurr.

"Aw, come *on*," said Devis, throwing his hands up.

But the barbarian was already striding toward the weapon.

"It's clearly an ancient relic of incredible power," said Devis, trotting after him. "So we need to sell it to the highest bidder and split the money!"

"Comrades, we simply cannot barter away such a remarkable weapon," said Vela, who hurried after the other two. "The Axe of Destiny has a higher purpose. According to legend, its wielder can turn the tide of one unwinnable battle. At a critical moment it could stanch the onslaught of evil!"

"Or, and hear me out on this one," said Devis, "each of us could buy a boat."

"As usual, you mortals ignore the obvious," said Sorrowshade, whose keen eyes darted around the chamber as she drew her bow.

"What is that, elf?" said Thromdurr as he grabbed the handle of the axe and pulled.

"Do you truly think we can just waltz in here, grab the priceless artifact, and be on our merry way without facing the ancient evil of the temple?" said Sorrowshade.

"Huh?" said Thromdurr, straining with all his might. "Was not the sphinx the evil?"

"It was certainly rude," said Devis. "I mean, if four professional adventurers can't guess your dungeon riddle, maybe it's not their fault. Maybe it's *yours* and you need to rethink—oh." The thief slapped his forehead. "Guys, the answer was 'Sand.'"

"Sand!" said Vela and Thromdurr in unison, slapping their foreheads as well.

And at this moment the Axe of Destiny came free from the pedestal with an audible click.

"Still, all is well that ends well," said Thromdurr. "The axe is ours."

And the barbarian held the battle axe above his head. The weapon gleamed in the shaft of improbable sunlight, and none who saw it could deny that it looked extremely heroic. But Sorrowshade's eyes were elsewhere.

"It's not the end," said the gloom elf, nocking an arrow. "We're just getting started."

The other heroes turned to see that all the sarcophagi lining the walls of the chamber had opened. Each contained a desiccated figure, clad in rotting bandages and royal garb. Their sunken eyes glowed red with hatred for the living. The corpses began to lurch toward the adventurers.

"Mummies!" said Vela. "Don't look them directly in the eyes. That's how they use their curse power, which they can each do three times a day. To destroy a mummy, you must strike for the heart. Now, Sorrowshade, you strafe left. Devis, you strafe right. I'll press down the middle and attempt to rebuke them with my holy symbol to create an opening for—"

"DIE AGAIN, DUSTY GHOULS!" roared Thromdurr, swinging the Axe of Destiny with both hands and charging forward.

"Thomdurr, no!" cried Vela. "If the Axe of Destiny is wielded in a battle that is *not* unwinnable, it will curse its wielder with certain defeat!"

"Kind of a lot of rules for an axe," said Devis.

"BAH! I COULD BEAT THEM WITH MY BARE HANDS!" bellowed Thromdurr, dropping the axe and unslinging his mighty croquet mallet. "BUT BONESHATTER II WILL BE FASTER!"

And so the four heroes fought a desperate battle against the ancient queens and pharaohs of the Sanctum of the Shifting Sands. Sorrowshade's arrows flew fast, pincushioning their undead foes, while Thromdurr's mallet swatted them down in twos and threes. Devis the thief fought with guile and finesse, while Vela the Valiant called upon the Powers of Light to sear the vile creatures with luminous power from her holy symbol. Yet each time a mummy was defeated, it was only a moment until it rose again to attack with renewed vigor. And as the battle raged on, the heroes found themselves on the defensive, guzzling healing potions, forced to fight enemies they had already beaten.

It was only then that Vela put together that the horrid creatures didn't carry their hearts within their bodies. And while the others kept up the fight, Devis snuck from sarcophagus to sarcophagus, smashing clay jars until he found the particular vessel that held each monarch's dried-out heart. And in this way, one by one, were the mummies truly defeated.

The party was victorious, but the battle had taken its toll. Vela's sword had been broken in the fight, and Sorrowshade had used all but four of her arrows. Thromdurr bled from a dozen wounds, and Devis's pockets were so filled with gold and jewels plundered from the sarcophagi that he could barely move.

"Okay," said the paladin, exhausted from the fighting. "Those mummies must have been the true evil of the Sanctum of the Shifting Sands."

And that was when the giant scorpion appeared.

"Seriously?" said Devis.

A colossal arthropod the size of a horse cart scuttled up from the dark pit they had crossed. In front it had two pincers, big enough to shear a person in half. In the back, it had a stinger full of deadly poison that could strike at its enemies lightning quick. Worst of all, the monster had blocked the heroes' only exit from the chamber, back across the rope bridge.

Vela charged in, wielding her broken sword. A slashing strike from the scorpion's pincer tore a wicked gash across her chest, while she barely managed to raise her shield in time to avoid the deadly stinger. Thromdurr swung his mallet, yet the creature's chitinous shell was as tough as plate armor and the haft of Boneshatter II snapped. The scorpion barely seemed to notice. As Devis watched Sorrowshade's last four arrows ricochet off the monster's hide, he knew his own daggers would be of little use.

The scorpion danced back, surprisingly agile for a creature its size, still blocking the bridge. In its crude intelligence it knew the weary heroes' attacks were ineffective and was content to bide its time and pick them off one by one.

"I am sorry to have led you here," said Vela as she regrouped with the others. "We cannot win. Nor can we hope to escape."

"Sounds pretty unwinnable to me," said Devis. "Would now be a good time to break out the good old Axe of Destiny, or what?"

Vela sighed, uncertain, and picked up the enchanted

weapon, but Thromdurr stopped her.

"Nay," said Thromdurr. "We cannot risk the axe's curse. There is a way to win this fight. Though the price will be great." The barbarian threw down his broken croquet mallet. "Know that I have valued my time with you more than gold or precious salves. Truly, in your own way, each of you has the spirit of a warrior. Tell the same to the wizard Albiorix, if you ever see him again."

"Thromdurr, what are you saying?" cried Vela.

"FOR THE SKY BEAR!" bellowed Thromdurr.

Before anyone could stop him, the barbarian charged toward the giant scorpion. Instantly it snapped a pincer around his chest, pinning him tight. Thromdurr winced as the barbs bit into his flesh, but somehow he kept pressing forward. Though caught in the monster's iron grasp, he used his incredible strength to force the creature backward a single step. Then, two steps. Then three . . .

"Look!" cried Devis. "He's unblocked the bridge."

"The fool is sacrificing himself to save the rest of us," said Sorrowshade.

Tears welled in Vela's eyes. "I cannot leave him here to die!"

"We have to!" cried Devis, who was already emptying his pockets of their burden of treasure as he darted toward the bridge. "Or the rest of us will die too!"

"*The fool,*" hissed Sorrowshade. And she raced after the thief.

Vela waited another instant, agonizing over what to do. She closed her eyes.

"By the Powers of Light," said Vela, "I swear your sacrifice will not have been in vain."

And Vela followed the others. As they sped across the swaying bridge, she gave one last look over her shoulder.

Thromdurr still stood on the lip of the chasm, crushed in the scorpion's claw. Yet even in his pain, he managed a smile. His eyes met Vela's.

"Go," said Thromdurr. "But do not forget me."

And at that moment, the scorpion plunged its stinger into the barbarian's heart. Instantly Thromdurr's skin turned a sickly gray from its venom. He stumbled a half step and his eyes rolled back in his head.

"No," said Vela under her breath.

But Thromdurr didn't give up. Though poison coursed through his system, the barbarian blinked and shook his head.

"YOU ARE A WORTHY FOE, PINCER BEAST," roared the barbarian at the giant scorpion. "BUT SO AM I. PERHAPS WE SHALL FIGHT AGAIN IN THE UNDERWORLD!"

And with his last ounce of strength, Thromdurr forced

the giant scorpion over the edge of the pit. Vela watched the pair of them plummet away into darkness and certain death.

And so Thromdurr, son of Heimdurr, berserker of the Sky Bear clan and barbarian of the Steppes of Ursk, gave his life to save three others.

Chapter 2

A word of warning to the faint of heart: Blowing It is much, much easier in Advanced Homerooms & Hall Passes. Players who expect a friendly Hall Master to hold their widdle-biddy baby hands and fudge the rolls to save them are in for a rude awakening! When you run this game, your goal is to depict the merciless challenges of high school no matter how arbitrary, harsh or unfair. Every time one of your players has to roll up a new character, you can take pride in a job well done. . . .

—*Excerpt from* The Advanced Hall Master's Guide

❧

"OKAY, FOR A ROUTINE resurrection spell," said the Priest of Light, "that's going to run you eight thousand six hundred and forty-four gold pieces."

There was a moment of awkward silence.

". . . Excuse me, how much?" said Vela.

"Eight thousand six hundred and forty-four gold pieces," said the priest.

Vela frowned. Sorrowshade whistled. Devis rubbed his temples. The three of them stood in the grand Temple of Light in the city of Far Draïz. Their fourth companion—what was left of him, anyway—lay on a table nearby.

"And why, exactly, does resurrection cost that much?" said Devis, gritting his teeth.

The priest blinked. "We are literally bringing a soul back from the dead and . . . and the ritual uses a *lot* of incense."

"Please excuse us for a moment," said Vela. "My comrades and I must confer."

The adventurers removed themselves to the far side of the chamber, while the priest rocked on his heels and tried not to eavesdrop.

"Look," said Devis, "Thromdurr was great. He really was. But I think he would want us to try to move on and enjoy our lives without him."

"Devis!" cried Vela.

"We went to the trouble of climbing down a three-hundred-foot pit, fishing all the Thromdurr bits out of the giant scorpion goo, and lugging his *incredibly* heavy remains the whole way back across the desert to civilization," said Sorrowshade. "So if we actually don't bring him back to life, at this point, I'm going to be really, *really* annoyed."

"But death is a part of life," said Devis. "Pretty sure that was a Snow Badger clan thing that my old buddy Thromdurr always used to say. He was wise, in his dumb way."

"He paid the ultimate price to save all of us!" said Vela. "That would have been a total party kill back there."

"I know, I know," said Devis. "And I think the best way to repay that sacrifice is if we all got our own boats. I'm thinking of calling mine the *Loud Barbarian*. Pretty poignant, huh?"

"Look, I hate to put a damper on things," said Sorrowshade, "but do we even have enough money?"

The adventurers ran a quick inventory of all the treasure they had recovered from the Sanctum of the Shifting Sands—magnificent goblets, beautiful jewelry, gleaming crowns and scepters, and coins of ancient mint. Setting aside the Axe of Destiny, which Vela would only sell or barter as a last resort, the grand loot total came to 10,665 gold pieces. It was enough. As they counted out enough treasure to pay the priest, Devis closed his eyes. He couldn't bear to watch.

And so the Priest of Light pulled closed the sacred curtain and the adventurers listened to him chant a holy ritual in Celaestine, the language of the divine, and indeed a thick cloud of incense filled the room. And after five minutes or so, the priest yanked the curtain back with a flourish. The resurrection was complete.

"WHOA!" said Thromdurr, sitting bolt upright.

"Welcome back, buddy," said Devis. "You owe me two thousand one hundred and sixty-one gold pieces."

"WHAT?" said Thromdurr.

"Sorry to rip you from the velvet embrace of death," said Sorrowshade. "How was the afterlife? Was it dark? Tell me it was dark."

"I DON'T REMEMBER!" said Thromdurr, leaping to his feet. "DID I KILL THE SCORPION THING? WHERE AM I? I'M STILL PRETTY AMPED UP FROM THAT FIGHT! MY FEET FEEL WEIRD!"

Vela put a hand on the barbarian's arm to calm him. "You gave your life to save us all."

"THE ULTIMATE HERO'S DEATH!" roared Thromdurr. The barbarian did a heroic fist pump.

"Is the yelling a side effect of the resurrection?" asked Sorrowshade.

"No, I think that is merely his personality," said the priest.

And so the party of adventurers made their way toward the exit. As they did, the Priest of Light stood by the door and cleared his throat and held out his hand. There was another awkward moment of silence.

"Seriously?" said Devis. "You want a tip?"

The Priest said nothing. But he did not retract his hand.

Vela fished into her coin purse. "How much do people usually, ah . . . ?"

"Twenty percent is customary," said the priest. "But whatever you feel won't risk the wrath of the gods."

"The Cloak of Covertness is eight hundred gold pieces," said the merchant.

"Mmm," said Devis. "And do you have any sort of installment plan?"

The merchant's eyes narrowed.

"How much for a three-month lease?" said Devis.

The merchant folded the magic cloak and put it away. Devis moved on through the market warren of Far Draïz, a winding maze of shop stalls shaded from the blazing sun.

After the cost of Thromdurr's resurrection spell (plus gratuity) the grand total of their dungeon haul came to 293 gold pieces. Divided four ways, each of the adventurers received 73 ¼ gold pieces for their efforts. Not a great return on the months of work they'd put into finding the keys and the Sanctum of the Shifting Sands. Devis was grumbling to himself about this very subject as he caught up with his other companions.

Sorrowshade was eyeing a pair of matte black krakenskin boots she couldn't afford. Vela had given up on purchasing a new shield and was haggling uncomfortably with a blacksmith over the cost of getting her old shield unbent. And Thromdurr the barbarian was, for the fifth or sixth time since they had left the Temple of Light, recounting his amazing death.

"And then . . . I was all like, 'Run, little friends! Run for your tiny lives! Thromdurr the barbarian will save you!'" cried Thromdurr.

"Not *exactly* how I remember it," said Sorrowshade.

"And you all fled like rabbits—"

"We didn't flee like rabbits," said Sorrowshade.

"Fine! Like mice, then!" cried Thromdurr. "You fled like timid mice and left me to face the monstrosity alone: a scorpion the size of a galley ship. . . ."

"It was nowhere near that big," said Sorrowshade.

"He's still talking about this, huh?" said Devis.

Sorrowshade nodded and pantomimed shooting a bow and arrow at her own head, as Thromdurr continued his tale, oblivious to who was listening.

"Well, I got a lightly used longsword and my shield unbent for only five gold pieces," said Vela as she rejoined them. The paladin squinted at her shield, which honestly still looked a bit off.

"I bought some new arrows and some foot salve," said Sorrowshade. "My old boots make blisters."

"You know, the bard in my last party had a policy," said

Devis. "When we went on a quest, everyone just kept whatever treasure they found. It worked out fine."

"Truly?" said Vela. "It seems such a rule would create an atmosphere of ruthless backstabbing and intraparty conflict."

"Those were the days," said Devis, wiping the corner of his eye.

"Well, if we pool all the money we have left, I believe we can afford two healing potions," said Vela. "We drank our last ones in the dungeon."

And so they did.

"Well, this adventure has been a total bust," said Sorrowshade. "Predictable."

"I disagree," said Vela. "We recovered the Axe of Destiny and destroyed the evil of the Sanctum of the Shifting Sands!"

"That evil wasn't bothering anybody," said Sorrowshade, kicking a pebble.

"Ooh, that reminds me," said Vela. The paladin brought out her Journal of Deeds and began to write down the party's exploits in the dungeon. "Hopefully this will be enough for the Order of the Golden Sun."

". . . and the beast plunged its stinger into my very heart!" cried Thromdurr, who was still telling his story. "The heart! One of my most vital internal organs, dear friends!"

"Sorry, I'm just going to use my last three coppers to buy some cotton balls to stick into my ears," said Devis.

And so the party of bold adventurers made their way out of the market warren and onward to whatever challenge awaited them next. Though they could not guess it would find them so soon.

At the edge of the market, a merchant with a large and colorful headdress stepped in front of them, blocking their way.

"Greetings, friends," she said. "Might I interest you in my wares? They are unique among all the sellers of this bazaar."

"Sorry, but we are a bit tapped out at the moment," said Vela. "Perhaps next time."

"Truly you do not want to miss these items," said the merchant. "We have treasures from lands far away. Behold!"

And with a flourish, she waved to a nearby table. On it was a pair of sneakers. Beside that was a hoodie with the words Pine Hill High School emblazoned on it. And beside that was a Spinco Roastmeister home rotisserie, still in the box.

The adventurers all looked at each other.

"Mmm," said the merchant, with a little smile. "Something has caught your eye."

"It has," said Vela. Her voice sounded uneasy.

The paladin picked up a smartphone from the corner of the table. It was in a protective case with a shiny holographic pattern. On the back was a goofy, faded *Oink Pop* pig sticker. The entire party recognized the object.

It was June Westray's phone.

Chapter 3

Big Surprises are a huge part of what makes Advanced Homerooms & Hall Passes so much more fun than the dumb old games your grandsire used to play! As Hall Master, you must always be ready to spring something totally unexpected on your players. Ideally, you want to keep them perpetually disoriented and occasionally terrified. . . .

—*Excerpt from* The Advanced Hall Master's Guide

THE OLD BLIND MAN sat by the fire of the tavern, his raven croaking on his shoulder. Outside, a thunderstorm raged.

"Come hither, me lad, and I'll tell you a tale," said the old man, stroking his long white beard. "A tale of treasure lost and glory found; a tale of two star-crossed lovers, one a doughty dwarf, the other a lizard woman most fair, who together discovered an ancient kingdom beneath the—"

"Sorry, I don't mean to be rude," said Albiorix, cutting the man off, "but is this going to be a quest?"

The old man blinked. "Well, yes."

"I don't do quests," said Albiorix.

"Strange," said the old man, "you have the brave—"

"—and hardy look of an adventurer," said Albiorix, finishing the man's sentence. "I know. I think maybe what you're reacting to is that all my clothes look sort of wizard-y."

The man nodded. "Are ye not a wizard?"

"Nope. Common mistake," said Albiorix. "I'm a tavern lad. Speaking of which, can I take your order?"

The old man seemed a bit flustered. "Er, sorry, I hadn't thought about it yet. I was preparing my quest pitch, you see."

"Do you need a few more minutes to decide?" said Albiorix.

"No, no, I'll just go with the mutton shank," said the old man.

"An excellent choice," said Albiorix. "And anything to drink? Or are we just going to stick with water tonight?"

"Water is fine," said the old man.

"Water is fine," repeated his raven.

Albiorix relayed the order to the innkeeper of the Wyvern's Wrist, whose name was Frumhilde.

"Did you tell him about the specials?" said Frumhilde.

Albiorix slapped his forehead. "I forgot to mention the ambrosia-glazed cockatrice in lotus fruit reduction."

"That were yesterday's special," said Frumhilde, gritting her teeth. "Today it's boiled yams."

Albiorix apologized again and grabbed the food for his other two tables. He delivered a rare aurochs steak to a noblewoman whose ancestral lands had been overrun by bloodthirsty hobgoblins, and a small fruit salad to a hobgoblin whose cavern home had been overrun by bloodthirsty humans. Albiorix politely declined their quests, for the second time, as he refilled their drinks.

After Albiorix lost his apprenticeship with the Archmage Velaxis, Frumhilde had taken pity on him and offered him a job as a tavern lad. She'd even given him free lodging in the dusty attic of the Wyvern's Wrist. Though she apparently had a soft spot for him, it turned out that Albiorix wasn't an especially good tavern lad. He often mixed up orders and forgot to upsell the customers from ordering the house mead. Once he'd spilled an entire bowl of turnip soup all over the lap of a Ytherian warlord and had to talk the man down from returning with his howling armies to burn the place to the ground and pillage the surrounding countryside.

And then there were the quests. All day long Albiorix got quests thrown at him in the form of rumors, cryptic letters, crumbling maps, and the hardest of all to refuse: sob stories. Part of Albiorix really wanted to help those in need, but he just wasn't an adventurer anymore.

He didn't have the inclination. He didn't have an adventuring party. And at a practical level, since his apprenticeship had ended, his magical skills had gotten very rusty indeed. He occasionally tried a little something from his spellbook in the privacy of his attic room. Often the spell simply fizzled. When he did manage to cast the spell, it was usually somehow *off*. His lightning bolts arced backward and ended up shocking him. His conjured fog clouds had an incredibly unpleasant odor, like damp bugbear in summer. He created the illusion of a dancing frog but somehow ended up quadrupling the length of his own tongue, a side effect that luckily wore off after a few days. Without the Archmage breathing down his neck, Albiorix found the necessary mystical meditations and endless practice of wizardry to be very tedious.

It wasn't that Albiorix saw tavern lad as a long-term career path. He just didn't quite know what else to do with himself. He missed his old party. He missed the Realm of Suburbia. He missed June Westray.

So the former wizard spent his free time trying to design his own game. Conscious of not hewing too close to Homerooms & Hall Passes—how could he compete with the greatest game ever?—Albiorix was working on an abstract board game he called Octagono. The object was for each player to maneuver all of their octagons into their corral while preventing their opponents' octagons from preventing their octagons from entering their corral. Or their opponents' corral.

That was the simplest way Albiorix had of explaining it, at least. By the time he had gotten that far, most listeners' eyes had glazed over. Frumhilde occasionally told him to read the rules of Octagono aloud when she wanted to clear out the tavern common room of the Wyvern's Wrist at the end of the night. All but one of the people Albiorix had invited to "playtest" Octagono with him had politely told him it was the most boring, unfun, overly complicated nonsense they had ever encountered. None had ever asked to play it again. A few had never even spoken to him again. So it was clear he still had a little more work to do on the game.

As Albiorix was delivering the mutton shank to the old man with his raven, thunder crashed. The door of the tavern blew open dramatically. Four rain-soaked figures stood in the darkness outside. Albiorix cursed his luck. It was a slow night. But more patrons at the Wyvern's Wrist likely meant more quests he would be forced to awkwardly decline.

But when the new arrivals stepped into the light and warmth of the inn, Albiorix saw four familiar faces: a noble paladin, a dour gloom elf, a shifty thief, and a hulking barbarian.

"Well met, Albiorix," said Vela with a smile.

"Don't you 'well met' me. Come in here for the real thing!" said Albiorix as he hugged them all. "Welcome, welcome! Have a seat! Dinner's on me!"

"Normally, I would politely decline such an offer," said Vela. "But . . ."

"We're broke," said Devis.

"No worries. No worries at all," said Albiorix. "Here, let's get you out of those wet cloaks. The special today is boiled yams!"

Albiorix seated his friends, and together they feasted. In fact, he was a little surprised about how hungrily they gobbled their food. Devis must not have been joking about the state of their finances. But that was the life of an adventurer. Very unstable. The only one who seemed eager to talk during the meal was Thromdurr, who recounted an amazing tale of sacrificing himself to save the others. As soon as he finished the story, he started it again from the beginning. Albiorix politely nodded through a second telling. Before having to listen to it a third time, Albiorix cut him off.

"So, ah, what brings you all back to Pighaven?" said Albiorix.

"It is a matter of some concern," said Vela. "Please do not be alarmed, but—"

"June Westray is dead," said Sorrowshade.

"What?" said Albiorix. His heart sank. The world reeled.

He felt like he was going to be sick.

"Well, she's *probably* dead," said Sorrowshade. "We don't actually know."

"So say *that* then!" said Albiorix.

"Sorry," said Sorrowshade, with a shrug. "If we *assume* she's dead, then maybe we'll be pleasantly surprised when she's not?"

And so the adventurers told Albiorix of finding June Westray's phone, along with several other Suburban items, in the unlikeliest of places—at a random merchant's stall across the Western Ocean in the city of Far Draïz. Albiorix almost didn't believe it until Vela plunked the phone down onto the table. His heart sank again, though not quite so far this time. It was definitely June's.

"We do not quite know what it means," said Vela, "though clearly someone, somehow has traveled to Suburbia. Someone has gone back inside our Homerooms & Hall Passes game. We hoped it might be you."

"It wasn't," said Albiorix. "I meant what I said about Bríandalör and Suburbia not mixing."

"You sure you haven't been sneaking back there to see your girlfriend?" said Devis.

"Not my girlfriend!" cried Albiorix, a bit too loud. "I mean, er . . . did the merchant say where she got the items?"

"Apparently she imported them from a seller in

Wharfharbor," said Vela. "Not far from here."

"This isn't good," said Albiorix. "It means my worst fears are founded."

"Ooh, I love a good worst fear," said Sorrowshade as she speared a boiled yam with her fork. "Do tell."

"Ever since we got back from Suburbia, I've had a lingering worry in the back of my mind," said Albiorix.

"That June doesn't feel the same way?" said Devis. "Not going to lie, I *did* kind of get that vibe from her. I feel like she'd be into shorter men."

"Well, maybe June's dead and it's a moot point," said Sorrowshade.

"It's not that!" said Albiorix. "When we defeated Azathor the Devourer and I asked him for his boon, I said, 'All who are not of this place—be they demon, warlock, or adventurer—shall return from whence they came.'"

"Of course," said Thromdurr. "Otherwise we would still be stuck inside our game and I never would have gotten to do my amazing hero death."

"Right," said Albiorix. "But I realized later that I worded it wrong. Demon, warlock, and adventurer included Azathor, Zazirak, and all of us. But it didn't cover everything."

"How so?" asked Vela.

"Well, I didn't say 'evil spellbooks,'" said Albiorix, burying his head in his hands. "So I'm pretty sure the

Malonomicon is still in Suburbia. And I can't help but think these two things are related."

"Wish wording," said Vela, shaking her head. "So important to an adventurer, but they do not teach it in school."

"And that's not all," said Albiorix. "A month ago, all my Hall Master's notes from our Homerooms & Hall Passes game were stolen."

"What does it all mean?" said Vela.

"It means that until we get to the bottom of this, Suburbia is in danger," said Albiorix, rising from the table. "Finish your yams. We leave for Wharfharbor tonight."

Chapter 4

Characters need cash! Without it, they won't be able to purchase necessary equipment like sneakers and noise-canceling headphones. In the Realm of Suburbia, you can't just stroll down to your local dungeon and kill a few goblins to get your walking-around money. Luckily, Advanced Homerooms & Hall Passes features new employment options for player characters. As high schoolers, they can choose from such lucrative vocations as lifeguard, babysitter, dog walker, ice cream scooper, carnival game attendant, and more.

—Excerpt from The Advanced Hall Master's Guide

❧

I N THE SEEDIEST QUARTER of the exceptionally seedy city of Wharfharbor—between a burned-out tenement and a coffin maker's store—there stood a little pawnshop called Wurt's Wares. It was the kind of place where items were bought and sold with no questions asked and no reasons given. Retail was a tough business, but Wurt made it work. The desperate and the unlucky always ensured that his shelves got restocked.

Lately, though, the pawnshop owner had had a remarkable run of good fortune. Wurt had recently become the sole purveyor of items available nowhere else in Bríandalör. His source was a mysterious supplier, who came to his shop at odd hours with more inventory to sell.

At first Wurt stocked the shelves of his little shop with these wondrous new things: brightly colored clothing and strange gadgets and small glowing rectangles called "phones." These usually stopped glowing for good after a day or so, but Wurt never mentioned that to the customers. It said No Refunds right there on the wall, so who could complain?

Business boomed. Eventually, though, Wurt found more profit in reselling these foreign goods to other merchants at a tremendous markup. Now he shipped them all over the land, and the gold kept piling up. A stroke of good fortune indeed.

Why had Wurt been chosen by this particular supplier? He didn't know. He never asked, of course. But he suspected it was his natural discretion. For a pawn shop owner, keeping your mouth shut was a professional necessity.

The bell of the shop door jingled as the cloaked fellow entered. Right on time. He was older than a boy but younger than a man, and he had the daring look of an adventurer about him. Wurt's Wares saw its fair share of adventurers, but they were mostly thieves, looking to discreetly offload valuables they had recently, er, obtained. This lad had a bit more panache than your average thief, though. He carried a rapier and a finely crafted lute and called himself Tybal. Wurt knew it was an alias. But who could blame the lad? Wurt wasn't exactly his real name either.

"Well, well, well," said Wurt. "What've you got for me this time, my boy?"

"Treasures beyond your wildest imagination," said Tybal with a half smile. "The single greatest haul yet. I guarantee you will not be disappointed."

Tybal flopped his floppy hair to one side and swung a heavy sack onto the counter. Wurt licked his lips as he waited to see what curiosities it might hold. Rich nobles all over Bríandalör paid top price for this lad's rare foreign merchandise.

"Behold!" said Tybal, yanking the drawstring away with a flourish. The sack fell open to reveal a pile of bracelets. Wurt was confused, and honestly a bit disappointed. Bracelets didn't quite have the exotic quality he'd come to expect from Tybal's deliveries. But then he picked one up. On it was a tiny clockface, the size of a coin. The hands ticked the seconds away. Wurt gasped.

"By the gods," said Wurt, "they're amazing."

"They're called . . . watches," said Tybal.

Just then the bell on the door of Wurt's Wares jingled again. Wurt scowled. In his eagerness, he had forgotten to lock up and flip the sign from Open to Closed, as he usually did when Tybal paid him a visit.

"Go away," said Wurt. "We're closed."

"Sorry to bother you, good sir," said a girl clad all in armor, "but I am afraid your shop has something we're looking for."

Behind her stood four others, about the same age as Tybal himself. Adventurers, if Wurt had to guess.

"What's that?" said Wurt. Perhaps he could offload a few "watches" immediately. Provided these five could pay the exorbitant price he had in mind.

"We're looking for him," said a grim-looking elf with a black bow on her shoulder.

Wurt's eyes met Tybal's. Tybal smirked.

"Out the back," hissed Wurt.

Tybal somersaulted over the counter and dashed for the back door of the pawnshop, which led into one of Wharfharbor's countless unnamed back alleys.

The five adventurers raced toward the counter just as

Wurt slammed and latched the iron cage door that func-
tioned as his security system in the (very frequent) event of
a robbery.

"I said we're closed," said Wurt with a yellow grin.

The adventurers had no choice but turn around and
leave the way they had come: out the front door of the pawnshop they'd been watching for days.

"I know that guy," cried Albiorix as they exited into the
darkened streets of Wharfharbor. "With the hood of his
cloak up I couldn't quite tell before, but I met him a few
months ago at the Wyvern's Wrist. Right before my H&H
notes got lifted!"

The party circled the pawnshop, headed for the alley
behind. But when they got there, they found it empty. Tybal
was gone.

"Up there," said Sorrowshade, whose eyes were keener in
darkness than in light.

They looked up to see the hem of a cloak disappear over
the eave of the roof.

"Sorrowshade, can you scale the wall if we give you a
boost?" cried Vela, looking around. "Where is Thromdurr?"

It was a few seconds more before the berserker came
around at a leisurely jog. It was very unlike the barbarian to
lag behind his companions.

"Pick up the pace," said Sorrowshade. "You're running

slower than Albiorix!"

"Hey!" said Albiorix, still out of breath.

The barbarian shrugged. "Faster? Slower? It makes little difference. Either we will catch the fellow or we won't. In truth, I doubt this adventure will top my amazing scorpion death," said Thromdurr. "Besides, I outran Devis, did I not?"

The thief was nowhere to be seen. But the others had little time to look for him or to address the barbarian's shocking apathy. Tybal was getting away. With Vela and Albiorix's help, Sorrowshade spidered her way up onto the roof. She looped a rope around a chimney and tossed down the other end. The paladin and the wizard followed her up. Presumably Thromdurr did as well, but no one looked back to check.

They saw that Tybal had already crossed two more roofs. He turned to blow them a kiss before nimbly springing across another alley and catching the eave of a higher building. Tybal swung his feet up and started to run.

"I've got this. Nobody messes with my H&H stuff and gets away with it," cried Albiorix, pulling out his spellbook. *"E dekaerer ma'rn a'ph aeri!"*

Albiorix's eyes glowed icy blue. A helix of frigid magical energy swirled around his outstretched palm as he cast the frostbolt spell and . . . somehow froze both his feet to the roof he was standing on.

"Ugh! What?" cried Albiorix. The wizard tried to move.

He was stuck fast. "Go on without me!"

So Vela and Sorrowshade left their immobilized companion behind as they continued after their quarry. The gloom elf and the paladin made the same long jumps across the intervening alleys and clambered up onto the higher roof.

Ahead, Tybal had nearly crossed this rooftop as well. He sped up for another leap across another alley. Sorrowshade froze and nocked an arrow. Just as Tybal's boots left the ground, the assassin let fly. The arrow pinned his trailing cloak to a nearby rain gutter. With an awkward snap, Tybal was yanked backward out of the air and landed flat on his back with a thud.

Vela caught up to him a moment later. "Stop right there, floppy-haired stranger!" she cried, drawing her sword. "And tell us what you have been up to in our Homerooms & Hall Passes game!"

"Please, don't hurt me," groveled Tybal. "I—I don't want to be doing this. I'm not a bad person. I have no choice. They're—they're forcing me." He looked up at the paladin with fear in his eyes.

"Who?" cried Vela. "What are they forcing you to do? Are they making you search for the Malonomicon in Suburbia? Do they possess the book already?"

"No," said Tybal in a quavering voice. "They're forcing me to . . . to . . . to do this!"

Tybal sprang toward the surprised paladin and shoved her off the edge of the roof.

For an instant Vela was airborne. Yet instead of plummeting to her death, she somehow managed to catch the edge of the rooftop with her hand. Her lightly used sword clattered down to the alley fifty feet below as she hung by one arm.

Tybal peeped over the edge of the roof and smiled down at Vela. "The Malonomicon, eh? Infamous spellbook chock-full of vile, forbidden knowledge? Yes, I do believe I've heard of it. In Suburbia, you say? Good to know. Could fetch a nice price for the right buyer. Somebody evil. But more important, somebody rich. Thanks for the tip." He nodded. "I owe you one."

"Not so fast, you oily fop," hissed Sorrowshade as she stepped out of the shadow of a nearby chimney. Her bow was trained on Tybal's heart.

"Ooh, dramatic entrance. I respect that," said Tybal, throwing both his hands up. "Points for style. But I'm not a fop. Unlike you, I happen to take pride in my personal appearance. The gods grant but one chance to make a first impression." He shot her a gleaming smile. "Now that I've made mine, I'm afraid I really must go. I do hope you make the right choice."

"What choice?" said Sorrowshade.

"Capture me or save your friend," said Tybal. And then

he stomped on Vela's fingers.

Vela screamed and let go of the roof. Sorrowshade had a split second to react. Anyone slower would not have been able to help the paladin. But with inhuman deftness, the gloom elf dropped her bow and dove to catch Vela's arm. Vela was saved, but her bulky armor made her too heavy for Sorrowshade alone to haul back up onto the roof.

"The power of friendship. Personally I don't get it, but to each their own," said Tybal. "Well, this has been moderately amusing, but know this: Suburbia belongs to me now. Don't get in my way, or things will go worse for you than they did today, which, let's be honest, was quite badly. Wouldn't you agree?"

"You're a corpse full of arrows, even if you don't even know it yet," hissed Sorrowshade as she strained to hold Vela.

"Yikes. So menacing. I love it," said Tybal. "In fact, you've inspired me, m'lady." He unslung his lute from his back and began to strum. Then he sang:

"Now gather 'round children and you'll hear a tale
Of an elf maid grim and daaaaark!
She had a mane of greasy black hair
And the charm of a hammerhead shaaaaark . . ."

Sorrowshade seriously considered dropping Vela to choke Tybal as he turned his back to her and casually sauntered away singing his (irritatingly beautiful) song. But before she'd made her choice, another figure called out.

"Stop right there!"

Devis the thief had appeared from somewhere. He stood in Tybal's path, fists balled at his sides. Tybal paused.

"Sorry, that came out a little harsh," said Devis, staring at his feet. "I feel like maybe this is all just a big misunderstanding and we can work it out, so, you know . . . would you, uh, *mind* stopping? Please?"

"I would mind," said Tybal, tousling Devis's hair. "You were right about this party, Goblinface. A few splashes of inspiration here and there, but ultimately quite boring. Let me know if you ever want to earn some real gold again. Farewell."

Tybal sauntered past—the thief didn't move to block him—and walked another dozen paces or so, still strumming his lute. Then he turned and gave a wink and disappeared into thin air.

Albiorix arrived a moment later—stumbling on feet still numb from the magical ice he'd conjured—and helped Devis and Sorrowshade drag Vela back up onto the roof.

". . . I *really* didn't like that guy," said Sorrowshade, who was quietly deciding on which of her poisons she would use on him the next time they met.

"He was somehow both utterly infuriating and quite

charming," said Vela. "I cannot believe he took advantage of my trusting nature to shove me off a roof!"

"When that guy came through the Wyvern's Wrist a while back, he complimented my robes and laughed at all my jokes," said Albiorix. "Eventually I got around to telling him about the new board game I'm designing. He played Octagono and said he loved it. He was the only person who ever said that, and I'm starting to suspect it was all a ruse to gain access to my Homerooms & Hall Passes notes to somehow get to Suburbia. But how could he have known about our adventure inside the game?"

Sorrowshade's eyes narrowed. "And how did he know you, Devis?"

"Did he know me?" said Devis, who still stared at his feet. "Oh yeah, I guess maybe he did."

"Who is this Tybal, really?" said Albiorix.

Devis cleared his throat. "His name is Tristane Trouvère. And he's the bard from my old party."

Chapter 5

Friends are crucial to surviving high school. Without them, the academic and social grind can easily over-whelm hapless player characters. As in the real world, the bond of true friendship is irreplaceable. When a true friend is present, player characters get a +1 bonus to all Social Ability Checks and a −1 penalty to all Saves versus Peer Pressure.

—Excerpt from The Advanced Hall Master's Guide

❧

*T*HE PARTY SAT IN the common room of a rough-and-tumble inn on the waterfront called the Sailor's Sad Song. After locating Thromdurr—during the rooftop chase, the barbarian had wandered into a clothing shop and started browsing the scarf section—they had retired here for the evening. The other patrons were all shady nautical types. Many had parrots. The heroes had only been there an hour, and they'd already seen three fist-fights break out.

The light of the fireplace twinkled in Devis's eyes. "So, you want to hear the story of Tristane Trouvère?"

The rest of the party nodded.

"Remember a while back, after we left Albiorix, when you guys were off exploring the Bog of Feculence?"

"Yes," said Vela, crinkling her nose. "Mayhap our smelliest quest ever. We tried to breathe through our mouths as we scoured the putrid swamp for the fourth key to the Sanctum of the Shifting Sands."

"The Sanctum of the Shifting Sands!" cried Thromdurr, suddenly tuning in to the conversation. "That is where my legendary giant scorpion battle and subsequent death took place—"

"Stow it," said Sorrowshade.

"As I recall, Devis, you could not accompany us because your bum knee was acting up," said Vela.

"Yeah, I was faking it," said Devis, "because the Bog of Feculence sounded, well, kind of gross."

"I cannot believe you took advantage of my trusting nature to feign injury and shirk your duties!" cried Vela.

"I know," said Devis. "But I promise I won't ever lie to you again."

"I am glad to hear it, friend," said Vela, brightening.

". . . Um, I think he might be doing it right now," said Albiorix.

Vela cocked her head. Devis shrugged and nodded. Vela sighed.

"Well, anyway," said Devis, "while you guys were off slopping around in the mud, I was relaxing in a tavern in Far Draïz. And that's where I happened to run into Tristane Trouvère. We went on a lot of adventures together back in the day, and say what you will about him, he's a lot of fun."

"He shoved Vela off a roof," said Albiorix.

"Right," said Devis. "But aside from that, he has plenty of personal style, and he's always ready with a witty quip, and you heard him sing. The guy has got pipes."

"Not a big fan of his singing," hissed Sorrowshade, who looked like she might poison Devis now.

"Fine, but he's always been really nice to me," said Devis.

"Didn't he call you Goblinface?" said Albiorix.

"Yeah, that's a funny inside joke we have," said Devis. "He gave me that nickname because he says my face looks all scrunched up and weird, like a goblin's face."

"Not going to disagree," said Sorrowshade. "Still seems a bit harsh."

Devis shrugged. "We always had a playful back-and-forth! Anyway, Tristane and I were catching up, and it turns out the rest of the old party died in a dungeon collapse and he was the sole survivor. Poor guy. That's actually happened to him a couple of times, which, now that I'm saying it, does sound sort of suspicious. But he told me this amazing story about how he tricked a cloud giant into giving him this magic flying chariot—the guy is quite a storyteller. So then, when he asked me what I'd been up to, I didn't quite know what to say."

Albiorix crossed his arms. "Yet you still said something, didn't you?"

"I may have mentioned, ahem, a tiny bit about our Homerooms & Hall Passes adventure in Suburbia," said Devis.

"What exactly did you tell him?" said Albiorix.

"Um, well, let me think. It might have been . . . everything . . . in exhaustive detail," said Devis. "Up to and including all of your names and the precise location of the Temple of Azathor where we translated the Old Dragonian curse that ultimately trapped us inside the game."

"Oh, Devis," said Vela with a sigh.

"You don't understand!" said Devis. "Tristane Trouvère is just so *cool*. You can't help but want to impress him. I mean, did you see his hair?"

At this, there was a moment of uncomfortable silence in the group. Though they were loath to admit it, each member of the party knew in their hearts that Tristane Trouvère *did* have very impressive hair.

"Well, now he's threatening the people of Suburbia," said Albiorix. "Including June." The wizard held up her smartphone.

"And to make matters worse," said Vela, "I inadvertently revealed to him that we left the Malonomicon there."

"See!" said Devis, "It's easy to accidentally tell him stuff."

"Now I'd give it an eighty, maybe eighty-five percent chance that spellbook's eldritch evil will once more be unleashed," said Albiorix. "It's easier than you'd think!"

Sorrowshade squinted at the wizard. "If you're willing to cast spells you can't read."

When the party was in Suburbia, Albiorix had mistranslated an arcane ritual and accidentally resurrected the undead warlock Zazirak, an unfortunate turn of events that had nearly killed them all.

"Yes! I agree!" said Devis. "Let's all shift focus onto how Albiorix screwed up last time. Albiorix, I'm still really, really disappointed in you." The thief gave the wizard a very serious look.

"Stop," said Albiorix. "It doesn't matter how we got to this point. It matters what we do next. June is in trouble. We need to get back inside the game. We have to save the Realm of Suburbia once more."

The heroes all looked at each other.

"Is the game world even real?" said Devis. "Where did we land on that?"

"It's real!" said Albiorix, knocking June's smartphone against the table for emphasis.

"I confess I am hesitant to return," said Thromdurr. "In a realm without monsters or dungeons, there is a vanishingly small chance of me topping my glorious death."

Sorrowshade glared. "You know, if you *really* want to die again, I can arrange something."

"Thromdurr, it's a whole different world," said Albiorix, "so maybe there's something super glorious you can do in Suburbia that doesn't even exist here—something even better than shoving a giant bug off a ledge."

Thromdurr considered this. "I doubt it, friend. But I have always known you to be wise. Fair enough. I accept this likely fruitless quest. I pledge to give it moderate effort!"

"That will have to do," said Albiorix. "How about you, Sorrowshade?"

"Saving Suburbia is all well and good," said the gloom elf assassin, "but I want revenge on that handsome crooning creep. I'm in."

"And I as well," said Vela. "The innocent people of the Realm of Suburbia are at risk, and more than that, if Tristane Trouvère obtains the Malonomicon, that puts all of Bríandalör in danger too. Imagine a villain even more powerful than Zazirak getting their hands on that dark book."

They all turned back to Devis now. The thief shifted uncomfortably in his seat.

"Look, he's not that bad a guy once you get to know him!" said Devis.

His companions now glared.

"Fine, fine," said Devis. "At least I'll finally get to eat some real soup again. In Bríandalör we can make unicorn saddles and floating castles, but somehow we can't manage a half-decent clam chowder? It's ridiculous." The thief shook his head. "So what's the plan, Magic Man?"

"Well," said Albiorix, "it appears that Tristane Trouvère needed my Hall Master notes to exploit the same curse that trapped us inside our own Homerooms & Hall Passes game."

"Except it seems he can come and go as he pleases," said Vela.

"Right, that's different," said Albiorix. "There must be something more at play."

"Too bad June's phone is dead," said Sorrowshade. "It might tell us something useful. Like how June died."

"Please stop saying that," said Albiorix. "But . . . it's not a bad idea. Perhaps if I used a fine-tuned lightning spell, I could charge the phone enough for us to learn something."

Instinctively, the others backed away from the table.

"What?" said Albiorix.

"It's just . . . ," said Vela. "Well, we saw what happened when you, ahem, attempted to cast frostbolt, back there on the roof. . . ."

"The rest of us don't want to get fried!" said Devis.

"For what it's worth, I do not care that much," said Thromdurr, cuffing Albiorix on the back.

"Look, I'm a little rusty at magic, that's all," said Albiorix. "But I trained for years in the arcane arts. I know what I'm doing."

Albiorix pulled out his spellbook and flipped to the appropriate page: "Call Lightning." Just as the Archmage Velaxis had taught him, he centered his mind and visualized the branching fractals of electricity arcing between two thunderheads. Then he bent all his mental focus on harnessing the arcane weave of magic to produce the smallest amount of electricity possible. Albiorix pointed his fingertip at the phone's charging port and read aloud: *"Tyael ael e raekyntaetk ma'rn na' phsh ha'oi."*

A tiny spark of electricity crackled up his fingertip and arced to the phone. A moment later, the dead battery image appeared onscreen. Zero percent charged . . . then one percent . . . then three. It was taking all of Albiorix's mental focus, but the spell was working. He was still a wizard yet. The screen of the phone lit up.

On it was a text message exchange, dated September 14:

Morton: **hey whats up?**

June: **nothin u?**

Morton: 🐵

June: 🦖

"Interesting," said Devis, who was reading over Albiorix's shoulder. "Looks like she's got a serious boyfriend."

With a deafening thunderclap and a blinding flash, Albiorix's lightning spell surged. The phone screen exploded, and a cloud of acrid smoke rose from the charred device. The common room of the Sailor's Sad Song went silent as everyone turned to stare at the adventurers.

Vela stood. "Apologies, friends. Our companion's girl-friend appears to have met someone new."

"Please don't tell them that," said Albiorix, burying his head in his hands.

"I cannot lie," said Vela.

The other patrons nodded sympathetically and went back to drinking and carousing and fistfighting—all save one. A man in a wide-brimmed hat with a wooden peg leg stumped across the tavern toward their table.

"Avast, landlubbers," said the man, scanning the table. "Be one of ye Vela the Valiant?"

"I be . . . er, am," said Vela.

"A parcel for ye arrived aboard the good ship *Sea Goose*,

this eve," said the man. He dropped an envelope on the table, gave a curt nod, and stumped away.

The envelope was large and heavy, sealed with a sunburst insignia. Vela held it up and took a deep breath.

"It's from the Order of the Golden Sun," said the paladin. She ripped it open. After a moment of uncertainty, her face lit up. "They granted my promotion! I am now officially ranked a Knight-Commander of Justice and Righteousness!"

"And aside from how tedious it is to say," said Sorrowshade, "how exactly is Knight-Commander of Justice and Righteousness different from Justiciar of Honor and Virtue?"

"It is one rank up!" cried Vela. "In truth, I suspected I had been granted the title once I saw the envelope. If it is good news, they always send a big envelope."

"Congratulations, Vela," said Albiorix. "Sorry to cut the celebration short, but, well, I think we have more pressing matters to consider."

"You are right," said Vela. "I have enjoyed this recognition, but I must now set my sights upon earning the title of Grand Seneschal of the Gleaming Sword!"

"Uh, no," said Albiorix. "I mean saving June and everyone else from Tristane Trouvère and the Malonomicon."

"Oh, yes, of course," said Vela, catching herself. "To

return to the Realm of Suburbia, it seems we must get back to the Temple of Azathor and trigger the curse yet again?"

"That's the only way I know," said Albiorix.

"Yet this time there will be no Archmages, nor any demon lords to bring us back to Bríandalör," said Vela.

"Right," said Albiorix. "We'll just have to find another way. You mentioned seeing a Pine Hill High School sweatshirt where you found June's phone, right?"

"And a Spinco Roastmeister home rotisserie!" said Thromdurr.

"Well, I think that hoodie means Tristane Trouvère isn't inside Homerooms & Hall Passes at all," said Albiorix.

The rest of the party was confused now.

". . . He's not?" said Vela.

"Not exactly," said Albiorix. "It seems the bard has been playing Advanced Homerooms & Hall Passes."

The next morning, the party stood on a crowded Wharf-harbor street outside a small, dingy shop. Above it hung a crudely painted wooden sign that read Grull Games.

Albiorix gave a wistful sigh. "Boy, this place really takes me back. It's where I bought my first Homerooms & Hall Passes book ever: *The Fulsome Folio of Foods.*"

"Why was *that* the first book you bought?" said Devis.

Albiorix shrugged. "It had the coolest cover. The big

bowl of macaroni and cheese just looked so . . . *evocative*."

"And explain to me again why we can't just use the three hundred H&H books you already own to track down and crush Tristane Trouvère?" said Sorrowshade.

"I only own twenty-seven, and they won't help us much," said Albiorix. "First edition Homerooms & Hall Passes takes place in middle school. But they just released a whole new edition of the game called Advanced Homerooms & Hall Passes. It's compatible with the original game so you can keep your beloved characters and continue your campaign, but it takes place in high school."

"Seems like a scam to sell a new set of books to people who already bought a bunch," said Sorrowshade.

"It's not!" said Albiorix. "The new version of the game is way more intense: more class options, more complex social dynamics, more high-stakes standardized testing. It's time to take your players to the next level: high school!"

"Are you just repeating their advertising copy, word for word?" said Vela.

"Maybe," said Albiorix. "But it doesn't matter. Pine Hill High School seems to be where Tristane Trouvère is making mischief. It won't do us much good if we're still eighth graders stuck at J. A. Dewar Middle School. To catch him, we need *The Advanced Hall Master's Guide* and the first AH&H adventure module they published. It's a sequel to the classic

The Semester of Stultification. It's called *The Freshman Year of Futility.*"

"Perhaps this is an obvious question," said Vela, "but why have you not already bought these books?"

"Believe me, I wanted to. But since our old campaign effectively manifested an alternate dimension full of sentient beings, I figured I probably shouldn't be toying with metaphysical realities beyond my comprehension," said Albiorix. "That, and . . . I don't have anybody to play with."

"Oh, wow," said Devis. "That's sad."

"Come here, sorcerous friend," said Thromdurr, giving Albiorix a crushing hug. "You are a unique and precious flower. You know that, right?"

"Thanks," said Albiorix. "It's good to see you guys again."

Sorrowshade peeped through the window. "We ready?"

"Yeah," said Albiorix. "Grull is a great guy, but this place can be a little intimidating at first if you're not used to, uh, game store culture. Just follow my lead."

The party slipped inside the dimly lit shop. The shelves were lined with exotic board games with names like Bean Counter, Salt Merchant, and Docent! that none in the party had ever heard of, save Albiorix, who knew every single one of them. Though this place was in a completely different world, it somehow reminded them all of another store they had encountered not so long ago: Pan-Galactic Comics and Collectibles.

"You know, I come from a lightless forest full of giant albino spiders," said Sorrowshade, "but I must say, this shop even gives me the creeps."

"By the Powers of Light!" Vela's hand instinctively moved to her sword as she caught sight of the owner.

Behind the counter stood a vicious-looking nine-foot-tall ogre, who was painting a tiny statuette of a substitute teacher with an impossibly small brush. The monster turned and glared at the party with beady black eyes.

"WHO GOES THERE?" roared the ogre.

Everyone drew his or her weapon, except Albiorix.

"Grull, don't you recognize me?" said Albiorix.

The ogre squinted.

"Oh, hey, man!" said Grull with a big smile of sharp, rotten teeth. "Long time no see! How's the whole apprentice wizard thing going?"

"Um, not great?" said Albiorix. "I'm an ex-apprentice wizard now."

"I feel you, man. I feel you," said Grull. "My parents wanted me to be a lawyer, but I had to follow my passion: hobby games retail!"

"Speaking of which," said Albiorix, "I'm here to buy *The Advanced Hall Masters Guide* and *The Freshman Year of Futility*."

Grull looked pained. "Oof, no can do, man. All sold out

of both." The ogre pointed to a conspicuously empty shelf behind him.

"What?" said Albiorix. "But I thought they printed up loads and loads of copies of the new edition."

"They did," said Grull. "I had tons of the books until one guy came through and bought them all up."

"Let me guess," said Sorrowshade. "Floppy hair. Lute. Stabbable face."

"Yep," said Grull. "He was super friendly, but for some reason I still wanted to, like, grind his bones to make my bread or whatever."

"Tristane Trouvère must be trying to cover his trail so nobody can follow him back into the game," said Albiorix. "Well, thanks anyway, Grull. I really hate to do this, but I guess I'll probably have to go to Harkon's Hobbies to get the books I need."

"They don't have any copies either, man," said Grull. "Way I hear it, the guy bought up every single Advanced Homerooms & Hall Passes book in the whole city of Wharf-harbor."

The party looked at each other. Albiorix frowned.

"Not good," said the wizard. "Each minute we waste looking for game books puts June and the rest of Suburbia at further risk. Thanks for trying to help, Grull."

The heroes turned and started to leave the store.

"Wait," said Grull. "Do you need the books for something important?"

"We do," said Albiorix.

Grull nodded. "I wouldn't do this for just anyone. But ever since I saw you run the Field Trip of Disappointment at LothlóriCon, two years ago, I knew you were the real deal when it came to Hall Masters."

The ogre reached under the counter and pulled out a slightly worn copy of *The Advanced Hall Master's Guide* and *The Freshman Year of Futility*.

"These are my own personal books that I use to run my home game," said Grull.

"Oh, wow, this is . . ." Albiorix trailed off, overcome with emotion. "Thank you, Grull. I promise I'll get them back to you."

Grull nodded. "Roll on, my man."

"Roll on," said Albiorix.

And so the five brave heroes journeyed forth from the city of Wharfharbor into the trackless wilderness. And there they faced many perils, including brigands, harpies, and a pack of surprisingly aggressive carnivorous mushrooms. At last, after many days of hard travel, they came upon the mole-faced entrance to the forgotten Temple of Azathor (though it seemed less and less forgotten these days). And here the hardy band descended into the darkness of the dungeon.

Below the earth they gave a cursory thrashing to a now-familiar tribe of goblins and somehow almost triggered the reactivated poison dart trap before re-disarming it. (Indeed, this sparked an interesting discussion within the group: who resets dungeon traps?) Luckily, no one had bothered to change the answer to the magical door's riddle ("Love") though, and all agreed it was much fairer than the stupid "Sand" one the sphinx had posed.

Deeper they delved, until at last they came to the very heart of the place: a dark hall of fallen columns and piled bones. And there, of course, was the hidden chamber with its curse carved in Old Dragonian.

Albiorix laid out the borrowed game books and his pile of dice. "Okay, first we need to play the game." The wizard passed out four blank character sheets. "Unfortunately, you have to remake your old characters. Your sheets got stolen along with my notes, so you'll have to do it from memory."

"I'm pretty sure my guy had eighteens in all his stats and was a millionaire," said Devis.

"Please don't cheat, Devis," said Albiorix. "It's not just a game anymore. We're messing with other people's reality now, so we have to be extremely careful going forward."

Using the new Advanced Homerooms & Hall Passes rule set, the other heroes set about re-creating their old game characters: Valerie Stumpf-Turner the Overachiever, Stinky

Smith the Class Clown, Melissa McElmurray the Loner, and Douglas Schiller the Nerd. Thanks to the experience points they had earned defeating Zazirak, Albiorix declared they were all Level 9 now.

"What else?" The wizard drummed his pencil on *The Advanced Hall Master's Guide* as he racked his brain. "Oh yeah, can somebody please add Armando Boort's Canadian passport to their Equipment list. I won't have a character, and I'm not eager to have to prove I exist all over again."

"It shall be done!" cried Thromdurr as he scribbled it down on his sheet.

"Thanks," said Albiorix. "And I think there's just one more thing: September 14 was the date of those text messages we saw on June's phone."

"The texts from June's new, serious boyfriend!" said Thromdurr.

"We don't know that," said Albiorix, who realized how defensive he sounded. "But hey, good for her if he is, because I don't care. I mean, I'm happy. Very happy!"

"Riiiight," said Sorrowshade.

The wizard did some quick math in his brand-new blank game notebook. "Anyway, based on how long ago you guys found the phone, I'm estimating it's currently . . . October 5 in the town of Hibbettsfield. Which means I'm going to have to come up with some reason why you are all enrolling at Pine Hill High School three weeks late."

"What if we all caught some horrific wasting disease?" said Sorrowshade. "That would be fun."

"Ooh, that's a great reason for missing the first few days of school," said Albiorix. "Very creative. You'd make a good Hall Master."

"Seems like a lot of work," said Sorrowshade.

And so Albiorix laid out the setting for them: the placid and tedious town of Hibbettsfield in the utterly banal Realm of Suburbia. The season was summer, a sweaty time of mini golf and pool parties. The group played through the story of how each of their characters had spent the break after their eighth-grade year.

Valerie played on a club soccer team while attending a two-month program that simulated what it was really like to be a college freshman. Stinky got a part-time job at a frozen yogurt shop that had virtually no customers, freeing him up to goof off all day long with the other young employees. Douglas Schiller went to a very selective astronaut camp and excelled at the math and science portions but was too nausea prone for any of the flight simulators. Meanwhile, Melissa McElmurray mostly stayed in in her room, listening to depressing music while avoiding direct sunlight and conversation with her family.

At first it was a bit awkward to return to the game of

Homerooms & Hall Passes after so long. But soon the group fell into an easy rhythm. Sitting among the ancient ruins, they played for hours. They laughed and did funny voices and rolled piles of dice, eventually losing themselves in the fictional world. Sorrowshade even smiled. Twice.

And at the end of summer vacation, all their characters spontaneously came down with a made-up Homerooms & Hall Passes disease called mono that occasionally afflicted the teenagers of this realm. The simultaneous timing of their illness was a little implausible, but this was a world that asked you to believe there were no magic swords, so you couldn't really quibble about verisimilitude. And thus, Valerie Stumpf-Turner, Doug Schiller, Stinky Smith, and Melissa McElmurray all ended up missing the first three weeks of high school.

". . . And as you enter the Pine Hill cafeteria for the very first time, you are impressed by the sights and sounds of your new environment. Everything you thought you knew about school feels different here. There are different cliques, different rules, and higher stakes. It's clear that this place will bring a whole new set of challenges," said Albiorix as he closed the scenario book. "And I think we've played enough, so that's where we're going to end it for now."

"Wait!" cried Thromdurr, who sounded a bit like his old self. "We did not get to choose our lunches! Which food options will not inflame Douglas the Nerd's many allergies?"

"We'll have to find out next time we play," said Albiorix. "Or, actually, once we're trapped inside the game with no obvious way back to the real world."

"So the next step is to loot the room, is it not?" said Vela.

"I'm on it," said Devis.

The thief entered the empty chamber. The last time they'd been here, this hidden treasure vault had been thoroughly cleaned out by the dungeon goblins they'd beaten earlier. (Who knows what game the poor creatures got trapped inside by the curse? Some strange goblin version of checkers?) But the adventurers had a plan for this: they'd recovered some of the room's stolen loot from the goblins they defeated earlier.

"Hopefully this counts," said Devis. He dropped a jeweled goblet, a platinum tiara, and a pile of gold coins on the ground. The thief tapped his foot as he waited a few seconds. Then he picked the treasure up again and walked out of the chamber. "Room: technically looted."

"Excellent," said Albiorix. "Now I think it's time for us to change."

Each of them found a secluded corner of the hall and changed from their normal clothing to the odd, brightly colored garments they had brought back with them from Suburbia before.

As they reconvened, they almost looked like the five average high school kids pictured on the cover of *The Freshman Year of Futility*.

"Is everybody ready?" said Albiorix.

"I am somewhat enthusiastic!" cried Thromdurr.

"I'd call myself willing but skeptical," said Devis. "Again, I don't really think Tristane Trouvère is the prob—"

"I'm ready," hissed Sorrowshade, *"to gut that pretty boy and wear his skin."*

The other heroes all looked at her.

"And save everyone or whatever," said the gloom elf.

"I too am eager to undertake this quest to protect the innocent and thwart evil," said Vela, "and if I happen to receive another promotion, that would be fine too!"

"I noticed you have not been scribbling in your little book of late," said Thromdurr. "Have you finally realized your meager exploits cannot ever compare to my amazing scorpion death?"

"No, it is because earning the rank of Grand Seneschal of the Gleaming Sword only requires one deed," said Vela. "Performing a miracle."

"Oh, is that all?" said Albiorix.

Vela smiled and nodded. Sarcasm still eluded the Knight-Commander of Justice and Righteousness.

"Well, hopefully we won't need a miracle to locate

Tristane Trouvère and the Malonomicon and get out without causing too much trouble," said Albiorix. The wizard took a deep breath. He realized that for the first time in a long time, he felt happy. Though their purpose was serious, he had been dreaming of returning to Suburbia ever since they'd left.

From memory, Albiorix recited the curse: "Woe to thee who loots this room. . . . Let thy respite be thy doom."

And as expected, in a puff of magical smoke, they were gone.

Chapter 6

The transition from a middle school to high school is not for weak-willed players. One moment, H&H characters are eighth graders, supreme in their academic environment, lording it over the pathetic sixth and seventh graders beneath them. The next, they are dropped into a place where they are at the absolute bottom of a totally new social hierarchy dominated by seniors, some of whom are legal adults with cars and mustaches and everything! The worst mistake an Advanced Homerooms & Hall Passes player character can make is assuming you are more important than you really are.

—Excerpt from The Advanced Hall Master's Guide

❧

THE FIVE HEROES INSTANTLY found themselves standing in a crowded lunch line, in a world that was not their own. The transition was disorienting, and it took them a moment to find their bearings. But this wasn't their first adventure trapped inside a fantasy role-playing game of nonadventure. Past experience gave them some sense of how to act.

"I am behaving normally!" said Thromdurr. "I, Douglas the Nerd, am behaving normally!" The barbarian picked up a salt shaker and showed his peers he knew what it was.

"Nobody cares," said an older kid with blotchy skin.

A few other kids snickered.

Sorrowshade stood on her tiptoes to take a look at what meal was on offer. "Well, the food's still disgusting in this world. I'm both disappointed and comforted. Also, I'm definitely not eating any of *that*." She pointed to a tray of glistening, gray pasta salad.

Vela crinkled her nose and nodded. "A paladin often fasts to reaffirm her connection to the gods. So maybe I will just do that."

"No, no, guys," said Albiorix. "Everybody get lunch. Don't act weird."

"The only weird thing is your giant grin," said Sorrowshade. "You look deranged."

"What? I'm not—" Albiorix realized he did have a big smile plastered across his face. "Okay, fair point." He dropped it and tried to mimic the blank, vaguely hostile expression he saw on the faces of many of the other kids.

Apparently high schoolers were trusted to serve

themselves their own food, a privilege Devis was happy to abuse. The thief piled his tray high with hot dogs and quesadillas and breadsticks. The other four chose more modest lunches, and they all headed out into the main cafeteria.

As they stepped out into the grand chamber, they were momentarily overwhelmed. Everything was bigger here. The kids were bigger. The room was bigger. Even the tables were bigger. The noise of the place was almost deafening. The group made a slow, awkward tour, searching for the right place to sit. Making the wrong choice somehow seemed like it might have dire consequences.

"Does anyone see Tristane Trouvère?" said Vela, scanning the crowd.

The shifty bard was nowhere to be found. But they did spot a few familiar faces.

"Hey, look, there's that kid we embarrassed," said Devis.

"Greetings, Brent Sydlowski!" called out Thromdurr.

Brent Sydlowski gave a confused wave and then turned back toward the quesadilla on his tray.

Vela frowned. "In eighth grade, Brent was easygoing and friendly, the most popular student in class. But now his spirit looks . . . broken. Is that because of what we did?"

"I don't think so," said Albiorix. "None of the freshmen look very happy, do they?"

Indeed, Sharad Marwah had a miserable scowl on his

face. Jackie Barrera looked terrified. Derrick Day stared off into the middle distance like he might just fade away into nothing.

"Oh perfect."

The heroes turned to see Olivia Gorman behind them, looking unhappier than any J. A. Dewar alumnus they'd seen so far.

"You five are back to ruin my life again," said Olivia. "I was hoping maybe you all went to a special magnet school for jerks."

Before any of them could respond, Olivia had already elbowed past them to go sit at an empty cafeteria table by herself.

"Boy, I'm kind of realizing we hurt a lot of people's feelings last time," said Devis. "You guys should try to be more sensitive."

"Regular folk are often intimidated by greatness!" said Thromdurr. "And as I recall, we also told many, many lies."

"That we did," said Vela with a sigh.

At last the party found their own empty table.

"So, Albiorix, should we keep our distance from one another, as before, so as not to arouse suspicion?" asked Vela.

"I don't think it matters," said Albiorix. "We're all ninth graders now. So we're pretty much socially irrelevant. Nobody is paying much attention to who we talk to or hang out with."

"Um, do you guys mind if I sit here?" said Nicole Davenport.

Their blood ran cold and none of the heroes knew quite knew what to say. In the moment of uncomfortable silence, Nicole looked timid. Her eyes darted around the cafeteria, ever conscious of who might be watching. Vela started to say something, but Sorrowshade stopped her.

"This is a trap," hissed the gloom elf.

Nicole sighed. "You know what? It's fine. I get it. I can go somewhere else." She turned and disappeared into the crowd.

"Nicole Davenport, the prettiest and most ruthless girl at J. A. Dewar Middle School . . . is just a common loser here?" said Sorrowshade.

"Guess so," said Albiorix.

"That begs the question," said Vela. "Who holds the power here at Pine Hill High School?"

The heroes looked at the various cliques around the cafeteria. They saw the Populars, with their expensive clothes and perfect teeth, and their allies the Jocks, shouting and jostling each other in their letterman jackets. They saw the Nerds clumped together at their own tables, quietly discussing their esoteric Nerd interests, and the Overachievers trying to somehow hold themselves above the Nerds, yet not quite able to impress the Populars. Even the Loners, who sneered at all the rest, seemed to be a powerful faction in their own right here.

"It seems the various social distinctions of middle school have hardened here," said Vela.

"I think you're right," said Albiorix. "According to *The Advanced Hall Master's Guide*, high schoolers are desperately trying to build their own unique identity, while being painfully conscious of what other people think."

"Sounds like a nightmare," said Sorrowshade.

"Do you think everyone would laugh if I dumped ketchup on my head?" said Devis.

"Please don't," said Albiorix. "We need to get in and get out with as little fuss as possible, thereby posing no further risk to this world. So I think it's best if we split up to look for Tristane Trouvère and the Malonomicon."

And so they did.

Chapter

7

Table 242i: Random Hallway Encounters

Whenever characters travel between high school locations, roll three times and consult the following table to determine who/what they encounter along the way.

1 to 3: 1 to 3 students taking selfies

4 to 5: A panicked freshman who has forgotten their locker combination

6 to 9: 1 to 4 Jocks attempting to jump high enough to touch a wall-mounted clock

10 to 13: A lone student sobbing over a perceived insult (roll once and consult Table 322g: Perceived Insults to determine the nature of the slight)

14 to 15: 1 to 4 upperclassmen snickering about one of the characters

16: A Class Clown in the official school mascot costume

—*Excerpt from* The Advanced Hall Master's Guide

"Lo there, Nerds," cried Thromdurr from down the hall. A group of five kids—who were playing a giant-robot-themed collectible card game on the floor near their lockers—all looked at each other.

"Hey, man, that's, uh . . . kind of hurtful?" said a kid in a superhero T-shirt.

"Apologies," said Thromdurr. "It is a point of pride for me. Our mighty minds set us apart from even the brightest of Overachievers!"

"I—I guess?" said the kid.

"Anyway, my name is Douglas Schiller, son of Ron Schiller, and I too am a Nerd. You do not know me because the first few weeks of school, I was afflicted with a terrible wasting disease called mono!"

Thromdurr stuck out his hand. Nobody shook it.

"Well, anyway," said Thromdurr. "I am searching for someone here at Pine Hill High School. I do not say this lightly, but his hair is immacu—"

"Clear out, dorks. I'm walking here."

The Nerds scrambled to clean up their cards. Thromdurr turned to see a group of Jocks—led by a short, muscular boy with a buzz cut—deliberately cutting a path straight through the Nerds' game. A few of the players weren't quite quick enough and their cards got stepped on.

"Can you believe these dweebs spend all this time obsessing over a totally made-up game?" said the short boy.

"Anyway, like I was saying, our team's gonna crush Harbor High this Friday."

The other Jocks grunted in agreement. Thromdurr recognized one of their voices. Sure enough, Evan Cunningham trailed behind the others, wearing an ill-fitting JV basketball jersey and looking like he was trying hard to fit in.

"Evan!" cried Thromdurr. "Remember me? We went to middle school together. You were most unpleasant then. Perhaps you have changed?"

"Shut up, Schiller," said Evan.

The leader turned to Evan. "No, *you* shut up, Evan."

Evan stared at the ground. The short boy turned back to Thromdurr and glared up at him. The barbarian was at least a foot taller.

"That little twerp is a part of my crew now. So anything you say to him, you say to me. Get it, bro?"

"As you wish," said Thromdurr. "And what is your name, friend?"

At this, the Jocks burst out laughing again. Thromdurr noticed that all the other Nerds had somehow disappeared.

"Check this guy out, walking around Pine Hill High acting like he doesn't know who I am," said the short boy. "You trying to prove something, jumbo shrimp?"

"I have nothing to prove," said Thromdurr, who caught himself before launching into the thrilling tale of his giant scorpion death.

"Well, my name's Teddy McGirk," said the short boy, "and I ain't your friend, pal."

Quick as a snake, Teddy grabbed Thromdurr's wrist. The barbarian was expecting a weak physique, typical of Suburbia. Instead, Teddy twisted and then wrenched his arm with incredible power, causing Thromdurr to gasp in pain. The boy was as strong as any Bríandalörian adventurer.

Teddy moved close to Thromdurr's ear and whispered, "You know my name now, right? And I'm going to make sure you don't forget it, Schiller."

He held Thromdurr in the painful wrist lock for a moment more. Then he let go. He and his crew of Jocks chuckled and continued on their way. Thromdurr rubbed his forearm, stunned and confused.

Meanwhile, in another part of Pine Hill High School, Vela the Valiant smoothed her sweater and prepared to approach a fellow Overachiever—a girl in glasses and a crisp Oxford shirt—as she strode down the hallway with purpose.

Vela cleared her throat. "Hello. My name is Valerie Stumpf-Turner. I'm new here at Pine Hill High School."

The girl gave a quick glance at Vela but didn't slow down. "And?"

"And . . . um, I thought after I said my own name you might introduce yourself?"

"Christina Christopoulos," said the girl, who looked

annoyed that her name took so long to say. "And I don't have time to talk. Right now I'm on my way to Algebra II. After that I have German class, then history class, then German Club, then play practice, then cross-country, then fifteen minutes for dinner, and after that I'm prepping for the debate team match against Westview High until I go to bed."

"That sounds like a very full schedule," said Vela. "I am impressed."

"Wish I could say the same," said Christina, who had increased her walking speed by at least thirty percent since the conversation began.

"Well, I was hoping you might be able to, ah, help me out." Vela had to practically jog to keep up with her now.

"Mmm," said the girl. "Afraid not."

"But you do not even know what I want help with!"

"I have a *very* extensive to-do list, and as long as it is, you're not on it," said Christina. "Have a great day, Vanessa."

"It's Valerie," said Vela. But Christina Christopoulos was already out of earshot.

Meanwhile, elsewhere on campus—out behind the recycling bins—a group of misfits loitered. From a distance they watched the other students coming and going, alternating between disdainful jokes and quasi-profound statements about the hopeless nature of life.

"Look at them all," said Sorrowshade, who had crept up to

this group of Loners unseen. "Just a bunch of mindless sheep."

"Wow," said a wild-haired girl in a faded army jacket. "What an original metaphor."

Sorrowshade was taken aback. She didn't often encounter anything approaching her own level of sarcasm. It stung. "I—I wasn't trying to be original."

"Oh yeah? Then you're no better than *them*." The girl pointed toward the distant crowd. The rest of the Loners nodded knowingly.

"Am too!" said Sorrowshade. "My thing is, I'm doomed to walk through this life of misery and pain alone. So."

"Who are you trying to convince?" said the girl in the army jacket.

"You! I mean, nobody!" said Sorrowshade. "I don't care what anybody thinks."

The girl in the army jacket crossed her arms. "You know what your problem is? I don't think you're actually unhappy at all."

"How dare you!" said Sorrowshade.

The girl stared Sorrowshade right in the eyes. "Underneath the hair and the frown, you're just a bunch of butterflies and rainbows, aren't you?"

"No way! I'm *so* unhappy, I'm miserable," said Sorrowshade. "Name something and I probably hate it. Fedoras? Despise them. Those backpacks with the little wheels? Gross. What else? The beach? Ugh! Don't even get me started!"

"She sounds, like, defensive, Moonglove," said a tall, thin boy with stringy green hair.

"She's just another phony," said the girl, apparently named Moonglove, as she turned away from Sorrowshade. "Disregard."

And so the other Loners disregarded her. The gloom elf stood there for a few moments longer until it became unbearably awkward. Still, she had a mission.

"Look, I'll just get right to it: I'm trying to find someone," said Sorrowshade. "Strong jaw, floppy hair, makes irritatingly catchy music."

"He sounds very conventionally attractive," said Moonglove. "I bet you have a crush on him."

Sorrowshade might have been a tad defensive before, but this made her furious. "I do not!"

"Don't worry. I think it's adorable," said Moonglove.

"I hate him worse than I hate fedoras!" cried Sorrowshade.

None of the Loners believed her. They merely rolled their eyes and scoffed until the assassin stumbled backward into the shadows and disappeared.

At the very same time, Devis was supposed to be pumping the high school's scattered contingent of Class Clowns for clues to the bard's whereabouts. But honestly, what use would that be? Chuckleheads and goofballs didn't pay close attention to much, and they were hardly reliable sources of information. So instead he hung back in the cafeteria and went through the line several more times—each trip utilizing a hastily improvised disguise and a brand-new alias—to get more and more helpings of delicious hot dogs and quesadillas. It wasn't that Devis didn't want to find Tristane Trouvère. Far from it. He was just super hungry.

And it was cliqueless Albiorix, wandering the halls of Pine Hill High School alone, who spotted Tristane Trouvère at last. Sitting on some outdoor steps was a handsome boy with floppy hair. He played an acoustic guitar and sang with his eyes soulfully closed. A pack of girls crowded around the bard, enthralled by the performance.

"Hey! You!" cried Albiorix. The wizard had never been very good at coming up with snappy one-liners to hurl at villains.

Tristane Trouvère stopped playing his song and gazed up at Albiorix, utterly confused. "Excuse me?"

"You're the bard from . . ." Albiorix caught himself before he said anything that might raise too many questions with the other students. The wizard put his hands on his hips. "You know who you are, buddy."

"Yes . . . ," said Tristane very slowly. "My name is Travis Tyson."

"And you're not from around here, are you?" said Albiorix.

"That's right," said Tristane. "I'm from California. I miss my dog, Boomer. We had to give him to my uncle when we moved."

"Aw," said one of the girls.

"No! Don't feel sympathy for him," said Albiorix. "He never had a dog, and he's not a good guy."

The bard's audience remained unconvinced.

Tristane put up both his hands. "Hey, man, I don't know you and I don't know what you *think* I did, but I'm sure we can work this out. I'm all about peace and love, okay?"

Albiorix didn't know what was going on. Had he made some mistake? Was Tristane Trouvère somehow using this Travis Tyson's appearance? Had the boy been ensorcelled by the bard? Or someone else?

"I . . . Maybe we could talk about it somewhere more private?" said Albiroix.

"Sure, man," said Tristane. "Anything you—"

CRACK! Tristane fell to the ground, clutching his jaw like Albiorix had slugged him.

"Ow!" cried Tristane Trouvère from the ground. "Why'd you do that, man?"

"What?" said Albiorix.

"What a bully!" said one of the girls.

"Who, me?" said Albiorix, confused.

Tristane writhed on the ground in pain. Tears welled in his eyes. It was so convincing that Albiorix even wondered for a moment whether he *had* punched the kid. But that was absurd.

"He's faking it! I've never punched anyone in my life," said Albiorix. "These are not punching fists!" Albiorix flapped his delicate wizard hands.

"I'm getting the vice principal," said another girl. "Stay right there, bully."

"I'm not a—"

The girl had already run off down the hall. Tristane Trouvère moaned.

"Stop that," said Albiorix. "Get up." He grabbed Tristane by his elbow and tried to drag him to his feet, but the bard went limp like a dead fish.

"You're hurting him!" cried another girl.

"Oooooh, I think my jaw's broken," wailed Tristane. "I don't know if I'll ever be able to sing again."

The remaining girls gasped.

"You're a monster," said one of them to Albiorix.

"I'm really not," said Albiorix. "He's the monster. I'm a good guy."

"I'll be the judge of that," said a small, cheerful-looking woman wearing a pantsuit and a wooden beaded necklace. "I'm going to need both of you to accompany me to my office."

Chapter 8

Discipline is no joke. Back in original Homerooms & Hall Passes you might threaten players by telling them something would go on their (nonexistent) "permanent records." For you as an Advanced Homerooms & Hall Passes Hall Master, that won't cut it anymore, pal. In high school, the mischief characters get up to can literally be charged as a crime! Tell your players to keep their noses clean and stay out of trouble or they will Blow It. If any of them give you lip, don't be afraid to make an example of them.

—Excerpt from The Advanced Hall Master's Guide

⁓

"S o I'm GOING TO open this dialogue with two words, and I want you two to repeat them," said Pine Hill High School's vice principal, Teri Sloane. "Conflict resolution."

"Conflict resolution," repeated Albiorix and Tristane Trouvère in robotic unison.

The two of them sat on beanbag chairs in her warm, comfortable office, decorated all in earth tones and hand-woven rugs. Soothing New Age music played from a speaker in the corner, and a friendly fern thrived in a planter by the window. As vice principals' offices went, it was a stark contrast with Myron Flanagan's sparse, military aesthetic.

As the bard clutched his jaw and continued to feign serious injury, the wizard glared at him. They'd been back in Suburbia less than an hour, and Albiorix had already been sent to the vice principal. A part of him understood he was in danger of Blowing It, but another part was almost too angry to care.

"Now, do either of you feel like violence is an appropriate form of conflict resolution?" said Sloane.

Tristane Trouvère shook his head woefully. "No, ma'am."

Violence was often the default option in Bríandalör, but here, in this world, it was largely frowned upon.

"No," said Albiorix. "Which is why I didn't hit anybody."

Vice Principal Sloane clucked her tongue. "It isn't constructive to try to squash this dialogue before it even starts . . . ah, hmm. You know, I'm not sure I actually caught your name."

"Armando Boort, Canadian exchange student," said Albiorix. "I think you'll find my paperwork is in order."

He handed her a folder that contained his passport and a fully completed school enrollment form. At least he'd had enough foresight not to take any chances with this aspect of the quest.

The vice principal regarded his passport. "Beautiful. Maple syrup; poutine. We embrace and respect other cultures here at Pine Hill High School. But I'm not sure you're being a very good ambassador for Edmonton, Alberta, when you physically attack the students at your new school."

"For the last time, I did *not* attack him," said Albiorix. "I yelled at him, and he flopped around on the ground. He's just a really good actor."

"Vice Principal Sloane," said Tristane Trouvère in a quavering voice, "I think I may have a concussion. I'm seeing flashing lights. I think—I think I hear my grandfather's voice calling to me. He died two years ago. . . ."

"Oh, come *on!*" said Albiorix. "Check his face. You won't even find a bruise."

Vice Principal Sloane considered this. "Travis, would you mind if I took a look at your jaw?"

Albiorix caught a flash of annoyance on Tristane's face. Reluctantly, the bard removed his hand. Vice Principal Sloane gave his chin a close look.

"Armando is right," she said. "I don't *see* any visible injury."

"Maybe it's a bone bruise, ma'am?" said Tristane Trouvère. "Because it *hurts.*" He clutched his jaw again as a fresh batch of crocodile tears streamed down his face.

Vice Principal Sloane drummed her fingers on her desk. "He does appear to be in quite a lot of pain, Armando."

"'Appear' is the right word," said Albiorix, "because he was clutching the other side of his face before."

Vice Principal Sloane paused and gave a slight frown. "You're right."

At this, Tristane Trouvère slowly lowered his hands to his lap. He wasn't crying anymore. Now the bard had an utterly neutral expression on his face. The transition from sobbing to nothing was jarring.

"Now, I don't know what actually happened between you two," said Vice Principal Sloane. "As it turns out, nobody actually saw Armando throw the punch. So it's one student's word against another's. I cannot take disciplinary measures on that basis. But we do have a situation on our hands. And it's clear to me that neither one of you is using the right tools for conflict resolution yet. So, Armando, I want you to apologize."

"What?" cried Albiorix.

"Apologize now, or I will expel you from Pine Hill High School," said Vice Principal Sloane. She was still smiling, but her touchy-feely tone had been replaced by one as hard as Myron Flanagan's. Albiorix hesitated. Tristane Trouvère smirked. Now the wizard really did want to punch him.

". . . I'm sorry, Travis," said Albiorix. He felt like throwing up.

"Thank you. Contrition is the first step toward healing," said Sloane. "Now, Travis, I want you to apologize to Armando."

"I'm story, Armando," said Tristane.

"Excellent," said Sloane. "That was very brave of you to—"

"Wait, he didn't say it!" said Albiorix. "He didn't say 'sorry.' He said, 'I'm *story*.' With a T!"

Tristane looked confused. "Why would I say that?"

"Why would he say that, Armando?" said Vice Principal Sloane.

"To irritate me!" said Albiorix.

Teri Sloane sighed. "Let it go, Armando. Forgiveness is the second step. Now I'm going to leave you both with a strong suggestion: learn to get along." Her tone suddenly grew hard once more. "Learn to get along, or we're all going to have a *serious* problem."

With that, she dismissed the two boys. They walked out of the school office together in tense silence. Tristane Trouvère still wore an infuriating smirk on his face. Albiorix seethed.

Once they were in the hallway (and out of any authority figure's earshot) Tristane Trouvère turned with a flourish. His smirk was now a maddening grin. "Well, that was fun. Thanks for the compliment, by the way."

"Compliment?" said Albiorix, who was determined not to let the slippery bard out of his sight.

"You said I'm a good actor. That means so much to me. I try to honor the craft." Tristane bowed.

"Look, we're on to you," said Albiorix. "The jig is up. So you can come with me peacefully, and nobody needs to get hurt."

Tristane Trouvère shook his head. "Where's the fun in that?"

"You don't belong here. I don't belong here," said Albiorix. "This isn't our world."

"Agree to disagree. I think you'll see that I pretty much own this place," said Tristane. "But I take your point about leaving. Honestly, I find that to be the hardest part of acting."

"What?" said Albiorix.

"Knowing how to make an exit," said Tristane. And with that, he vanished into thin air.

Albiorix looked around. No sign of the bard. The wizard cursed. They'd lost Tristane Trouvère yet again. He started down the hall at a jog one way and then spun around and went the other. As he rounded a corner, he bumped into a girl, nearly bowling her over.

"Sorry," said Albiorix as he bent to help her pick up the books and papers that she had dropped.

"It's okay," said June Westray.

Albiorix did a double take. "June! You're alive!"

June smiled, though she looked a bit confused. "I mean, last I checked. Wait, so you're . . . back?"

Albiorix was overcome with relief. The wizard had thought about what he might say to June for months, but suddenly he couldn't think of anything. "Mmm-hmm," said Albiorix. "Back-a-roonie." Instantly he regretted his words.

"Okay, *why* are you back?" asked June. "Another quest?"

"Oh yeah, well, there's this sleazy bard from Bríandalör named—"

"June, wait up!" A baby-faced boy in an anime T-shirt jogged over to them. The kid was an archetypal Nerd. "Sorry, I'm moving kinda slow today. I think there was something in that quesadilla. No way I'm going to make it through bio awake."

"Armando," said June, "this is my friend Morton."

"Hey, man," said the boy. "Morton Blanc." He gave a friendly smile and extended his hand. Albiorix hesitated. Then he shook it.

"Morton," said Albiorix.

"Actually, now that I think of it, you two would really

get along," said June. "You're both into stuff that regular people find mind-numbingly dull."

"You like board games?" said Morton.

Albiorix gritted his teeth. "Yes."

"Awesome. Well, I just got this new one for my birthday called Bubble Bulber. It's a trading game all about the seventeenth-century Dutch tulip craze," said Morton. "For some reason I can't get June to play it with me."

"Just hearing about it makes me sad," said June.

"It won game of the year at the Frankfurt Games Festival," said Morton. "That's like the Oscars of European board games."

"Getting sadder, over here," said June.

"Yeah, well, it doesn't matter," said Albiorix, "because I don't think I'll be able to play it anyway. I'm very busy."

"Doing what?" said June.

"Stuff," said Albiorix. "The stuff I was about to tell you about before . . ." He gave a none-too-subtle nod toward Morton.

The wizard expected June to discreetly tell Morton Blanc to get lost, so they could freely discuss the party's new mission to retrieve the Malonomicon and banish Tristane Trouvère from Suburbia. She didn't, though. Instead, June just shrugged. There was a moment of awkward silence.

Morton tried to fill it. "Yeah, man, stuff. I get that. Sounds pretty hectic. But, hey, that's life, right? Wow, I sound like one of the phrases embroidered on my grandma's throw pillows."

"So what have you been up to?" said Albiorix to June, and definitely not to Morton Blanc.

"A little of this, a little of that," said June. "I'm really into collage these days."

"Because we found your phone," said Albiorix. He held up June's smartphone that the party had purchased in the bazaar of Far Draïz. "We found it in *our neighborhood.*"

June caught his meaning. "Really? That's super weird."

"We were very worried," said Albiorix.

"Why?" asked June.

"We thought somebody might have stolen it," said Albiorix. "Somebody bad."

"Nope," said June. "That phone died months ago. RIP, old phone. I spilled green smoothie all over it and it just wouldn't turn on again. So I got a new one and tossed that one in a drawer, where it's been gathering dust. I guess maybe my mom tried to recycle it or something?"

"Okay, but that doesn't totally explain it," said Albiorix.

June shrugged again. "Maybe it was magic?"

Morton gave an awkward chuckle. He stopped when he realized no one else was laughing with him.

"But I'm telling you, there's no reason to worry," said June.

"So you're not in any danger?" said Albiorix.

"Danger?" said Morton. "Guys, I'm a little lost here?"

Albiorix ignored him.

"Nope. No danger," said June. "I've actually been doing great. I'm vegan now, which is a little harrowing sometimes. You know, ice cream and so forth. Oh, and I've been teaching myself to play guitar online."

"She's really good," said Morton.

Albiorix ignored him yet again. "Well, I'm just glad to hear you're okay."

June grinned again and cocked her head. "You didn't come here thinking you were going to save me, like some sort of princess or something, did you?"

Albiorix gave a nervous laugh. "What? No. No, of course not. That wasn't . . . Nope."

"Cool," said June. "Because you understand I can handle myself."

"Right," said Albiorix. "Obviously. Yep."

"Okay. I've got to get to class," said June. "But I'm psyched you guys are back. We should hang out."

"Maybe this afternoon?" said Albiorix.

"Sure," said June.

She gave Albiorix a hug, and then she and Morton headed off down the hall, leaving Albiorix alone with mixed feelings. It wasn't quite how he had imagined his reunion with June Westray going. That was the Morton she had been texting with. Albiorix couldn't quite tell if the kid was June's boyfriend—and again, good for her if that was the case!—but he wasn't definitely *not* her boyfriend. Either way, there was something about Morton Blanc that rubbed Albiorix the wrong way. The most annoying thing of all was that, if Albiorix was being honest, he kind of liked the kid.

The wizard rechecked his class schedule and realized that this period his computer class was in room 114, all the way on the opposite side of the building. He set out at a run and got there forty seconds after the tardy bell rang.

It was an unlucky prelude to a tedious and grueling day. The academic portion of high school was much like middle school, only more so. The increased number of class options at Pine Hill High School meant that the heroes only saw each other intermittently and they rarely had a chance to speak freely. Much to Vela's dismay, due to a scheduling error, she'd been enrolled in shop class instead of AP US History. The administration assured her they were working on fixing the problem.

After the last bell, Albiorix and the other Bríandalörians reconvened in the secluded east stairwell of the building. Albiorix updated them on Tristane Trouvère and June Westray.

"Well, I am certainly glad June is alive!" said Thromdurr.

"Disappointed to hear that Tristane Trouvère is, though," said Sorrowshade. "Hopefully I'll get a chance to slowly disembowel him with a rusty fork."

"Our goal is not to murder him but to ensure the safety of this place," said Vela. "We must apprehend him and take him back to our world."

"That's going to be tough if he can literally disappear at will," said Albiorix. "Any idea how he does it, Devis?"

"What?" said Devis. "Oh yeah. Well, I'm pretty sure he has a cap of invisibility."

"That's a very powerful magic item," said Albiorix. "Perhaps you could have mentioned it to us earlier."

"Sorry. Slipped my mind," said Devis. "But it's a funny story. I was actually there when he found it. Our old party was exploring this haunted keep, and we'd just won a harrowing victory against an ice troll. We were dividing up the loot when we found a cap of invisibility. And I was like, 'Oh, wow, that would be perfect for me, because I'm a thief.' But then Tristane was all like, 'Nope, I'm keeping it.' And so he kept it." Devis chuckled. "So Tristane."

There was a moment of awkward silence.

"I fail to see the humor in the tale," said Thromdurr. "It seems to me as though the bard bullied you mercilessly."

"Like friends do!" said Devis, throwing his hands up.

"Tristane Trouvère might be elusive, but I don't think he

98

has the Malonomicon yet," said Albiorix. "We have to get to it before he does. Our only advantage is that we know where it was the last time we were here. That's where I think we should start the search."

Vela made the sign of the Golden Sun. "And so we must return to that forsaken place of great evil: the Old Mall."

"Yep," said Albiorix. "But first we all need to check in at our respective homes like real high schoolers would."

"Wait," said Sorrowshade. "You're not going to sleep in a closet and eat vending machine food? You have a home this time?"

Albiorix glanced at Thromdurr. "I hope so," said the wizard.

Chapter 9

The world of Advanced Homerooms & Hall Passes has no shortage of antagonists: cruel Populars, vindictive teachers, menacing bullies. But for many high schoolers, they will face no foe more unyielding and formidable during their teenage years than their own parents.
—Excerpt from The Advanced Hall Master's Guide

A LBIORIX SAT AT THE kitchen table of the modest ranch house at 45 Crescent Drive, thumbing through his spellbook, trying to refresh his magical memory. He was so out of practice he had forgotten the names of half the spells he used to cast. Meanwhile, Thromdurr wrote a long and detailed note to Doug's father. Though Ron Schiller wasn't due home for another half hour, he walked in the door around six p.m., surprising them both.

"Hey, Doug. Ned Sharkey tried to heat up a baked

potato in the microwave. Only he left the aluminum foil on. Nearly burned the break room down. Long story short, Mr. Flores decided to close up the shop early today," said Ron Schiller. He noticed Albiorix. "Oh, hi again."

Albiorix hid his spellbook behind his back. "Hello, Mr. Schiller!"

"Greetings, Father," said Thromdurr. "Thank you for telling me of Ned Sharkey's combustible potato. I trust you remember Armando Boort? He is a Canadian exchange student who will be living in our home for the next few months to provide me with a hearty dose of cross-cultural enrichment."

Ron Schiller frowned and scratched the side of his face. "Huh."

"Of course you are free to rescind this offer of hospitality and banish Armando to the frozen northland from whence he came," said Thromdurr. "Within these walls, Ron Schiller's word is law."

"Right," said Ron. "Well, son, to be honest, I would have preferred if you'd run this by me before he, um, got here."

"I try not to trouble you with such details," said Thromdurr. "But I promise you he is quiet and eats little."

"It's true," said Albiorix in an extra-quiet voice.

"Okay," said Ron. "I hear enrichment is good. So, um, welcome to our home, Armando."

"Happy to be here," said Albiorix.

"Furthermore," said Thromdurr, "the pair of us shall venture forth this eve to follow one of my obscure and Nerdly pursuits. But worry not, our activity will be safely supervised by countless responsible adults."

"Sounds good," said Ron. "Did you finally decide you want to join Math League or something?"

"Yes, yes," said Thromdurr. "That is precisely it. Math League. Farewell, Father! Enjoy the great recliner in my absence."

Albiorix and Thromdurr headed for the door.

"You sure you boys don't want me to heat you up a bowl of chili first?" said Ron.

The barbarian and the wizard looked at each other for a moment. Then they hurried back to the kitchen table for a quick serving of Ron Schiller's finest.

Not so far away, at 800 North Pineknoll Avenue, another Bríandalörian was handed another warm bowl.

"Here you go, Stinky," said Dad Stinky. "This is my take on a traditional Creole gumbo."

Devis took a sip. The soup was warm and spicy, full of shrimp and sausage cooked to perfection.

"Mmm," said Devis. "Delicious. Immaculate. Revelatory. Three and a half stars."

"Out of five?" asked Dad Stinky.

Devis nodded. "I feel like I'm losing the celery flavor with all the cayenne pepper. And if this is Creole gumbo, why does it have andouille in it? Sausage is for Cajun gumbo. You know that, Dad."

Dad Stinky bowed his head. "I'm sorry, son." He moved for the bowl. "Do you want me to me to dump this slop down the garbage disposal and start again?"

Devis stopped him. "No need for that, just . . . try to do better, okay?"

"I will," said Dad Stinky. "I promise."

"I'm putting three gallons of corn chowder in the freezer, for when your father and I are away," called Mom Stinky from the kitchen. "Is that enough corn chowder for two days?"

"Probably not," said Devis. "Where are you guys going again?"

"We've been over this," said Dad Stinky. "You *really* don't remember?"

"Nope. Pretend I just got here from a whole different world where there are dragons and dungeons and such," said Devis. "Oh, and instead of your son, I'm a lovable, morally flexible rascal who brings a much-needed dose of levity to a band of overserious adventurers."

"Very specific, but sure?" said Dad Stinky. "Just like every year, we're going to SoupExpo, the premier international soup/stew festival/trade show/media event of the year.

Your mother's on a soup panel!"

"Your father's on a soup panel!" said Mom Stinky.

"We're both on soup panels!" they said, in cheerful unison.

"So I'll have this whole place to myself while you're gone?" said Devis.

"You'll be the ranking Stinky," said Dad Stinky.

"Try not to get into trouble," said Mom Stinky.

"Who, me?" said Devis. The thief took another sip of gumbo and grinned.

Meanwhile, in another part of the town of Hibbettsfield—17 South Euclid Street, to be exact—another Bríandalörian hero was talking to her own parents.

"It's a school night, sweetheart," said Marie Stumpf-Turner. "And you shouldn't have free time anyway. If we somehow left a hole in your after-school schedule, that's our mistake, but I'd be happy to sign you up for a coding class or fencing lessons."

"I don't *need* fencing lessons," said Vela. "And I must go out tonight, because I have to locate a very important book." It wasn't a lie, but it omitted a large enough portion of the truth to make the paladin uncomfortable.

"Isn't everything online these days?" said Marie.

"Not this book," said Vela.

"I'm sorry, but no," said Andy Stumpf-Turner, pressing the back of his hand against Vela's forehead. "I forbid it. I'm still reeling from this shop class scheduling snafu. And you're still not at a hundred percent. I don't want you to have a mono relapse and miss more school."

"On my honor, I will *not* fall to mono again," said Vela. "But I must go."

Marie shook her head. "Listen to you argue. When did you become such a teenager, Valerie? Our answer is fina— Wait, it's not your *Coughlin PSAT Study Guide*, it it?"

Vela held both her hands out in a noncommittal gesture. Still not a lie.

"You *need* that study guide!" cried Marie. "I guarantee you Olivia Gorman and Kyle Chung will be poring over it all night. You already missed the first three weeks of ninth grade. We cannot allow a study-guide gap. Go, go, go!"

Marie shooed her daughter out the door.

"And if you touch anything or anyone," called Andy from the front door, "use hand sanitizer!" He tossed Vela a small bottle of clear liquid as she hurried down the block.

Things were far less confrontational in the beautiful Victorian house at 29 Sierra Avenue. Melissa McElmurray's bleak bedroom sat empty, but beautiful smells wafted through the house from the kitchen.

"Aw, they *do* look just like little elves," said Sorrowshade, as Pam McElmurray pulled a fresh tray of cookies out of the oven.

"It was a great idea to give them chocolate-chip noses," said Pam. "And to bake holiday cookies three months early. What made you think of it?"

"Elves are just so darn cute!" said Sorrowshade. She gave Pam a big hug.

Pam smiled, a little confused. "I don't exactly know what's gotten into you, Melissa, but . . . I'm happy that you're happy."

"I'm happy I'm happy too!" said Sorrowshade. "Just please don't tell anybody. If anyone asks, life is a merciless parade of grief and disappointment, okay?"

"Got it," said Pam, no less confused. "Should we try one?"

Sorrowshade and Pam each took an elf cookie, still a little warm and gooey from the oven. They were delicious.

"Mmm," said Sorrowshade. "I'd love to stay here and bake more but there's something important I really need to go do tonight. Is that okay, Mom?"

Pam thought about it. "You haven't asked my permission for anything you've done since you were eight. But sure, go right ahead. Have fun, dear."

"I will, Mom," said Sorrowshade. "I love having fun."

She gave Pam another hug and bounded for the door.

By the time Sorrowshade was outside, her posture had reslouched, her eyes had renarrowed, and her usual dour expression had returned. She threw the hood of her sweatshirt up, plunging her face into shadow, and none who saw her would ever guess that her mind was composing a new poem, one about how yummy cookies were in her tummy.

The Old Mall sat grim and silent on the edge of town. The parking lot was empty now, with weeds pushing up through cracks in the pavement. The streetlights cast long shadows as the sun dipped beneath the horizon. Inside the building, all the lights were off.

One by one, the five Bríandalörians convened by the main entrance to the Hibbettsfield Galleria.

Vela peered through the glass of the doors. "Looks like the mall has been abandoned since our battle with Azathor the Devourer."

Devis shivered. "The place is only slightly creepier than when it was open."

Almost on cue, some animal—a dog or a coyote, perhaps—howled in the distance.

"I kind of like it," said Sorrowshade. "I could definitely imagine shopping here now. I should wear more cobwebs."

Devis pulled out his set of thieves' tools and nodded toward the locked door. "Shall I?"

"Can we give it just a few more minutes?" asked Albiorix.

The wizard scanned the horizon and saw what he was looking for. Down the block, a city bus pulled over at a lonely bus stop, and a single passenger got off. The wizard grinned.

"Hey, guys!" cried June.

June greeted Vela, Thromdurr, Devis, and even Sorrowshade with a big hug.

"I'm so glad you came, June," said Albiorix. "I sent you that email, but I didn't know if you got it, so I wasn't sure how long to wait, because I thought, hey, maybe her email isn't working for some reason, even though the odds of that are probably pretty—"

"Relax," said June. "There's no way I'd miss this. The six of us adventure people back together, going on a quest like we used to in eighth grade. I should've brought my . . . uh, what do you call the spikey thing on a chain?"

"Do you mean a morning star?" said Vela.

"Right, I should have brought one of those!" said June. "So I could bop somebody!" June pantomimed a bopping motion.

Vela shook her head. "Though we brought our weapons, I hope there will be no bopping this evening, June. We are on a mission of subterfuge and reconnaissance."

"STEALTH IS THE ORDER OF THE DAY, JUNE!" cried Thromdurr.

"Shh," said Sorrowshade.

"Man, I just wish Morton could be here," said June. "He'd love something like this."

"Morton can't know about any of it!" said Albiorix. It came out way too harsh and drew a look from June and even his fellow Bríandalörians.

"Even though, ah, I'm sure he's a very cool, ahem, gentleman," said Albiorix.

"Cool gentleman?" said Devis.

Albiorix waved him off.

"No, no, I get it," said June. "Heroes only for this one."

While Devis worked on the lock, the others filled June in on the plan: locate the Malonomicon before something terrible happened or Tristane Trouvère beat them to it.

"You mean that guy Travis who's always playing cheesy guitar on the steps at lunch is really a secret villain from Bríandalör?" said June. "Figures. At first I had a big crush on him."

"What?" cried Albiorix. "I mean . . . hmm? How about that?"

"I know," said June. "But it took me, like, forty seconds to realize he's a total creep. I can't understand how *anybody* is dumb enough to fall for his shtick."

"He's not that bad!" said Devis.

The tumblers of the lock clicked and the door swung open, allowing the party to slip inside. The Old Mall was dark and reeked of dust and mold. Albiorix cast a light spell—he remembered that much magic, at least—bathing the path ahead in silvery moonglow. The stores were all vacant now. The merchants had cleaned out their inventory, leaving behind only empty clothing racks and stained carpeting. From somewhere they heard the faint sound of water dripping.

"You know, it was pretty nuts after you guys left," said June. "Nobody wanted to talk about the dead rising from their graves and roaming the earth. When I brought it up, people tried their best to come up with a rational explanation for what had happened."

"Like what?" asked Vela.

"Pranksters in Halloween costumes, somebody making a student film, or . . . my personal favorite . . . bears out looking for trash to eat, during the big storm. I mean at a certain point, you have to accept that an evil necromancer from another world *is* the most logical explanation, right? It was maddening to be the only person in the whole world who knew the truth."

"That sounds tough," said Albiorix. A wave of guilt swept over the wizard. He'd second-guessed their choice to leave this world and return to Bríandalör a thousand times in the preceding months. But he'd only contemplated the decision from his own point of view. He'd never thought that June might feel abandoned.

"Yeah, well, nobody said being an adventurer would be easy, right?" said June. "The few times I could get anybody to talk about it at all, they focused on the weird weather aspect—the lightning and the green clouds—instead of anything else. My new theory is that talking about weather is how most people seem to psychologically process things. Me? I make art." June paused. "Oh, wait, that reminds me, I've got an opening . . . sorry, that sounds super pretentious. Let me start over. Some of my collages are going on display at this coffee shop called the Daily Grind in two weeks. Please come, you guys!"

The party agreed they would as they reached the former location of Style Shack. This was the site of their fight against a pack of animated mannequins. The floor was still littered with broken glass and plastic body parts. Albiorix nudged a severed mannequin hand with his toe.

"This is a good sign," said the wizard. "Looks like they barely cleaned anything up before they closed down the Old Mall. It's a long shot, but maybe the Malonomicon is still here somewhere."

"Speaking of long shots, June," said Thromdurr. "You know what was a long shot? When I saved these three from a giant scorpion and certain doom. . . ."

And so June listened, captivated, to Thromdurr's heroic tale, while the other four (even Vela) rolled their eyes and tried their best to let him have this moment. They all knew that soon enough June Westray would be as tired of the story as the rest of them.

Up ahead, the party saw the shattered escalators still entwined in a death embrace.

Vela threw her grappling hook up to the balcony railing, and the party climbed up the rope to the second floor. At last they came to a dry fountain near the burned-out Cheesecakery, the place where they had battled the undead warlock Zazirak. Here there was a big, charred fissure in the floor marking Azathor the Devourer's entry into this realm from the infernal plane. They could still smell a faint sulfurous tang in the air. Again they heard a mournful howl from somewhere not far away.

"The book's not here," said Sorrowshade.

"Are you certain?" said Vela.

The party had little reason to doubt the gloom elf's superior senses.

"Maybe somebody tossed it in the garbage and it's in the bottom of a landfill right now," said Devis. He turned to June. "You guys love stuffing trash in big holes and pretending it's gone, right?"

"I wouldn't say we *love* it," said June. She sounded a bit self-conscious.

"My point is," said Devis, "this could be a Boneshatter I situation, right?"

"I commend your optimism, Devis," said Vela. "But evil tomes of forbidden knowledge are rarely done away with so easily. Until we know for sure, we must assume the book is still out there."

"Again, I wish Morton was here," said June. "He's super good at finding stuff. Like, one time I lost my sunglasses and he went all the way back to the Hibbettsfield Cinema Fourteen and found them under the claw machine where they somehow fell out of my pocket while I was winning a stuffed dolphin."

"You went to the movies with Morton?" asked Albiorix.

"Yeah?" said June.

"Not the time, Albiorix," said Sorrowshade.

"Anyway," said June, "is there a way Albiorix could, like, do a cool magic spell to find the book?"

There was a moment of awkward silence from the rest of the party.

Thromdurr laughed. "Oh, June. Sweet, naive June. Since my wizardly companion is suddenly taciturn, I shall speak on his behalf: The answer is a resounding no. In the intervening months, Albiorix has let his magical skills lapse while attempting to develop an original board game about octagons. We are lucky he cast that light spell without some-how injuring himself."

"Not true!" said Albiorix. "I could do a spell. I have loads of good spells because I'm still really good at doing spells.

I'm basically a raging tornado of unbridled mystical power."

"Easy, guy," said Devis.

Albiorix flipped through his spellbook. "So many fantastic spells. Ah, here we go: find lost object. Exactly what we need for this situation, wouldn't you say? I'm going to cast it. Because I can."

"Sure," said Sorrowshade. "Let me just take cover first." The gloom elf ducked behind a cement column.

"Nice knowing you guys," said Devis, from . . . *somewhere*. The thief had already hidden himself completely.

Vela gave a nod. "It is a sound plan. You can do this, Albiorix." Though the wizard noticed that even the paladin was backing away and ever so slightly hunching behind her dented shield.

Thromdurr stood his ground and smiled. "Death holds no fear for me. Have at it, friend!"

"Yeah, I remember the lightning bolts and stuff during the big fight, last time," said June. "But a spell that lets you find a thing you lost would be *way* more useful. Think about how much money we, as a society, would save on umbrellas."

"Glad *someone* believes in me," said Albiorix. "Okay, June, prepare to be dazzled."

Despite the show of confidence, his palms were sweating. His hands were shaking. It was a difficult spell. Even when he was training with the Archmage every day, Albiorix

114

had only managed to successfully cast find lost object a couple of times. He realized he was desperate to impress June. Paradoxically, such a distraction would make it harder for him to cast the spell. He'd already committed, though. He'd look like a fool if he backed out now.

Albiorix closed his eyes and centered his mind and read the arcane words inscribed in his spellbook. *"Ta' phaet zyen ael ra'ln a'ti doil nysh'a."* He traced the secret sigil of finding in the air with his fingertips, touching the arcane weave of the universe. At the same time, the wizard bent his consciousness toward locating that which was most important to find. There was a flash of purple light from his fingertips. Albiorix had done it. He'd cast the spell.

"Consider me dazzled," June whispered.

Albiorix spoke in a faraway voice, his eyes still closed. "The book . . . is . . . here."

The party looked at each other.

"Tell us where," said Vela.

Albiorix concentrated on the spell. "Ten paces to my right."

Thromdurr started at Albiorix and marked ten paces to his right. He nearly bumped into June.

"June, do you possess the book?" asked Vela.

"Nope," said June.

"Are you standing upon it?" asked Thromdurr.

June stepped to the side. No Malonomicon.

"The book just moved!" said Albiorix, eyes still shut.

"Check your backpack," said Vela.

"Guys, it's a ten-pound book with screaming faces on the cover," said June. "I'd know if it was in my backpack." She opened her backpack to show them. No Malonomicon.

The party was baffled.

"Did you eat it, perhaps?" said Thromdurr.

"No!" said June.

"Maybe you ate it and forgot," said Devis from his hiding place. "I do that sometimes."

"I didn't eat the evil spellbook!" said June.

Sorrowshade stepped out from behind the column. The gloom elf shook her head. "Albiorix cast the spell on June."

Albiorix opened his eyes, ending the spell with a fizzle. "What?"

"You did cast find lost object, but not on the Malonomicon," said Sorrowshade. "You bent the mystical fiber of reality to locate June Westray. Even though she's standing right beside you."

"Huh," said June.

"I . . . that wasn't . . . I didn't mean to . . . uh . . ." Albiorix trailed off.

Thromdurr scratched his chin. "Wait! Albiorix, perhaps you were subconsciously obsessing over June so much that you inadvertently foiled your spell!"

Albiorix stared at the ground. This particular magical failure was far more humiliating than freezing both his feet to the ground or quadrupling the length of his tongue.

"No worries," said June, patting the wizard on the arm. "I'm sure it'll work better next time."

Devis had stepped out from wherever he was hiding. "Hey, Albiorix, I'm looking for Vela. Maybe you could cast a magic spell to find her."

"All right," said Albiorix. "Ha ha."

"Do you think maybe you could cast a spell to help me find my house?" asked Sorrowshade. "The address is 29 Sierra Avenue."

"I get it," said Albiorix.

"What's that over there?" said Vela.

Albiorix buried his face in his palm. "Oh, not you too, Vela."

The paladin drew her sword. The party turned. A dark, hulking shape crept out of the shadows.

It was a wolflike beast, as big as a pony, and its yellow eyes glowed with malevolent intelligence. The beast let out a bloodcurdling howl.

Chapter 10

Of course, three unexcused absences and an Advanced Homerooms & Hall Passes character will Blow It and be eliminated from the game. But even excused absences carry a terrible price, too great for many to pay. That price is called "makeup work."

—Excerpt from The Advanced Hall Master's Guide

"IT APPEARS I MAY have spoken too soon," said Vela, dropping into a fighting stance. "There may yet be some bopping."

"Guys, what *is* that thing?" said June.

The others had all readied their weapons, for they knew quite well what the creature was.

"A warg," said Vela. "A horrid wolfish beast that haunts the darkest forests of Bríandalör."

"Why is it at the mall?" asked June.

Before anyone could answer, the warg snarled and charged. June screamed and leaped out of the way. Luckily, the monster went for Vela. The warg was swift, but somehow the paladin got her shield up in time to block its snapping jaws. Still, the beast's mass and incredible strength knocked her off her feet, sending her sword clattering away across the floor. The warg scrabbled on top of her shield, pinning her to the ground.

Sorrowshade nocked an arrow, then paused. "Ugh. I don't have the shot. I don't want to hit Vela. Can you pull that thing off her?"

It took Thromdurr a moment to realize that she was talking to him. "Who, me? Ah yes, of course. I am very mighty and so forth." The barbarian trotted toward the warg and wrapped his beefy arms around the beast's shoulders.

"Begone, vile monstrosi—"

The warg bucked its body and flung Thromdurr off, sending him tumbling backward. The party had never seen Thromdurr foiled so easily in a contest of strength. With a growl, the warg turned its slavering jaws back to Vela.

"Help me, comrades," cried the paladin. "Please!"

"Albiorix, anything?" asked Devis.

"Uh," said Albiorix. In truth he was paralyzed with the fear of what might happen if he botched one of his more combat-oriented spells. He could end up accidentally

119

incinerating or electrocuting his friends.

"That's a no," said Sorrowshade.

"Then I guess it's up to me," said Devis. The thief drew his daggers. "Deeeeevvvvviiiissss!"

Devis darted toward the warg. With a quick slash, he nicked the creature's leg, drawing a thin line of blood. The cut was more annoying than serious, but the attack turned the warg's attention toward the thief. The beast snapped its jaws at where Devis had just been, but he'd been quick enough to nimbly somersault underneath its legs and out of harm's way.

This gave Vela the chance she needed. She wrenched her shield free and used its edge to bash the creature under its jaw. The warg stumbled back, dazed. *Thwip!* Sorrowshade buried an arrow in its flank. The warg snarled and ran.

Sorrowshade loosed too more arrows, but they missed as the warg leaped over the second-story balcony railing. Vela got to the edge just in time to see it disappear into the shadows below. Swift as the creature was, there was no hope of catching it.

After the battle, the party regrouped.

June was nearly hyperventilating, but she had a huge grin plastered across her face. "We beat it! I mean, you guys beat it. I mean, that wolf thing was like 'Raaarrgh!' and Vela was like 'Oh no!' and then Devis jumped in there like

'Yaaaah!' And staring down mortal danger is still new to me, but that was kind of close, right?"

"Too close," said Vela, sheathing her sword. "A lone warg should hardly present a challenge to a party of our ability. I am disappointed."

"Vela can soft-pedal it, but I won't," said Sorrowshade. "That was pathetic." The gloom elf sneered at Thromdurr and poked him in the chest with her finger. "What happened?"

"The monster proved to be, ah, stronger than anticipated," said Thromdurr.

"You can't keep giving it half of what you've got," said Sorrowshade.

Thromdurr pondered this. "Half my effort should be roughly equivalent to one normal person's."

"Not good enough! You died and it was great and now you need to get over it. Otherwise you're liable to get the rest of us killed," said Sorrowshade. "Speaking of which . . ." The gloom elf turned to Albiorix. "I suggest you figure out exactly what it is you do."

Albiorix stared at the floor and cleared his throat. "Spells," he said very quietly.

"You sure about that? Because I didn't see you doing any spells, just now. All I heard was a loud choking sound." Sorrowshade now turned to Devis. "And you?"

"Yes?" said Devis.

"You actually did pretty well," said Sorrowshade, "which only highlights how disappointing you normally are."

"If the floor is open for constructive criticism," said Devis, "at times, I find you to be overly negative."

"Take that back or I'll poison you, you sawed-off klepto-maniac," said Sorrowshade.

June stepped between them. "Guys, relax. You won."

The Bríandalörians all looked at her.

"And nobody has answered my question," said June. "What is a vicious Bríandalörian monster doing here?"

"We must assume it followed us," said Vela, glancing behind her.

"Wargs are servants of evil," said Albiorix. "It could be looking for the Malonomicon too."

"Or merely choosing a conveniently deserted place to finish us off," said Vela. "Does Tristane Trouvère possess some power over animals?"

"He's a very talented guy, great hair, snappy dresser," said Devis. "But I don't remember controlling beasts being one of his things."

"Then a greater evil is afoot," said Vela. "And while a single warg is no match for our party, it could easily pick off any one of us if it caught us alone. We must be vigilant now. There is more going on here than we realize."

Victorious but hardly triumphant, the adventurers returned to their homes that night and arose early the next morning for their second day at Pine Hill High School.

They found it difficult and confusing. In their language arts classes, they studied grammatical rules as arbitrary and particular as any alchemist's formula. In Algebra II, they tried to wrap their simple Bríandalörian minds around the idea of "imaginary" numbers. In biology, they learned that all creatures were but a collection of cells, little bits so small you couldn't even see them (touches like this really put the "fantasy" in a fantasy role-playing game). In shop, Vela made a lamp.

Every class generated homework every night, and to make matters worse, their protracted mono absence had left them mounds of makeup work they needed to complete in their free time to avoid flunking their classes and thus, of course, ceasing to exist. They'd just arrived and they were already overwhelmed.

One morning, between first and second periods, Vela spotted Tristane Trouvère in the hall. But before she could confront him, he gave her an annoying smirk and disappeared again. Albiorix saw him at lunch, playing guitar on a bench to another group of adoring girls, and yet again he managed to vanish into thin air. It was clear that Tristane Trouvère was wary and cunning, which made sense for a seasoned adventurer. Thereafter, the heroes could never manage to get close before he donned his cap of invisibility to make his escape. So they watched him from afar and tried to learn what they could.

It seemed that the bard was able to use his natural charm and musical talents to manipulate practically everyone he met. He played his cheesy guitar songs on the steps, while his growing legion of devoted fans showered him with gifts—new clothes, jewelry, video games. Sorrowshade even listened as one girl gave him her parents' credit card number. Between periods he was nowhere to be found. Then, while everyone else was in class, Tristane Trouvère roamed the halls with impunity, disarming any teachers he happened to meet with a quick joke or a compliment and a plausible (but false) excuse. Occasionally one of the heroes would catch sight of him outside their classroom, and he'd give a little wink before strolling on. It was maddening.

They searched for the Malonomicon, too, but made little progress. After much arguing, Devis finally agreed to pick the lock on Tristane's locker to see if it was in there. It wasn't, of course. However, the heroes did find a stack of flyers for an upcoming performance. It appeared that Tristane Trouvère was planning on making his musical debut in a few weeks with a "secret, all-ages show" at a local music venue called the Monarch.

After the warg attack, there were no more portents of evil. Apart from Tristane Trouvère's petty scams, nothing particularly untoward seemed to be happening in the sleepy Realm of Suburbia. They wondered if Devis might be right. Perhaps the spellbook had been incinerated or recycled by now. But how could they ever know?

As experienced adventurers, they weren't quite used to all forward progress on an adventure slowly grinding to an anticlimactic halt, though June assured them that this was quite normal in her world. "Take it one day at a time," she told them. "Stay positive. Stay hydrated. Try to get enough sleep."

One day at lunch the party sat in silence, each one contemplating their lack of progression in the quest.

Devis dropped his fish sandwich on his tray. "All right, I'll say it. What happens if we never actually find the Malonomicon?"

Sorrowshade considered this. "I suppose we would spin out the remainder of our meaningless lives in this sad, gray place as either telemarketers or social media managers? Pass the human ketchup, please."

June passed her the ketchup. "C'mon. There's more to this world than that," said June. "With all of your amazing abilities, you guys could totally end up as claims adjusters for a midsized regional insurance company."

"Our disappointing future career options are moot," said Vela. "We *will* find the book. Albiorix, have you made any headway in relearning the find lost object spell?"

Albiorix nearly spat out his milk. "Yes, good, very good. Good headway." In truth, he had attempted the spell several more times and had never been as successful as his first attempt at the Old Mall. Was he somehow getting dumber?

"So you can successfully cast the spell now, then?" asked Thromdurr. He clapped Albiorix on the back. "Kudos! A stunning reversal to your recent string of wizardly humiliations."

Albiorix swallowed. "Um, not quite. I feel like I'm maybe eighty . . . no, seventy-nine percent of the way there."

"Which is to say: zero," said Devis. "Look, Tristane Trouvère obviously has some method of getting back and forth between here and Bríandalör. Maybe if we called a truce, I could talk to the guy and figure a way out of this—"

"No!" said Albiorix. "The bard is a menace. I won't let him exploit the good people of this world."

"Agreed," said Vela. "We cannot stand idly by while evil reigns upon the land."

"He's just stealing," said Devis. "That's not a crime!"

Vela buried her face in her hands. "Oh, Devis."

"Sure it's just lies and short cons for now," said Albiorix, "but he's capable of much worse. He sent a warg to kill us!"

"We don't know that was him," said Devis.

"I'm not going to cut some deal with that lying, perfect-haired jerk," said Albiorix.

"I second that," said Sorrowshade. "I plan to crush Tristane Trouvère beneath my bootheel and laugh in his face while I destroy everything he holds dear. Pass the human mustard, please."

June passed her the mustard.

Devis crossed his arms. "Well then, even if we find the Malonomicon, we have no way of getting back to Brían-dalör."

"It's the same fallback plan as last time," said Albiorix. "We end the scenario and get home by completing the objectives from the nonadventure module *The Freshman Year of Futility*."

"Which are what?" asked Vela.

Albiorix blinked. "We've been so busy I haven't even had time to check. Hang on." The wizard whipped out *The Freshman Year of Futility* and paged to the end.

Sorrowshade scowled. "How can you not know this already? I thought reading these tedious game books was your reason for living. If you can't fight or cast spells or deploy your Homerooms & Hall Passes meta-game knowledge to our advantage, then you're basically just June."

"Excuse me?" said June. "I beat the main bad guy last time!"

"Here we go. Victory conditions," said Albiorix. The

wizard read the page silently. At last he let out a quiet *"oof."*

The rest of the party looked at each other.

"Was that an *'oof'* of hope, Albiorix?" asked Vela.

"No," said Albiorix. The wizard read aloud: "'To win this nonadventure, player characters must complete three of the five objectives: One, get a perfect score on the Academic Basic Skill Evaluation Exam. Two, throw an epic high school party with at least one hundred attendees. Three, be a member of a state championship team. Four, get crowned homecoming king or queen. Five, win Battle of the Bands.'"

Devis whistled.

"I guess they tried to make Advanced Homerooms & Hall Passes more difficult to appeal to the hardcore gamers," said Albiorix. "Like me."

"Well, does our situation appeal to you?" asked Sorrowshade.

Albiorix frowned.

"It seems we face a difficult road ahead," said Vela. "Achieving any one of those goals would be a daunting challenge, much less three of them. Still, we must not despair."

"So, who's excited to become a social media manager?" asked Sorrowshade.

"No, guys, Vela's right," said Albiorix. "I think we can do this. Sure, a couple of these objectives are a little hard to imagine. Not sure I see us winning homecoming king or queen, which is basically just a glorified popularity contest, when the five of us collectively only have one friend."

"You guys have a friend?" said June. "Oh, right. Me. Well, I could get Morton to vote for one of you too. He loves you guys."

"Mmm," said Albiorix. "Still, I think we hold off on that one until we all somehow become much more likable."

"Just a theory," said Thromdurr. "Perhaps Sorrowshade is bringing down the average?"

"If I ever become likable, please load me into a catapult and fling me into an active volcano," said Sorrowshade.

"Doesn't matter," said Devis. "I'm charismatic enough for all of us. The secret is telling people what they want to hear."

"You mean lying all the time," said Vela.

"That's very insightful of you, Vela," said Devis. "Out of all the party, I've always thought you were the most perceptive."

"Why, thank you," said Vela.

"And sure, maybe I'm not exactly a homecoming king type," said Devis, "but Stinky Smith could totally throw an awesome party that a hundred people would come to."

"I admire that confidence," said Albiorix. "But I am extremely dubious." The wizard continued down the list. "Is Battle of the Bands a possibility? Do any of us possess any musical talent?"

"I'm a fantastic lute player!" said Devis.

"Are you just telling me what I want to hear?" asked Albiorix.

"That's very insightful of you, Albiorix," said Devis. "Out of all the party, I've always thought you were the most perceptive."

"Right," said Albiorix. "How about you, Vela?"

"Well, Valerie *was* first chair flute in the marching band," said Vela, "until people, ahem, heard me play my instrument."

"Okay. Thromdurr?"

"I can perform the traditional war yodel of the Sky Bear clan," said Thromdurr. "It is extremely loud."

"I'll bet it is," said Albiorix. "June?"

"As I mentioned, I've been teaching myself guitar," said June. "I can get all the way through 'House of the Rising Sun.' Almost."

"Noted." Albiorix turned to Sorrowshade. "And how about you—"

"No," said the gloom elf. "No music." Her look suggested he should not press it further.

"Yeesh. Okay, so Battle of the Bands is out for now," said Albiorix.

"What, pray tell, is the Academic Basic Skill Evaluation Exam?" asked Thromdurr.

"Oh, I can answer that," said June. "It's the big statewide

standardized test for ninth graders. Totally grueling. They call it the ABSEE for short."

"If we all study super hard like we did for our big algebra test last year," said Albiorix, "then at least one of us can ace it."

"Sounds like a lot of effort," said Thromdurr. "Perhaps you should take point on that one, friend wizard."

"Fine, I will," said Albiorix. "The ABSEE isn't for a while, though. And neither is homecoming. At the moment, I think our best bet is a state championship team."

"That's smart," said June. "There are loads of teams, and unlike in school-school, your cool fantasy adventurer skills might actually help you with them."

Vela brightened. "I am a champion of light and goodness. Perhaps I could also be champion of . . . volleyball?"

"Right on," said June. "Sorrowshade, I'm pretty sure that Pine Hill has an archery team."

"The thought of being on a team of any sort makes me want to crawl out of my skin and then turn around and throw up into the empty skin I just vacated," said Sorrowshade.

"Vivid imagery." June pushed her tray away. "I think I'm done with lunch."

"But . . . I suppose I can check it out," said the gloom elf.

"And Thromdurr, you're twice the size of anyone at this school, including faculty," said June. "Any sport would be lucky to have you. It's a no-brainer."

"A no-brainer sounds like a good choice for me," said Thromdurr.

June sized up Devis. "And dude, with your acrobatic skills, I'm thinking you go out for spirit squad."

"Ooh," said Devis. "If that is some sort of organized ghost-hunting team, then count me in!"

"Hmm," said June, who didn't want to correct him. "And Albiorix, I hope this isn't an offensive stereotype, but . . . wizards are super good at chess, right?"

Albiorix threw his hands up. "June, how dare you!"

"Oh gosh, sorry," said June. "I just . . . I think I saw it on a black light poster at my cousin's house and I figured—"

"Nah, I'm just kidding," said Albiorix. "Of course wizards are good at chess. Although in Bríandalör we call it gryphon chess."

"Then you can join chess club," said June.

And so the bold adventurers had formed a plan: while their search for the Malonomicon was stalled and their efforts to stop Tristane Trouvère's misdeeds were thwarted, they would lay the groundwork for their eventual departure, through statewide extracurricular success.

Chapter 11

Chapter Eight of the Advanced Hall Master's Guide details 387 of the most common extracurricular activities available to characters in the game. But please note this list is far from exhaustive! As Hall Master, feel free to make up your own. When you are creating a new extracurricular, the only requirements are that it looks good on a college application and costs dozens of hours of your player characters' precious free time.

—Excerpt from The Advanced Hall Master's Guide

❧

"I'M SORRY," SAID COACH Uribe. "Unfortunately, it's too late to join the archery team, Melissa."

"Aw," said Sorrowshade. "Too bad."

The gloom elf rejoined her companions. "No dice. Looks like I'm doomed to miss out on forced camaraderie, weekend practices, and rambling, cliché-ridden pep talks.

Instead I'll focus on searching for the Malonomicon."

Albiorix shook his head. "I wish I'd thought about how missing the first three weeks of school would mean we'd lose the chance to sign up for so many extracurriculars."

"By my reckoning, it is also too late for football, cross-country, soccer, tennis, and volleyball," said Vela. "Since I have conquered my fear of public speaking, I plan to audition for the speech and debate team this afternoon. I have four hours to master all of this strange fictional world's current events."

June handed Vela her phone. "Here. Try Wikipedia."

"No spots left on the gryphon chess club, either," said Albiorix. "So I need to somehow convince Ms. Kozlowski I deserve to be there."

"Ooh, I also heard through the grapevine that since Katie Ng broke her toe, spirit squad needs one more member," said June. "They're actually holding tryouts for her replacement this afternoon, Devis."

"Spirit squad tryouts?" said Devis. "Is that, like, exploring a haunted mansion and helping all the restless souls trapped inside pass on to the next world?"

"Don't tell him," said Albiorix.

"Okay," said June.

"And I shall attempt to joint the wrestling team," said Thromdurr. "Will I be successful? Perhaps! Perhaps not!

So it goes, friends. So it goes."

June took Albiorix aside. "Dude, what happened to Thromdurr?"

Albiorix sighed. "It's possible dying may have depressed him a little."

And so the party split up to continue their school day, with a plan to meet later that night at June's house. Between third and fourth periods, Albiorix sought out the chess coach, Ms. Kozlowski, who normally taught physics. He entreated her to let him join the team.

"You're too late," said Ms. Kozlowski. "Registration is closed. Try again next year."

"I thought you might say that," said Albiorix. "So how about we play a game of gryphon chess, and if I beat you, I can join the club."

"*Gryphon* chess?"

"Uh, sorry," said Albiorix. "I meant regular, normal chess. Obviously. It's not called gryphon chess, and gryphons don't exist."

"I know that, Armando," said Ms. Kozlowski. "You know, I think you may have read one too many fairy tales. In the real world, things don't come down to dramatic contests of skill. There are sign-up periods, official deadlines, and paperwork that needs to be sent to the statewide chess association."

"I see," said Albiorix. "You're afraid you're going to lose."

Ms. Kozlowski's eyes narrowed. She pulled out a small magnetic chessboard from her desk drawer. "You have until the tardy bell rings."

The game was a little different than gryphon chess. The gryphon was called a "queen." Gnomes were "pawns." Rocs were "rooks." But the basic mechanics were the same. Albiorix didn't need until the tardy bell, though. He beat Ms. Kozlowski in four moves.

"Impressive," said Ms. Kozlowski. "You've got skill, Armando, I'll give you that. But you've already missed six practices. I'll take you as an alternate, so long as you don't miss any more. Got it?"

"Got it," said Albiorix.

After school, Thromdurr made his way to the gym, where he found Jeff Bohannon, the wrestling coach, reading the sports section of the newspaper before practice. When Coach Bohannon caught sight of the barbarian, he dropped the paper and did a double take.

"Oh, wow," said Coach Bohannon. "Look at you."

"My name is Douglas Schiller," said Thromdurr. "And I have come to join your wrestling team so that we might win a state championship. Perhaps such glory can alleviate the gnawing sense of purposelessness I have felt of late."

"That's the spirit," said Mr. Bohannon. "Not that it's a

deal breaker, but do you have any wrestling experience?"

"I recently wrestled a gigantic scorpion off a cliff," said Thromdurr.

"I'll bet you did," said Coach Bohannon. "Look, technically, the sign-up period is closed. But to be honest, Sean Holland has little tiny noodle arms and you—well, I'm not sure I've seen biceps like yours on a ninth grader before. What kind of workout do you do, son?"

"Climbing. Hammering. Hefting large treasure chests overflowing with gold," said Thromdurr.

"So, sort of a crossfit thing," said Coach Bohannon. "Interesting. Well, let me just introduce you to the guys, and then we can get you fitted for a uniform."

Coach Bohannon led Thromdurr into a stuffy practice room with mats on the floor. It was filled with high school boys in purple singlets and boots and protective headgear who were already stretching and warming up for practice.

"All right, fellas," said the coach. "I want to introduce you to the newest member of the Pine Hill Harriers wrestling team. His name's Schiller, and well, you've all got eyes, right? With a kid like this on the team, we're going all the way to state. What do you say?"

Coach Bohannon seemed to be waiting for a cheer. It never came. The wrestling team merely stared at Thromdurr with quiet skepticism.

Teddy McGirk stepped forward. He was both the

shortest kid on the team and the most muscular. "Nah, I don't think so, Coach."

"What do you mean you don't think so, McGirk?" said Coach Bohannon.

"I don't think he's right for the team," said Teddy. "The dork might be big, but he's weak. Plus I don't like his haircut."

"I am not weak," said Thromdurr, who suddenly felt a spark of his old competitive nature flare. "And my hair is thick and lustrous."

"Sure, he hasn't had much practice," said Coach Bohannon. "But with his size, I think he could really help us—"

"Nope," said Teddy. "Veto."

"Veto? I'm the coach of this team," said Coach Bohannon. Though Thromdurr thought he heard a touch of uncertainty in the man's voice.

"I'm the coach of this team," said Teddy in a mocking voice. The other wrestlers laughed.

"That is incredibly disrespectful," said Coach Bohannon. "I will not tolerate—"

Teddy suddenly lunged toward Coach Bohannon, causing him to flinch backward and almost trip. The other wrestlers laughed again.

"Look, Coach, I'm going to lay it out for you like you're dumb," said Teddy. "I'm your best wrestler in any weight class, correct? When I wrestle, I win. You need to win. 'Cause if you have another season like you did last year? Hoo boy. Well, let's just say you're going to go from Coach Bohannon to Job Search Bohannon."

Coach Bohannon stared at the ground and spoke quietly. "There were a lot of factors that led to last year's disappointing season. But we've learned from our mistakes and we strive to do better."

"Uh-huh," said Teddy McGirk. "But, hey, I like you, Coach, so I'm going to throw you a bone. I'll give the jumbo shrimp one shot to pin me. If he doesn't embarrass himself, he can wear the uniform. Sound fair?"

Coach Bohannon nodded but didn't make eye contact. "Looks like you're up, Schiller."

"I shall relish the opportunity," said Thromdurr. "Despite your diminutive stature, I do not intend to hold back."

"Oh no," said Teddy. "I'm shaking in my unitard."

Thromdurr and Teddy McGirk headed to the mat while the rest of the team crowded around. Teddy rolled his neck and smiled. Thromdurr lowered himself into a fighting stance. Coach Bohannon blew the whistle.

With blinding speed, Teddy threw himself at the barbarian's midriff. Thromdurr grappled at him, but before he could get a hold, Teddy McGirk had spun around behind him. Teddy used his lower center of gravity to lift Thromdurr off his feet and slam him backward onto the mat. Throm-durr's legs flailed helplessly in the air. His arms were locked at his sides. He couldn't move. He was pinned. The whole thing had taken all of two seconds.

Coach Bohannon blew his whistle. "All right, McGirk, you made your point."

But Teddy held Thromdurr for a long moment, just to prove he could. "Nerds don't belong on the wrestling team," he whispered in Thromdurr's ear.

Teddy released his grip, and the barbarian scrambled to his feet. Thromdurr fled the practice room while the rest of the team jeered and laughed. Teddy McGirk watched him go with his arms crossed and a joyless grin on his face.

Meanwhile, in the auditorium on the other side of the Pine Hill High School campus, Vela the Valiant prepared to audition for the speech and debate team. Mr. Divekar, the speech and debate coach, introduced her to the rest of the team.

"Okay, folks, this is Valerie," said Mr. Divekar. "She's a freshman who's very, very eager to join us."

All the team members greeted Vela politely save one.

"You again?" said Christina Christopoulos.

Before Vela could answer, Christina checked her watch.

"So, Valerie," said Mr. Divekar, "typically, we present

prospective members with a sample debate topic, give them a few minutes to digest it, and then there's a short mock debate against one of our current team members. No pressure—we're open to all skill levels here. It's just a helpful way for us to see where you're at with this stuff. Sound good?"

"I am ready to orate," said Vela. "May my tongue be guided by the twin spirits of logic and clear elocution!" She bowed.

"Um, great," said Mr. Divekar. "Do I have any volunteers for a mock debate with Valerie?"

Christina sighed loudly.

"Anybody?" asked Mr. Divekar.

"That loud sigh was me saying yes, I'll debate her," said Christina, "as long as it doesn't make practice run long. You know I've got equestrian lessons at five p.m."

"You'll make it to your horses, Christina," said Mr. Divekar. "All right, Valerie, here's your topic. Should our country use existing antitrust laws to police tech giants?"

Vela beamed. She had read several articles about this very subject on June's phone earlier and had already formed a hard and rational opinion on the matter.

"Mr. Divekar, I need no time to digest," said Vela. "For I am prepared to argue my . . ." The paladin trailed off.

"Position?" asked Mr. Divekar.

Vela said nothing. Somehow her words failed her. She

knew exactly what she wanted to say, but she simply couldn't say it. Mr. Divekar looked at her expectantly. He wiggled his fingers as if he could somehow coax the sound out of her with the gesture. Yet no sound came. The other team members looked uncomfortable. For her part, Christina Christopoulos stared daggers at Vela.

The paladin took a deep breath and tried to start over. Still nothing. Mr. Divekar frowned.

"Is she okay?" asked one of the other debate team members.

"This happened to her in middle school too," said another. "During announcements."

"She's taking too long!" cried Christina at last.

"Sorry," said Vela. "I know what I want to say, I just . . . I can't seem to say it."

"Well, saying stuff is, ahem, pretty much the gist of what we do here," said Mr. Divekar. "If you don't like public speaking, then maybe speech and debate isn't the team for you, Valerie. But there are plenty of quiet extracurricular activities you can do. Like meditation club."

Vela shook her head. "I thought I had conquered this."

"While Vanessa works through her personal demons, can the rest of us get on with practice?" asked Christina. "I do not want to lose to Westview High."

And so Vela left the auditorium, unable to join the Pine Hill High School speech and debate team. In the hallway, as she walked away, she was able to fully articulate her argument in favor of enforcing existing antitrust laws against the ever-growing power of the tech giants. But of course it was too late.

Meanwhile, in the gymnasium, the Pine Hill spirit squad held special tryouts for the open spot on the team recently vacated by Katie Ng. (Get well soon, Katie!) After reviewing several excellent routines, they ultimately chose Kimberly Savage, who could do a back handspring. For his part, Devis had completely forgotten about spirit squad by then. The clever thief had something else in mind entirely.

And so of all the Bríandalörians, only the wizard Albiorix managed to find his place on a team. Sorrowshade was indifferent; Vela was perplexed; Devis was occupied with other matters. Only Thromdurr the barbarian took his failure to heart.

The barbarian had never encountered a foe quite like Teddy McGirk, and certainly not in the Realm of Suburbia, where the people were soft and squishy. It was true he had struggled to care about most of the challenges that had presented themselves to the party since his valorous death, but today was different. Thromdurr had genuinely meant to defeat the boy in single combat—he'd even felt a flash of his old berserker rage!—but he'd been bested. It hadn't been through luck or trickery. It had been sheer skill in battle.

And Teddy McGirk had done it easily.

Thromdurr wandered the empty halls alone after school, stricken with self-pity. If he could not win a simple wrestling match against a boy half his size, how could he call himself a hero? Perhaps even his scorpion death had been a fluke? Or, at best, the pinnacle of his life? Maybe all his deeds meant nothing and would soon be forgotten, like the builders of that dusty old temple? In this fugue of melodramatic melancholy, the barbarian closed his eyes and called toward the heavens.

"O great Sky Bear, ancestral totem of my clan!" said Thromdurr. "It seems my warrior spirit has fled me, leaving only the mewling specter of self-doubt. How can I battle the opponent within? The opponent who is me! If you can hear this humble berserker, show me the path forward."

It was at this moment that Thromdurr accidentally walked into a door.

"Ow," said Thromdurr, opening his eyes.

He saw a piece of notebook paper taped to the door. On it was written:

Math League Practice
Room 117

"A competition of mathematical prowess," said Thromdurr. "I may no longer be a worthy warrior, but I *was* pretty good at algebra, wasn't I? Yes, this must be the answer."

And so the barbarian headed to room 117, a tiny conference room off the school library. Mr. Marsella, the geometry teacher, snoozed in a swivel chair with a crime novel open on his chest, while two freshmen quietly did practice math problems from a workbook.

"Oh, hey, man," said Morton Blanc.

"Greetings, Morton Blanc," said Thromdurr.

"Not you," said Olivia Gorman.

"None other," said Thromdurr. "I have come to join the league of math."

"Oh, cool!" said Morton. "We need another—"

"Not cool," said Olivia. "It's not going happen, Doug. You're not even good at math. Go do something else."

"I tried," said Thromdurr. "Is Mr. Marsella the coach of this team? I shall rouse him from his slumber and make my case directly."

Thromdurr moved toward Mr. Marsella, but Olivia stepped between them.

"Don't you dare wake that man up," said Olivia. "Look, Doug, I don't want you on this team because you're dishonest. You and your friends ruined my life last year. You made me a laughingstock. You did it by cheating."

Thromdurr frowned. "I apologize. Though, in our defense, we acted for reasons you cannot understand."

"Oh, I understand, all right," said Olivia. "I understand

145

that the cool kids like you and your friends can do whatever you want, and the rest of us dorks are the ones who pay the price."

"Cool kids?" said Thromdurr. "Olivia, I assure you, my companions and I are not cool at all. By the standards of this place, our lameness knows no bounds."

"It took me a whole year to crawl out from under the class president scandal," said Olivia. "There wasn't even going to be a math league team until I begged Mr. Marsella to let me start one. This is my thing. I can't let you ruin it for me."

"Believe me, I do not wish to ruin it," said Thromdurr. "I want nothing more than for our Pine Hill High School to win the state championship."

Olivia squinted. "I don't get it. Last year you came to me begging for help with algebra."

"And you taught me well," said Thromdurr. "Please, give me a chance to prove myself. I . . . I need this."

"We need him too, Olivia," said Morton. "You know as well as I do that we can't even compete if we don't have the minimum three-member roster on the team."

Olivia let out long sigh. "Fine," she said. Then she paged through the workbook and picked out a problem. "What's the solution to $3^x = x^3$?"

Thromdurr considered this for a moment and then let

out a booming laugh that actually woke up Mr. Marsella.

"You phrased your question as though it has but one solution," said Thromdurr. "A clever ruse, Olivia Gorman. But the equation has two solutions: x equals three and x equals infinity!"

Morton checked the workbook. "Yep. He's right."

Thromdurr grinned and bowed. "As I said, Olivia Gorman, you taught me well."

There was a long pause.

"Okay, Doug," said Olivia. "You're on the team. Until you inevitably screw it up and we all go down in flames."

Thromdurr raised his fist toward the sky, triumphant. "Until we all go down in flames!"

"What's happening?" asked Mr. Marsella. "I wasn't asleep. Who is this kid?"

"I am Douglas Schiller," said Thromdurr. "The newest member of the math league."

Albiorix walked through the darkened streets of Hibbettsfield. The wizard kept a wary eye out for wargs or any other enemies who might unexpectedly appear. No ambush came, however, and he arrived safely at 410 North Rush Street.

As he entered June Westray's house, he couldn't help but notice that her mother, Amy, greeted him a bit coldly. Cheese, June's fat orange tabby cat, was as friendly as ever, though, rubbing his head against the wizard's ankles. Albiorix found the other adventurers eating cookies in the Westray living room, updating one another on their progress.

"Devis, why didn't you go to the spirit squad tryouts?" asked June.

"What? Oh, the ghost-hunting thing?" said Devis. "Nah, I've been working on something way better. Trust me."

"Here we go," said Sorrowshade. "June, you might want to cover your ears in case the authorities question you later."

"It's not like that," said Devis. "So my parents, Stinky and Stinky, are out of town this weekend. They're going to this big annual soup conference."

"Did that sentence make sense to anyone else?" asked June.

The others nodded.

June shrugged. "Fine. Continue."

"While the Stinkys are away, the Stinky will play," said Devis. "Sounded better in my head. Anyway, this is the perfect chance to throw an epic high school party and check off a scenario objective."

"Sounds great," said Sorrowshade. "One question: how are you going to convince anyone other than us to hang out with you?"

"Yeah, Devis," said Albiorix. "Ethical concerns aside, if

this is some sort of kidnapping plot, I feel like you're going to run into a problem of scale."

"I'm not kidnapping anyone to come to my party," said Devis. "I'm generating buzz. With these." He grinned and held up a dark blue paper invitation shaped like a question mark. Devis flipped it around. On the reverse it had a day (Friday), a time (seven p.m.), an address (800 North Pineknoll Avenue), and two words in capital letters:

DREAM HUGE

"Dream huge?" asked Albiorix. "What does that even mean?"

"It's like 'dream big,' but bigger," said Devis.

"And what does 'dream huge' have to do with your party?" asked Thromdurr.

Devis shrugged. "I don't know. It's just, like, a vibe, man."

"I am credulous to a fault," said Vela. "And this invitation is perhaps the least persuasive thing I have ever seen."

"That's because you don't understand marketing," said Devis. "The less people know, the more they *want* to know. Just like the bard in my old party used to . . ." The thief trailed off as he realized the other heroes were glaring at him. "Well, it doesn't matter who said it, it's true. These invitations are so vague and mysterious, people won't be able to stay away."

"I mean, I guess it's worth a shot," said Albiorix. "If nobody knows it's your party, they might actually come."

Vela frowned. "The tactic is borderline dishonest. But I suppose it doesn't quite cross the threshold into lying."

"Exactly!" said Devis. "Marketing!"

"In a twisted way, it's sort of genius," said Sorrowshade.

"Of course it is," said Devis. "I've already slipped these into the lockers of all the coolest kids at Pine Hill High School. They'll tell all their friends, and those friends will tell their friends. Come Friday, we will be turning people away at the door of 800 North Pineknoll Avenue."

"Well, Morton and I will be there," said June. "So you only need ninety-eight more guests."

"Morton's coming?" said Albiorix.

"Yes, of course," said June.

"Hmm," said Albiorix. "I guess that's fine. Just don't tell him what it's really about. We don't want word to get out that it's actually us throwing the party."

June cocked her head. "Morton wouldn't tell anybody."

"I don't know," said Albiorix. "The guy looks like he can't keep a secret."

"How can somebody look like they can't keep a secret?" asked June.

Albiorix shrugged. And the other four Bríandalörians glanced at each other and it was a bit awkward. But all in all, the adventuring party had passed a relatively successful day in the Realm of Suburbia, and spirits were high. Between chess club and math league and Devis's unexpected knack for party planning, they now had a plausible path to completing two of the three scenario objectives from *The Freshman Year of Futility.*

Yet the Malonomicon was still lost. And as they laughed and joked in June Westray's living room, outside in the shadows someone watched them and quietly plotted their downfall.

Chapter 12

When you hear the word "party," you naturally think of a bold band of adventurers with a complementary set of skills for conquering any dungeon. But in the high school world of Advanced Homerooms & Hall Passes, the word "party" has an altogether different connotation.

—*Excerpt from* The Advanced Hall Master's Guide

❧

DING! THROMDURR SLAMMED HIS bell a hair quicker than Morton.

"The solution is n equals seven!" cried Thromdurr.

"You are correct, Doug," said Olivia, who was moderating the practice match. "But do you have to be so loud about it?"

"Sorry," said Thromdurr. "The thrill of mathematical competition makes it hard for me to moderate the volume of my voice."

"I almost beat you to it, too," said Morton, scribbling something on his practice sheet. "Although I was going to say n equals eleven. Which was wrong. So maybe not answering was the best move? Life is complicated. Hey, sounds like I came up with another grandma throw pillow."

Olivia glanced at the clock. "Well, it's five. That's it for today."

"Already?" asked Thromdurr. "Can we not stay and do more math?"

"This guy is a beast," said Morton as he stood and collected his things. "Glad to have you on the team, Doug. But the rest of us need to eat and sleep occasionally."

"And now some parting words from our math league coach, Mr. Marsella," said Olivia. She gestured toward Mr. Marsella. Despite all the bells and yelling, he was still fast asleep in his swivel chair. He looked as peaceful as a forty-five-year-old mustachioed baby.

"Very inspiring," said Olivia. "Next practice is Tuesday afternoon. And since we now meet the minimum number of team members required to officially compete, looks like we're going to face off against Riverview High School for the Arts in two weeks. I want to be ready."

Thromdurr pounded his bell. "We shall crush them without mercy. When the match is done, the auditorium will ring with the powerful lamentations of their parents."

"I repeat: this guy is a beast," said Morton. "Hey, are you

guys going to that Dream Huge thing tonight?"

"What's that?" asked Olivia.

"Yes, and I too do not know what that is, and would also like to know," muttered Thromdurr, who had many talents, of which lying was not one.

"Some mysterious party that everybody's going to," said Morton. "There were all these anonymous invitations in people's lockers the other day. June told me about it."

"Well, count me out," said Olivia. "They don't want people like us there."

"I think you should attend," said Thromdurr. "Perhaps the party's organizers merely need a minimum of one hundred people there, and they are indifferent to who—"

"Nope. It's just another way for the cool kids to make the rest of us feel excluded," said Olivia. "Can I ask, Morton, did you actually receive an invitation of your own?"

"Well, no," said Morton.

"How about you, Doug?" asked Olivia.

"Technically, I did not," said Thromdurr.

"And we never will," said Olivia. "Nerds like us have to grind away for any shred of respect we ever get, while the Populars get to have fun all the time. Everything is just handed to them on a silver platter because of their rich parents and perfect faces. It's completely unfair."

Morton shrugged. "I don't know. I just thought it might be fun."

"Fun? I'd rather eat 6.022×10^{23} particles of dirt," said Olivia. "What is Dream Huge anyway? It's not a phrase. It's not even grammatically correct. Those two words don't mean anything together!"

"Perhaps it is like 'dream big,' but even bigger," said Thromdurr quietly.

"My huge dream is getting into a good college and leaving Pine Hill High behind so I don't have to deal with this ridiculous teenage caste system *ever* again," said Olivia. "Enjoy your evening."

And with that, she left.

Morton and Thromdurr looked at each other. Mr. Marsella stirred a little in his sleep.

"Dude, what was that about?" asked Morton.

Thromdurr sighed. "I believe Olivia still harbors some resentment over events that transpired last year. Events for which my companions and I were, ahem, unfortunately responsible."

"Oh, the class president thing?" asked Morton. "Yeah, she told me about it. Why did you guys do that?"

"Winning class president seemed like life or death at the time," said Thromdurr. "Perhaps I can atone by leading our math league team to victory."

"I think that would make Olivia happy," said Morton. "At least, as happy as she gets. To be perfectly honest, I don't even think Nerds actually get treated too badly here."

"You have not encountered Teddy McGirk," said Thromdurr.

"I guess I just stay in my lane," said Morton. "Maybe Olivia's right. Maybe I shouldn't go to this party?"

"Nay, friend Morton," said Thromdurr. "We shall attend together."

"Cool," said Morton. "It's either going to be legendary or a total disaster. Either way, should be fun to watch, right?"

Thromdurr paused. "And why would the party be a disaster?"

"Any time something gets this hyped up, there's basically no way for it to meet expectations," said Morton.

"Huh," said Thromdurr.

And the barbarian did have a tingling sensation that might or might not have been a sense of impending doom. But he brushed it off, and he and Morton Blanc set out across the town of Hibbettsfield toward 800 North Pineknoll Avenue.

June Westray and the four other Bríandalörians were already there. Devis—who had been uncharacteristically nervous all week—flitted around the house, putting up balloons and decorations and making sure all the last-minute preparations for his party were in place. The others watched.

"Where's a good place for Pin the Tail on the Donkey?" asked the thief. "I'm thinking in the den, beside the piñata."

"Putting a blindfolded person with a pin next to another blindfolded person with a baseball bat might not be the ideal combination," said Albiorix.

Devis frowned. "My party's going to be a failure, isn't it?"

"No, no, it's going to be great," said Albiorix. The wizard hoped he sounded convincing.

"Totally," said June. "Except . . . why are you having Pin the Tail on the Donkey and piñatas again?"

"I don't know!" said Devis. "I just went to the party store and got a bunch of stuff for a party, okay? Please don't tell me I should've sprung for the bouncy castle."

June cocked her head. "So you planned this entire thing without any real idea of what high schoolers actually want at a party?"

"Of course I know what high schoolers want at a party," said Devis. "You can see that I made over a dozen party soups!" He indicated the various pots, bowls, and tureens strategically placed around the room.

"Huh," said June. She gave Albiorix a warning look. The wizard shrugged.

"Now people just need to show up before the cream of celery gets cold and the gazpacho gets warm," said Devis. The thief kept glancing from the clock to the door to the clock again. The seconds ticked by at an agonizing pace.

"It's 7:01 and nobody's here," hissed Sorrowshade in

Devis's ear. "Your party's a failure."

"Aaagh! I knew it!" cried Devis.

"Do not lose heart, Devis," said Vela. "Of course I would arrive promptly at the time on the invitation, but few possess my unwavering commitment to punctuality."

Just then the doorbell rang. Devis's eyes lit up. He rushed to answer it.

"Greetings!" said Thromdurr.

"Oh, it's just you," said Devis, slumping.

"Good to see you too, friend," said Thromdurr.

"Hi?" said Morton as he followed the barbarian in. "Wait, this is your house, Stinky?"

"Yep," said Devis. "Can I offer you some lobster bisque?"

"Uh, sure," said Morton.

Devis handed Morton a bowl full of soup and a spoon.

"June, did you know Stinky organized this mysterious underground party?" asked Morton.

"Yes, I wanted to tell you, but I was sworn to secrecy," said June. "Armando thought you'd spill the beans."

"What, no, I didn't . . . I was just . . . We were being extra careful, is all," said Albiorix.

"No, no, I get it," said Morton. "I kind of look like I can't keep a secret, right?"

"Yes!" cried Albiorix.

"You're not wrong," said Morton. "I don't mean to, but

158

I've blown more pranks and spoiled more twist endings than I care to remember. I'm just kind of naturally honest."

"An admirable quality, Morton," said Vela.

"Eh," said Devis.

Morton looked around. "Are there any other guests here?"

"Nope," said Sorrowshade. "The party's a bust. It's mortifying."

Devis buried his face in his hands. "I hoped the first invitation would be enough. But after the second invitation, I was sure people would come."

"What second invitation?" asked Vela.

But before Devis could respond, the doorbell rang. Devis answered it.

Marc Mansour, an extremely cool junior who played on the basketball team, stood outside.

"Hello, hello, welcome, please come in," said Devis. "Can I interest you in some tom yum, a traditional Thai hot and sour soup made with shrimp and lemongrass?"

"Nah, I'm good," said Marc as he stepped inside and looked around. "Is Dream Huge your party?"

"Yep," said Devis.

"Cool," said Marc.

"My name is Stinky," said Devis.

"Uh-huh," said Marc.

This was followed by a long, awkward silence.

After a minute or so, June could bear it no longer. "Do you want to play Pin the Tail on the Donkey?" she asked, and immediately regretted asking.

"Nah, I'm . . . I'm good," said Marc. He shifted a little and put his hands in his pockets.

The doorbell rang again. There were four more people outside, all upperclassmen. As soon as Devis had greeted them and offered them soup, the doorbell rang yet again. By seven twenty-five, there were at least forty people crowding the foyer of 800 North Pineknoll Avenue. Many stared at their phones. A few made awkward small talk. Mostly they looked confused and a bit impatient.

"I figured it was a long shot, but somehow he's pulled it off," said Albiorix to June.

"It's weird, though. Nobody seems to really want to be here," said June. "But they aren't leaving yet. If they keep coming at this rate, you'll get your hundred guests by eight o'clock."

"Hey, is it cool if I just snag my free phone and leave?" asked a senior named Monica Hilaire.

"Yeah, where are the free phones?" asked Marc Mansour.

"Oh, how careless of me," said Devis. "I forgot to put them out."

Devis disappeared upstairs and came back with a large

bowl. Instead of soup, though, it was filled with dozens of new smartphones, still in their packaging.

Before he could offer them to the guests, Vela grabbed Devis by the arm and yanked him aside. June and the other Bríandalörians crowded into the hall closet.

"Hey, why'd you grab me?" asked Devis. "I'm hosting here!"

"Free phones?" asked Vela. "Devis, what precisely are you doing?"

"Oh, well, when you throw a party in this world, it's polite to offer your guests some token of appreciation," said Devis. "They're called party favors."

"Party favors?" said Albiorix. "Each of these costs, like, six hundred dollars!"

"What can I say?" said Devis. "I'm *very* polite."

"Explain yourself now, Devis," said Vela.

"We wanted people to come to this party, right?" said Devis. "But I was worried nobody would show up. So yesterday I slipped another invitation into all the cool kids' lockers."

Devis showed them a new invitation. It was printed on the same dark blue paper, only it was shaped like a dollar sign this time. In addition to the date, time and address, it read:

FREE PHONES FOR THE FIRST 100 GUESTS

"People love freebies," said Devis.

"He's not wrong," said June.

"See? Another genius marketing move by me," said Devis. "You're welcome."

Vela's eyes narrowed. "Where did you get a hundred new phones?"

"I bet I know," said Sorrowshade.

"No, no, no! It's not what you guys think," said Devis. "I *stole* them."

Vela blinked. "That is exactly what I thought."

"Me too," said Albiorix.

"Also me," said Sorrowshade.

"I thought perhaps an eccentric millionaire gave them to you," said Thromdurr. "But stealing makes a lot of sense."

"Turns out Valu-Barn only has one security guard at night, and he's usually pretty distracted by updating his online dating profile," said Devis. "Poor guy. Hope he finds that special someone."

Vela snatched the bowl of phones away from Devis. "You must return these stolen goods, at once."

The thief sighed. "Was it wrong to steal these phones? Sure, maybe, if you subscribe to a simplistic black-and-white version of morality."

"I do," said Vela.

"But you can't argue with results," said Devis. "Look out

there. Thanks to me, we're definitely going to get a hundred people to come to this party."

"He's right," said Albiorix. "I wish he wasn't."

"No," said Vela. "If we steal from the people of Suburbia, we're no better than Tristane Trouvère!"

"Ooh, that reminds me," said Devis. "He's not here yet, is he? Did anybody see him come in?"

Sorrowshade's eyes narrowed. "Please tell me you invited Tristane Trouvère to this party for the purpose of springing a surprise attack on him."

"Oh, right," said Devis. "Yes, that's totally why I did it."

"You just wanted him to come to your party, didn't you?" asked Sorrowshade.

"Well, he is one of the most popular kids in school, a real Pine Hill High tastemaker," said Devis. "Plus I thought maybe if we got him here, we could all sit down and talk to each other, like civilized—"

"If I see that sleazeball, I'm not going to be doing any talking," said Sorrowshade.

"He hates us, Devis," said Albiorix.

"He hates you guys," said Devis. "He likes me. Anyway, if I'm not allowed to give out the free phones, then one of you can go and tell everyone."

The party exited the hall closet to find an even bigger crowd forcing their way into the house. The guests seemed

163

agitated now. They grumbled darkly amongst themselves. Vela nudged her way up the stairs so she could address them all.

"Greetings and welcome," said Vela in a loud, commanding voice.

"Where are the phones?" called a girl in a denim baseball cap.

"This party's lame!" yelled Marc Mansour. "I want my phone!"

"Regarding the phones you were promised," said Vela. "I regret to inform you that unfortunately we will not be giving them away after all."

At this, the crowd erupted in incredulous fury. A furious chant broke out: "Free phones! Free phones! Free phones!"

Albiorix approached Vela and whispered in her ear. "I just counted and there are eighty-two people here. If we can just hold out a little while longer, I think we'll get to a hundred."

Vela spoke over the crowd in a clear and commanding voice. "Would anyone like to hit a piñata instead? I do not wish to ruin the surprise, but I believe its hollow interior is filled with candy treats."

"How about we hit you and see what you're filled with?" cried Monica Hilaire.

"That seems a bit aggressive," said Vela.

"I don't trust her!" cried Devis, who had somehow joined the angry crowd. "What has she done with our phones?"

The other Bríandalörians closed ranks around Vela, who was now the target of the guests' ire.

"Please, let us remain calm," said Vela. "Perhaps some controlled breathing exercises would be in order."

"You know an invitation constitutes a legally binding contract in our state, right?" yelled a boy in a puffy orange vest as he waved around the second invitation.

"Er, I did not know that," said Vela. "But if you like freebies, there is, ahem, plenty of free soup."

The chanting grew louder, but it was almost drowned out by a piercing cry of wordless rage.

"We're losing them," said Albiorix. "They're going to riot."

Morton elbowed his way to the front of the rowdy crowd. He looked terrified.

"Uh, sorry, guys, I think I'm going to, uh, head home," said Morton.

"It is just as you predicted," said Thromdurr. "A total disaster."

"I mean, we all kind of knew it was going to end this way, didn't we?" said Sorrowshade.

"Sorry, Morton," said June. "I'll see you tomorrow."

"What are you guys doing tomorrow?" asked Albiorix.

"None of your business," said June.

"Can this wait?" asked Sorrowshade. "We have an angry mob on our hands."

Morton looked around. "Well, anyway, tell Stinky the soup was delici—"

He flinched at another deafening cry that sounded barely human.

Sorrowshade cocked her head. "Guys, that noise isn't coming from any of the guests."

"Is it the warg?" cried Vela, looking around frantically.

"No," said Sorrowshade. "I think it's the lobster bisque."

There came an even louder cry. This time the odd, squelching quality was enough to startle everyone at the party into silence. The whole house was eerily quiet. The adventurers and their guests slowly turned their attention toward the pot of lobster bisque sitting on an end table in the living room.

"Guys, why is the soup screaming?" asked June.

With a bubbling sploosh the lobster bisque erupted out of the pot and onto the floor.

"Aw, man, that's a Persian rug," said Devis. "Mom Stinky and Dad Stinky are going to kill me."

Suddenly there were splooshes all around the house. The tom yum flew out of its pot. So did the cream of celery. So did the beef noodle and the vichyssoise. All twelve soups had violently ejected themselves onto the floor.

"What kind of party is this?" asked Marc Mansour.

But the strangeness was only just beginning. The crowd watched in stunned horror as each puddle of soup slithered its way along the floor, all of them converging on a central point in the middle of the living room. The soups all merged together into one formless, undulating shape. And slowly that slimy shape rose up toward the ceiling. What stood before them now was a dripping, vaguely humanoid monster made entirely out of soup. The soup thing let out another inhuman scream.

And this is when the crowd panicked.

Chapter 13

*Over the years, many fans have suggested we intro-
duce magic into the game to make it more realistic, and
they hoped this change would be included in the new
edition. Fat chance, folks! People don't actually want
realism in games. They want to escape from the every-
day into a fantasy world filled with such whimsical
absurdities as "prescription sunglasses" and "parking
tickets."*

—*Excerpt from* The Advanced Hall Master's Guide

MRS. MULLIGAN, THE NOSIEST neighbor on the block,
had spent the better part of an hour watching the
house next door through a tiny crack in her blinds. Teenagers had been arriving in droves. It was a party at the Smith
house. She just knew it. No maroon hatchback in the driveway
meant the parents were away—the perfect chance for that boy

of theirs to pull something like this. Mrs. Mulligan called her neighbor Grace Neumann and told her there was a party at 800 North Pineknoll. She called Jodi Barnes and Tad Mora, so they would know too. A party next door would mean loud music late into the night. Unacceptable! Once nine thirty p.m. rolled around, Mrs. Mulligan would strike with righteous fury. She would do what she had done to countless other house parties on Pineknoll Avenue over the past fifty years: call the cops to come shut it down. She grinned in anticipation. She had the police on speed dial for just such an occasion.

But when the kids started running out the front door well before eight p.m., Mrs. Mulligan didn't quite know what to do. She frowned. Was the party already over? Maybe she wouldn't get to shut it down after all. The children did look awfully scared, though. Some of them were crying. Should she call the authorities, just in case? She hesitated. Mrs. Mulligan had received a strongly worded reprimand from the Hibbettsfield police chief after she had tried to call the department on Ralph Buckner for leaving his Christmas lights up until March.

In the end, Mrs. Mulligan thought better of it and moved to a different window, where she could clearly observe the Kozic family. They were having a barbecue in their backyard. Sure, it seemed harmless for now, but who knew when things might get out of hand?

For once, Mrs. Mulligan probably should have called the authorities, for the scene inside the house at 800 North Pineknoll Avenue was pure pandemonium. Terrified teenagers screamed and fled for their lives as a horrific soup monster rampaged.

The Bríandalörian heroes snatched their weapons from the umbrella stand where they'd hidden them and surrounded the creature in the living room. The soup thing roared and flipped the family's piano in a frightening display of strength.

"I just wanted a free phone," whimpered Marc Mansour, who cowered in the corner behind it. He had somehow gotten trapped so the soup monster was between him and the front door.

"By the gods," said Thromdurr, "what is this abhorrent soupstrocity, Devis?"

"I don't know!" said Devis. "I mean, I maybe used a little too much cumin in the tortilla soup, but that can't be it, right?"

"This is sorcery at work," said Albiorix, who had no weapon, so instead had grabbed an umbrella.

"We must slay the soup thing before anyone gets hurt," cried Vela, raising her sword.

"Try not to get any on the curtains!" cried Devis.

The paladin lunged in and swung her blade. The sword

sliced through the creature's arm and came harmlessly out the other side, coated in soup. No damage done. The monster gurgled and swung a backhanded blow at Vela, sending her sprawling backward over the couch. From the stairs, Sorrowshade loosed two arrows that sank into the creature's viscous body. The creature strained for moment, and the two arrows came flying back out. The gloom elf had to duck as they lodged in a Stinky family photo hanging on the wall behind her head.

"My precious memories!" cried Devis.

"This may sound obvious," said Sorrowshade, "but it's like fighting soup."

For some reason, it was at this moment that Marc Mansour decided to make his break for it. He jumped up and ran. Marc was a gifted athlete and fast on his feet. He had almost made it to the front hall when the soup monster whirled and caught him in one of its sticky armlike appendages. The creature pulled him in. Marc gave a muffled yelp as the soup thing's body began to engulf the boy. In only a few moments, he was completely swallowed up inside it.

Vela leaped over the couch and reared her sword back to strike again, but Albiorix stopped her.

"Don't!" cried Albiorix. "You might accidentally hit that kid!"

The paladin stopped. "You are right. We must get him

out of there before his air runs out."

"I shall save you, random party guest!" roared Thromdurr. The barbarian feinted under a swatting blow from the soup thing, then plunged both his arms into its torso. With a mighty heave he pulled Marc Mansour free. The boy came out sputtering and coughing.

"Look at that," said Sorrowshade. "Thromdurr actually did something!"

The barbarian looked as surprised as any of them. "I acted without thinking—the best kind of action! Perhaps math league has somehow rekindled my innate sense of competi—"

The soup thing bellowed and swung at Thromdurr, smashing him backward into the wall and knocking down three ceramic chickens that hung there.

"Careful, those are antiques!" cried Devis.

"Also, Thromdurr might have been hurt," cried Vela.

"That too!" said Devis.

Indeed, the barbarian lay in a dazed, soup-coated heap on the ground. But in the meantime, June had managed to drag Marc Mansour out of the fray.

"I'll help the others get to safety," said June. "Kill this soup, please!"

She threw Marc's arm around her shoulder and helped him toward the door. The soup creature wailed and swung at Devis, who danced back out of its reach. The blow ended up shattering a lamp.

"How do you defeat a creature you can't hit with weapons?" asked Sorrowshade, who hesitated to shoot any more arrows at the soup thing for fear that they might come flying back at her.

Albiorix took a deep breath. "You defeat it with magic."

The other heroes looked at him.

"Are you sure?" asked Vela. "There are several innocent bystanders here, Albiorix. If you cast a spell, and if it were to backfire . . ."

"That's what I'm counting on," said Albiorix. "Stand back." The wizard pulled out his spellbook and strode toward the soup creature. He began the mystical incantation for the frostbolt spell: *"E dekaerer ma'rn . . ."*

Albiorix's eyes glowed blue, and icy waves of magical energy began to curl around his fingertips. The soup thing regarded him for a moment and then started to engulf him, just as it had done to Marc Mansour. With his last breath, Albiorix managed to get out the final words.

". . . a'ph aeri!"

Albiroix finished the spell just as he too was swallowed into the soup thing's form. The creature gave a gurgling roar and turned back toward the others. They readied their weapons.

But then came a crackling sound from somewhere inside the creature. The heroes watched as a wave of frosty energy—presumably starting from Albiorix's feet—swept up the soup creature's body. It lurched another half step toward them before it was frozen solid.

With a mighty overhand swing of his war hammer, Thromdurr smashed the soup thing into icy shrapnel. The blow revealed a shivering Albiorix half stuck inside it. The other heroes carefully pulled him out. Vela threw a wool afghan around his shoulders.

"You *knew* your ice spell would backfire," said Vela. "Just as it did on the rooftops of Wharfharbor."

"I was hoping it would," said Albiorix. He smiled, though his teeth were still chattering. "I figured if I could freeze myself while I was inside it, that might be enough to freeze it too."

June returned. "You killed the soup!"

"And my living room," said Devis, surveying the damage.

"All the guests have been safely evacuated," said June. "Although I'm afraid the reviews of your party aren't going to be particularly positive. The verdict on social media so far has been both swift and harsh."

"Did we at least get a hundred guests?" asked Devis.

June frowned. "By my count, you guys topped out at eighty-seven. Sorry."

Devis sighed. "So my house got destroyed for nothing. Fantastic."

"We shall help you rebuild," said Thromdurr. He picked up two pieces of ceramic chicken and tried to stick them back together. They didn't fit.

Vela shook her head. "This is an escalation on Tristane Trouvère's part. The warg attack was one thing. We were alone in a deserted mall. But this? An innocent could have gotten seriously hurt."

"We don't know it was him," said Devis.

"Stop saying that," said Sorrowshade. "You gave him an invitation to the party. He knew exactly where we would be and when."

"I . . . Okay, that's true," said Devis. "But he's a bard. He doesn't have the power to create evil soup monsters. That's wizard stuff, right, Albiorix?"

"It would seem so. We don't know exactly what's going on, but I'd bet Tristane Trouvère had a hand in it." Albiorix waved toward the frozen chunks of soup monster. "We can't keep treating that bard with kid gloves. It's time to bring the fight to him."

"A worthy goal," said Thromdurr. "But how is such a thing possible, when the slippery coward can vanish at will?"

"The problem is that when Tristane Trouvère puts on his cap of invisibility, we don't know where he is," said Albiorix.

175

"But there is one place we know he will be."

"Where?" asked Vela.

Albiorix reached into his pocket and pulled out a crumpled flyer. It was the one they'd found by Tristane Trouvère's locker advertising his "secret show" at the Monarch, Saturday at eight (doors seven thirty). Tomorrow.

By seven forty-five, the Monarch—a dingy music club occupying a former sewing factory in an industrial part of Hibbettsfield—was almost full. It was an "all-ages show," and the crowd was all teenagers. Travis Tyson's usual contingent of lunchtime fans gathered near the front, of course. But Teddy McGirk and his pack of Jock cronies were here too, jostling and forcefully high-fiving each other. There was also a contingent of Loners, led by Moonglove Bernbaum. They hung out near the back of the club and made snide jokes among themselves. The Overachiever of all Overachievers, Christina Christopoulos, had even taken time out of her unfathomably busy schedule to catch this show. The heroes of Bríandalör recognized many of the same faces from Devis's ill-fated soirée the night before. They tried their best to avoid eye contact with those people.

Those who had been brave enough to check social media found that Dream Huge had quickly been deemed the worst, lamest, most pathetic party in history. The party was

176

now colloquially known as Fail Huge. Oddly, the fact that a nightmarish soup creature had menaced the guests seemed to be a secondary complaint. Mostly people were mad about not getting their free phones.

After the adventurers had cleaned up the Smith house as best they could, Vela commanded Devis to break back into Valu-Barn to return all the phones he had stolen. The thief was happy to point out that this would technically mean committing another crime, but in the end he did as he was told. Afterward, they all got down to planning their "secret show" ambush in earnest. Albiorix thought they'd come up with a pretty good plan.

First off, the Bríandalörians would wear disguises to the show so as not to tip off Tristane Trouvère to their presence. June had been in charge of this aspect of the plan, and she relished her role. In addition to new clothes, she had gone so far as to create completely fake names, personas, and biographies for each of them. According to June, Albiorix was supposed to be Logan Chins-Ranton, future heir to a considerable molasses fortune. She'd given him an odd ponytailed wig and a fedora to wear. Albiorix tried to tell June that these false identities weren't necessary and were maybe even a little silly, until she reminded him that this was pretty much exactly the same thing as playing Homerooms & Hall Passes. Albiorix had to admit she was right.

It was nearly eight now. The wizard gave a nod to his companions, and Devis (Callum Markinswell III), Thromdurr (Percy Finn), Vela (Rowena Thornton), Sorrowshade (Dame Seraphina Durchville), and June (Maddie Jensen) took their positions around the venue. The four Bríandalörians stationed themselves strategically at the club's four exits, to prevent Tristane Trouvère from escaping. The bard might be able to turn invisible, but as far as they knew, he still couldn't walk through walls. He would need to exit the building through one of the doors if he meant to flee, and they would be right there to catch him if he tried, invisible or not.

Meanwhile, June took her place as lookout beside the club's one wall of fixed windows. The glass panes had been painted over by the Monarch's owners, but enough of the paint was peeling off that it still gave a view of the street outside if you stood close enough.

Albiorix would play a key role in the ambush. The party couldn't risk any civilian casualties, so the wizard's objective would be to safely separate Tristane Trouvère from the crowd before any confrontation occurred. He would do it using magic.

While the others had worked out the finer points of the ambush, Albiorix had spent all day practicing the arcane arts alone. And it had gone well. He felt proud that his magic had only backfired once out of the six times he'd attempted to cast the spell he would use.

And the wizard wasn't the only one on an upswing. Thromdurr too seemed newly energized. At long last the barbarian was emerging from his post-death existential crisis. He seemed eager to confront and defeat Tristane Trouvère. He hadn't mentioned giant scorpions once all day. When he digressed, it was mostly to talk about his upcoming math league match against Riverview High School for the Arts (they were "weak" and "destined for defeat," apparently).

Vela and Sorrowshade were similarly committed to bringing down the bard. Only Devis seemed reluctant. Perhaps he was a bit despondent over how Dream Huge had turned out. But Albiorix suspected that the thief still didn't want to confront his old friend and mentor.

At eight p.m., the lights dimmed. From somewhere in the back of the club, the manager took the mic: "Ladies and gentlemen, please welcome to the Monarch stage: Travis Tyyyyysoooooooon!"

The lights onstage came up, and Tristane Trouvère walked out carrying his acoustic guitar and smiling brightly. He wore a crisp white T-shirt and artfully ripped jeans. His amazing hair somehow looked even more amazing under the stage lights. As Tristane adjusted the microphone, Albiorix tipped his head down to hide his face under the brim of his fedora. He hoped the bard wouldn't recognize anyone in the party.

"Hello, Hibbettsfield!" said Tristane. "Thanks for

coming out to see me play. Here's a little number I wrote that's very close to my heart. I dedicate this one to my dog, Boomer, who I left back in California. I miss you, buddy."

"Awww," said the crowd.

Tristane wiped away a single tear. Then he started to strum his guitar and sing:

"Girl, you know you're my everything.
Girl, you know you're my diamond ring.
But if you want to make a splash with me . . .
Girl, you can throw some cash at me."

The song was beautiful, ethereal, mesmerizing. The audience sang along, and Albiorix was surprised to find himself humming it under his breath too. Tristane's voice was perfect. The tune was insanely catchy. The lyrics were so deep.

"Girl, we could ride a hot-air balloon . . .
Romantic views that will make you swoon.
Above this world is where we float,
Then you toss me a C-note."

Albiorix knew the song would be stuck in his head for weeks. Maybe months. He didn't care. He loved the idea. The wizard joined the rest of the crowd in singing along at full volume with the chorus ("Throw cash at me" x 3). Fans were now tossing handfuls of bills onto the stage. Some jewelry too. Tristane Trouvère grinned as the money fluttered down at his feet.

The guy was so cool! Albiorix felt his own hand reaching toward his pocket. He stopped himself. There was something he was supposed to do. What was it again? Create a disruption? But why would he want to disrupt this beautiful music, this amazing performance, this perfect moment? Albiorix wanted to listen to Tristane Trouvère play the song "I Love U Girl (Throw Cash)" forever.

Luckily, something deep inside the wizard, some kernel of willpower, rejected this. Albiorix shook his head and managed to snap himself out of whatever glamour Tristane Trouvère's bardic performance had spun around the audience. Instantly he could see the situation for what it was. The creep had written a dumb song to hypnotize the crowd into giving him free money. It was as laughable as it was petty.

The time to act was now. Albiorix pulled out his spellbook and began to recite the words of the first spell he had ever been able to master. *"Bherr nyi va'zis aetlaevi di I lidda't la'di vaerrmo a'geh!"*

As he finished the incantation, he felt his consciousness touch the unfathomable mystical fabric of the cosmos, and he knew the spell had worked. Albiorix scanned the ground and spotted one: a tiny gray shape skittering across the floor of the club. Then he saw another. And another. Albiorix smiled. He'd done it. He'd successfully cast the spell summon pill bugs.

Albiorix grabbed the arm of the boy beside him and yelled over the music. "OMG! Look at that! So gross!"

The kid looked and saw a writhing swarm of pill bugs crawling over his feet. "Whoa!" the boy screamed. "What?"

The boy jumped, causing others around him to look. They too noticed the growing mass of tiny crawling creatures and scrambled back, bumping into others and bringing more attention to the pill-bug swarm. Create a disruption. So far, so good.

The crowd was beginning to panic, shattering whatever enchantment Tristane Trouvère's musical performance had spun over them. Nobody had ever seen anything like this: some kids were screaming and others were running for the doors. Albiorix kept a close eye on the stage, where the bard kept on singing his ridiculous song. At last Tristane Trouvère threw down his guitar in frustration.

The bard squinted out into the audience. "Guys, the energy you give to me is what I give back to you. What exactly is going on out there?"

"This club is infested!" shrieked a girl.

"It's roaches!" cried another girl.

"It's killer bees!" screamed someone else.

"Why can't we have just one normal night in this town?" cried Marc Mansour.

At this point, the unseen club manager took up his microphone again. "Everyone please remain calm and make an orderly exit so we can figure out . . . AAAAAH, ONE OF THEM WENT UP MY PANTS! GET IT OUT! GET IT—"

The mic squealed as he dropped it. The crowd ran for the exits in earnest, shoving one another to get out (Albiorix spotted the Monarch's manager among them). The wizard expected Tristane Trouvère to make a break for it, but he didn't. The bard remained onstage, watching the pandemonium with a slightly disappointed look on his face.

The music club was almost empty now; only a few stragglers remained. Aside from Tristane Trouvère and his own companions, Albiorix counted three others: Teddy McGirk, Moonglove Bernbaum, and Christina Christopoulos.

They didn't seem to be going anywhere, though. What? This wasn't part of the plan. Everyone was supposed to leave. Albiorix would have to improvise.

"Guys, are you seeing the gross bugs?" yelled the wizard. "We should probably all leave!"

The three bystanders didn't react. They merely stared

back at him with looks of blank incomprehension on their faces.

Tristane Trouvère blinked. "Wait, I know you!" cried the bard. "It's one thing for you and your friends to try to capture me. But to interrupt a stage performance? *That is unforgivable.*"

Albiorix tipped his hat down again and stared at the floor. "Afraid you must be mistaken, old pip, I'm just—my name is, uh, Logan Chins-Ranton. My family made their fortune in the, uh, molasses industry."

Sorrowshade sighed. "He knows who you are, man."

"We don't want to fight you, Tristane," said Devis, stepping forward with both hands up.

"Speak for yourself," said Sorrowshade.

"Guys, I see something out the window!" cried June.

"What?" cried Albiorix.

"It's the—"

June's voice was drowned out by a bloodcurdling howl from outside.

"Oh no," said June.

She just managed to dive out of the way. An instant later the warg leaped right through the window of the Monarch with a horrendous crash. Broken glass sprayed all over the floor.

"Teddy, Moonglove, Christina, you all need to leave

now!" cried Vela, striding forward to confront the beast. "This beast is dangerous!"

The warg shook the shards from its fur and looked around, licking its chops as it chose a victim. Then it charged straight for Moonglove Bernbaum.

Chapter

14

In Advanced Homerooms & Hall Passes, players will inevitably butt heads. As Hall Master, you should try your best to mediate disputes so that everyone feels satisfied. But you can't let their bickering mess things up for the other players. If two players consistently can't get along, they should settle their conflict outside the game in a mature and responsible way: with a duel.

—*Excerpt from* The Advanced Hall Master's Guide

❦

"LEAVE HER BE!" CRIED Vela as she ran to intercept the warg. But there was no way the paladin would make it in time. The racing beast would reach Moonglove first. To Albiorix, it all appeared to unfold in slow motion. The beast opened its jaws wide as it crashed into Moonglove.

Now Moonglove was wrestling with the warg and scratching behind its ears. It licked at her face, coating her in slobber. A scream rang out. No, not a scream. Laughter? Moonglove Bernbaum was laughing.

"Come here," said Moonglove. "Who's a good boy? Who's a big good boy?"

The warg snorted and snuffled and licked her again like a gigantic golden retriever.

"Wait," said June. "What?"

"Wait, what, indeed?" said Tristane Trouvère. The bard now had a theatrical smile on his face as he spoke into his microphone.

Sorrowshade watched Moonglove cuddle the warg. She glanced back at Tristane Trouvère onstage. Her eyes narrowed. "You two are in cahoots?"

"Even though he's a conventionally attractive lame-o Popular and I'm a cool detached Loner," said Moonglove. "Quite a twist, isn't it?"

"But you accused me of having a crush on that creep," said Sorrowshade.

Moonglove winked. "I still think you might." Then she raised a crossbow.

"June, run," said Albiorix.

June hesitated. "But I'm a member of this adventuring party too—"

"Go, June," said Vela.

June turned and raced for the exit.

Tristane Trouvère laughed at her as she went. "Oh, don't leave now," said the bard. "You'll miss the most exciting part of the show!"

"Ach, enough blathering, man," said Teddy McGirk. "Can we get down to it already?" Teddy rolled his shoulders and kicked off his shoes. Suddenly the Jock was at least five inches shorter. Barefoot, Teddy McGirk stood four foot seven, tops.

"You wear special shoes to artificially increase your height?" said Thromdurr. "Devious."

"They call 'em lifts here," said Teddy, pulling a wicked-looking axe from inside his letterman jacket. "And you're gonna need a pair, once I cut you down to size."

Vela looked at Moonglove, Teddy, and Tristane. Then her gaze fell upon Christina Christopoulos. "You are with them too, aren't you?"

Christina smiled and nodded. "Your powers of deductive reasoning seem a bit sluggish. Glad you're not on the debate team." Christina's fingertips began to crackle with arcane power. "I must say, hex of tongue-tying did the trick quite nicely."

"A magical curse!" cried Vela. "I *knew* I wasn't afraid of public speaking anymore."

Tristane Trouvère somersaulted off the stage. He landed with a rapier drawn and the microphone still clutched in his other hand. "Since you've made your entrance, I suppose it's time for a formal introduction to *my* adventuring party. Roll call!"

Moonglove cocked her crossbow. "Azheena the ranger. And this is my beast companion, Amarok. Don't worry, he's just a big old sweetheart. Unless I tell him to rip your throats out." She turned to the warg. "Hey, Amarok. Rip their throats out." The beast snarled and bared his fangs at the heroes.

"Skegg the Surly," said Teddy, stepping forward. "Dwarf warrior." He scratched vigorously at his jaw. "You've nae idea how many times a day I shave to keep up this daft human disguise."

"And I am Calyxia, sorceress extraordinaire," said Christina, pulling out her spellbook. Albiorix couldn't help but notice it was twice as thick as his own. "I have completed mystical training under the tutelage of the Archmage Reginus, Oephra the Evocator, and the Warlock Vecnarrion, better known as the Blightlord of the Manglewood. I understand you are a pupil of the Archmage Velaxis."

"Ex-pupil," said Albiorix.

"Well, I look forward to destroying you all the same," said Calyxia. "It may prove instructive."

The two sides stood facing each other, weapons drawn.

"Surrender now," said Vela, "or prepare to do battle

against a band of seasoned adventurers."

Tristane Trouvère rolled his eyes. "Samesies."

"Hey, boss, didn't you say these five cream puffs couldn't even handle you on your own?" asked Azheena.

"That's right. I beat all of them by myself on the rooftops of Wharfharbor," said Tristane. "I couldn't say which one was the most useless: the elf, the oaf, the naif, or the bumbling wizard. If I had to choose, I suppose it would be my dear old friend Goblinface."

"You still consider me a friend?" said Devis. "That's nice to hear."

"Have some self-respect, man," said Sorrowshade. "I'm with short stack, over here." She nodded toward Skegg. "Less yapping, more fighting."

"Won't take long," said Skegg. He smiled at Thromdurr. "Last time I beat jumbo shrimp in two seconds flat. Didn't even need me axe."

Thromdurr looked down at his hands. They were shaking. He felt the vein in his forehead. It was throbbing. He beamed. "Your taunts and jibes have had their desired effect, dwarf," said the barbarian. "I AM FINALLY FURIOUS AGAIN! HOORAY! NOW PREPARE FOR YOUR SMASHING!"

And with that, Thromdurr raised his war hammer and charged at Skegg the Surly. The dwarf dodged out of the way and came up with a slashing blow of his axe. Throm-durr blocked it with the haft of his hammer.

The fight had begun.

Azheena raised her crossbow and fired at Sorrowshade. The gloom elf ducked behind an amplifier, and the bolt whistled over her head. Sorrowshade rose and returned fire with her longbow, but the ranger leaped behind a column. The gloom elf's arrow passed harmlessly through her trailing army jacket.

"Do you mind telling me what the most advanced spell in your spellbook is?" asked Calyxia as she casually advanced toward Albiorix.

"And give you a strategic advantage? No way!" said Albiorix. *"Na lya'a'n ha'oi zaeny e phaesima'rn koih!"*

A magical ball of fire leaped from Albiorix's hand toward Calyxia. The wizard felt his heart jump. Almost without thinking, he'd successfully cast an offensive spell.

"Ya'ois lvirr aelt'n ka'aetk na' za'sg voiddh," said Calyxia.

And just as quickly, Albiorix's heart sank again, as his ball of magical fire fizzled into nothing. Calyxia had countered his spell.

The sorceress laughed. "Oh no, don't misunderstand me. I'm not worried about you defeating me. I can't die from pill bugs." She stomped one of the creatures still swarming over the club floor. "I'd just like to know if I'll get to copy down any new spells once I pry that spellbook of yours from your charred, lifeless corpse."

Meanwhile Tristane Trouvère was locked in a fierce swordfight with Vela the Valiant. The bard's flashing rapier was quicker, but the paladin had the edge in strength and endurance.

"So you're the leader of this mismatched band of incompetents, eh?" asked Tristane as he lunged toward her. "Congratulations to you."

"Many thanks, villain," said Vela. The paladin parried the blow. "You've picked an unwise conflict that will mean your downfall. We shall prevail, for our party fights for truth, goodness, and honor!" She returned a slashing strike with her own sword.

Tristane Trouvère ducked under the blade and clucked his tongue. "That may be what *you* fight for, paladin. Even I can see that your companions all have their own agendas. That's what makes your side weak."

The bard feinted, then counterattacked. Vela blocked his blow with her shield.

"Unlike you, our little fellowship is united in purpose," said Tristane Trouvère, dancing back out of Vela's reach. "We fight for a goal that is far purer than yours: money."

"Nothing is purer than truth, goodness, and honor!" cried Vela. She leaped forward and came down with a fierce overhead strike. Tristane Trouvère just managed to parry by catching the blade of his rapier in his other hand. The strength of the paladin's blow caused him to stumble back a step.

"Truth is boring, goodness is debatable, and honor is the enemy of success," said the bard. "Speaking of which, this midfight banter was merely meant to distract you long enough for an ally to mount an unfair surprise attack."

"Huh?" said Vela. Just as she turned, Amarok the warg bit into her shoulder.

"Good boy!" called Azheena from across the club. The ranger laughed. "Hey, Sorrowshade, my puppy-wuppy's going to eat your tedious friend. But hey, who needs friends when you're a Loner, right?"

The gloom elf turned to see the warg mauling Vela. "Amarok, was it? Stupid name. You probably picked it. He'll make a nice rug."

Sorrowshade rose and loosed an arrow at the warg. The shaft buried itself in Amarok's side. The beast yelped in pain and released his grip on the paladin's arm. But before Sorrowshade had time to duck down again, she felt a burning sting in her arm. One of Azheena's crossbow bolts had grazed her flesh. A thin trickle of blood dripped down her sleeve.

Sorrowshade crouched behind the amplifier as another

one of the ranger's bolts flew overhead. "Using your pet as bait to lure me out?" called Sorrowshade. "Pathetic. You missed, by the way."

"Eh, I can always summon another beast companion," called Azheena. "Maybe I'll go for a giant snake next time . . . or hey, a shark would be pretty cool, right? Anyway, I heard you like poison. Is that right?"

"What, are you stalking me?" said Sorrowshade as she nocked another arrow. "Creepy."

"Well, I *hope* you like poison," said Azheena. "Because you know that crossbow bolt that just nicked your arm? It was totally poisoned."

Sorrowshade tried to stand, and she felt her head swim. A wave of nausea hit her stomach. She glanced at the wound, and indeed it was starting to fester an ugly green. Plagueseed extract? Or maybe tincture of bleeding kiss? She only had a few minutes to find the right antidote. The gloom elf dropped her bow and began to frantically rummage through her poisoner's kit.

"What, no more playful back-and-forth?" called Azheena from the other side of the room. "Aw. You're not dead already, are you? That would be so lame."

Meanwhile, Thromdurr and Skegg traded axe and hammer blows.

"YOU HAVE REIGNITED MY RAGE, TINY FOE!"

194

roared Thromdurr. "A GRAVE MISTAKE!"

He swung his war hammer wildly, missing the dwarf but bashing a footwide hole in the wall. Skegg the Surly used the opening for an expert counterattack, gashing the barbarian's leg with his axe.

"That's right, big boy," said Skegg. "Get mad. Get reckless. Get dead."

Thromdurr swung again, and Skegg parried. On the backswing, the dwarf's axe caught Thromdurr in the shoulder, opening another cut.

"NICKS AND SCRATCHES ONLY FEED MY FURY!" cried Thromdurr.

A two-handed swing of his hammer came down with incredible force. Skegg sidestepped the blow.

"Yep," said Skegg as he vaulted up and kicked Thromdurr in the face with his bare foot. "That's the bloody idea."

The barbarian staggered back—now bleeding from his nostrils—and bellowed with inchoate rage.

"Tyael ael e raekyntaetk ma'rn na' phsh ha'oi!" cried Albiorix. The wizard's lightning spell sputtered out of existence as it flashed toward Calyxia. So far she'd countered everything he'd thrown at her but had refrained from casting any spells at him. Instead she seemed distracted—engrossed in her own hefty spellbook—as they fought.

"Hmm. Acid spritz," said Calyxia as she flipped through

the pages. "Plasma cloud? I don't think so. Searing strike? Blech. No."

"Why aren't you attacking me?" cried Albiorix. Her relentless defense had him flustered and more than a little intimidated.

"I'm searching for an interesting spell to finish you with," said Calyxia. "Ah! This one should be fun." The sorceress looked up at Albiorix. Her eyes now glowed purple. *"Wa'avl ta'z ha'oisi e yivkiya'k ha'oi da'sat."*

Albiorix tried to cast a ward of protection on himself. *"Tsag'h mog toimt go—"*

But he wasn't quick enough. A tendril of purple energy snaked from Calyxia's fingertip and coiled around Albiorix's leg. It slithered up his torso and into his mouth. And then, in a bright purple flash, the wizard seemed to wink into nothing.

Calyxia steepled her fingers and giggled. "Excellent. Now comes the real fun!"

From the corner of her eye, Vela saw the Albiorix's empty clothes fall to the ground.

"Albiorix!" cried the paladin. "Where are you? What happened?"

No answer. Amarok snapped his jaws at Vela. She blocked the bite with her shield and swung at the warg with her sword. The beast dodged backward a few paces. After the first surprise bite on on her shoulder, Amarok hadn't been able to hurt her again. With her shield and sword in hand, Vela had been able to keep the vicious warg at bay. But neither did Amarok relent. Vela could see now that the beast was keeping her occupied, trapped in a corner where she couldn't aid her companions. This was probably an intentional strategy. She needed a way out. If Albiorix was even still alive, he needed her help.

Tristane Trouvère surveyed the battle with a sly grin on his face. He liked what he saw. Amarok had the paladin effectively separated and pinned down. Azheena had poisoned the elf with something nasty. Skegg was leading the raging barbarian around by the nose, and Calyxia had magicked their so-called wizard (potentially the biggest threat, if he ever managed to get his act together) right out of the fight. His companions were on the cusp of victory. Tristane Trouvère paused. He wrinkled his nose.

"Unless I'm counting wrong, there should be one more," said the bard.

It was then that Tristane Trouvère felt the point of a dagger pressing into his back. The bard froze and slowly raised his hands.

"Call them off," said Devis.

Tristane sighed. Then he smiled. "I can't do that, Devis. We have a good thing going here, and your friends are trying to muck it up. This is my livelihood we're talking about."

"I know, but couldn't you just pick somewhere else to run this scam?" asked Devis. "I'm asking you as a friend. Please."

"And as a friend, I'll extend the same offer I did in Wharfharbor," said Tristane Trouvère. "Switch sides. Join our team. I know you're not in it for any of that truth and justice nonsense. You want money. Just like us."

Devis paused.

Vela needed a way to distract the warg so that she could help the others. But Amarok was relentless. Perhaps if she somehow threatened the animal's master? But how? Azheena was thirty feet away, and Vela only had her sword and her shield in hand.

"Sometimes the best defense is a good offense," said Vela.

And then the paladin hurled her shield at the ranger. It whistled through the air—straight into her unsuspecting enemy's head, knocking her right off her feet with a metallic clang. Amarok instantly broke off his attack and raced to Azheena's aid.

It had cost her her shield, but Vela still had her sword. She ran toward Calyxia and whatever was left of Albiorix.

"I'm coming for you, Albiorix!" cried Vela.

Calyxia turned toward Vela and sighed. "I really don't have time for this. *Na'z I'd ka'aetk na' oili yoissaereti zaetvl a't ha'oi.*"

A gust of hurricane-force wind blew from Calyxia's outstretched palm. The blast of air stopped Vela in her tracks and then started to push her back. With a final push, the paladin pressed forward, only to be blown off her feet. She slid back across the length of the club. Her sword slipped from her fingertips as she did.

Calyxia dropped the wind spell and crouched beside the pile of Albiorix's rumpled clothing. She reached into the neck hole of his T-shirt and felt around until she had him. The sorceress smiled as she stood. Calyxia now held a hedgehog in her hand.

Albiorix screamed in horror. It came out as a cute little squeak.

Calyxia stroked his quills. "Instant hedgehogification. An incredibly obscure and difficult spell developed by the Archmage Maylendra during the reign of King Vulas the Vindictive. As I understand her magical theory, she was able to combine the core mystical principles underlying the instant frogification spell and the summon pinecone spell. Only seven arcanists in history have ever successfully cast this particular spell. I am now the eighth."

Albiorix squeaked uselessly in Calyxia's palm.

"Apologies. You probably don't understand the significance of what I'm talking about because you're a magical washout," said the sorceress. "Bottom line: casting this spell will do wonders for my arcane reputation. But I am not content to stop there. Oh no. I aim to be one of the greats of wizardry, so I must surpass the Archmage Maylendra. The duration of instant hedgehogification is normally only an hour. By deploying my own highly attenuated variation on the petrification spell, I will now attempt to make your transformation permanent. Congratulations, you're about to become part of magical history."

Calyxia cracked her knuckles, flipped her spellbook to another page, and started to incant. *"Na'z nyael lvirr zaerr mira'di visdetin et ha'oi . . ."*

Albiorix would be doomed to live out the rest of his life as a hedgehog. Eating grubs. Sleeping in hollow logs. Puffing up into a ball when startled. An adorable nightmare. He had to do something. Anything. So he bit the sorceress on the thumb.

"Ow!" cried Calyxia.

Reflexively, she dropped hedgehog Albiorix. And so the wizard ran away from her as fast as his four little legs would carry him.

Meanwhile, Devis the thief still held his old mentor at dagger point.

"I'm getting bored," said Tristane Trouvère. "What's your answer, old friend?"

"Look, I get it. My adventuring party can be annoying

sometimes," said Devis. "Okay, they're *usually* annoying. Vela's a goody-goody, Thromdurr's an dope, Sorrowshade's a downer, and Albiorix is a doofus, but . . . I like them."

Tristane Trouvère clucked his tongue. "Then you're not going to enjoy how this battle will end. Look around. Your side is losing."

Devis did. Sorrowshade was slumped behind her amplifier. Her skin had taken on a sickly green cast. Vela had just been blown across the floor like a human tumbleweed. Her weapon was gone. Thromdurr was foaming at the mouth and flailing uselessly while Skegg the Surly wore him down with dozens of cuts and gashes. And Albiorix was apparently now a small woodland creature. They'd knocked out Azheena, but Amarok was already licking her face, and Devis could see the ranger was starting to stir. She'd be back in the fight momentarily. Their odds were bad and getting worse.

"Look, I've got you at the pointy end of a dagger," said Devis. "I'm the one who calls the shots. So tell your friends to stand down, or . . ."

"Or what?" asked Tristane Trouvère.

"I don't want to hurt you, man," said Devis.

Tristane Trouvère nodded. "I know you don't. That's why you're not going to. But I respect our history, so I'll sweeten your offer: If you join us, I promise to leave your friends alive."

"You will?" said Devis.

Tristane nodded. "As long as they agree to exit the Realm of Suburbia and never interfere with our business again."

After a moment, Devis slowly lowered the dagger.

"Okay," said Devis. "I'll do it."

Tristane Trouvère smiled. Then the bard whirled and kicked the blade out of Devis's hands. "I can't believe you fell for that. It's clear I taught you *nothing*."

And with a lunging thrust, Tristane Trouvère ran Devis through the side with his rapier. The thief let out a startled gasp as he slumped to his knees.

"Devis!" cried Vela.

The thief fell forward onto the ground, already unconscious.

"It's over," said Tristane Trouvère. "We've beaten you."

And Vela knew he was right. They would need a miracle to win now.

But miracles did happen. Hadn't Grefn the Great turned the tide of the Battle of Digrvǫllr when her sword began to glow with the divine light of the gods? And hadn't Zentha Blacktree held off an entire army of raging orcs at Helgur's Pass with just ten soldiers under her command? And so the paladin got on one knee, closed her eyes, and prayed for a miracle.

"Powers of Light," said Vela. "If ever there was a time

when the forces of good could use your help, that time is now. Please, as your humble servant I beseech you . . . send us your aid."

"RRAAAGGGH!" roared Thromdurr. His eyes bulged wildly as he swung his hammer. But the barbarian was moving slower now. He was exhausted, and blood dripped from countless axe cuts all over his body. Skegg kept his distance, controlled and ruthless, leading the barbarian ever backward.

"That's it, ye big ox," said Skegg. "That's it. . . ."

Thromdurr swung again at Skegg's head. The dwarf ducked, and Thromdurr's hammer smashed into Vela's face. The blow instantly knocked the paladin unconscious.

Skegg laughed. "Nice work, mate. Saves me the trouble."

Instantly the barbarian's rage faded, and he was overcome with shame and fear. "What have I done?" whispered Thromdurr.

"Ye've lost, that's what. And now's the part where I split your skull," said Skegg. "Doubt I'll find anything in there, but reckon I might as well check."

Skegg the Surly raised his axe over his head for a killing blow and—

"Skreeeeeee!" A dark, shrieking shape flew through the air and latched onto the dwarf's head. The creature scrabbled at Skegg's face with its claws, causing the dwarf to drop his axe. Skegg cursed and stumbled. After a moment of fighting, the dwarf threw the thing off.

It was an inky demon with glowing red eyes and a long curling tail, about the size of a monkey.

"E daquir aeuir aaeak," it screeched, a simple curse in Fiendish, the unholy language of devils. Then the thing crouched to pounce again.

"What in the Thirteen Hells?" cried Skegg as he wiped blood off his face with the back of his hand. The dwarf looked around, confused.

"Guys!" cried June. "I couldn't get out."

She had been forced back through the door by another one of the dark imps. Now there were dozens more of the horrid things pouring into the Monarch, through all four doors.

Chapter 15

In Advanced Homerooms & Hall Passes, the success
or failure of an action is determined by a roll of the die.
Sometimes players will roll poorly. Sometimes they will
roll extremely poorly. Sometimes they will roll a one
sixteen times in a row, resulting in a baroque string of
unmitigated disasters for their (likely doomed) charac-
ter. This is all part of the fun of the game!
    —*Excerpt from* The Advanced Hall Master's Guide

❧

SKEGG THE SURLY KICKED his axe into his hand and
then buried the blade in the imp's back. The creature
squealed and burst into a puff of foul-smelling black smoke.
Skegg coughed as he moved to attack Thromdurr again, but
two more imps had already gotten between them.

"Curse ye, wee smoke demons!" cried the dwarf. "This
ain't over, jumbo shrimp!"

Skegg swung his axe, decapitating an imp in another burst of noxious vapor. The other one bit into the dwarf's leg, causing him to grunt in pain.

An imp flew at Thromdurr. Instinctively, the barbarian batted it away with his hammer. But he was still reeling. His recklessness had felled a companion. It was lucky Vela had merely been knocked unconscious and not injured worse.

"Help me!" cried June as she raced toward Thromdurr. Two of the imps were on her heels.

Thromdurr turned to look at June. Tears welled in his eyes as he stood motionless. Useless.

"C'mon, man! Do something!" yelled June.

Thromdurr shook himself. With an overhand swing of his hammer, he crushed one of the imps into a cloud of black smoke. A powerful kick sent the other one sprawling across the floor.

Luckily, the villains were engaged in their own fight with the creatures now. More and more of the smoke imps streamed in through all the Monarch's exits, shrieking profanities in Fiendish. Tristane Trouvère slashed at them with his rapier. Amarok held one in his jaws and worried it violently. Skegg the Surly was methodically chopping them down, even as he moved to help the dazed ranger, Azheena, to her feet. The sorceress Calyxia vaporized a group of them with a magical blast of acid. Yet still they came.

A pack of the imps had surrounded Thromdurr and June too. Thromdurr swept his hammer from side to side in a wide circle. For the moment the little demons kept their distance. They seemed to be wary of the barbarian's long reach.

"What happened?" cried June. "Where are the others?"

But even as she asked, June saw them. Vela was down. Devis was down. Sorrowshade wasn't moving. Albiorix was nowhere to be seen, and for some reason a stray hedgehog was tugging at her pant leg. She gently nudged it away with her foot.

"We lost, June," said Thromdurr. "By the great Sky Bear, we lost."

"Not yet we haven't!" said June. She picked up Vela's sword and swung it clumsily at a nearby imp. She missed it by a wide margin. "Look, I'm not so good at fighting, so I'm going to need you to handle that part. Got it?"

Still half in a daze, Thromdurr nodded.

"Now grab Vela and let's go!" cried June.

Thromdurr hefted the paladin's limp form onto his shoulder. Three of the imps saw their chance. They sprang at him with scratching claws and biting teeth. Thromdurr bashed two with his hammer, and June somehow managed to stab the one in the leg with Vela's sword. All of them popped into stinking clouds of sulfurous smoke.

Individually, the little creatures were weak, but there were far too many of the imps to defeat, especially in the party's already wounded state. To survive, they needed to escape.

"Now let's get Devis," said June, holding her nose against the stink. She looked down to see that the hedgehog was pulling on her pant leg again. "But where's Albiorix? Is he—"

At that moment, an imp pounced onto June's back and sank its fangs into her neck. June screamed. The imp burst into smoke as a black arrow lodged in its chest.

"You're . . . welcome," said Sorrowshade. The gloom elf stumbled toward them. Her speech was labored and her skin had an ugly greenish cast. Her fingers fumbled as she tried to nock another arrow.

"Are you okay?" asked June.

"I'm . . . fine," said Sorrowshade. "Just a routine . . . fatal dose . . . of plague-seed extract. . . . No big . . . deal. . . . I had the antid—*aaaugh* . . ." Sorrowshade doubled over and vomited onto the floor.

June looked away and noticed that the hedgehog was still tugging at her pants. "Okay, seriously, whose hedgehog is this?" She noticed that the creature now stood on its hind legs. It was waving its front paws.

"Oh no . . . Albiorix?"

The hedgehog nodded. Not typical hedgehog behavior. June forced herself not to react as she picked Albiorix up and tucked him into her shirt pocket.

A sea of hostile imps now separated the party from the evil adventurers. The villains were fighting for their lives now. The music club had filled with a haze of dark smoke from each imp they'd defeated. Somewhere above, the Monarch's fire alarm was beeping.

The heroes pressed their way toward Devis's prone form, bashing and stabbing and shooting arrows at the imps as the went. They found the thief unconscious. While the others defended her, June crouched and felt that his shirt was slick with blood. She looked up, horrified.

"Is he . . . ?"

"Not . . . quite," said Sorrowshade. "Check . . . his pockets. . . . He should have . . . a healing potion."

June rummaged around in Devis's pockets. She found a mysterious puzzle box, a gold-plated dragon's tooth, a fake will, seventeen dollars in cash, and a piece of oddly warm pizza. At last she located a small, stoppered flask full of viscous red fluid. She held it up. Sorrowshade nodded and made a "glug-glug" motion with her hands.

"Really?" said June. "I'm not sure it's safe to pour liquid down an unconscious person's throat. Couldn't he choke?"

"We do it . . . all the time," said Sorrowshade. "It's . . . fine."

While Sorrowshade and Thromdurr kept the imps at bay, June popped open the flask and emptied it into Devis's mouth.

An instant later, he sat bolt upright and yelled, "Bouillabaisse!"

"Come on," said June as she helped the thief to his feet. "Show's over. Time to go."

Tristane Trouvère's party had opted to fight their way out the side exit that opened onto Terrace Street. They were cutting down imps as fast as they came, but that only drew more of the creatures to them. It left the heroes an opening on the opposite side of the club.

Albiorix squeaked and waved his hands toward the big window that Amarok had shattered.

"He's right," said June. "The other exits are all full of imps. We've got to get out that way."

And so the party battled their way through the scratching and biting mass of smoke demons. Devis fought them with his daggers, and June swung Vela's sword with enthusiasm, if not skill. Many of Sorrowshade's arrows missed their mark, and an exhausted Thromdurr was almost dragged down under a clinging mass of imps more than once as he carried Vela. In the sulfurous haze, they could barely see more than a few feet in front of themselves now.

At last the thick smoke finally set off the Monarch's sprinkler system. Water sprayed down from the ceiling, and emergency sirens wailed on the street outside.

The party slipped out the window and escaped into the night just as the first of the fire trucks arrived.

Firefighters kicked in the door of the Monarch—only to find the club empty and filled with stinky black smoke and (strangely) the worst pill-bug infestation any of them had ever seen. They shook their heads. Another "all-ages show" gone awry.

Thankfully June Westray's mother, Amy, was out for the evening—on a very boring date with a software engineer named Tim—or she would have seen a most alarming sight. Her own daughter and four other wounded teenagers, soot stained and sopping wet, arriving at her house on foot. Her own daughter bore a wicked-looking bite mark on the back of her neck. The others looked far worse. Douglas Schiller was covered in too many cuts and gashes to count. Stinky Smith's sweatshirt was crusty with dried blood. Melissa McElmurray looked like death warmed over as she stopped to dry heave every few paces. Valerie Stumpf-Turner was groggy, with a wicked-looking bruise covering half her face. Oh, and for some reason they had a hedgehog with them.

The party made their way to June's living room, where they sat and ate cookies in grim silence. Then there came a crackle of purple energy, and suddenly the hedgehog was very human and very naked. Devis had snagged Albiorix's (waterlogged) spellbook on the way out of the club, but nobody had thought to grab his clothes. June disappeared and discreetly returned with one of her mom's bathrobes, which Albiorix quickly put on.

None of the adventurers knew quite what to say. They had been well and truly beaten.

At last, June broke the silence. "Does anybody have 'I Love U Girl (Throw Cash)' still stuck in their head?"

They all nodded.

Suddenly Thromdurr stood with his head bowed. His voice cracked as he spoke. "I . . . am so sorry, Vela. My foolish error nearly cost you your life. The penalty for such recklessness amongst the Sky Bear clan is death!"

He handed Vela her sword and stuck out his neck for her to chop. It was a bit much.

Vela smiled, though she winced as she did it. "I do not plan on executing you, friend. I know it was an accident." She gave the barbarian a big hug. "Forgiveness is a blessing. And what is a war hammer to the face, now and again, between friends?"

"I thought . . . I thought I was doing what I was

supposed to do," said Thromdurr. "My fighting spirit had finally returned, my heart burned with the fury of a thousand bonfires, yet still my foe bested me. He was the more skilled fighter. I am . . . pathetic."

"Join the club," said Albiorix. "I was casting spell after spell, and they weren't even backfiring or malfunctioning, but it just didn't matter. Calyxia is so far beyond me in terms of ability. Honestly, I'm . . . fifteen, maybe ten percent of the wizard she is."

"They mopped the floor with us," said Sorrowshade. "And Devis could've stopped it."

"Huh?" said Devis. A cookie fell out of his open mouth onto the carpet.

"I saw you," said Sorrowshade. "You had your dagger to Tristane Trouvère's back, but you didn't have the guts to use it. He agreed to join their evil party, by the way."

"I didn't!" cried Devis.

"Just because I've been dosed with enough poison to drop an oliphaunt, that doesn't mean my pointy ears don't work," said Sorrowshade.

"I mean, I agreed, yes, because I was trying to save your lives," said Devis. "You're all welcome, by the way!"

"You should've buried your blade in his kidneys," said Sorrowshade.

"Mercy is not weakness, Devis," said Vela.

"Oh, is that what the Powers of Light teach us?" asked Sorrowshade. "Because they sure came through with an amazing miracle back there." Sorrowshade looked up at the ceiling and gave a thumbs-up. "Thanks, guys."

Vela's eyes narrowed. "You are being very disrespectful. If you had a belief system beyond sarcasm, I would be sorely tempted to mock it. I would refrain, however."

"Ouch," said Sorrowshade.

"You know, Sorrowshade, for somebody who knows what everyone else should've done," said Devis, "you sure spent a lot of that fight puking into your boots."

"Again: I was poisoned!" cried Sorrowshade.

"Oh yeah?" said Devis. "Maybe they'll use something a little stronger next time."

"Maybe we won't waste a healing potion on *you* next time," said Sorrowshade. "Only one left, right?"

"Guys, enough!" cried June. "There are four evil adventurers, one giant wolf thingie, and about a million little smoke demons out there who want to kill you. You don't need to fight among yourselves too."

"She's right," said Albiorix. "But I think that might not be the worst of it."

The other adventurers all turned to stare at him.

"Glad to know we haven't hit rock bottom yet," said Sorrowshade. "Please tell us what we have to look forward to."

"The smoke demons," said Albiorix, "they weren't just attacking us. They were fighting Tristane Trouvère's party as well."

"You're right," said June. "I didn't even think about that. Where do those things even come from?"

"The Thirteen Hells," said Albiorix. "So, I studied the Malonomicon a little last year, and one of the most basic spells in the book was called summon smoke imp."

"Oh no," said Vela.

"Oh yes," said Albiorix. "And the soup monster from Dream Huge? I think that might have been another spell from the Malonomicon—the spell that brings inanimate objects to life and turns them evil."

"Like the mannequins and the escalators that ambushed us at the Old Mall!" cried Thromdurr.

Albiorix nodded.

Devis scratched his chin. "I've never thought of soup as an inanimate object before, but I suppose it technically counts."

"That means there's some good news and some bad news," said Albiorix.

"For morale's sake, I think we could all use a bit of good news," said Vela.

"Tristane Trouvère and his crew still don't possess the Malonomicon," said Albiorix. "Not yet, anyway. Imps aside, if they had it, I have no doubt Calyxia would've been casting its nastiest curses against us in that fight. She craves knowledge above all else, and that book is full of evil magic you can't find anywhere else."

"So what's the bad news?" asked Vela.

Albiorix swallowed. "I'm afraid that the warlock Zazirak has returned."

Chapter 16

In the world of Advanced Homerooms & Hall Passes, much communication is done via "social media." This is a concept that is particularly difficult for novice players to grasp. Think of it this way: In the real world, two people have a conversation. But just imagine how much more efficient things would be if everyone in the world was constantly talking to one another at the same time.

—Excerpt from The Advanced Hall Master's Guide

***

IT WAS A DARK time in the Realm of Suburbia. The undead warlock who had once threatened all life in this world was seemingly back from the dead yet again. It was only a matter of time before he tried to pull off some flashy new apocalyptic scheme. That was just what evil warlocks did.

For the time being, Zazirak was apparently biding his time and working in secret, though. But the only ones strong enough to defeat him had been utterly demoralized by their recent defeat. Indeed, it was the worst drubbing they had suffered since they'd had to run from the Kraken of Krence, an undersea leviathan that had lashed them with hundreds of poison-barbed tentacles. Somehow this stung worse.

Back in Bríandalör, once a foe bested you, that was that. Maybe you were dead. Maybe you weren't. Maybe you plotted your revenge. But you definitely didn't get up the next Monday at six thirty a.m. and go spend all day in the same building with them, trying to avoid eye contact as you passed them in the halls. But here in Suburbia, the adventurers needed to keep attending Pine Hill High School. After all, three unexcused absences would mean their doom.

And so they went to school. And sure enough, Tristane Trouvère, Azheena, Skegg the Surly, and Calyxia were openly hostile now. As proud adventurers, some in the party had the understandable instinct to go for a rematch. But to attack would have been folly. A swordfight in the cafeteria or the library would have led directly to expulsion by Vice Principal Sloane, and yet again they would have Blown It. Even worse, deep down, they all feared it was a battle they might not win.

So instead they endured a constant stream of low-grade antagonism. They tried to keep their distance, but Pine Hill High School was only so big (smaller than most dungeons back home). There were snide comments and veiled threats. Dark looks from across the lunchroom. When Albiorix accidentally sprayed ink all over his shirt from a faulty pen, he wondered if some subtle and insidious spell from the sorceress Calyxia was responsible.

And it wasn't just the four evil adventurers themselves. The four cliques they controlled—the Overacheivers, the Populars, the Jocks, and the Loners—followed the example set by their leaders and took it upon themselves to make life miserable for the heroes at every turn. They started a social media whisper campaign against Valerie Stumpf-Turner, about how she got sent home early from college camp for shoplifting, and they filled Douglas Schiller's backpack with garbage when he left it unattended. While Melissa McElmurray was in a bathroom stall, somebody tipped a bucket of ice water over the door and then ran before she could find out who did it.

It left the party with a sense of chronic unease. They were surrounded by enemies who they could never truly confront. They could no longer hope to relax.

In the cafeteria, the party now kept to themselves, ever wary of some new indignity or insult. Only June Westray seemed unfazed by all the negativity. As they ate their lunch on Thursday, Sorrowshade broke the silence.

"We should poison their food," said the gloom elf.

"No," said Vela. "We are not murderers." It wasn't the first time the paladin had shot down a similar idea.

"Three drops of gorgon blood would turn them to stone," said Sorrowshade. "Not *technically* murder."

"Uh, not to weigh in on the not-technically-murder side, here," said June, "but don't you guys normally spend most of your time killing monsters?"

"Killing monsters is not murder!" said Vela, close to being offended.

"I mean, can't most of them talk or whatever?" asked June. "If they're self-aware, how do their families feel when you—"

Thromdurr placed a friendly hand on June's shoulder. "You are overthinking it, friend June. And I cannot blame you. I find myself overthinking everything these days. My own head is a strong-jawed, lustrous-haired prison of introspection! How I long for the days when I was a simple berserker whose only desire was to crush his foes into the dirt at the slightest provocation and then feast upon large quantities of charred meat."

"Cafeteria potato salad not doing it for you, huh?" said June.

"What is the meaning of life after you have tasted the ultimate glory?" asked Thromdurr. "And how do you keep going after you have suffered the most abject defeat? I am lucky I have math league to cling to amid my mighty emotional turmoils!"

"I wish they'd just get it over with and attack us already," said Devis. "The worst part is all the waiting."

"Waiting is worse than getting stabbed to death?" said June. "Sometimes I really don't *get* you guys."

"Wait a second," said Albiorix. "I think you're on to something. We know why *we're* not attacking *them*. But why aren't *they* attacking *us*?"

Devis considered this. "Maybe, deep down, Tristane Trouvère has realized how much my friendship truly means to him and he's—"

"Nope, that's not it," said Albiorix. "I think they're playing by the same rules as we are."

"They are treacherous, ruthless, and greedy," said Thromdurr. "They play by no rules, wizard."

"Sorry. I mean *literally* the same rules," said Albiorix. "However it is that they're traveling back and forth between Suburbia and Bríandalör now, they got here the exact same way we did. By playing Homerooms & Hall Passes and then triggering the Cave of Azathor curse. They're player characters too."

"So that means they can Blow It?" said Vela.

"Exactly," said Albiorix. "Think about it. The only places they've openly attacked us have been deserted: the Old Mall, the Monarch once it cleared out. And for the most part, Tristane seems to be trying to keep all his scams a secret. I think they're trying not to get into too much trouble."

"If that's the case, then I suppose we're relatively safe at school," said Vela.

Albiorix nodded. "At least from direct physical harm."

"But outside the walls of Pine Hill High School, all bets are still off," said Vela. "When we are not here, we should stick close to our homes and refrain from venturing out into strange and potentially indefensible environments."

The rest of the party agreed. Except June.

"Staying at home is all well and good," said June, "but my art opening is tonight at seven o'clock."

"Art opening?" said Thromdurr. "What is this art opening of which you speak?"

"My collages at the Daily Grind," said June. "I told you guys about it."

"Alas, I did not add it to my day planner," said Thromdurr, hanging his head. "Yet another failure! I am truly sorry, June."

"Enough of the apologies, man," said June. "Just be there. You all said you'd come."

The other adventurers looked at each other.

"Of course we want to support you, June," said Albiorix, "but . . ."

"Is there any way you would postpone the event?" asked Vela. "Between the evil adventurers and Zazirak, hosting such a gathering seems like a safety risk. I mean, you saw what a disaster Devis's party turned out to be."

"Hey!" said Devis.

June crossed her arms. "Postpone? Absolutely not. I put the invite up on social media a month ago. I've got family coming in from out of town. My mom bought special paper napkins and everything. Nope. I'm not going to let a magic dead guy or pack of fantasy-land bullies tell me how to live my life."

Thromdurr slammed the table. "By the great Sky Bear, I respect your fiery commitment to the art of collage!"

"Me too, June," said Albiorix. "I have chess club first, but I'll be there."

Vela nodded. "You must do what you believe. We will all be there at the Daily Grind to protect you."

"Please," said June. "I'm going to have to protect *you* from getting stuck in a terrible conversation about patent law with my uncle Albert."

"Hey, guys," said Morton Blanc as he sat down beside them. "What are we talking about? Sports? Current events? The last season of *Crescent City Mob*?"

"My big art opening," said June. "After I'm a super-famous artist with a hundred assistants who actually do my art, I promise I won't forget all of you. I'll only forget two or three of you, tops."

"Oh yeah, tonight's the big night," said Morton. "I can't wait. How much are you selling your pieces for? I heard a certain amateur art collector might use some of his birthday money to buy one."

"Bidding starts at ten thousand dollars," said June.

"Cool," said Morton. "On second thought, maybe I'll get you a muffin instead."

"Ha ha. Witty banter. Awesome," said Albiorix. "Later." And the wizard got up and abruptly left.

Morton watched him go. "Guys, did I do something to Armando?"

Thromdurr laughed. "Bah! He is merely jealous of—"

Sorrowshade elbowed the barbarian.

"Ahem," said Thromdurr. "He is jealous of your . . . powerful physique."

Morton looked at his arms. He flexed one and made a small muscle. "All I do is a little yo-yo sometimes."

"You can *really* tell," said Devis.

And so the adventurers passed the rest of the school day, staying wary of villains and ghostly necromancers while trying to focus their minds upon such mind-numbing subjects as language arts and geometry.

Albiorix had chess club practice directly after school. If

Morton Blanc bid on one of the collages, maybe he could outbid him. Would that be gallant, or would it just come across as desperate and lame? What if he made her a collage? No, that would send the message that just anyone could cut out little pieces of paper and glue them to other paper. Couldn't they, though?

All these thoughts were running through Albiorix's head as he made his way to his locker to grab his backpack after the last bell. Whatever else was going on in the game world, at least he had his own locker this time around. It was a small comfort.

Albiorix opened the locker door and was surprised to see a large plantlike growth—it resembled an oversized bloodred Venus flytrap—emerging from a heavy clay pot. The wizard recognized it instantly: a fungus from Bríandalör known as a slurper. Slurpers were a deadly dungeon hazard that opportunistically fed on whatever unlucky creature happened to pass by. Often this meant careless adventurers.

Albiorix didn't have time to run. He didn't even have time to scream, because a slurper strikes fast. Quick as lightning, the fungus opened its pod, grabbed Albiorix with its tentacles, and slurped him up. The momentum of the attack slammed his locker door shut behind him.

So much for being safe at school.

Chapter 17

In the highly regimented world of Advanced Home-rooms & Hall Passes, even leaving the house for an after-school nonadventure can present a challenge. If a character's parent or guardian objects, have the character make a Persuasion Check modified by their GPA Bonus to change their mind. Otherwise a Deception or Stealth roll is in order.

—*Excerpt from* The Advanced Hall Master's Guide

❧

BY THE NEXT MORNING, the other adventurers were very worried. Albiorix had planned to meet up with Thromdurr and head to June's art opening with him. He didn't show, which definitely put a damper on the evening. It was hard to enjoy sparkling cider and the art of collage when your absent friend might have fallen victim to an evil warlock attack. The heroes soon found out he hadn't been at chess club practice either. They spent much of the night searching in vain for the missing wizard.

They arrived at school early the next morning—the last place anyone had seen Albiorix—and scoured the halls for any sign of him. It was June who noticed his locker ajar. She opened it to find a grotesquely swollen red fungus with a distinctly Albiorix-shaped lump inside it. June gathered the other party members, and Devis used a dagger to carefully cut an incision in the slurper. Albiorix's limp form came tumbling out, covered in whatever foul goop was inside slurpers.

After a moment, he coughed out a cloud of reddish spores. The wizard was alive. The party breathed a sigh of relief.

"You missed my opening," said June as she helped Albiorix to his feet. "It's okay, though. Seems like you had a good excuse."

"I was . . . going to buy . . . one of your collages," said Albiorix.

"Too bad," said June. "My uncle Albert bought them all for his new offices. It was a little anticlimactic."

"You're alive," said Sorrowshade. "Better than the alternative."

"Yeah," said Albiorix, wiping slime off his face. "A slurper takes weeks to fully dissolve a meal. In the last fourteen hours, I think I've only been very lightly digested."

"Such horrid fungi grow in forgotten underground

places in Bríandalör," said Vela, "Not in school lockers in Suburbia."

"Pretty sure this one was put here special, just for me," said Albiorix. "And I have a guess as to who did it."

The wizard checked under the dead slurper's pot. As expected, he found a handwritten note. In a beautiful, florid script, it read:

From one gamesman to another, I shall elucidate:
You tried to compete, but your team got beat.
It's time to give up. Checkmate.
—T.T.

"T.T.? Could it be?" said Thromdurr. "Talking Turtle? That is to say, the turtles that we endowed with the power of communication by leaving a magical Ring of Turtle Speech here last time?"

Sorrowshade shook her head. "How can you simultaneously be so smart and so dumb?"

"I am nothing if not complex," said Thromdurr.

"I think it stands for Tristane Trouvère," said Albiorix.

Devis examined the card. "Yep. This is his handwriting."

"Elucidate?" said Sorrowshade, rolling her eyes. "So pretentious."

"Disagree," said Devis. "I think the poem's pretty good.

I mean, honestly, what can't the guy do? Poetry, music, fencing, he's a triple threat!"

"Devis, he literally tried to kill you," said Vela.

"Yeah, I guess he didn't quite pull that one off," said Devis. "Couldn't manage to whack Albiorix either."

"I don't think the goal was to kill me," said Albiorix. "I think he just wanted me to miss chess club."

"Why?" asked June. "You think he's a big Monopoly guy?"

"The clue is right there in the poem: checkmate," said Albiorix, balling up the note. "He knew if I missed one more practice, I'd be off the team."

And sure enough, when Albiorix went to make his case to Ms. Kozlowski, the chess club coach, she was unmoved. No matter how good his excuse was (obviously he couldn't tell her the real reason), he was no longer a chess club alternate. And so another of the party's chances to complete a *Freshman Year of Futility* objective slipped away, foiled by Tristane Trouvère and his crew.

After this, Albiorix went from "We are not murderers" to the "Undecided" column in the debate of what to do about the evil adventurers.

Perhaps Sorrowshade sensed this change in her companion. After the last bell rang that afternoon, she found the wizard standing at his locker taking deep, calming breaths. He was understandably hesitant to open the locker door again but had nearly worked himself up to it. Sorrowshade tapped Albiorix on the shoulder, causing him to jump.

"That slurper was a fatal mistake," said Sorrowshade.

"Not to sound like Devis, but credit where credit is due," said Albiorix. "The slurper definitely achieved its purpose."

"Right. But those things constantly exude spores," said Sorrowshade. She crouched and wiped her finger on the floor. It came back with the hint of a dusty reddish smudge. "Your weak human senses can't detect them. But mine can." The gloom elf sniffed deeply. "I can smell them."

Albiorix cocked his head. "What do they smell like?"

"Revenge," said Sorrowshade. "I can track the trail of spores this slurper left all the way back to wherever it came from. I'm assuming the evil adventurers have an evil hideout somewhere."

"Yeah," said Albiorix. "You're probably right. If we locate it, we can spy on them. Learn more about what they're up to. Maybe figure out their weakness."

"We find where they relax," said Sorrowshade. "We watch. We wait. Then, when they're napping, a couple of drops of basilisk venom in the ear."

Albiorix frowned. "I don't know about that. What do the others think?"

Sorrowshade shook her head. "Devis can't be trusted. Thromdurr is going through an existential crisis. Vela will try to shut the whole thing down. It's just you and me on this one, wizard. Normally I wouldn't cut you in, but I figure after spending the night inside a man-eating fungus, you might be up for a little payback."

Albiorix nodded. She was right. "What about June?"

Sorrowshade frowned. "This mission already has one useless human who can't fight or cast spells."

"I *can* cast spells now," said Albiorix. "And June is a member of the party too, you know."

"Are you trying to make up for missing her art opening by inviting her to go on an adventure?" said Sorrowshade.

Albiorix shrugged. "Maybe."

Sorrowshade sighed. "Fine. But if she dies, you have to bury her."

"Not totally sure that's how things work here," said Albiorix.

Albiorix caught up with June on the front steps of the building she was leaving for the day.

"Hey, any chance you want to go on an ultrasecret reconnaissance mission to thwart evil tonight?" asked Albiorix.

"Uh," said June. "I totally would, but . . ."

"But?"

"But I'd planned to watch the premiere of *Crescent City Mob* with Morton tonight."

Albiorix caught himself before he made a face. "No worries. The fate of the world hangs in the balance, but I understand they ended last season on a big cliffhanger, so . . ."

June chewed her lip. "Do you think we could wrap up the adventure by nine?"

"Yeah, definitely," said Albiorix. He wasn't actually sure.

"Okay, then count me in," said June. She did an awkward sort of adventurer salute. Albiorix returned it as best he could.

And so that evening, after darkness had fallen over the Realm of Suburbia, Sorrowshade the elf, Albiorix the wizard, and June the NPC made their various excuses and stealthily reconvened at Pine Hill High School. Sorrowshade sniffed the air for spores and pointed southeast. June and Albiorix followed.

The spore trail led its winding way all over Hibbettsfield—down alleys, across yards, past a Burger Buds franchise, and under an overpass. Eventually they followed it to a big parking lot at the edge of town. A glowing sign, so tall it was visible from the interstate, said STOR-4-U. Beneath the sign was a sea of storage lockers surrounded by a tall chain-link fence.

Rather than enter by the main gate, they picked a

spot hidden by bushes and cut a hole in the fence. As they squeezed through, they heard a bloodcurdling howl in the distance.

"It's the wolf thingie," whispered June.

Sorrowshade smiled. "Good. Means we're on the right track."

Taking care to make sure they weren't seen, the group followed the trail of spores as it wound its way through the seemingly endless blocks of storage lockers. Sorrowshade, who led the group with her nose, suddenly held up a fist. Albiorix and June froze. The gloom elf pointed. Their human eyes weren't as sharp as hers, but even they could see an eerie blue light ahead.

They crept forward to see that storage locker 2-4283 was open and emitting a flickering blue glow. The hairs on Albiorix's arms stood on end. The wizard could sense powerful magic nearby. They saw movement too.

Locker 2-4283 was piled high with brand-new consumer goods—clothing, electronics, various As Seen on TV products still in their boxes. Two figures—Tristane Trouvère and Calyxia—were loading these items through a shimmering blue portal. On the other side, the heroes could just make out lush forests and towering mountains beneath breathtaking blue sky. It was the striking, vibrant landscape of Bríandalör.

They'd found the villains' lair *and* their secret way home!

Sorrowshade, Albiorix, and June quietly watched. This locker was apparently the staging point for the villains' transdimensional black market import-export operation. The goods were stolen or scammed here, and on the other side they'd be sold for piles of Bríandalörian gold. It was as simple as that. The evil adventurers had no grander purpose than lining their pockets. To that end, they were willing to endanger the entire Realm of Suburbia and all its inhabitants. The whole thing was so petty, it made Albiorix furious.

Once most of the merchandise was loaded through the portal, Calyxia stepped through. Presumably she would guide the newest shipment on to wherever it would be sold on the other side. Perhaps the grimy pawnshop in Wharfharbor? Meanwhile Tristane Trouvère stood guard on this side of the portal. After a few minutes of boredom, he sat down on a stack of Bluetooth speaker boxes, pulled out his guitar, and started to strum. The bard was apparently composing a new song.

"Account number and PIN," sang Tristane.

"Account number and PIN.
Open up your heart and girl, let me in.
Open up your wallet and tell me it again.
Girl, we go together like account number and PIN . . ."

As always, even this ridiculous half-formed scrap of a song was extremely catchy. Albiorix couldn't help bobbing his head in time to the music. He noticed June had unconsciously taken the emergency credit card her mom had given her out of her pocket. The wizard nudged her and she caught herself. Meanwhile, Sorrowshade was using a little glass dropper to coat the head of an arrow with some vile black poison. It seemed the assassin meant to assassinate.

But at that moment Albiorix noticed something hanging from a nail on the storage locker wall. It was a pointy bycocket hat made of some silvery fabric that almost seemed to shimmer in the blue glow. Albiorix sensed a magical aura, distinct from the portal, emanating from the hat. It had to be Tristane Trouvère's cap of invisibility!

Albiorix pointed at the hat. Sorrowshade shrugged. He pointed again, more emphatically. Sorrowshade pantomimed shooting an arrow and Tristane Trouvère dying a slow, painful death. Albiorix shook his head. Calyxia—in Albiorix's estimation the most dangerous member of the evil party—was just on the other side of the magic portal, an entire world but only a few feet away.

If Sorrowshade was lucky, she might be able to take out Tristane with her poison arrow, but then they'd have to face the sorceress. And supposing she missed? Against Tristane Trouvère and Calyxia together, they didn't stand a chance.

Albiorix gave them a five, maybe three percent chance of making it out of that fight alive. Not to mention the fact that Amarok the warg was roaming somewhere nearby. Attacking now was far too risky.

Sorrowshade disagreed. But Albiorix ignored the gloom elf's death glare and snuck forward. Stealth was more Devis or Sorrowshade's thing, of course, but Albiorix did his best. He was inside locker 2-4283 now. Tristane Trouvère worked on the chorus of his song with his back to the wizard, and Albiorix slowly crawled forward and reached up. He was so close he could feel the pleasant Bríandalörian breeze blowing through the portal.

Albiorix snagged the cap of invisibility. And then he slowly crawled backward out of the locker. Such a powerful magic item could give them a real edge, especially before Tristane Trouvère knew they possessed it. Albiorix rejoined the others. Sorrowshade looked so angry, he was a little worried that she might use the coated arrow on him. The wizard shrugged.

Just then the party heard a noise. Someone was right behind them. They'd been caught!

Chapter 18

Keeping track of the food your character eats has always been a beloved part of any Homerooms & Hall Passes game. But we always felt this was only one side of the coin. With Advanced Homerooms & Hall Passes, we are proud to debut a complete rules system for going to the bathroom.

—Excerpt from The Advanced Hall Master's Guide

❧

"*G*uys?" whispered Morton Blanc. "What's happe—"

Sorrowshade clapped a gloved hand over his mouth. Then the four of them squeezed between two nearby storage lockers. There wasn't enough room, though. Albiorix couldn't fit. He heard Tristane Trouvère drop his guitar.

The bard stepped out of 2-4283 and saw nothing. Albiorix quickly donned the cap of invisibility an instant before Tristane Trouvère appeared. The bard scanned the darkness and listened carefully. His eyes fell on Albiorix, and he stared for a long moment before turning and walking back toward the portal. A minute later, "Account Number and PIN" started up again, this time with a slightly different chord progression.

Albiorix doffed the hat, and the group beat a quiet but hasty retreat back toward the hole in the fence. They'd made it a few blocks at a jog before Morton broke the silence.

"What . . . what exactly was I looking at back there?" said Morton. "I saw that guy Travis from school and something that appeared to be—but definitely wasn't—an interdimensional portal to another world. It totally wasn't that, right?"

Nobody said anything. Morton stopped walking. He was shaking all over.

"*Right?*" he asked again.

"Right," said Albiorix. "What you saw was just a very, very high-resolution plasma-screen TV that—"

"I don't want to lie to him," said June.

Albiorix ignored her. "Hey, speaking of TV, who wants to go watch the premiere of *Crescent City Mob* tonight? I bet the one guy will try to shoot the other guy. What do you think?"

"I think," said Morton, "I think . . . maybe I need to sit down first."

And so Morton sat down. Right in the middle of the sidewalk.

"On your feet, human," hissed Sorrowshade. "We need to make haste. They could be following us."

"They?" said Morton.

"The evil adventurers," said June.

"June!" said Albiorix.

"He's my friend," said June. "I owe him the truth."

"Evil?" said Morton. "You guys are joking. Tell me you're—"

A howl from Amarok split the night. The beast didn't sound close, but he didn't exactly sound far away either.

Sorrowshade hauled Morton to his feet. "Not joking."

"Wait," said Albiorix, "why were you following us, anyway?"

"I live a couple of blocks from Burger Buds," said Morton. "I was eating a Junior Bacon Bud with Cheese when I looked out the window and saw you three crossing the parking lot. But by the time I made it outside, you were already way down the street. I ran after you to say hi."

"Huh," said Sorrowshade. "Well, now you're caught up in a life-or-death struggle for the fate of the world." The gloom elf shrugged. "Guess you should've gone to Taco Maravilloso instead."

And so as they walked across town, June filled Morton in on the details of who exactly they were and where exactly they came from. In between Morton's stunned ohs and uh-huhs, June sent word, via text message, to summon the other party members to her house.

Vela, Devis, and Thromdurr were already at 410 North Rush Street, the home they had affectionately dubbed Castle Westray, tensely snacking on cookies in the living room, when the others arrived.

"June told this guy everything," said Sorrowshade, nodding toward Morton.

"So you're *all*, like, secret fantasy hero guys?" asked Morton. "Even you, Doug?"

Thromdurr sighed. "What is a hero, really, Morton?"

"Ignore him," said Devis. "Yes, we're all amazing, muscular heroes and I'm sort of the de facto leader. The president of the other heroes, if you will. You may call me Devis the Handsome."

Vela squinted at Sorrowshade. "Why did you split the party?"

"Here we go," said Sorrowshade. "Another party-splitting lecture. It's not realistic for five adventurers with individual needs and goals to constantly do everything together, all the time!"

"Splitting the party is dangerous!" said Vela. "And logistically complicated! Totally unmanageable! You could die!"

"But we didn't," said Albiorix. "And we nabbed this." He held up the shimmery bycocket hat.

"A funny hat!" said Thromdurr. "Very humorous. At

times laughter is our only companion. Kudos to you."

"It's not just any funny hat," said Albiorix, "This is Tristane Trouvère's cap of invisibility."

"Guys, that's stealing!" cried Devis.

The other four Bríandalörians turned to stare at him.

". . . What?" said Devis.

"We also learned they have a storage locker hideout full of hot merch," said June, "with this, like, warp gate back to, um, I can never say it right . . . *Bree-an-duh-lurr*?"

The others looked at her, confused.

"I think she means Bríandalör," said Albiorix.

"Ah," said Vela. "Setting aside my stern disapproval at your careless decision to secretly undertake such a foolhardy quest, good work. Any idea how such a portal came to be?"

Albiorix frowned. "I believe Calyxia is using the spell dimensional door."

"Are there centaurs where you guys come from?" asked Morton quietly, apropos of nothing.

"Yes," said Albiorix before turning back to Vela. "Dimensional door is the same spell the Archmage Velaxis used to travel here, last time around. It's extremely high-level magic. Calyxia must be more powerful than I even imagined."

"Yay," said Sorrowshade.

"And with your expulsion from chess club," said Vela,

"our odds of successfully completing *The Freshman Year of Futility* have only gotten worse."

"We still have math league!" cried Thromdurr. The barbarian threw his arm around Morton's shoulder. "Our match against Riverview High School for the Arts is tomorrow."

"I just learned we inhabit a multiverse full of centaurs," said Morton, "and you're still thinking about math league?"

"Indeed," said Thromdurr. "It may well be our only hope to ever return to our own world."

Morton winced. "Well, that's a lot of pressure."

"You'll get used to it," said June. "Here, have a cookie." She handed Morton one.

"To beat the scenario, we do pretty much have to win math league now," said Albiorix. "It's our last shot at a state championship. And one of us also has to ace the ABSEE. The test is coming up soon."

"To that end, I have taken it upon myself to prepare a rigorous ABSEE group study plan," said Vela. She passed out a photocopied sheet to each of the Bríandalörians. "We cannot rely on last-minute cramming and overnighters for this. We must all study hard, every day, from now until the test. For the next several weeks, you'll see that your spare time has been planned out, down to fifteen-minute increments."

"Dare I ask what the third objective we hope to complete is?" said Sorrowshade.

"Realistically," said Albiorix, "we need to win homecoming king or queen."

At this, Morton burst out laughing. "Sorry," said Morton. "Of all the stuff I learned today . . . that one seems a tad far-fetched."

And so the party returned to Pine Hill High School the following morning. After a string of defeats, they'd finally scored a victory—albeit a minor one—against their foes. The villains' secret hideout had been discovered, and the group had obtained a powerful magic item. Such was often the key turning point in an otherwise impossible quest.

That night, Olivia, Morton, and Thromdurr faced off against Riverview High School for the Arts in their first math league match of the season. It was an intense battle of calculation and reflexes. In the second round, Thromdurr hit the bell so hard it shattered, necessitating an unprecedented ten-minute delay while a new bell was located.

The match was close at first, but despite having two fewer team members, Pine Hill High School ran away with it in the end. They won handily—188 to 93—though many present considered Douglas Schiller's savage victory whoops to be a bit unseemly. That night the team received several emails from other Pine Hill students who wanted to join up.

Yet the day after that, there was an even more momentous development. In the daily drama of high school, it was easy for an adventurer to lose sight of the true goal of their quest. But still, when Sorrowshade wasn't studying for the ABSEE with her fellow party members or secretly writing poems about how much she loved sunshine and warm cocoa, the gloom elf kept up the search.

And that afternoon, in a scraggly patch of woods outside school, she finally found what she had been looking for: evidence of a vile, arcane ritual. In a small clearing, she saw a complicated magic circle inscribed on the ground in chalk, surrounded by the nubs of nine candles. In the middle was a single word written in Shadownese, the language of darkness that happened to also be the gloom elf's native tongue. It said CONQUEST.

Barely a quarter mile from Pine Hill High School, someone had invoked the dark power of the Malonomicon.

Chapter 19

The selection of a homecoming king and queen is an important yearly ritual in the Realm of Suburbia. The crown is an alluring goal for many a Popular and Jock. But please remind players that these titles are largely ceremonial. Otherwise, after their coronation, they may be surprised to find that, unlike in the real world, they lack the power to declare war, levy taxes upon the peasantry, or order summary executions.

—Excerpt from The Advanced Hall Master's Guide

IN THE WEEKS THAT followed, the naked hostility from their evil counterparts waned. The good guys were on an upswing, and perhaps their increased confidence acted as a natural ward against bullying. The insults came less frequently, the pranks stopped altogether. If Tristane Trouvère knew they possessed his cap of invisibility, he wasn't letting on. Though the bard did seem to have lost some of his mojo. Albiorix wasn't sure, but he felt like he saw fewer Travis Tyson superfans mooning over the bard's lunchtime acoustic sets.

Math league enjoyed an impressive string of victories. They defeated Summit High. They mopped the floor with Williamson High. Their match against Westview was a close thing, but they squeaked it out in the end. So many more Nerds joined up that they had to start turning away new members. The core of the team remained Morton Blanc, Olivia Gorman, and Douglas Schiller. Math league even made the school newspaper, an outlet often loath to cover nonathletic competitions.

Thanks to Vela's methodical plan, the heroes' ABSEE studies proceeded well too. Though the process was dry and tedious, their scores were consistently improving on the practice tests included in the official *Academic Basic Skill Evaluation Exam Companion Workbook* ($89.99). June and Morton pitched in to help them study. On one such test, Albiorix managed to get a perfect score in all five sections: language arts, reading, math, science, and social sciences.

And so homecoming approached. It was to be a week of pageantry and celebration, capped off by a momentous football game played by the beloved Pine Hill Harriers against their hated rivals, the vile Elk Grove Elks. And perhaps more important, after the game, the homecoming dance would be the most special and magical ball this side of junior prom. The entire school was abuzz with gossip over who was asking whom to the dance.

The homecoming court would be selected in two rounds of voting, conducted during homecoming week. In the first round, students could vote for anyone nominated. The top vote getters would then appear on the much shorter, final ballot. The homecoming king and queen winners would be crowned during halftime at the football game. Unlike the thinly veiled popularity contest for class president, homecoming court did not claim to be anything other. And even with the Bríandalörians' extraordinary abilities—boundless valor, incomparable strength, deadly accuracy, superhuman reflexes, and arcane knowledge—they were woefully ill equipped to win such a popularity contest.

June and the Bríandalörians walked down the hall between first and second period, grimly discussing their homecoming strategy.

"Step one," said Albiorix, "we all have to nominate each other to get on the first homecoming ballot."

"Simple enough," said Vela. "What is step two?"

"Step two is . . . we somehow make everyone in this school love us," said Albiorix. The wizard sighed.

"I've spent years with you humans," said Sorrowshade.

"We've shared triumph and tragedy. Each of you has saved my life on numerous occasions. And I *barely* like you."

"Gee, if only someone had been allowed to give away a hundred free phones," said Devis. "Something like that could have really turned the tide of public opinion."

"Perhaps our recent string of math league victories could translate into popularity," said Thromdurr, "thus propelling the Nerd Douglas Schiller to homecoming king victory!"

"Oh, Thromdurr," said June, shaking her head.

"I don't know how we do it," said Albiorix, "but somehow we have to win this thing."

"Not going to happen," said Tristane Trouvère.

The party saw that their path was blocked. Skegg the Surly, Calyxia, and Azheena stood shoulder to shoulder with the bard, spanning the width of the hall. The heroes glanced at each other. They hadn't seen the evil party all together like this since their disastrous fight at the Monarch. A crowded hallway was hardly the place for a battle, but if the villains attacked, they'd have no choice but to defend themselves. There was a moment of tense silence.

"Excuse us," said Vela.

"Wow, so polite," said Azheena. "Nauseating."

Sorrowshade stepped forward. Her nose was barely an inch from the ranger's. "My friend means to say: get out of the way if you don't want to end up an ironically detached grease stain on the linoleum."

"Ooh, this one's a flask of fire oil," said Skegg. "Shame we didn't get to tangle last time. Wasted all me time on jumbo shrimp."

Thromdurr said nothing.

"Now is not the time to fight," said Vela. "You know this as well as we do."

Tristane Trouvère cupped his hand to his ear. "Loser says what?"

The other villains snickered. The bard relished their laughter.

"I'm kidding, of course!" said Tristane Trouvère. "For once, we agree. We'll have plenty of time to finish what we started, later." The bard winked at Devis. "But we aren't going to let you win *The Freshman Year of Futility*."

"Huh? What . . . what are you talking about?" said Albiorix. His faux ignorance didn't sound convincing.

"Please. Bluffing isn't your strong suit," said Tristane Trouvère. "Wait, what *is* your strong suit, wizard?"

"Personally, I would hesitate to even call him a wizard," said Calyxia.

"I'll cut to the chase." Tristane Trouvère held up his own copy of *The Freshman Year of Futility*. "We know you're trying to complete three objectives to win the scenario, thereby ending the curse and returning all the Homerooms & Hall

Passes players, i.e., us, back to Bríandalör, once and for all. But we won't let that happen. It's why we kept you off the teams. It's why we won't let you win homecoming king or queen. The scenario can't end. We need this place to stay open for business."

All Albiorix could muster was a feeble shrug.

Tristane Trouvère grinned. "I mean, how could you possibly win, anyway? I am the coolest, most beloved, and—at the risk of sounding immodest—handsomest kid in the whole school. With the votes of the Populars, the Jocks, and let's be honest, most of the girls who go to Pine Hill, I'll easily win homecoming king. Calyxia, paragon of academic virtue and all-around golden girl, will lock down the remaining votes from the Overachiever and Nerd contingents to become homecoming queen. Do the math. You losers don't have the numbers."

And so the evil adventurers elbowed their way past and proceeded down the hallway, leaving a group of flustered heroes behind them.

"Well, that was *highly discourteous*," said Vela through gritted teeth.

"I know lying is out, but does your paladin code have anything against understatements?" said June. "Why did they even do that? That was some straight-up eighties high school movie bullying."

"I think Tristane is trying to psych us out," said Albiorix.

"Then I commend him on his success," said Thromdurr. "There is simply no conceivable way any of us can get elected to homecoming court. I feel sad and a little hungry. Sorrowshade, is this what it feels like to relinquish all hope?"

Sorrowshade smiled. "I knew you'd get there, one day."

"Okay, I got it," said Devis. "What if we secretly fill the school with eels? And then we get rid of the eels? And who gets elected to homecoming court? The brave eel heroes who saved everyone from the eels!"

June cocked her head. "Why is that the best plan you guys have come up with so far?"

"When in doubt, I choose blind optimism," said Vela. "But I must agree with Thromdurr. We have many admirable qualities, but we are not . . . well liked. Unless something changes, we will not win."

"What needs to change is our tactics," said Sorrowshade. "We keep losing because we always try to play it straight. We need to beat them at their own game. We need to fight fire with fire. We need to go dark."

"Please tell me you are not talking about coating their toothbrushes with hydra venom again," said Vela. "We've been over this—"

"I'm talking about something worse," said Sorrowshade.

"Are you saying we somehow find the Malonomicon

and—and use it against them?" asked Albiorix.

"Worse," said Sorrowshade.

"What could be worse than a tome of ancient evil?" said Vela.

"There is a force in this world so ruthless, so devious, and so sinister that to meddle with it is perhaps to risk our very souls," said Sorrowshade. "But I fear it is our only hope."

"Sorrowshade, you're kind of scaring me," said June.

"You should be afraid, mortal," said Sorrowshade. "More than the rest of you, I walk a path of darkness. So I will attempt to harness this evil to our advantage."

"I will not sacrifice my morals," asked Vela. "But it does appear we require a new strategy. Are you certain this is the only way?"

The gloom elf nodded.

"Then may the Powers of Light watch over you," said Vela.

That night, after many cheerful rounds of Traders of Ogoo with the rest of the McElmurray family, the gloom elf snuck out the window of her room and shimmied down the drainpipe. Bringing all the stealth of her years of assassin training to bear, she slipped from shadow to shadow across the town of Hibbettsfield, until at last she came to a beautiful gabled house on tree-lined Kenmare Street.

Sorrowshade stepped out of the darkness and onto the

sidewalk. She composed herself. And then she rang the doorbell. At this moment, she was flooded with grave misgivings at what she was about to do. But the assassin steeled herself. She had already come this far. There was no turning back now. She heard footsteps inside.

Nicole Davenport opened the door.

Chapter

DAVENPORT, Nicole Alexandra

CLASS: Popular

ATTRIBUTES: Cunning: 18, Intelligence: 12, Likability: 18, Willpower: 15, Fitness: 13

SKILLS: Apple Polishing +1, Athletics +1, Computer +2, Deception +11, Note Passing +5, Persuasion +9, Style +7, Trivia (Designer Clothing) +4

BIOGRAPHY: Nicole Davenport first realized her true calling at age 5, when she successfully started a rumor that Chelsea Azarian still wore diapers. With Chelsea's reputation in tatters, young Nicole was able to swiftly consolidate power and conquer the social hierarchy of Ms. Kwok's kindergarten class. . . .

—*Excerpt from* The Cyclopedia of Students

*n*ICOLE CROSSED HER ARMS. "Ugh. What are *you* doing here?"

"I crave popularity," hissed the gloom elf.

"Sorry. Can't help you with that anymore." Nicole held up her phone. It showed a well-composed selfie—Nicole smiling in a lavender dress. "I just posted a picture of my homecoming gown. Three likes. Not that anybody's even *asked* me to the dance yet."

"Perhaps because your personality is abhorrent," said Sorrowshade.

Nicole gave a wistful sigh. "I know. Never used to matter. But these days, I'm nothing but a regular old loser. Just like you."

"Yes, you are a loser," said Sorrowshade. "And how it must sting all the more, after having been the most popular girl in middle school. You soared so close to the sun, only to be cast down into the muck and slime with the rest of us patheti—"

"What is your point?" asked Nicole.

"You may not *be* popular," said Sorrowshade. "But you know *how* to be popular."

Nicole cocked her head.

"Even if I lost my bow, I'd still know how to hit a bull's-eye at five hundred feet," said Sorrowshade. "So you must know how one would dominate the vicious high school social hierarchy, even if you no longer sit at the top."

"You're so weird," said Nicole. "It's gross."

"You're not telling me to leave," said Sorrowshade.

Nicole tapped her foot. "Fine. Come inside."

As Sorrowshade passed through the beautiful house to Nicole's bedroom, she had a flash of déjà vu. She'd spent many hours here the previous year, back when she and Nicole were "besties."

Nicole sat down on her bed. "Look, it's not all about everyone loving you. The key is preemptively destroying other people who everyone might want to love *instead* of you, okay?"

"And how do we do that?" asked Sorrowshade.

"Just use that creepy little book you have, that has everybody's darkest secrets, again," said Nicole.

The gloom elf shook her head. "They haven't published *The Advanced Cyclopedia of Students* yet, so we only have potential blackmail material for those who attended J. A. Dewar Middle School. And anyway, such a book wouldn't help us with who we're trying to take down."

"And who are you trying to take down?" asked Nicole.

"Travis Tyson," said Sorrowshade.

Nicole's eyes nearly shot out of her head. "Are you insane? Travis Tyson is *literally* the cutest boy in school. Maybe on earth."

"He is a greedy, deceptive parasite who manipulates everyone he meets," said Sorrowshade.

"What does that have to do with what I said?" asked Nicole.

"He must be stopped from winning homecoming king," said Sorrowshade.

"Why?" asked Nicole. "He deserves to win. His hair is perfect."

"Christina Christopoulos must also be prevented from winning homecoming queen," said Sorrowshade.

Nicole considered this. "She's a little square. I mean, seriously, lose the glasses, sweetheart. But overall, strong favorables. She's pretty. Teachers like her. Nerds like her. Overachievers like her. Not as much of a shoo-in as Travis, but easily a top-three homecoming queen contender. Only Hope Kaufman and Imani Booker could give her a run for her money."

"You've already given this some thought," said Sorrowshade.

"Even a lion at the zoo thinks about hunting," said Nicole.

"So can you do it or not?" asked Sorrowshade.

"Do what?" asked Nicole.

"Can you get one of us onto homecoming court?"

At this, Nicole burst out laughing. Sorrowshade scowled.

Still Nicole laughed. Sorrowshade checked the clock on the wall. A full minute passed. Still Nicole Davenport laughed.

"Enough mirth, mortal!" cried the gloom elf.

Nicole wiped her eyes, still giggling a little. "OMG, one of *you* on homecoming court? Can you *imagine*? I only invited you inside because I knew you'd humiliate yourself. And you did not disappoint, you little pointy-eared weirdo."

"Are you sure you didn't invite me in because you have no friends?" asked Sorrowshade.

Nicole's smile dropped. "Okay, Melissa. Time to get out of my house. You didn't steal anything on the way in, did you? I know you're, like, *poorer* than me."

She started to shoo Sorrowshade toward the door.

"What good is perfect-hair Travis Tyson or high-favorables Christina Christopoulos if neither one of them will give *you* the time of day?" asked Sorrowshade.

"What are you talking about?"

"I've seen you try," said Sorrowshade. "You introduce yourself. You like the right social media posts. You ingratiate yourself and try to climb the little ladder. Yet no one cares. You should be running the school. Instead, you're invisible."

Nicole's eyes flashed. "I *should* be running the school."

"My friends and I may be losers," said Sorrowshade. "But we are capable of extraordinary things. You have the knowledge. We have the power. If we work together to take

258

down the current cool-kid regime, that leaves a void. A void that could be filled by you."

Nicole considered this for a long time. "Of course I know how to do it," said Nicole. "But it's not going to be easy, it's not going to be cheap. And it's not going to be pretty. My fingerprints can't be on it."

"Understood," said Sorrowshade.

"Oh, and there's something I want," said Nicole.

"Homecoming queen," said Sorrowshade, over the noise of the cafeteria. "Nicole wants to be homecoming queen."

The other party members stared at the gloom elf.

"But if she is the queen, then you or I cannot be," said Vela.

"Frankly, the thought of standing in front of the school in a frilly dress and a tiara makes me wish I was eaten by minotaurs along with the rest of my family," said Sorrowshade. "But only one of our party actually needs to win."

Morton spat out a bite of his sandwich. "Wait. I'm sorry, your family was eaten by what now?"

"Minotaurs. Try to keep up," said Sorrowshade. "Anyway, we have no choice but to accede to Nicole's demand. Unless any of you have a better plan?"

"Did I already pitch you guys the school-full-of-eels idea?" asked Devis.

Sorrowshade ignored him. "In exchange, Nicole will help one of our party win homecoming king."

Albiorix, Devis, and Thromdurr all looked at each other.

"Me!" said the thief and the barbarian in unison.

"I am the most physically impressive," said Thromdurr. "And only my flowing mane can match Tristane Trouvère's impeccable coif in one-on-one competition."

"Oh yeah? Well, I can do this with my thumbs," said Devis. He waggled his double-jointed thumbs.

Sorrowshade shook her head. "Nope. Nicole said it's got to be Albiorix."

"What?" said Albiorix.

"What?" said June.

"Doug is a Nerd, so he's out," said Sorrowshade. "Stinky is too short, so he's out."

"Injustice!" cried Thromdurr.

"Unbelievable!" said Devis.

"Nicole's words, not mine," said Sorrowshade. "But she says Armando Boort is basically a blank canvas—an anonymous nobody, without a memorable personality, who no one knows anything about."

"Well, now, that also feels a tad hurtful," said Albiorix.

Sorrowshade shrugged. "We don't have much time. Nicole said we need to start boosting Armando Boort's profile as soon as possible. He has to make it past the first round of voting and get onto the final ballot," said Sorrowshade. "Albiorix, she gave me a checklist of things you need to do by tomorrow."

The gloom elf handed the wizard a scrap of paper. It was a long list with things like "Velocity Select Sky-Max Low Top Sneakers (Gray)" and "McCabe Slim-Fit Tapered Leg Jogging Pants (Red)" and "Always smile" and "Avoid sounding too smart; people *hate* that."

Albiorix sighed. "Fine."

June peeked at the list over his shoulder. "So you're just going to pretend to be a totally different person?"

"Wouldn't be the first time," said Albiorix.

"In the meantime," said Sorrowshade, "if we want to take down Tristane Trouvère and Calyxia socially, Nicole says the key is not to attack an opponent from their weakness but from their strength."

"Nicole Davenport truly has a warrior's cunning," said Thromdurr.

"Vela," said Sorrowshade, "you should probably leave if you don't want to tarnish your soul or whatever."

"Farewell, comrades," said Vela. "I shall return to the salad bar." And so the paladin stood and left them to their scheming.

And so the others discussed their strategy for upending the entire social order.

The next day, the students of Pine Hill were struck by the arrival of a hip, handsome, interesting new student. His name was Armando Boort (cool name) and he came from Canada (apparently a cool country). The kid was decked out in the latest styles, and he had the freshest haircut ever. Armando smiled a lot and he seemed smart (but not too smart), and everyone who saw him walk down the hall in his gray Velocity Select Sky-Max Low Top Sneakers wanted to know more.

The previous night June and the other heroes had accompanied Albiorix to the Towne Centre Mall, where the wizard had spent a small fortune on expensive brand-name clothing and a designer haircut to complete his new look. After the makeover, the wizard barely recognized himself.

As Albiorix proceeded to his locker, he was a bit flum-moxed at all the newfound attention. Depressingly, Nicole had been absolutely right. Many of his fellow students hadn't even registered the old Armando's existence. Now they were intrigued.

"Hi," said a girl with a green-and-pink backpack.

"Who, me?" said Albiorix, taken aback at a stranger talking to him. He kept his smile up, though. Always smile.

"Cool haircut," said Marc Mansour.

"Uh. Thanks, guy," said Albiorix.

"Guy," said Marc. "I'm going to start saying that. Later, guy."

"My friend wants to know if you've asked anyone to the homecoming dance yet," said Laura Hong, a junior.

"Not sure," said Albiorix, trying his best to sound like a cool guy. "But I guess I'm kind of thinking about asking Nicole Davenport."

Laura crinkled her nose. "Nicole Davenport? Who's that?"

And this too was part of the plan.

But the debut of this fascinating new tastemaker on the Pine Hill social scene wasn't even the most exciting thing that happened at school that day. It was also a day that a pillar of the academic community would fall.

The student body was shocked to learn that Christina Christopoulos—MVP of the speech and debate team, master equestrian, likely future Ivy Leaguer—had cheated on a chemistry test. Her answers were exactly the same as the ones Monica Hilaire had turned in, and everyone saw Monica sitting right in front of her. It was unbelievable. Why would Christina Christopoulos need to cheat? But then again, it kind of made sense. Nobody could actually be as perfect as her, could they? Of course she hadn't played by the rules to get where she was. What other corners had she cut? they all wondered.

Those who happened to catch a glimpse of Christina being escorted from Mrs. Ijendu's chemistry class to Vice Principal Sloane's office were struck most by her face. She had always been impatient, yes, and maybe a little curt. But now her eyes almost seemed to glow with incandescent rage. Clearly she wasn't the golden girl they'd all taken her to be.

It had been a fairly simple matter for Devis to slip inside the classroom unseen and change the answers on Christina's test that morning. The villains apparently hadn't expected the heroes to use the same underhanded tactics they had employed—a major blind spot.

And as the week rolled on, the results of the first homecoming court ballot came in. The final choices for homecoming king were Travis Tyson, Rhys King, Marc Mansour, Caleb Greene, and Armando Boort. For homecoming queen, the school would vote on Hope Kaufman, Imani Booker, Lena Garza, Cecilia Hasdeu, and a relatively unknown dark-horse candidate, a freshman named Nicole Davenport, who many believed to be romantically linked with the fascinating Canadian newcomer.

"Armando!" called out a boy in orange sunglasses.

"How's it hanging, my guy?" called Albiorix back as he walked down the hall with June by his side.

"Who was that?" asked June once they'd passed.

"No idea," said Albiorix.

"So you put on some new clothes and pay someone a hundred and thirty dollars to cut your hair, and now you suddenly have a bunch of new friends?" said June.

"It's your world, not mine," said Albiorix. "And hey, maybe this is the real me, only I just didn't know it until now."

"I wish rolling my eyes made a sound," said June as she rolled her eyes. "I can't believe you're actually *pretending* that Nicole Davenport is your girlfriend."

In the past few days there had been a flurry of social media activity hinting at a tumultuous on-again off-again romance between Nicole Davenport and Armando Boort. Nicole herself was running both accounts to keep all the crazy plot twists straight and ensure maximum continuity. They'd "split up" and "gotten back together" no less than three times already during the week. It was like a real-life soap opera playing out in front of the entire school, and as Nicole had predicted, people couldn't get enough.

"Uh, I think we may actually be broken up at the moment," said Albiorix, "It's hard to keep track. And look, Nicole isn't exactly my favorite person in the world, but she is helping us."

Bree Mitchell waved as the wizard walked past. Albiorix shot her a thumbs-up. Bree giggled.

June shook her head. "She's helping you by making you into a complete phony."

Albiorix shrugged. "I guess. It kind of beats scraping by as an anonymous loser, though."

"Is that what you think I am?" asked June.

"What? No," said Albiorix. The wizard turned to high-five Ray Rojas as he walked past. "Ray! Love the McCabe Arc Logo Color Block Hoodie, guy."

"Thanks, guy," said Ray.

When Albiorix turned back around, June was gone. The wizard sighed. No time to look for her, though. He was on his way to meet the others.

The rest of the Bríandalörians—minus Vela, of course—had convened in a secluded corner of the hallway, not far from the ninth-grade lockers. Their takedown of Christina Christopoulos had been more successful than they had possibly hoped. It was clear that Nicole Davenport was an evil genius when it came to this stuff. She'd given Sorrowshade her next set of instructions for the greater challenge: destroying Travis Tyson.

"As we all saw, attacking Calyxia from her strength proved highly effective," said Sorrowshade. "The plan is to do the same to Tristane Trouvère. Any guesses as to what his greatest strength is?"

"His boundless charm?" asked Devis.

The gloom elf shook her head.

"His musical talents?" asked Albiorix.

The gloom elf shook her head.

"His classical good looks?" asked Thromdurr.

"Close, but not quite it," said Sorrowshade. "We're going to beat him with these." The gloom elf held up several loose tufts of hair, the same color as Tristane Trouvère's.

Thromdurr squinted. "Are those some breed of exotic local wildlife? Greetings, little caterpillars!" The barbarian waved at the hair tufts.

"Nope," said Sorrowshade. "The humans call them hair extensions."

"And what are we going to use them for?" asked Devis. "You planning to tickle Tristane Trouvère into submission?"

Sorrowshade shook her head. "After what we're about to do, he's definitely not going to be laughing."

A rumor began to spread among the students of Pine Hill High School. It came through anonymous posts on social media and comments whispered in the halls between classes. This rumor was so outrageous that those who heard it couldn't help but pass it on. Little did they know that it had been deliberately crafted this way, by a veteran master of spreading gossip.

People were saying that Travis Tyson's beautiful hair was not his own. This was, on the face of it, obviously crazy. But then again, why did people keep saying it?

For his part, the normally chill and friendly Travis seemed to bristle at the implication, which only piqued people's curiosity. Was he hiding something?

On more than one occasion, when he was regaling listeners with a beautiful song (his new one, "Account Number and PIN," was a real banger) on his guitar, he stopped suddenly and invited someone, anyone, to yank on his hair to prove that it was real. It was strange and off-putting and no one really wanted to do it, which only seemed to agitate Travis more. The audiences for his impromptu performances dwindled further, and even those who stayed had to admit that Travis Tyson had been *off* ever since that cool guy Armando showed up. Some even had a distant memory of some sort of fistfight in the halls between the two of them. Was Travis jealous of the Canadian stealing his thunder?

It was on one such occasion, at lunchtime on the Wednesday before homecoming, when Travis was loudly demanding someone pull his hair "as hard as they could," that his guitar case popped open and dozens of hair extensions spilled out. He tried to deny they were his, but they were exactly the same color as his hair. Then Travis exploded, yelling at everyone present. He said they were puppets, or worse, part of a conspiracy cooked up by his enemies. He even accused Armando Boort and several others of not actually being Pine Hill High School students. Instead he claimed that they secretly came from some strange fantasy world called "Bríandalör" and they were tricking everybody—making fools of the entire school. It was a total mental breakdown. And unfortunately for Travis Tyson, more than one person filmed it on their phone.

As the scene unfolded, it was all Sorrowshade—wearing Tristane Trouvère's own cap of invisibility—could do to keep herself from bursting out laughing.

Homecoming week wore on. The heroes continued their rigorous ABSEE studies for the test the following week, math league annihilated the hapless team from Alston Montgomery High, and Sorrowshade kept looking for the Malonomicon. She'd found evidence of at least three other dark rituals in the area surrounding the school.

As Friday arrived, the heroes' anticipation was almost unbearable. Nicole Davenport's devious campaign of guerilla social warfare had worked. Christina Christopoulos's reputation had been ruined, and Travis Tyson was now seen by many as a raving maniac with fake hair. In the meantime, the whole student body obsessively followed the ups and downs of Armando Boort and Nicole's (totally made-up) "relationship."

And so Pine Hill High School cast their final votes for homecoming court. The glorified popularity contest had finally come to an end.

On Friday, during the morning bulletin, the results were announced. The Pine Hill High School homecoming king and queen would be Armando Boort and Nicole Davenport.

Chapter

21

*Of all the tricky social encounters that present them-
selves in an Advanced Homerooms & Hall Passes game,
none can match the potential awkwardness of high
school dances. Such events are just as likely to leave
a player character giddy and elated (+5 to all Checks
and Saves) as they are to leave them heartbroken and
humiliated (-5 to all Checks and Saves).*

—*Excerpt from* The Advanced Hall Master's Guide

T HE FLOODLIGHTS OF THE football field glared as
Albiorix stepped forward for his coronation. Last year's
homecoming king, Luis Sanz—now a college freshman—
placed the sparkly plastic crown upon the wizard's lowered
head. The audience erupted in applause.

"Congratulations, Armando," said Luis. "Enjoy this.
But remember: the crown you wear carries with it a huge
amount of responsibility."

"It does?" said Albiorix.

Luis grinned. "Nah, it actually doesn't matter at all. To tell you the truth, I'm a little embarrassed to even be here."

As Nicole Davenport, resplendent in her purple gown and elaborate hairstyle, received her own crown to more thunderous clapping, Albiorix scanned the crowd. He caught sight of Tristane Trouvère. The bard stared daggers at him.

Afterward, Albiorix sat in the bleachers with Nicole and watched the rest of the game. They didn't talk. Nicole managed her social media accounts while Albiorix attempted to make sense of the football game—a sport so brutal it could almost have been Bríandalörian. The Pine Hill Harriers got stomped by the Elk Grove Elks. Final score, 49 to 3.

But athletics were a secondary concern to most that night. After the game, the students made their way to the darkened gymnasium, now a forest of balloons and crepe paper. A DJ blared pop music over a sound system while a twirling disco ball made thousands of tiny sparkles swim across the floor. This was the long-awaited homecoming dance.

Albiorix entered arm in arm with Nicole. And once again, the student body erupted in applause. The wizard smiled.

"Hey, uh, thanks," whispered Albiorix. "I know we've had our differences, but obviously we couldn't have, uh, done this without—"

"The only thing that could ruin this moment for me is you talking," hissed Nicole through her brilliant smile.

A slow song came on and Nicole and Albiorix headed to the dance floor, along with other pairs of students. The wizard put his arms on Nicole's shoulders and did his best to sway in time to the music, while she joylessly rage-smiled in his general direction.

As they slowly spun, the wizard saw Tristane Trouvère, Skegg the Surly, Azheena, and Calyxia all huddled in a dark corner of the gym, glaring at him. It wasn't the place to start a fight, but the evil adventurers looked furious. Albiorix stared right back at them and did something Tristane Trouvère himself might have done: he laughed. Somehow the villains looked even angrier.

On the other side of the gym, Albiorix saw his companions. Vela gave him an encouraging nod. Sorrowshade smirked. Devis mouthed, "It should have been me." Thromdurr, who stood with his fellow members of math league, jumped up and down and waved his arms wildly. Albiorix grinned. After so many setbacks, the party had finally completed one of the objectives of *The Freshman Year of Futility*. It felt good.

June was there too, but she didn't exactly look happy. As he danced with Nicole, she looked at him with an unreadable expression on her face and her arms crossed. Albiorix tried to give her a little "isn't this crazy?" shrug. June turned away and started chatting with Morton Blanc.

"This music is so lame," said June. "You want to go do something else?"

"Uh, sure," said Morton. "What?"

"Anything," said June. And she started toward the exit.

Morton quickly followed, leaving Thromdurr standing alone with Olivia Gorman. Olivia scowled as she watched June and Morton go. Then she turned her withering gaze upon the new homecoming king and queen as they slow danced in the middle of the gym floor. She looked like she'd just tasted something awful.

"Doug, tell me the truth," said Olivia. "Did your friends somehow rig this homecoming vote too?"

"What?" cried Thromdurr. "Nay! Armando beat the competition fair and square. Everyone agrees he is a very intriguing fellow. Did you know he's Canadian?"

"Yeah, right," said Olivia. "Look, if we beat Valley View Magnet School this week, you know what that means?"

Thromdurr grinned. "We shall bring glory and honor to Pine Hill High School as math league heads to the state championship!"

Olivia turned to stare hard at the barbarian. "You've been an important part of the team. Invaluable, even. I never thought I'd say this, but you're almost as good at math as I am."

"High praise, Olivia," said Thromdurr, who actually felt

himself starting to choke up. "High praise, indeed."

"But if you have something up your sleeve, some trick or scam you and your friends are planning to pull at the last minute, tell me now, Doug." She almost looked desperate. "I need this. And I can't let anyone screw it up for me."

"I need this too," said Thromdurr. "No tricks, Olivia. I swear upon my ancestors, I will let no dishonor come to the sacred Spirit of Mathematics."

"Your ancestors?" said Olivia.

"The Schillers!" said Thromdurr a bit too quickly. "Such as my uncle Leonard and, ah, my great-aunt Mabel!"

"All right, Doug," said Olivia. "I hope you don't disappoint me, like everyone eventually does." And with that, Olivia turned to leave the dance as well.

On Monday morning, Albiorix arrived at school with a confidence he had not felt in a long time. He'd bested his foes and been validated by the entire school. Also his shoes were really cool. He almost felt like a real king as he walked down the hall to his locker.

At lunch, it was all the wizard could do to dodge his legions of newfound friends and admirers to take his usual seat at the secluded table with the rest of the party.

"Boy, it's like I'm some sort of celebrity around here. It's almost annoying," said Albiorix as he set his tray down on the table. "I wonder if me not sitting with Nicole will start the rumor mill guessing."

"Here's a thought," said Devis. "If you don't like the attention, stop wearing your hipster costume, and then nobody will care about you anymore."

"I mean, I *own* the clothes. I might as well keep wearing the clothes I own, right?" said Albiorix. "Where's June?"

The others shrugged.

Vela cleared her throat. "Well, you won, Albiorix. We joined ourselves with an unscrupulous ally and deployed trickery and lies, so the victory does not come without shame. But . . . I very lightly commend you."

"Hooray?" said Sorrowshade.

"We have completed one of the scenario objectives, but there is no time to waste," said Vela. "Our next challenge awaits."

"We need to ace the Academic Basic Something Exam Exam," said Devis. "Wait, did I get the acronym right?"

Vela scowled. "The test is tomorrow. I fear we are not ready. I missed five questions on the most recent ABSEE practice test we took. Not good enough."

"I achieved a perfect score on the math section!" cried Thromdurr.

"Yeah, but you really blew it on the social studies," said Sorrowshade.

"So did you, elf," said Thromdurr.

Sorrowshade shrugged. "Look, I can hear a sparrow sneeze at five hundred paces and walk across newly fallen snow without leaving any footprints. You want me to be good at standardized tests too?"

"Don't worry, guys. I've got this," said Albiorix. "I aced my last three ABSEE practice tests. We're all good."

"I'm ready too," said Devis. "Because it absolutely doesn't matter how I do on the test as long as Albiorix gets a perfect score."

Vela nodded. "If—and I hesitate to tempt the gods, who cannot abide the pride of mortals—but *if* Albiorix is successful, then we will have completed two of the three scenario objectives."

"And after math league vanquishes puny Valley View Magnet School, we are headed to the state championship," said Thromdurr. "The third and final objective is within our grasp, friends."

"Then we must defeat Zazirak and obtain the Malonomicon before then," said Vela. "Otherwise we leave the warlock and the evil grimoire behind to wreak havoc upon the defenseless people of Suburbia."

"The spellbook is here," said Sorrowshade. "It's at school. I know it."

"You mean Zazirak has possessed one of the students or

faculty members at Pine Hill?" said Vela, gazing out over the crowded auditorium.

The teachers and other kids laughed and chatted among themselves at a deafening volume. It was chilling to think that one of them secretly harbored the ghost of an undead warlock.

"I keep finding the remnants of evil magic nearby," said Sorrowshade. "The Malonomicon must be here. Albiorix, you say you can do magic now. Why don't you try to cast that find lost object spell again?"

Albiorix nodded. The wizard glanced around to make sure nobody was watching. Then he closed his eyes and quietly muttered an incantation from his own spellbook as he focused his mind's eye upon the Malonomicon.

"Ta' phaet zyen ael ra'ln a'ti doil nysh'a," said Albiorix as he traced the outline of the sigil for finding.

"Hey, guys, what's shaking?" said Morton, putting his tray down on the table nearby.

"Albiorix is casting a spell to find a legendary book of evil magic that threatens the very existence of your world," said Vela.

Morton slumped. "My fault for asking."

". . . It feels like the book is here, but—no, wait." The wizard shook his head. "I thought I had something, but I don't know. I'm not really getting anything."

Devis shook his head. "The guy still can't do magic. It's okay. His new special power is, ah, cool sneakers."

Albiorix opened his eyes again and dropped the spell. "The magic did work, but . . . but I couldn't find the book. Sorry, I'm not sure what to tell you."

"The Malonomicon is here," repeated Sorrowshade.

"Then we must find it quickly," said Vela. "And in the meantime, it is imperative that we eat a balanced meal. Everyone finish your green vegetables and try to get as much sleep as possible before tomorrow."

"Happy to start right now," said Devis, and the thief gently lowered his head onto the table and soon started to snore.

The next morning, the party's homeroom teacher, Ms. Lane, passed out their Academic Basic Skill Evaluation Exam booklets. Each of the five sections was individually timed and had its own multiple-choice answer sheet. The entire test was to be administered over a single brutal day.

There was a nervous energy in the air. The ABSEE had put all of ninth grade on edge. Vela had her eyes closed as she prayed to the Powers of Light for help with the biology questions. Devis chewed on one of his double-jointed thumbs. Thromdurr had a look of either intense concentration or intense indigestion etched upon his face. The wizard even caught the normally unflappable Sorrowshade's eye twitching. He tried to catch June's attention, but she didn't look up.

"Okay, guys," said Ms. Lane, "this test isn't everything. But . . . it's close."

Albiorix knew he was the party's best hope. It didn't matter if he had won homecoming king; if he couldn't pull this off, the heroes would likely be stuck in Suburbia forever. Yet somehow the wizard felt totally calm. He had studied. He had practiced. He was ready.

"Hey, man," whispered Morton, who was sitting at the desk in front of Albiorix, "I'm not sure I totally get the stakes of this whole thing for you guys, but I just wanted to say, ah, good luck."

Albiorix was surprised that he didn't feel like rolling his eyes or making a face or coming back with a cutting retort. Instead he said, "Thanks, Morton. Good luck to you too."

First was language arts. Ms. Lane said the class would have exactly one hour for this section. The timer started. Pages turned. Pencils flew. Albiorix worked his way through a seemingly endless series of questions about grammar and vocabulary. For each one he filled in a little oval on the answer sheet to indicate A, B, C, or D. His mind danced from gerunds to infinitives to definitions. A phone alarm chimed.

"Pencils down, everyone," said Ms. Lane.

There were a few sighs and some frantic erasing before the last of the pencils finally came to rest. The hour had flown by. But Albiorix had finished the test eleven minutes ago. There hadn't been a single language arts question he didn't know the answer to. He was in the ABSEE zone.

"Please pass your answer sheets forward," said Ms. Lane.

Albiorix handed his to Morton. All the ninth graders passed their little sheets of filled-in ovals toward the front of the class, where ultimately the papers would be sealed in an official-looking envelope and shipped off for computer grading.

They repeated this grueling process again for reading, then math, science, and social studies. At the end of the day, many of Albiorix's classmates looked shell-shocked and haggard.

After the last bell, the Bríandalörians made their way to the ninth-grade lockers. The wizard's companions looked grim.

"That was as rough a slog as the time we marched all the way from Mountains of Desolation to the Fathomless Sea," said Vela. "If the children of this realm regularly endure such tests, perhaps they are made of stronger stuff than I had realized. I am sorry to say that I do not feel confident in my answers."

"Me neither," said Devis. "I was trying to take the test, but then I got really distracted."

"When?" asked Sorrowshade.

"The whole time," said Devis.

"You got distracted for five hours?" said Sorrowshade.

"Yeah, I'm pretty focused when it comes to getting distracted." Devis turned to Thromdurr. "How about you, big guy?"

"I slew the feeble math section and then cracked open its bones to slurp out the delicious math marrow inside!" said the barbarian. "But the language arts are beyond my ken. This strange world's punctuation rules still elude me. I KNOW NOT WHEN IT IS APPROPRIATE TO USE EXCLAMATION POINTS!"

"Well, I'm not going to sugarcoat it," said Sorrowshade. "The science section was an unmitigated disaster for me. Stupid physical laws of the stupid universe. All made up anyway."

"Looks like it all comes down to the homecoming king," said Devis.

The others turned to stare at the wizard. Albiorix grinned.

"I did it," he said. "We obviously have to wait for the official results for it to count but . . . I aced the ABSEE."

"How confident are you?" asked Vela.

"One hundred percent," said Albiorix.

The party gasped. In their long experience, the wizard had never been one hundred percent sure of anything before.

"Lo, the smart one returns," said Devis.

"Then it falls to me and the other math league stalwarts to finish our quest," said Thromdurr. "We will not fail you, friends!"

Indeed, that night the Pine Hill math league team would face their toughest opponent yet: the team from Valley View Magnet School, a high school that drew all the best and brightest from the surrounding region. The auditorium was almost full. The Pine Hill team's winning streak had generated an unprecedented level of interest in something that wasn't even a sport. Thromdurr, Morton, and Olivia took the stage—along with recent additions to the team George Stedman and Sharad Marwah, rounding out the five-person roster—and sat at one of two long tables. The Valley View team took the other.

The other Bríandalörians sat together in the audience to watch the match.

"How boring is this going to be?" whispered Devis.

"When I start to feel bored," said Vela, "I list my flaws and reflect upon how I may work to correct them."

"That might work for you, but I don't have any flaws," said Devis. "I'll do Sorrowshade's instead."

The thief turned to stare at the gloom elf and pulled out a small pad and pen. Sorrowshade glared at him.

"Glares too much," said Devis as he wrote. "Maybe sunglasses could fix that."

June took an empty seat beside the party.

"Hey, June, how's it going?" whispered Albiorix.

"Not bad," said June. "Shocked the mighty homecoming king would deign to show up for something as geeky as this. Where's your little girlfriend?"

"Nicole is *not* my girlfriend," said Albiorix. "She can't stand me."

"Not what my phone says. You just won her a prize at the carnival." June showed Albiorix a social media post of Nicole laughing and cuddling an overstuffed teddy bear that she claimed was from Armando Boort. "Very romantic," said June.

Albiorix sighed. "She's making all that stuff up."

"Why?" said June. "Homecoming is over and done."

"Don't ask me," said Albiorix.

"Nicole Davenport has always got an angle," said Sorrowshade. "You know that by now, right?"

Albiorix frowned. "Hey, come on. Private conversation over here."

"With elf hearing, there are no private conversations," said Sorrowshade.

Devis made another note. "Likes to eavesdrop. Earplugs, perhaps?"

Just then the moderator called the math league match to order. The teams were introduced, and the first problem was given: Solve $-4 < 4 + 3x \leq 7$.

After a few seconds of tense scribbling, Thromdurr chimed the bell and roared, "The answer is $-8/3 < x \leq 1$."

Correct!

The match was close. The Valley View team was whip smart and quick on the bell. But from the outset, it was clear that the Pine Hill team was the stronger competitor. They opened a lead early, and they maintained it the whole match. The final score was 224 to 181.

As Pine Hill was officially declared the winner, the auditorium erupted into applause. Everyone knew they would head to the state championship the following week. The Bríandalörians cheered too, and they rushed toward the stage to congratulate Thromdurr on the win.

In the jostling of the crowd, Albiorix felt a hand grip his shoulder. He turned to see Tristane Trouvère standing behind him.

"Enjoy it," said the bard.

"Thanks. Means a lot," said Albiorix. "Say, did you get a new haircut or did some of your extensions fall out? Either way, looking good, guy."

Tristane smiled. "It's all very amusing to pretend like we're students at this school. As an actor, I love the performance. 'Oh no, I missed the tardy bell!' 'Did you study for the big quiz?' But deep down, we're really Bríandalörians, aren't we? And in the end we will settle this thing the Bríandalörian way."

"What are you talking about?" said Albiorix.

Tristane nodded toward the stage. "The math league championship is being held at a hotel in a city twenty miles from here. It would certainly be a shame if something *bad* happened there."

The bard gave a little bow of his head and then melted back into the crowd.

Chapter
22

So, you're tired of the fantastically boring Realm of Suburbia and you wanna take your game on the road, huh, chief? Well, you better watch out. Little is known of the Big City that lies to the east, save that its narrow streets are said to be haunted by corporate lawyers and stand-up comedians and parking is a complete nightmare. Seriously, do not even get me started on parking. . . .

— *Excerpt from* The Advanced Hall Master's Guide

❧

THE COMMUTER TRAIN WOUND its way between trees and houses, and the heroes caught their first glimpse of the lands beyond Suburbia. Colossal towers of glass and steel sparkled in the distance.

"The Big City," said Vela. "It is *breathtaking.*"

"Yeah, it's pretty cool," said June. "I kind of miss it, to be honest."

"Did you inhabit one of those magnificent glass boxes?" asked Thromdurr.

"Nah," said June. "I lived in a third-floor walk-up above a Ukrainian restaurant. Almost as magnificent."

"And who rules this shiny city?" asked Sorrowshade.

"Well, there's a new mayor every few years," said June. "But everybody always hates his guts. It's kind of, like, a tradition."

"So if we want to fit in, we should insult him?" asked Sorrowshade.

"Sure," said June.

"Then the mayor is a mewling, gormless fool, barely fit for a ratcatcher, much less running an entire city!" hissed Sorrowshade.

"Perfect," said June. "You can also earn street cred by complaining about tourists. For example: get a load of this guy."

June nodded toward Albiorix, who fumbled with a large city map. He had it upside down.

"I'm just trying to figure out how we get to the math league championship once we're off the train. None of my Homerooms & Hall Passes books have any info about the Big City," said Albiorix. "Do you know where the Oracle Hotel and Conference Center is?"

"Yep. All we have to do is hop on the uptown select bus.

Pro tip: they never check tickets," said June. "Along the way, I can show you all the wonders of urban life—the cool graffiti, the mysterious street meat, the dudes in unauthorized mascot costumes you can pay to take your picture with."

"This place sounds amazing," said Devis.

"I agree," said Vela. "Cities where we come from are often filthy, loud, and disorganized. I am excited to see how clean and orderly this modern metropolis is."

"Um," said June.

"Sightseeing is all well and good, but we have to stay on our guard," said Albiorix. "The villains are definitely going to try something. Tristane Trouvère promised as much."

"Good thing we brought our . . . *camping gear*," said Sorrowshade, using the agreed-upon code word. She nudged the heavy duffel bag under her seat that contained the heroes' weapons and armor.

There was a moment of tense silence as the party contemplated another battle against their evil counterparts.

"Fine, I'll say it," said Devis. "There's no way we can win another fight with Tristane Trouvère and his crew. He's too smart. He's too ruthless. He's too tough."

"Sounds like you still worship the guy," said Sorrowshade.

"I don't," said Devis. "It's just . . . think about what happened last time." The thief's hand unconsciously moved to the spot where Tristane Trouvère's rapier had wounded him.

"Call that a practice round," said Sorrowshade. "They surprised us. Now that we know who we're facing, we'll destroy them." The gloom elf's face darkened. *"I'll destroy them."*

"I am afraid I must agree with Devis," said Thromdurr. "They trounced us handily. 'Tis folly to expect a different result this time around."

"For what it's worth, they probably won't have the wolf thingie with them," said June. "I've seen some crazy weird stuff in the city, but you can't have a pet like that running around off leash in broad daylight. You'd definitely get a ticket."

"Without Amarok, we outnumber them five to four," said Sorrowshade.

"Excuse me," said June. *"Six* to four."

"How could I forget?" said Sorrowshade. The gloom elf gave June a condescending pat on the head. "But it's really starting to annoy me that I am the only one approaching this situation with optimism."

"If their goal is to prevent us from completing the scenario objective, they will likely disrupt one of Thromdurr's math league matches," said Albiorix. "If he's occupied, the fight will be four to four."

"Hello? *Five* to four!" said June.

"Right, sorry," said Albiorix.

Vela sighed. "Comrades, I have given much consideration to the optimal combat strategy against our foes. Do we try to use flanking? Area of effect spells? Perhaps a phalanx formation? But in the end I am forced to conclude that Tristane Trouvère's party is an incredibly dangerous enemy. One strategy emerges."

Vela unzipped her backpack a few inches to reveal the glittering haft and blade of the Axe of Destiny inside.

"Whoa! Is that, like, a magic item?" asked June.

"Yes," said Vela. "It is a legendary weapon that is destined to turn the tide of a single unwinnable battle."

"Unwinnable?" said Sorrowshade. "You can't be serious. We can totally win this one. No need to break out the Axe of Destiny for these amateurs! Let's save it for a dragon or a god or when we finally fight the Tarasque. We're better than them. We just have to maintain our wits, and remember all our magic spells, and try to keep our feelings bottled up inside."

The gloom elf's companions didn't look so sure.

"If we use the axe in a battle that is not unwinnable," said Albiorix, "its magic will doom us to certain defeat."

Vela nodded. "The risk weighs heavily on me. But we have it if we need it. I only hope when the time comes, the Powers of Light show me the way."

The train pulled into the station, and the Bríandalörians were stunned to find themselves among the biggest crowds and tallest buildings they had ever seen. The sights and sounds of the Big City captivated their interest and threatened to overwhelm their senses. It was hard to stay wary for danger amid the honking cars and street performers and stinking bags of garbage piled high on the streets. Despite their superior Bríandalörian physiques, the party never seemed to be walking quite fast enough for the rest of the city. Locals huffed and sighed as they squeezed past them on the sidewalk.

The heroes made their way a few blocks east to the select bus. As it carried them uptown, June pointed out various sites of special significance. There was the place with the best one-dollar pizza slices. And there was the place with the worst one-dollar pizza slices. There was the greatest art museum in the entire country. And there was the playground where Michael Carnicelli had shoved her off a climbing structure in third grade and she broke her collarbone. Devis in particular was entranced by the seemingly endless opportunities the city presented for getting into trouble.

But the heroes had somewhere to be. They got off the bus in front of a tall, old hotel with THE ORACLE engraved in stone out front. All around, they saw others who were clearly math league competitors—often in dorky matching T-shirts—converging on this hotel for the state championship.

Morton, who had been driven in by his parents, was waiting on a bench out front when they arrived.

"Hey, guys, how was the ride in?" he asked.

"The train was full of wretched, malodorous tourists!" said Sorrowshade, loud enough for any nearby locals to hear.

"I wish I could have ridden with you," said Morton. "My parents won't let me ride public transit alone because they think I'm going to get mugged."

"Any sign of the villains?" asked Vela.

"Nope," said Morton. "Unless you're talking about the team from Borough Science. I hear they're the ones to beat this year."

"Then beat them we shall, friend Morton!" roared Thromdurr as he threw has arm around Morton. "Today is the day our names will be etched in history!"

"I love this guy," said Morton.

The group headed inside to a grand, if slightly shabby, lobby with a large banner that said Welcome Math League Competitors! Morton and Thromdurr rejoined Olivia and the rest of the Pine Hill Team. When Olivia saw the other adventurers, she scowled.

"What are *they* doing here?" asked Olivia.

"My friends are here to cheer us on to victory," said Thromdurr.

"They're not going to do anything crazy, are they?" asked Olivia. "They're not going to mess this up for me?"

Thromdurr hesitated. In all likelihood, the evil adventurers would mount some sort of assault on the competition, and his companions would respond in kind. Whatever happened, it would be crazy.

"Mmm," said the barbarian quietly.

The championship was a four-round single-elimination tournament among the best sixteen teams in the state. The Oracle's myriad conference rooms were packed with matches throughout the day. Pine Hill's first match was against Greenfield Academy in Conference Room D. June kept a lookout inside the room while the other Bríandalörians took strategic positions outside, by the exits. It was an ugly match. Neither team acquitted itself particularly well. But Pine Hill ground out a win. The final score was 181 to 168.

"No ambush," said Devis. "The suspense is killing me."

"Strategically, it makes sense," said Vela. "If Pine Hill loses and gets eliminated, we fail to complete this *Freshman Year of Futility* objective anyway. No need for Tristane Trouvère's party to risk a public attack."

"See?" said Sorrowshade. "They're scared."

"We must remain vigilant," said Vela. "But the assault will likely come during the final match. And probably only once our team seems likely to win."

As predicted, Pine Hill's quarterfinal match—against

East Bridge Charter School—passed uneventfully. Pine Hill won in a blowout, 221 to 171.

Their opponent in the semifinals would be Walter Morrison High. The audience was bigger now, as competitors from eliminated teams came to see the upstarts from Hibbettsfield compete. Pine Hill did not disappoint. They won the match 211 to 199. The team had made it to the finals.

After the match, June and the Bríandalörians congratulated Thromdurr and Morton.

"Nice work, big guy," asked Devis. "How did you know the answer to that last one?"

"I merely took the derivative of f(x) = 6 x 3 − 9x + 4!" said Thromdurr.

"Yeah, I was just being polite," said Devis. "Last time I ever do that."

"You're doing great, Morton," said June.

"Thanks," said Morton. "I feel like we're totally in the zone. We're, like, becoming this crazy math league robot dinosaur that's made up of smaller robots that aren't dinosaurs but they all fit together! You know what I mean?"

"Not really," said June as she gave Morton a big hug.

Albiorix winced. But at the end of the day, he had to admit he didn't actually dislike Morton. And if this was what June wanted, that was her choice. Even though it hurt, he wished her the best.

"Nice work," said the wizard as he shook Morton's hand.

Morton smiled. "Thanks, dude."

Vela approached Olivia. "I just want to offer my congratulations and wish you good fortune on your final match."

"Is this some kind of olive branch, Valerie?" said Olivia. "Well, I don't accept. I might be semi-okay with Doug, for now. But you? Oh, I'll never forgive you."

Vela nodded. "I understand."

The final match would play out between Pine Hill High School and Borough Science in the hotel's biggest event space, Conference Room L.

And so the heroes prepared themselves. They took strategic positions beside the conference room's two exits, which both opened onto the third-floor hallway. Vela made sure the Axe of Destiny was close at hand. Sorrowshade coated a number of arrows with different vile poisons. Albiorix pored over his spellbook, silently mouthing incantations. Devis readied his daggers and then disappeared behind a ficus plant for a surprise attack.

Inside Conference Room L, the atmosphere was tense. Pine Hill was clearly the underdog. Everyone knew the school hadn't even had a math league team until this year. Now they were in the finals. Meanwhile, Borough Science had won the state championship for the last seven years in a row. The general consensus was that they would do so again this time (though many secretly yearned to see the elite school taken down a peg or two).

The room was crowded with parents and members of other teams—sad that they had lost, but excited to see two titans of math league clash. Ron Schiller sat near the front. June scanned the crowd for any sign of Tristane Trouvère, Calyxia, Skegg the Surly, or Azheena. She saw no villains.

Pine Hill and Borough Science were welcomed to great applause. The teams took their tables. The moderator reminded them what an achievement it was to even get to the finals and then asked them the first question: "What is the surface area of a triangular prism with a height of five centimeters, whose base is an equilateral triangle with sides measuring two centimeters each?"

Morton rang in for Pine Hill and gave the answer: 31.723 cm^2. Incorrect. Borough Science answered 33.464 cm^2 to take an early lead. But two questions later, Pine Hill was back on top. It was an incredibly exciting match (or at least as exciting as watching two groups of kids trying to solve math problems could be). Pine Hill and Borough Science went back and forth like this, until somewhere in the third round Pine Hill opened a small lead and held on to it.

And sure enough, it was then that a loud pop occurred in the hall outside Conference Room L. The security camera overhead burst in a shower of sparks. Albiorix had no doubt it was magic.

"And so they arrive," said Vela.

A pinprick of shimmering blue light appeared in the air before the party. Vela considered pulling the Axe of Destiny out of her pack. Instead, she said a silent prayer to the Powers of Light and drew her sword. The blue light grew and split the space until it was a glowing portal. Four figures stepped through. Albiorix felt his heart racing in his chest.

Azheena looked around. "Well, they actually showed up, instead of chickening out. Tristane, I owe you a candy bar."

"We are not cowards," said Vela.

Tristane Trouvère shrugged. "That's what I told Azheena. Not cowards. Just fools."

Albiorix felt his fear give way to anger. "For fools, we've been doing pretty well lately."

"Fools are notoriously lucky," said Tristane Trouvère. "Just ask your friend Devis."

"Hi," said Devis, still unseen behind the ficus plant.

"But I'm afraid your luck has run out," said Tristane Trouvère.

Skegg the Surly grinned as he ran his thumb along the blade of his axe. "Been waiting for a rematch since our little dustup in the music club."

"Great day for you, then," said Sorrowshade.

And with that, the gloom elf let fly. Her aim was true. The black shaft whistled straight at the dwarf's head. But a few feet from him, it bounced off . . . nothing. The arrow clattered away harmlessly.

Calyxia sighed. "This is taking too long." She thumbed through her spellbook. "I shall vaporize them now."

"Wait!" Skegg turned to Tristane Trouvère in appeal. "You promised I could have some fun first. Axe fun."

"It isn't always about *fun*, Skegg," said Tristane Trouvère. "Sometimes it's about business. Calyxia, permission to do your thing."

The dwarf huffed.

The sorceress ignored him. "Very well. A bit pedestrian, but a plasma cloud seems optimal in this situation. *Ied ka'aetk na'vilnsa'h ha'oi zaeny e vrelde ra'oiv.*"

A cloud of molten plasma erupted from Calyxia's fingertips toward the heroes. Vela, Sorrowshade, and Albiorix all dove to avoid the blast. But the waves of superheated energy crashed against the same invisible barrier that had stopped Sorrowshade's arrow. The burning plasma cloud didn't reach them.

After a moment, the sorceress dropped the spell and the plasma cloud dissipated. She looked annoyed. "Well, well, well. It appears the dropout wizard has put up some sort of magical barrier between our two parties. Finally showing a bit of effort, are we?"

Albiorix said nothing.

"At least things have finally gotten mildly interesting,"

said Calyxia. "Allow me to dispel this unseen wall. *Uky a'geh phaeti ta'z ka'aetk na'vaelvir ha'ois lvirr.*" A thick greenish cloud of antimagic mist rolled out from the sorceress toward the barrier. She smiled. "There, the magical wall is now gone. Skegg, you may engage in your, ahem, axe fun for"— Calyxia checked her watch—"three minutes. After that I finish them off with a lightning orb."

The dwarf raised his axe and grinned. "Well, all right then!"

Vela braced herself as Skegg charged right at her. But somewhere in between, he smacked headfirst into the invisible barrier and fell down. From behind his plant, Devis couldn't help but laugh. A bolt from Azheena's crossbow whistled in the thief's direction but clattered off the barrier as well.

"I don't like this," said Azheena. "I told you we should have brought Amarok."

Tristane turned a withering glare on the ranger. "And what good would a warg do against an invisible wall, you idiot?"

The dwarf leaped to his feet, cursing at Calyxia. "You said the barrier was gone, you daft witch!"

"Watch your tone with me," said Calyxia.

"Hmm. It sounds like your team has a few interpersonal issues to work out," said Vela. "I recommend open, honest communication. After all, a leader's role is not merely to command but to listen."

"Shut up," snapped Tristane. The bard jabbed his rapier toward the barrier, nearly bending it double.

"Wow, he's so mad his hair extensions are going to fall out," said Sorrowshade.

At this, all the good guys began to laugh. Even Vela.

"Destroy them!" said Tristane.

"Ya'oi'si ka'aetk na' moist na' e rsaelv etv vaei ha'oi phsiegl," said Calyxia. She summoned a massive, crackling ball of lightning and hurled it at the heroes, but again, it dissipated harmlessly against the invisible barrier.

As the epic battle between good and evil outside failed to materialize, inside Conference Room L the competition was heating up. Borough Science had rallied. They'd gotten $13/9$, $c = -3$, and ≥ 11 all correct. Three right answers in a row had put them ahead of Pine Hill by two points.

The tension was nearly as thick as an invisible force field. It was the final question of the match. The math league state championship all came down to this.

Thromdurr looked at his companions. Olivia Gorman to his left. Morton Blanc to his right. Sharad Marwah and George Stedman rounding out the team. The barbarian gave them a nod of support. Whatever happened, they had given it their best. They had competed with skill and honor. They had done the sacred Spirit of Mathematics proud.

"Final question," said the moderator. "The sum of three numbers is twenty-eight. The largest minus the smallest is nine. The second largest minus the smallest is four. What are the three numbers?"

Both teams began to scribble furiously on their scrap paper. Thromdurr quickly worked it out. If x was the largest number, y was the second largest, and z was the smallest, then $x + y + z = 28$. He knew that $x - z = 9$ and $y - z = 4$, which meant that $x = 9 + z$ and—

A bell rang. It had only been a matter of seconds, but someone had beaten the barbarian to the punch. It wasn't the team from Borough Science, though. It was Olivia.

"Pine Hill," said the moderator.

"The answer," said Olivia, "is thirteen, eleven, and four."

The moderator paused for a moment as he checked the answer sheet. A smile slowly spread across his face.

"Correct," said the moderator.

The audience in Conference Room L erupted in applause. A chant began to break out among the crowd.

"Pine Hill . . . Pine Hill . . . Pine Hill . . ."

And so, as every empire must one day topple, Borough Science's reign was over. There was a new math league state champion.

Chapter
23

The Freshman Year of Futility is not meant to be challenging. It's meant to be insanely, arbitrarily, borderline unethically difficult! If you somehow allow your players to complete three objectives and win the scenario, you probably messed up, and you might want to reconsider your future as an Advanced Homerooms & Hall Passes Hall Master. Maybe a game like tic-tac-toe is more your speed?

—*Excerpt from* The Freshman Year of Futility

OUTSIDE CONFERENCE ROOM L, the chant echoed into the hall: "Pine Hill . . . Pine Hill . . . Pine Hill . . ."

The heroes and villains stood at the ready, geared up for a fight but still separated by an impenetrable, unseen barrier.

Azheena cocked her head to listen. "What just happened?"

Sorrowshade smirked. "They're probably chanting that because Pine Hill lost."

Azheena answered by firing another crossbow bolt, which ricocheted off the magical force field and knocked an artful black-and-white photo of the Big City's most famous bridge right off the wall.

"Nice comeback," said Sorrowshade.

"If your goal was to disrupt the match and prevent us from completing this objective," said Vela, "then it appears you have failed."

"She's right," said Calyxia.

Skegg shook his head and spat onto the floor. "Should've whacked 'em in the street earlier. Instead we acted like a pack of spineless weaklings."

"Are you questioning my leadership, Skegg?" asked Tristane Trouvère.

The dwarf stared at the bard for a long moment. "No, sir."

"I am," said Calyxia. "Your plan was a complete strategic failure."

"Was it? I thought you were the greatest spell caster since the Archmage Maywhosit or whoever," said Tristane. "Why couldn't you get rid of a simple magical wall? Perhaps you overstated your abilities."

"Please note," said Calyxia, "there is no impenetrable mystical barrier separating you and me."

The sorceress's eyes began to crackle with purple energy.

"Easy, easy," said Azheena as she put a hand on Calyxia's arm. "Not in front of the good guys."

"Nah, keep going," said Sorrowshade. "I could watch this all day."

"Doesn't matter," said Tristane Trouvère. "They'll never complete the final objective. Move out."

The bard glared at Calyxia. She hesitated for a moment.

"Lin di qoiln a'vit oiv e vaedlaea'ter va'a's saekyn ta'z ha'oi," incanted the sorceress.

With a flash, a new dimensional door opened, and the four villains vanished through it, leaving the heroes alone in the hallway.

"Hang on," said Devis. "Did we just . . . win?"

"I think—I think perhaps we did," said Vela. "Sort of."

"Nice work, Magic Man!" cried Devis.

"Hmm," said Albiorix.

The heroes entered Conference Room L to find the mood triumphant. Morton Blanc beamed. George Stedman and Sharad Marwah high-fived each other repeatedly. Even Olivia sported a rare ear-to-ear grin. Out in the audience, the team's coach, Mr. Marsella, was completely awake and competely thrilled. The other Pine Hill alternates cheered loudly beside him. June was out of her seat and jumping up and down in time to the Pine Hill chant. Ron Schiller looked so proud of his son he could burst.

But not all were happy with the outcome of the match. The team from Borough Science was crestfallen at their defeat, of course. But there was one other whose misery was even greater.

Thromdurr the barbarian scribbled over and over on his scrap paper. His face was dour. No matter how many times he worked it out, it ended up the same. With math, regardless of how many times you solved a problem, you would arrive at the same conclusion. It was this unbending consistency that the barbarian so admired.

"Excuse me," said Thromdurr into the microphone. His voice was barely audibly over the crowd. "EXCUSE ME!"

A hush fell over Conference Room L.

"Yes?" said the moderator.

"Our team's answer was not correct," said Thromdurr.

"What are you doing?" said Olivia.

"You made a mistake," said Thromdurr. "The correct solution is fourteen, nine, and five."

"Doug!" cried Olivia.

"*What is he thinking?*" hissed Sorrowshade to her companions.

The moderator shook his head. "I'm sorry, my sheet says the answer to the final question is thirteen, eleven, and four."

"Well, then your sheet is wrong," said Thromdurr.

"Let me just make sure I have this straight," asked the moderator. "You're challenging your own team's answer?"

"I—I suppose I am," said Thromdurr.

A gasp ran through the crowd.

The moderator shrugged. "Judges?"

The panel of three judges sitting at a small table behind the moderator quietly conferred for a few minutes. Afterward, one of them stood.

"The correct solution is thirteen, eleven, and four," she said.

"It is not!" said Thromdurr. "I can show you." The barbarian waved his crumpled scrap paper.

Tears streamed down Olivia's face now. "I cannot believe you're doing this to me. We won the state championship. We actually won. And now you're trying to take it from me. I knew you would try something like this. *I knew it.*"

"I swore an oath to you, Olivia," said Thromdurr, "that I would let no dishonor come to the sacred Spirit of Mathematics."

"Come on, Doug," said Morton. "Let it go. So there was a mistake—"

"There was no mistake!" cried Olivia.

"Do we truly want to win this way?" asked Thromdurr.

His other teammates looked back at him, confused and hurt.

Olivia's face had hardened. She wiped her eyes. "You're off the team, Doug. Effective immediately."

Thromdurr nodded. "Very well."

The barbarian carefully collected his scrap paper and walked silently down the center aisle toward the conference room exit.

"Uh, Doug, do you want me to . . . ," said Ron Schiller. "I guess—I guess I'll just see you at home?"

Thromdurr nodded as he strode out the door.

"Snatching defeat from the jaws of victory? You've got to be kidding me," said Devis as June and the other Bríandalörians followed him out.

The train ride back to Hibbettsfield was a far more somber one. The heroes watched in silence as town after town flew by, each too quickly to form anything but a vague impression.

"Well, you technically were on a championship team," said Devis. "For like, two minutes."

Thromdurr said nothing.

"Does it count?" asked Devis. "Albiorix, can we get a ruling?"

The wizard shrugged. "I don't know. I'm not the Hall Master of this place. Maybe it counts?"

"The correct answer is fourteen, nine, and five," said Thromdurr.

"Yeah, I heard that, somewhere," said Sorrowshade. "Certainly worth dooming us to an eternity exiled in another world."

"You did an honorable thing, Thromdurr," said Vela. "No need to feel ashamed."

"Regardless, I say it counted," said Devis. "They didn't accept your challenge. Pine Hill won. You were on the team when that happened. Plus we faced off against Tristane Trouvère and his crew, and we didn't die."

"Wait, I missed a big hero fight right outside while the match was going on?" said June.

"Hardly," said Sorrowshade.

"We didn't have to resort to violence," said Devis, "because Magic Man finally cast a spell that was actually useful. Summon invisi-wall or something like that!"

Albiorix shook his head. "I didn't cast any spell."

"What?" said Vela.

"It wasn't me," said Albiorix.

"Then who created the mystical barrier separating our two parties?" asked Vela.

"I don't know for sure," said Albiorix, "but I have a pretty good guess."

From the look on his face, the others understood. There was only one other—besides Albiorix and Calyxia—who was capable of such magic: the warlock Zazirak. At that moment, the commuter train passed into a tunnel shrouding their view the world outside in darkness.

"Regardless, we nailed the three objectives," said Devis. "Homecoming king, state championship team, and when the Albiorix's perfect ABSEE grade comes back Monday, we can finally say goodbye to this dump! No offense to you, June, but I'd really like to get back to the ogres and pit traps and treasure and such."

"That means we have one day to find the evil warlock and his spellbook," said Vela.

"Not sure where Zazirak is," said Sorrowshade. "But he is keeping the Malonomicon at school."

And so the next day—still the weekend, and thus a time of rest for most of Suburbia—the party returned to Pine Hill High School. Devis jimmied the lock and the party split up to scour every inch of the building. Albiorix searched the bathrooms. June searched the school office. Vela searched the gym. Thromdurr and Devis searched the classrooms.

But it was Sorrowshade who finally found the spellbook. Stuffed in an air duct inside room 117, there was an ancient tome, bound in cracked red leather. The stains on the cover resembled a sea of screaming souls.

The party had finally located the Malonomicon.

Chapter 24

Table 181w: Random Refrigerator Contents
To determine the contents of a refrigerator, roll five times
on the following table.
***1 to 3**: milk*
***4 to 5**: 1 to 4 yellow onions*
***6 to 9**: cheese (roll once on Table 362e: Random Cheese*
Varieties to determine what type)
***10**: two-day-old Chinese takeout*
***11 to 12**: baking chocolate (partially eaten)*
***13**: 1 to 6 ketchup packets*
    —Excerpt from The Advanced Hall Master's Guide

⁓

*T*HE MYSTERY OF WHY Albiorix's find lost object spell had failed was now clear. Inscribed in chalk on the cover of the Malonomicon in was a glyph of obfuscation, a ward against such magic. The consensus was that Vela was by far the least likely to be corrupted by its malign influence, so the paladin pocketed the grimoire.

After making off with the spellbook, the party expected a final, epic showdown with the warlock Zazirak. They stayed together well into the night—camped out in front of June's TV, gobbling cookies yet prepared to defend against such a confrontation.

But wherever Zazirak was and whatever he was doing, he wasn't battling adventurers. The evening passed without incident, and they all agreed that the whole thing felt a bit anticlimactic. Around ten fifteen, the group collectively decided it was time to go home.

"So what happens if you guys win the scenario but leave an evil spirit guy fluttering around here?" asked June as the others filed out her front door.

Vela held up the Malonomicon. "Without this spellbook, Zazirak's powers will be severely limited. He will not be capable of any world-ending magic, at least."

"And with all the other problems your world has," said Sorrowshade, "one angry ghost isn't going to make much of a difference."

"Cool?" said June.

"I agree the outcome is less than ideal," said Vela. "But we did save this world again. To put it in high school terms, I give our resolution of this quest a B-plus."

Devis considered this. "I get an A, you guys get Cs. Yep, average it out and that sounds about right to me. Later, June."

"Come, Albiorix, let us return to the House of Schiller," said Thromdurr. "The downstairs freezer is filled with ice cream bars ripe for the plucking!"

"I'll be there in a sec," said Albiorix.

The barbarian nodded and stepped out onto the porch, leaving Albiorix alone with June.

"Hey," said Albiorix. "So tomorrow we get our ABSEE scores back and, uh, if I'm right about how well I did, I guess . . . I guess that will be that."

"Yep," said June. "You guys win your game, the curse is over, and all the Advanced Homerooms & Hall Passes players go home. It will just be us lowly NPCs left around here."

"Well, hey," said Albiorix, "maybe your world will get threatened by the forces of darkness a third time, and we'll have to return!"

June cocked her head.

"Sorry," said Albiorix. "I really meant that as a joke. Anyway, I just wanted to say all the best to you and, uh, Morton."

"Huh?" said June.

"I mean, aren't you guys like . . . you know?"

"He's my friend, Albiorix," said June. "What, are you jealous?"

"Nah," said Albiorix. "Kind of. Yeah. Definitely." The wizard shrugged.

"Please," said June, "you're so cool now, you don't even need to hang out with me anymore."

"Of course I do!" said Albiorix. "Now that everyone loves me, I have no idea who actually likes me. When I was a loser, things were so much clearer."

June smiled. "You were never a loser, Albiorix."

She squeezed the wizard's hand, and he stepped out into the night.

The next day, the heroes arrived at school still half expecting to face off against Zazirak. The evil warlock didn't show.

During the morning bulletin, the Pine Hill math league team was congratulated on their incredible victory over Borough Science with mild, compulsory applause from the entire student body. Out of the corner of his eye, Albiorix saw Thromdurr quietly shake his head, still unable to accept the outcome of the championship match. On the other side of the room, Olivia Gorman sat stone-faced, unable to enjoy her victory either.

"So," said Ms. Lane, "it's the moment you've all been waiting for and/or dreading."

"Are you going to sing, Ms. Lane?" asked Devis.

"Ha ha, Stinky," said Ms. Lane. "Your ABSEE results are in."

She passed back everyone's scorecard. One by one, Albiorix watched Vela, Thromdurr, Sorrowshade, and Devis register disappointment on their faces. The rest of the party turned to him. Albiorix took a deep breath and looked at his results. He felt his heart sink. Armando Boort had gotten 994 out of 1000. He'd missed three questions in the final section. The wizard buried his face in his hands and slowly lowered his head onto his desk.

The rest of the morning passed in a blur, as Albiorix mentally ran and reran through all the questions he remembered from the test, trying to figure out how he could have missed one, let alone three. He had been so confident. But he'd let the party's last, best hope for making it home to Bríandalör slip through his fingers.

"Wait. Everything's going to be okay," said Albiorix, snapping out of his fugue in the middle of lunch. "We don't have to worry!"

"He is right," said Vela. "We must accept our fate. We can lead lives of quiet dignity as social media managers in this world."

"No, no, no," said Albiorix. "I'm still the homecoming king. I'm still popular. People still love Armando Boort!" He turned to Marc Mansour, who was sitting at a nearby table. "You still love Armando Boort, right?"

"Uh, sure," said Marc. "I guess."

Albiorix turned back to his companions. "See? I'm beloved."

His companions looked confused.

"Albiorix is losing it," said Devis. "Thromdurr, you should probably restrain him."

"So here's what we do," said Albiorix. "We use my awesome reputation to do the party thing again. Get a hundred guests to show up."

"Because that worked out so well last time," said Sorrowshade.

"We have the Malonomicon. There won't be another soup creature attack," said Albiorix. "That's the third objective! A party! If I can get Nicole Davenport to help promote it—"

"Didn't you guys already press your luck with her?" asked June.

"Maybe, but this is the only thing I can think of," said Albiorix. "It could work. It has to work."

Albiorix checked his hair (still pretty cool), brushed some (uncool) crumbs off his (cool) shirt, and walked (in what he thought was a cool way) over to Nicole's table. Unlike before, Nicole now sat amid several popular girls—many of them upperclassmen—confidently holding court, just as she had in middle school. Nicole had expertly leveraged her homecoming queen title to rapidly boost her social status.

"Hi, Nicole, my, ahem, girlfriend," said Albiorix.

"What's up, Armando?" said Nicole.

"Well, I was thinking we could, like, throw a cool party where a minimum of a hundred people show up?"

"Mmm, that's cute and oddly specific," said Nicole. "But I have something a little different in mind. In fact, I've been meaning to talk to you."

"You have?" said Albiorix.

Nicole leaped to her feet. "I still care about you, Armando," she yelled, "but what you did is unforgivable!"

Her voice was loud enough that a hush fell over the cafeteria.

"Uh," said Albiorix.

"I cannot believe you started the unfair, and untrue, rumor that Travis Tyson has hair extensions!" cried Nicole.

The crowd gasped.

"Wait," said Albiorix, "that's not— I didn't—"

"You did everything in your power to destroy that poor boy's reputation so you could become homecoming king instead of him," said Nicole. "It's time you come clean!"

Albiorix swallowed. "Okay, that is technically true, but—"

"I thought you were an honest person, Armando," said Nicole, who was now somehow actually crying. "But now I know you're not. And I'm not sure how I can ever trust you again."

With that, Nicole dramatically turned away and stormed out of the cafeteria.

"Wait, Nicole!" cried Tristane Trouvère from a few tables down. "Standing up for me was so brave of you."

The bard flashed Albiorix an almost imperceptible grin before running after her. It was a masterful performance that both of them had clearly rehearsed. And it left Albiorix standing alone in the middle of the cafeteria. The eyes of the whole school were on him.

"Those two cooked this whole thing up together," said Albiorix. "Nicole and I had an alliance, but now she made a new alliance with him. It's a classic Davenport double-cross."

"An alliance?" said Bree Mitchell. "That's how you talk about your girlfriend?"

"So cold," said Marc Mansour.

"What? No, she doesn't like me either!" cried Albiorix.

"Because you lied," said Monica Hilaire.

"Look, the bottom line is I still have a cool haircut and my clothes are super expensive," said Albiorix. "So you all have to come to this party I'm throwing this week. Okay?"

This prompted a chorus of of boos and hisses from the student body.

"So gross," said Monica.

And so the brief reign of Armando Boort as the most popular kid at Pine Hill High School came to its inevitable end.

The rest of the school day was a grim grind as the reality of the situation began to sink in. The heroes had recovered the Malonomicon, but they had no possible path toward achieving the third and final objective of *The Freshman Year of Futility*. Indeed, as the curse said, Advanced Homerooms & Hall Passes would truly be their doom. A part of Albiorix did love it here in the Realm of Suburbia, but then again, maybe he just cared about June. And if she didn't feel the same way . . .

The final bell rang, and instead of heading directly home with Thromdurr to collapse onto the Schillers' famous recliner to drown his sorrows in television and chili, Albiorix decided to follow up on a hunch that had been nagging him all day. He popped into Ms. Lane's room.

"Ah, hello again, Armando," said Ms. Lane as she packed up her oversized canvas teacher bag to go home. "Congratulations again on your ABSEE score. Best in the whole class. Er, probably shouldn't have told you that."

"Thanks," said Albiorix. "Unfortunately, it wasn't good enough."

"Oh, don't be so hard on yourself," said Ms. Lane. "Now, your friend Stinky, on the other hand, could stand to be much, much harder on himself. Hmm. Probably shouldn't have told you that, either."

"Is there some way for me to check which questions I

missed?" said Albiorix.

Ms. Lane glanced at her watch. "Well, I am trying to make it to a very full spin class before it fills up. Can this wait till tomorrow?"

Albiorix shook his head. Somehow Ms. Lane seemed to grasp the gravity of the situation. She nodded.

"Okay," said Ms. Lane. "One sec." She sat down at her school computer and used her ID to log onto the ABSEE website's educator portal. She scanned through her class's submitted tests until she found "Boort, Armando." She clicked on his name.

"Okay . . . seems you missed the last three questions in the language arts section," said Ms. Lane.

"The last three?" said Albiorix. What were the odds of that?

"Yeah," said Ms. Lane. "Did you run out of time? Looks like you left them blank."

Albiorix blinked. "I didn't leave them blank."

Ms. Lane shrugged. She turned the monitor toward Albiorix. It showed a scan of his section-one answer sheet. Sure enough, the tiny ovals of the last three questions were empty.

Ms. Lane shrugged. "I mean, it sure looks like you did."

"My test was sabotaged!" cried Albiorix.

Ms. Lane cocked her head. "It's only three questions in

one section, Armando. Between you and me, as long as you pass the ABSEE, your score doesn't *really* matter. You should relax. Go outside. Have an ice cream cone. Pet a dog."

But Albiorix was already out the door. And he wasn't on his way to pet a dog. His test had been tampered with, and there was only one person who could've done it.

Half an hour later the wizard was pounding on the front door of Castle Westray.

"Wow—are you mad at my door or something?" said June. "What's up?"

"Hi," said Albiorix. "Sorry to bother you, but is he here?"

June lowered her voice. "Who, Zazirak?"

"Morton Blanc," said Albiorix.

June nodded. "Oh, yeah, Morton's here. We're catching up on all the episodes of *Crescent City Mob* that I DVRed. All the recent adventuring has cut into my TV time."

"I need to talk to him," said Albiorix.

June led Albiorix back to the TV room, where Morton was sipping a cup of tea. The TV was paused on an image of a man in a fedora blazing away with a tommy gun.

"Armando!" said Morton. "How's it going, man? I don't know if you're all caught up with *CCM*, but we're pretty sure Tony the Beignet is about to get whacked!"

Albiorix didn't respond. Instead he turned to June and sighed. "June, I apologize for what's about to happen."

"Wow. Very calming way to start a conversation," said June. "Not ominous at all."

Albiorix turned back to Morton. "You sabotaged my ABSEE test."

Morton nearly spat out his tea. "What?"

"Admit it," said Albiorix.

June rolled her eyes. "Dude, I *know* you're jealous. But that doesn't give you the right to act like a jerk. Morton, I'm so sorry."

Albiorix ignored her. "Why'd you do it, Morton?"

"I don't know what you're talking about," said Morton.

"We passed our tests forward," said Albiorix. "You were the only person ahead of me. While I wasn't looking, you must've quickly erased some of my answers."

"You sound crazy, man," said Morton. "We're all friends here. I think you just need to try to stay calm."

Albiorix put himself between Morton and June. "Are you possessed by the evil spirit of an undead warlock?

"What? No!" cried Morton. "Trust me, I'm not possessed by Zazirak. I'm not possessed by anyone. I'm me! I'm Morton Blanc. "

Albiorix crossed his arms. "I never said his name was Zazirak."

"June . . . June must have mentioned it," said Morton. "Right, June?"

"No," said June. "I didn't."

Panic flashed in Morton's eyes. Albiorix quickly put himself in front of June and began casting the frostbolt spell. *"E dekaerer ma'rn—"*

Morton threw his hands up in terror. "Stop, stop! Okay, I'm *not* me!"

Albiorix's incantation trailed off.

"You're not?" said June.

Morton shook his head. "No. My real name is Brother Auros. I'm a junior acolyte of the Church of Light in Wharf-harbor."

"What is any of that?" said June.

"He's from Bríandalör too," said Albiorix.

Morton sighed. "I'm the fifth member of Tristane Trouvère's adventuring party."

Chapter

25

At a certain point, your players will feel like they've seen it all. Math tests are no longer harrowing. School dances are no longer interesting. That's exactly when you need to hit them with something that totally blows their minds. Consider having a previously innocuous NPC suddenly turn out to be a secret bad guy. It's a classic twist that can add drama to any campaign! But, like anything else, if overused it can become cliché.

—*Excerpt from* The Advanced Hall Master's Guide

❧

"ALBIORIX, CAN YOU PLEASE start casting that spell again?" said June. "I want you to fry this fraud."

"What?" said Brother Auros. "No!'

Alborix's eyes crackled with arcane power. "Tell me why I shouldn't, Brother Auros. And make it convincing."

"Because—well, because for one thing, I'm actually a

good guy," said Brother Auros.

"Uh-huh," said June. "Because good guys are *known* for leading double lives and lying to everyone around them."

"Okay, fair point. But didn't he do that too, at first?" Brother Auros pointed at Albiorix.

"Hey, this isn't about me," said Albiorix. "If you're such a good guy, then why are you part of an evil adventuring party?"

"I don't know," said Brother Auros. "It sounds dumb, but I just sort of fell in with the wrong crowd. Kind of like how the thief in your party used to run with Tristane."

"Devis probably shouldn't be your go-to example for moral clarity," said Albiorix.

"I cannot believe this," said June. "Albiorix, if you're not going to nuke him with some sort of a wizard-y fireball, I'm going to have to strangle him with my bare hands."

June lunged toward Brother Auros, but Albiorix stopped her.

"Wait," said the wizard. "I can't believe I'm saying this, but . . . maybe we should hear him out?"

"Huh?" cried June. "You've despised Morton Blanc since the moment I introduced you to him!"

"You have?" said Brother Auros, who seemed a little hurt.

Albiorix nodded. "Technically, *before* I ever met you.

Ever since I saw your text messages on June's old phone."

Now June glared at Albiorix. *"You read my texts?"*

"Uh. Whoops," said Albiorix. "Yeah. I thought you were in grave danger and . . . Doesn't matter. Sorry. I shouldn't have done that."

"Now I'm going to have to kill both of you," said June. "But Morton dies first."

"Look, all I'm saying is that he's maybe, kind of, a little bit right," said Albiorix. "You gave me the benefit of the doubt. I'm glad you did. Shouldn't we hear him out and then decide what to do?"

June glared at Brother Auros.

"I'm sorry, June," said Brother Auros. "I was going to tell you."

June shook her head. "Why do all my friends turn out to secretly be adventurers from a realm of magic and wonder? And don't say it's beacause I'm an NPC in somebody's stupid role-playing game!"

If anyone was thinking it, no one said it.

". . . Okay," said Albiorix, "you expect us to believe you're the one good guy in a party of cheats and scoundrels?"

"They're awful," said Brother Auros. "Just horrible people. Skegg the Surly eats his own scabs. He just eats them! Nobody knows how bad they are better than I do."

"But you *did* steal June's phone," said Albiorix.

Brother Auros winced. "I mean, after she spilled green smoothie on it, it didn't work. And she tossed it in a drawer and got a new one and I figured she wouldn't miss it. But . . . stealing is stealing. I knew it was wrong. They were pressuring me to come up with merchandise we could sell back in Bríandalör. I had to take something."

June crossed her arms. "You've also been spying on our party the whole time."

"Yes," said Brother Auros. "But I didn't tell them everything. I've barely been giving them anything lately. I didn't tell them you stole the cap of invisibility!"

"That's all well and good, but by sabotaging my ABSEE test, you did something much worse," said Albiorix. "Now we're stuck here in the Realm of Suburbia for the foreseeable future."

"Sorry," said Brother Auros. "But I did help math league win the state championship. So it's a wash, right? I was supposed to throw the match, but I couldn't do it. Man, Tristane was so mad about that, he told Calyxia to turn me into a cactus. I barely talked her out of it."

"Well, thanks for that," said Albiorix. "Were you the one who cast the magical force field at the hotel that day?"

"No, we all thought it was you," said Brother Auros. "I was never a very good acolyte. But my divine magic is especially weak here. I guess wherever we are, it's pretty far from

326

the Powers of Light. A few minor healing spells are all I've got. Like, if you've got foot fungus, I could probably cure that."

"I don't have foot fungus," said Albiorix.

"Me neither," said June. "So you've turned a corner, huh, *Brother Auros*? Well, why did you go along with all of it, if you knew it was wrong?

Brother Auros sighed. "I'm afraid of them. They don't like me anyway. Never did. They just used me. Because I'm weak."

"Used you for what?" asked Albiorix.

"Tristane Trouvère cooked up this scam after hearing about what happened to you guys last time," said Brother Auros. "But he didn't know anything about Homerooms & Hall Passes. He needed someone to run the game for his group so they could use the curse to get here."

"And you were their Hall Master," said Albiorix.

"Yep," said Brother Auros. "I just really wanted a group to play Advanced Homerooms & Hall Passes *with* because I'd heard great things about the new game mechanics and character class options."

"A lot of the design is really well thought out," said Albiorix. "It was a smart choice for them to add specific passive skill checks, because sometimes you don't want players to—"

"Stop nerding!" cried June.

"Sorry," said Albiorix and Brother Auros in unison.

"So what happens now?" said June. "We just take this explanation at face value?"

"I have to say, my gut says there's a ninety-five percent chance he's actually telling the truth," said Albiorix.

"It's a hundred. No, two hundred," said Brother Auros. "I'm totally done with them. You guys are the kind of adventuring party I should've been with all along. I've just never been that great at making friends, you know? And hey, maybe I could be useful to you now."

"How so?" said Albiorix.

"Well, Tristane and the others don't know I'm on your side now," said Brother Auros. "I could be, like, a double agent."

Albiorix considered this. He looked at June. She was still angry, but her expression had softened just a bit.

"I've still got one more question," said June. "Why Morton Blanc?"

"I'm a pretty good Hall Master," said Brother Auros, "but I'm no good at making up names on the fly."

"Me neither!" said Albiorix.

"Of course, I didn't have a character in the game I was running," said Brother Auros, "so when I showed up here, nobody knew who I was. I practically didn't exist. I've been living in that storage locker you guys found. You have no idea."

"I kind of do," said Albiorix.

"Well, anyway, I was in the grocery store the first time somebody in this world asked me my name, and I panicked. I looked around, and all I could see was this blue salt container on the shelf across the aisle. So I blurted out the name Morton."

"And the last name?" asked Albiorix.

"I had absolutely nothing," said Brother Auros. "Drew a total blank."

At this, Albiorix burst out laughing and then capped his hand over his mouth to stop himself. Brother Auros grinned. Even June couldn't help but smile.

"All right then," said Albiorix. "If you really are a good guy, it's time you give up anything useful you might have on your old party."

"Well," said Morton, "I'm a little bit out of the loop, but I know they're all practicing hard for Battle of the Bands."

"Battle of the Bands?" said Albiorix. "It seemed like such a long shot, I hadn't even considered it as a possibility. Why would Tristane Trouvère need to practice?"

"Yeah, say what you will about the creep," said June, "he's got some catchy tunes."

"Between your homecoming king coup and the math

league championship, you guys have them worried," said Brother Auros.

Albiorix considered this. "If Tristane Trouvère thinks we might beat him . . . maybe we can?"

The wizard looked at June.

She shrugged. "I *have* been teaching myself to play guitar online."

Chapter 26

Music is very important to the high schoolers of Advanced Homerooms & Hall Passes. For increased immersion, consider setting the ambience for your game with some mood music. Hire a small troupe of troubadours to play at modest volume while you run your game session. For an otherworldly flair, encourage these musicians to add a "bass drop" to the songs they play.

—Excerpt from The Advanced Hall Master's Guide

❧

*T*HE PARTY OF BRAVE adventurers had gathered in the garage of 45 Crescent Drive, the home of Douglas and Ron Schiller. June and Albiorix had informed the others of their ally-turned-enemy-turned-ally Morton Blanc's true identity. Devis the thief claimed (dubiously) to have known it all along. And then the wizard put forth the daunting task that lay before them.

"Since we didn't ace the ABSEE," said Albiorix, "this Saturday we have to beat Tristane Trouvère at Battle of the Bands."

The party stood stone-faced and stunned. Thromdurr gasped. Sorrowshade laughed darkly.

"I am trying to summon something optimistic to say here, Albiorix, but I find it is taking longer than usual," said Vela. "In the meantime, feel free to talk among yourselves."

"Take your time, Vela," said Albiorix. "Let me handle the whole inspirational battle speech this time." The wizard cleared his throat. "So, back home we're amazing at what we do, but in this world, it can sometimes feel like we're a bunch of pathetic losers perpetually taking one step forward and two steps back—"

"Off to a great motivational start," said Sorrowshade.

"—but if you really think about it, actually, we're not. Because we found the Malonomicon! We nailed two out of three scenario objectives!" Albiorix flipped open *The Freshman Year of Futility* and pointed at the relevant page for emphasis. "But now is our darkest hour—or our finest hour? One of the big hours. Because the last objective we need to check off is 'win Battle of the Bands.' We do that, and the scenario ends. Victory. All the Advanced Homerooms & Hall Passes players, good or bad, go home. This world will be saved, yet again. Personally, I think that if we knuckle down and practice hard, we have a ten . . . no, a twelve percent chance of winning. Which is much better than nothing."

The rest of the party stared back at Albiorix in silence.

"I am trying to summon something positive to say about your inspirational speech," said Vela, "but I find it is taking longer than usual."

Devis clapped his hands. "No, Albiorix is right! We can do this. We can beat Tristane Trouvère in a competition of musical skill. And after we win Battle of the Bands, we can conjure forth the demon Azathor the Devourer and defeat him in a pie-eating contest, just for fun."

"Maybe if we chop both Tristane Trouvère's hands off and then trick him into drinking acid right before he goes onstage?" said Sorrowshade.

"Yikes," said June.

"What?" said Sorrowshade. "I'm trying to be positive."

"Okay, forget my inspirational speech," said Albiorix.

"Already done," said Devis.

"Let me put it to you a different way," said Albiorix. "Does anybody have a better idea?"

Thromdurr stroked his jaw. "Personally, I find the demonic pie-eating contest very intriguing!"

In the end, none had a superior alternative.

"That's what I thought," said Albiorix as he pulled out

a pencil and notebook. "So if we're going to be a band, we need a plan. First off, June absolutely shreds, as they say, on guitar."

"I'm *learning* to absolutely shred on guitar. What I do on guitar right now is more of a gentle, ah, cheese-grating action," said June. "My best song is 'Turkey in the Straw.'"

"Is that a toe-tapping headbanger that's sure to get the crowd fired up?" asked Albiorix.

"Not at all," said June.

"Perhaps if it were something more exciting than a turkey?" said Thromdurr. "How about Klednar, Exile Prince of the Thunder Giants?"

"'Klednar, Exile Prince of the Thunder Giants in the Straw'?" said June.

"Love it!" said Albiorix. "I'm writing that down. No bad ideas. See? Now the creative juices are starting to flow. Vela, you play the flute, right?"

"On paper, my character, Valerie Stumpf-Turner, plays the flute," said Vela. "But whenever I try, it seems to make people very, very sad."

"Fantastic. You're making them feel *something*. That's the hardest part," said Albiorix. "Devis, you've mentioned that you play the lute."

"Learned from the best," said Devis. "And by that I mean Tristane Trouvère. Literally the best musician I have ever heard. The guy we're somehow going to beat with our unique spin on 'Turkey in the Straw.'"

"It's not the song, it's the singer," said Albiorix. "Speaking of which, our little ensemble needs a lead vocalist."

Thromdurr cleared his throat. "I claim no special musical talent. But many have described my voice as 'booming' and 'impossible to ignore.'" The barbarian belted out a few bars of what was, perhaps, a song.

"Uh-huh," said Albiorix. "That was . . . something. Does anybody else want to try?"

No one did.

"Anybody?" said Albiorix. "Anyone other than Thromdurr?"

There followed another thirty-odd seconds of silence.

"Then it seems I am the front man!" cried Thromdurr. "In truth, I feel I have the hair for it. And I promise that whatever song we choose, I will bellow it as loudly as an ice caribou giving birth to tripl—"

"Ugh, fine," said Sorrowshade. "I'll do it."

The others looked at the gloom elf.

"Kind of figured you for the bass player type," said Albiorix. "Is there something we don't know?"

The assassin sighed and crossed her arms. "All elves can sing beautifully. It's awful."

"Can you give us a little taste?" said Albiorix.

Sorrowshade frowned. And then she sang an ethereal, lilting song in Shadownese that filled them all with an overpowering sense of immortal melancholy.

"Wow," said Devis. "That was—"

"Shut up," said Sorrowshade.

"I was going to compliment you!" said Devis.

"I know," said Sorrowshade. "It's worse."

"Okay, Sorrowshade is *definitely* our lead vocalist," said Albiorix. "Although to win this thing, you're probably going to have to sing something the crowd can understand. Thromdurr, I'm moving you to drums."

"I can certainly swing a war hammer with devastating force," said Thromdurr. "Perhaps playing the drums is similar?"

"It's exactly the same," said Albiorix. "Well, I think that's everybody."

"Wait," said June. "What about you?"

"Oh," said Albiorix. "Well, check this out."

The wizard picked up a tambourine and started to play. It took two seconds before Devis kicked the instrument out of his hands. The tambourine flew across the garage and then rolled into the corner.

"Thank you, Devis!" cried Vela the Valiant, both fingers firmly plugged in her ears.

"Albiorix, how can your tambourine playing somehow be worse than Thromdurr's singing?" asked June.

Sorrowshade shook her head. "The instrument sounded like it was in pain."

Thromdurr eyed the tambourine where it lay near a pile of extension cords. "I fear we must destroy it now. It has been *contaminated*."

"Okay, jeez, sorry," said Albiorix. "I guess I was a little off beat?"

"Albiorix," said Vela, "when it comes to music, you have what can only be described as the opposite of talent. Perhaps you can play a more, ahem, supporting role in Battle of the Bands?"

"Yeah, after your little scene in the cafeteria with Nicole Davenport, I'm not sure having you up onstage will help our cause," said June. "People have turned on Armando Boort."

"Yeah, you're probably right," said Albiorix. "I'm more of a behind-the-scenes ideas guy anyway. I can be the songwriter for the band. I'll come up with an original song that captures the true essence and texture of life in the Realm of Suburbia. It'll knock the socks off all the NPCs!"

"Hey!" said June.

"Sorry," said Albiorix. The wizard clapped his hands. "Guys, I really think we can do this!"

And so Albiorix disappeared for the better part of an hour to furiously scribble page after page of song lyrics into his notebook. Meanwhile, the others attempted to "jam" together on their instruments. June's guitar playing was serviceable, if a little slow. Devis strummed the three lute chords he knew in different combinations. Vela tooted away on her flute and every so often let out a sour, high-pitched squeal. Thromdurr pounded mightily upon Ron Schiller's old drum kit, inadvertently breaking drumhead after drumhead until there were none left. And over it all, Sorrowshade sang "Turkey in the Straw" with haunting, eternal beauty.

At last Albiorix returned. In a fit of artistic expression, he'd written a sweeping epic, the first piece in what he described as a seven-part rock opera about an accountant journeying across the lands of Suburbia in search of the ultimate spreadsheet. He handed Sorrowshade a wad of crumpled handwritten lyrics.

And over the assembled cacophony of flute, lute, guitar, and broken snare drum, the gloom elf sang:

"I set forth from the offices of Hubbard and Moran
With a story in my heart and a briefcase in my hand.
I seek the mighty macro that will make us understand—
I seek the sacred spreadsheet from which all life began. . . ."

The music was dissonant, pretentious, and off tempo. In short, it was nearly unlistenable. And deep down each of them knew it. As they played their song, a quiet sense of despair began to creep over the bold heroes.

Chapter 27

Between school and homework, characters find them-selves with downtime on their hands. During such periods, players may attempt to improve their Skills through practice. To increase a Skill in this way, make a Skill check with a Difficulty equal to three times the current Skill bonus. Modify this Difficulty by −1 for each hour spent practicing. Success increases the Skill by +1. Failure indicates that the character got distracted, perhaps by watching cute animal videos or endlessly scrolling through their social media feeds.

—Excerpt from The Advanced Hall Master's Guide

❧

FOR THE REST OF the week, the adventurers' band prac-ticed hard. They spent every evening jamming for hours in the Schiller garage. And they did make progress. They got better, if not good, exactly. There were even times when, for a moment, they almost sounded like a real band. Though none of them said it, it was impossible to imagine the newly formed musical group pulling off anything to rival an earworm like "Account Number and PIN." But still they would try. They were heroes. after all.

Albiorix—with little to do other than listen to his friends repeatedly practice his eleven-minute song about metaphysical accountancy—instead focused on practicing magic. Experience told him to expect all manner of overt and subtle interference from Tristane Trouvère's party the day of the performance. The wizard wanted to be as ready for it as he could. He might not be as powerful a mage as the sorceress Calyxia, but he wouldn't make it easy for her.

So Albiorix ran through all the spells in in his spellbook, one by one, repeating them over and over again until he could cast them effortlessly. Oddly enough, for the first time in as long as he could remember, he found that he enjoyed it. When the Archmage Velaxis had been breathing down his neck, his magical studies had felt like a chore, someone else's burden he'd been shouldered with. But pushing himself to improve to protect his friends was a necessity. The innate resistance he now realized he'd always been putting up was falling away.

At last the day of Battle of the Bands arrived. There was a heavy feeling of fate in the air, as often came upon the party when they neared the end of a quest. Even the venue felt portentous: the competition was being held at the Monarch music club, site of the adventurers' most crushing defeat. As the group approached the entrance of the club, a sense of quiet dread fell over them. In some ways, it was a fear more sharp and palpable than that of monsters or traps. It was the fear of utter embarrassment.

This feeling only grew as they realized the place was packed. Nearly all of Pine Hill High School had turned out to see the competition. It was the Monarch's first "all-ages show" since Tristane Trouvère's disastrous solo performance, but even the memory of that night wasn't enough to keep the curious audience away. Few wanted to miss the epic musical showdown of the year—especially since disgraced Homecoming King Armando Boort's group would be facing off against the band fronted by Popular-turned-Pariah-turned-Popular kid Travis Tyson.

"So, I'm just spitballing here," said Devis, eyeing the capacity crowd, "but what if we didn't do this?"

"Didn't do what?" asked Albiorix.

"Didn't humiliate ourselves in front of all our peers," said June.

"What? No, you guys sound, uh, really, really great," said Albiorix. "And I honestly think—I think we are going to win. Yep."

Vela placed a gentle hand on Albiorix's shoulder. "I understand you do not follow the same code that I do, friend. But know that dishonesty can cause personal stress and put a strain on relationships. This is something I learned from the one lie I ever told."

"I'm not lying," said Albiorix, who didn't sound convincing even to himself. "We're definitely going to maybe, possibly do this. Maybe. For sure."

"You can admit it. We're doomed," said Sorrowshade. "Which, I'll be honest, is kind of my comfort zone."

"No way—look at this!" Albiorix pointed to a handwritten list posted on the wall near the exit. "It's the show order. And we got the best slot. Looks like we're playing last! Tell me that's not a good omen."

"Fantastic," said Devis. "More pressure."

The heroes took their places in the audience. Albiorix scanned the sea of familiar faces and briefly made eye contact with Nicole Davenport. She shot him a look that would have frightened a raging minotaur, and the wizard quickly looked away. Luckily, they only spotted one member of Tristane Trouvère's party. Brother Auros sidled up to them.

"Hey, guys," said Brother Auros.

"Hello, Morton Blanc, our friend!" said Thromdurr in a manner that was so loud and suspicious, several strangers turned to stare at him.

"Anybody need anything?" asked Brother Auros. "Water? Tea? I think they have a smoothie machine behind the bar."

The party quietly shook their heads. Most of them could not have kept anything as solid as a smoothie down at that particular moment.

"So you're ready, then," said Brother Auros.

"Not quite," said June. "Our band is like . . . whatever the opposite of a well-oiled machine is."

"A poorly watered plant?" said Thromdurr.

"We're not that bad," said Albiorix.

"Says the guy who's not going to be live onstage eating it in front of the entire school," said Sorrowshade.

"Well, Tristane ordered me to secretly sabotage all of your instruments ahead of the show," said Brother Auros. "So at least you won't have to deal with that."

"Actually, go ahead," said Devis. "Might actually make us sound better."

"You're all missing the point," said Albiorix. "Think about it! Tristane Trouvère is still worried. He still thinks we might be able to pull it off. He believes in us. Why don't you?"

The others looked at him like he was crazy. For some reason, an inverted vote of confidence from their hated archenemy didn't boost the group's morale.

At 3:05 p.m., the club manager of the Monarch—a

balding man with a ponytail—took the stage.

"Helloooooooo, Hibbettsfield!" said the club manager. "Welcome to the Monarch's annual Battle of the Baaaaaaaaands!"

The crowd applauded.

"Before we start the show, just some quick housekeeping. You gave us your feedback and we heard you, loud and clear. We have been working diligently with not one but *three* of the area's top pest-control companies. And I'm proud to report that the pill bug issue has been thoroughly dealt with. I repeat: the pill bug issue has been thoroughly deeeeeealt wiiiiith!"

Weak applause.

"Awesome," said the club manager. "So the way this competition works is simple: eight great local bands will perform. At the end, whoever gets the loudest applause wins the coveted title of Best Band! Are you reeeeeaaaady?"

The crowd applauded more loudly.

"Then welcome to the stage your first act: Format of Distortion!"

The club manager exited as four dour-looking teens in ripped clothing and black eyeliner took the stage and played a grim, throbbing industrial song called "Backstabber (Twist the Fork)."

Sorrowshade seemed to enjoy it—the elf clapped vigorously—but the rest of the audience had a more subdued reaction. The heroes then listened to sets by Crystal Panic, the Busted Boys, Recombinator, and The Where It's Ats. The groups' styles and genres varied, as did the audience's response. After the five performances, though, no clear favorite had emerged. Battle of the Bands was, theoretically, still anyone's competition to win.

The sixth act, Jenny and the Critters, took the stage, and the party made their way out to the parking lot to retrieve their instruments from Ron Schiller's pickup truck. Ron wanted to support his son but had been told by him numerous times that it would be "way too weird" to have a dad at the actual show. So he dutifully sat in his parked vehicle and listened to sports radio while eating an egg salad sandwich he had brought from home.

"Knock 'em dead in there, son," said Ron.

"Hopefully it will not come to that, Father," said Thromdurr. "I merely hope we are able to pull off an impressive musical performance."

"Um," said Ron. "Yeah?"

The group unloaded their instruments and returned through the side door of the Monarch. They were just in time to hear Jenny and the Critters finish their song to enthusiastic applause—the best act so far, apparently.

As the party made their way backstage, they nearly bumped into their mortal enemies, who were preparing to go on next. Tristane Trouvère had an electric guitar slung around his neck, Skegg the Surly carried a bass, Azheena clutched a pair of drumsticks, and Calyxia held a synthesizer case. They all wore matching red-and-black costumes, styled half as Bríandalörian armor and half as something more futuristic. There was no getting around it. The group looked incredibly cool.

"Hey, check it out," said Azheena. "I thought I smelled loser."

"Where's your dog?" asked Sorrowshade. "Doesn't a band need at least one attractive member?"

Skegg snickered. "Ha. That ain't half bad, elf. Very mean. You ever considered you might be evil? Why don't you join our merry band?"

"I would, but I heard you eat scabs," said Sorrowshade.

At this, the dwarf's jaw fell open. Skegg was speechless. Sorrowshade smiled.

"She has a point," said Calyxia. "It is a revolting habit."

"Which side are you on, witch?" roared Skegg.

Calyxia shrugged. "I had assumed the stronger. If so, shall we dispense with this silly music contest and end them now, *leader*?"

Albiorix thought he caught a note of contempt in that last word. From Tristane Trouvère's expression, her tone wasn't lost on the bard either.

"Try it," said Albiorix. "You'll just come up against the same indestructible force field I conjured last time." He waved his hands around in a way that he hoped looked both mystical and convincing.

Calyxia's eyes narrowed. "What spell was that? Tell me now."

"Wouldn't you like to know, Miss Smarty-Magic," said Albiorix.

"Miss Smarty-Magic?" said June quietly.

Albiorix's command of snappy comebacks had not improved.

But Calyxia took his point. "Or don't tell me. The knowledge can die with you." The sorceress's eyes crackled purple as though she was about to unleash a truly nasty spell.

Tristane waved her off. "No, no, no. Not right now. There are three hundred people out front. We can't risk it."

"You sound scared," said Albiorix, who surprised even himself with his boldness.

Tristane Trouvère cocked his head. "Have no doubt, we will destroy you. Your party is pathetic: an inept ex-wizard, a sad elf, a goody two-shoes knight, a brute who's better at math than he is at fighting. And of course, dear old Goblinface."

"I've been meaning to tell you," said Devis. "I don't, uh, much care for that nickname."

"I'll call you Fungusbreath, then," said Tristane Trouvère.

"And you forgot about me," said June.

Tristane smiled. "You're not a member of their party. You're just an NPC."

June glowered.

"In the end, you misfits don't stand a chance against us," said Tristane Trouvère. "But I mean to snuff out your last hope of escape first. Honestly, you hope to win a contest of musical skill. *Against me?*" The bard guffawed in a loud, stagy way. "This is your master plan to return home?"

"That's the same thing you said about homecoming king," said Albiorix.

Before Tristane could respond, an ecstatic (and sweaty) Jenny and the Critters edged past the two parties, high-fiving each other, on their way toward the exit.

"Give it up one more time for Jenny and the Critters!" said the club manager.

The crowd applauded again.

"And now," said the club manager, "please welcome our next act to the stage: Surprise Party!"

"Well, I'd love to continue this delightful repartee, but that's our cue," said Tristane Trouvère. "The public awaits."

"May the best band win," said Albiorix.

Tristane Trouvère shot him a wry smile and winked as he and his party took the stage.

"Hello, Hibbettsfield!" cried Tristane Trouvère. "You know me!"

The crowd roared. It seemed the hair extensions rumor had only caused a brief dip in Travis Tyson's popularity. His true fans had turned out in droves to support him.

"This is my band, Surprise Party," said Tristane Trouvère. "We want to play a brand-new song for the first time ever. It's a little number I like to call 'Girl U Know We Rule This Place.' And it's dedicated to a very special girl in my life. Her name is Nicole Davenport."

"Aww," said the crowd.

June nodded. "That explains it. That's what she got for humiliating you in the cafeteria."

"I thought I gave as good as I got in that, uh, particular exchange," said Albiorix.

All his companions shook their heads. Albiorix sighed. Nicole Davenport truly was an evil genius.

"One, two, three, four!" cried Tristane Trouvère.

Azheena laid down a driving beat on the drums. Skegg the Surly came in with a kicking baseline. Calyxia's fingers danced across the keys, playing an impossibly complex melody on her synthesizer.

Three seconds in, and Albiorix had to admit Surprise Party was good. Really good. And Tristane Trouvère hadn't even started singing yet. He checked his companions' expressions: a mixture of disbelief and despair. Thromdurr grimaced as he unconsciously tapped his foot.

Then Tristane's guitar came in and the bard started to sing:

"Girl you know we come from different worlds.
Where I come from there are different girls,
But I know that we were meant to be.
I know this moment is for you and me,
'Cause every time I look in your face
I remember that we rule this place!"

The crowd went nuts. They loved it. And Albiorix loved it too. The lyrics were fun (if you didn't think about them too much), and the melody was not unlike pure sugar for the ears. The wizard couldn't help it. A huge grin started to spread across his face. He tried to smoosh his mouth back into a frown. He couldn't. He was listening to his new favorite song.

"Such . . . beautiful . . . music," said Thromdurr.

"I cannot lie," said Vela. "This absolutely slaps."

"Do we still have to play next?" said Devis.

"I hate that I love it so much," said Sorrowshade.

"This is very bad," said Albiorix.

"Yep," said June.

The wizard shook his head. "Guys, I'm sorry. We can't do this. I know, we practiced and things were really starting to come together. But just listen to them. We might as well pack it in. This is the end. There's no way we can win Battle of the Bands."

"What did you say?" said Vela.

"I said we can't win," said Albiorix.

Vela blinked. "Yes. Yes, exactly!"

The paladin rummaged around in her backpack for a moment and then pulled out a gleaming bladed weapon. It was the Axe of Destiny.

"You want to attack them?" said Devis. "Right now? Doesn't seem very Vela-esque. Feels like more of a pre-crisis-of-confidence Thromdurr move."

"Agreed," said Thromdurr. "If attack we must, then can we at least wait until they finish playing this awful, beautiful song?"

"No!" hissed Sorrowshade. "I'm all for icing these creeps, but I've said it before: They're *not* better than us at fighting. We *can* beat them without it. If we use the Axe of Destiny now, its dumb curse will surely doom us. We don't need it!"

"We do," said Vela. "But first, Sorrowshade, give me six of your bowstrings. Devis, I also need your thieves' tools. Quickly!"

The gloom elf and the thief did as they were told and

provided Vela with the materials she asked for. While Surprise Party played out the remainder of "Girl U Know We Rule This Place," Vela the Valiant worked quickly and precisely, bringing all the skills she'd learned in shop class to bear. Albiorix had no idea what the paladin was going for, but before he could ask, her work was done.

"According to legend," said Vela, "the wielder of the Axe of Destiny can turn the tide of one unwinnable battle. Behold!"

She held the axe aloft. The paladin had pegged six bowstrings to the flat of the axe blade and strung them tight down the length of the handle, where she'd used Devis's thieves' tools to create six makeshift tuning keys. The party gasped. Vela had turned the legendary weapon into an improvised guitar.

"And so the Axe of Destiny has become the 'Axe' of Destiny!" cried Vela. "June, you are lead guitar. It is yours to wield."

She tossed the axe to June.

A look of panic spread across June's face as she caught it. "Uh, what? It's too heavy. Where are the frets? There's no way my capo's going to fit on this thing. How do I even play a G?"

Vela smiled. "Trust yourself." She turned to the others. "There is one other change I believe we should make before we take the stage. I do not think we should play 'The Ballad of Gabe Wyrzykowski, CPA.'"

"Why not?" cried Albiorix, who'd gone from defeatist to defensive in under a second. "That's the song we practiced all week!"

"We do not have much time, so you may find my explanation blunt." said Vela. "Your song is both boring and confusing."

"But hey, at least it's extremely long," said Devis.

"What's confusing about it?" said Albiorix. "Gabe Wyrzykowski is just a regular guy looking for a metaphorical spreadsheet that will reveal all the hidden secrets of the universe! I think it's *very* relatable."

"Comrades," said Vela, "I believe our best shot is if Sorrowshade sings a song of her own creation."

"Huh?" said Devis. "Look, we all know the accountant song is a snooze—

"Hey!" said Albiorix.

"—but it's all we've got," continued the thief. "A Sorrowshade original is going to be some depressing funeral dirge about spider-covered mushrooms growing out of a dead guy's eye sockets or something."

"I do not think so," said Vela. "I have had the privilege of reading some of Sorrowshade's song lyrics."

"Song lyrics?" said Sorrowshade. "You mean . . . my poetry?"

Vela nodded. "I think it is time to finally express your true feelings."

Before Sorrowshade could answer, the audience exploded into thunderous applause. Surprise Party had finished their song and, as anyone might have predicted, the crowd loved it. Tristane and company bowed, and bowed again. The applause continued for seconds, stretching into minutes, and it only seemed to get louder as the time passed. Surprise Party continued to bow.

At last Tristane Trouvère, Skegg the Surly, Azheena, and Calyxia exited the stage. The evil adventurers were beaming. And after such a performance, who could blame them? Surprise Party had been nothing short of incredible.

"Try to follow that," said Tristane Trouvère as the evil adventurers elbowed past.

And so they would.

"And now, please welcome our final act," said the club manager. "Give it up for the Hometown Heroes."

Albiorix waited in the wings as his five companions took the stage. His heart was in his throat. Perhaps Vela was right about the song he'd written. But was jettisoning the thing they'd practiced all week the right move? And would the Axe of Destiny make a difference? They would all know in a few seconds.

"Hello," said Sorrowshade into the microphone. "We're called the Hometown Heroes, but actually we come from a magical realm far beyond your dreary world. Except for June. She's local."

There was some sporadic applause.

"I'm actually from the Big City," said June. Albiorix could see that her hands were trembling. She didn't look thrilled at having to try to play a jury-rigged battle axe as a guitar.

"Oh. Right," said Sorrowshade. "Well, anyway, this is the first time anybody's ever heard this song, including us. So this ought to go well." The gloom elf turned back toward her companions. "Follow my lead, I guess?"

And then Sorrowshade started to sing, not with immortal melancholy but with a sense of childlike joy:

"Rainbows and dolphins and blankets with sleeves . . ."

Thromdurr came in on drums. He played a simple throbbing beat. It sounded like something a member of the Sky Bear clan might play on a hide drum beneath the stars on some clear, frozen night.

"Cupcakes and wholphins and bright autumn leaves . . ."

Devis and Vela came in on lute and flute respectively. So far, to the wizard's ear, the music had a distinctly Bríandalörian feel to it. Would the people of Suburbia respond to such an otherworldly sound?

"Your world is my world. I'm happy to be . . ."

And at last June came in on the Axe of Destiny. Her nervousness was gone, and she was absolutely shredding on the legendary guitar. June played the melody so fast that Albiorix could barely see her hand moving up and down the neck/haft of the axe, much less her strumming hand.

"Happy to be here! I'm happy happy happy to be here!"

The crowd went nuts. Albiorix peeked out and saw the entire audience dancing and clapping their hands and jumping up and down. Among them, near the back, he also spotted Tristane Trouvère and the rest of his party, darkly conferring among themselves. By now they realized that the Hometown Heroes were good, and they meant to do something about it. It seemed that the sorceress's argument had finally won the day: the good guys needed to be wiped out once and for all. In the darkness, Albiroix saw Calyxia's eyes flash purple.

A cloud of burning plasma leaped from her fingertips and soared over the heads of the crowd toward the stage, bathing the Monarch in flickering orange light.

"Ya'ois lvirr aelt'n ka'aetk na' za'sg voiddh!" incanted Albiorix from his own spellbook. A flash of blue energy erupted from his palm and met the plasma cloud midair.

With a blinding white flash, the cloud burst into a hundred thousand harmless sparks of light, which slowly rained down on the audience.

Albiorix almost couldn't believe it. He had successfully countered one of Calyxia's spells! Maybe, just maybe, he wasn't such a terrible wizard after all. Not only that, but the clash of the two spell casters had inadvertently created a mesmerizing pyrotechnic display/laser light show to accompany the Hometown Heroes' performance.

"Whoooooooa!" said the audience as the beautiful twinkling lights fluttered down. Many reached up and tried to catch the sparkles before they winked out of existence.

Calyxia looked more stunned than anyone. Quickly Albiorix cast the spell ward of protection over the entire party, including himself. It was a relatively simple incantation that would (hopefully) shield them from whatever spell was next thrown their way.

"Chocolate and podcasts and cool carabiners," sang Sorrowshade. *"Antibiotics and backyard bird feeders . . ."*

Calyxia began to incant once more, drawing a dark gray-green cloud about her from the ether. Albiorix cursed as he recognized the spell. It was an antimagic mist that would dispel his ward of protection and leave the Hometown Heroes wide open for another plasma cloud, or something even worse.

But just then, from out of nowhere, a figure rushed

through the crowd toward Calyxia. It was Brother Auros! He slapped Calyxia's heavy spellbook right out of her hands. The sorceress's casting was interrupted, and the gathering antimagic mist dissipated instantly. The spellbook spun away through the air and landed somewhere in the middle of the cheering, dancing crowd.

Calyxia was dumbfounded. She shrieked something that was drowned out by the music. Tristane Trouvère looked furious. An instant later Skegg the Surly and Azheena had wrenched Brother Auros's arms behind his back and put him in a headlock.

But Brother Auros had done it. He'd stopped Calyxia and bought the Hometown Heroes the time they needed to finish their song, whatever it was called.

"Your world is my world," sang Sorrowshade. *"I'm happy to be heeeeeere!"*

And just like that, the performance was over. The crowd roared. The Hometown Heroes took a bow. The clapping continued. Albiorix grinned at his companions from the wings. He shot them a Suburbia-style thumbs-up. They'd killed it.

The ponytailed Monarch manager took the mic again. "The Hometown Heroes, everyone! Wow, I can honestly say I've *never* heard anything like that before. Just phenomenal stuff, guys."

More thunderous applause as the adventuring party made their exit. Albiorix congratulated them as they headed backstage.

"That was absolutely incredible!" cried Albiorix.

"It felt . . . like a miracle," said Vela.

"I know," said Devis. "I was amazing, right? The rest of you were pretty okay too."

Thromdurr regarded his drumsticks with a giant grin. "I understand now. Percussion is not a matter of brute force. It is but timing—ensuring the length of time between each beat is the same. Drumming is a form of mathematics!"

"I'll take your word for it," said Albiorix.

Sorrowshade walked offstage scowling.

"Happy to be here, huh?" said Albiorix.

"Shut up," said the gloom elf.

June came last. She looked dazed. "I have no idea what happened out there. I blacked out. Did I drool or, uh, reveal any embarrassing family secrets?"

"You were unbelievable," said Albiorix. The wizard squeezed her hand.

"Cool," said June. "Sorry. This thing is still too heavy." She unslung the Axe of Destiny and handed it to Albiorix. "I think I've got to play a little *Oink Pop* to level out." She pulled out her phone and retreated into the comfort of digital pig tickling.

"Now comes the moment you've all been waiting for," said the club manager. "Time to pick the winner of this year's Battle of the Bands. And do we have some strong contenders, or what? These are honestly some of the best bands I've ever seen. But you guys are the judges here. So when you hear your favorite band's name, I want you to clap as loud as you can. Are you reeeeady?"

The crowd answered with a huge cheer. They were ready.

"Then give it up for Format of Distortion!" cried the club manager.

Most of the crowd went silent. Two people clapped. One of them quickly stopped.

The club manager ran down the list. Crystal Panic, the Busted Boys, Recombinator, and The Where It's Ats all got a tepid response. There was more enthusiasm for Jenny and the Critters. But it was clear which bands the final choice would come down to. The anticipation was palpable. Albiorix almost couldn't breathe. Whether or not the party was trapped in this realm forever would come down to this: how loud a bunch of kids clapped and yelled for them.

"All right, make some noise for Surprise Party!" cried the club manager.

This got a big round of applause. Albiorix spotted Nicole Davenport, amid the other Travis Tyson fans, jumping up and down and screaming her head off.

"Now, let's hear it for the Hometown Heroes!" cried the club manager.

The place exploded. The applause was almost deafening. The clapping and hooting were far louder than what Surprise Party got. Through the crowd, Albiorix could just make out the looks of confusion, anger, and despair on the faces of the evil adventurers. They'd lost, and they knew it. Brother Auros, still in a headlock, was grinning, though.

June looked up from her phone. "Did we do it?"

"I think . . . I maybe think we did," said Albiorix.

"Where's the axe?" asked June.

Albiorix looked down. He was no longer holding the legendary weapon. The Axe of Destiny was gone.

"Well, then I guess this is really it," said June. The wizard saw tears in her eyes. "Goodbye for real, dude."

"Yeah," said Albiorix. "Goodbye for real. I just . . ." The wizard trailed off. He felt himself starting to cry too.

June hugged him.

"I think the results are loud and clear," said the club manager. "You have made your voices heard. The winner of this year's Battle of the Bands is none other than . . . Olivia Gooooormaaaaaaan!"

Chapter 28

Though we hear them every day in our normal lives, the villains of an Advanced Homerooms & Hall Passes game should never, ever give the traditional soliloquy revealing all their monstrous and depraved plans. For starters, many of the bad guys in the Realm of Suburbia don't actually even consider themselves to be bad guys.

—*Excerpt from* The Advanced Hall Master's Guide

❧

"WAIT, WHAT?" SAID DEVIS.

A murmur of stunned confusion ran through the crowd.

"Oh no," said Albiorix. "Follow me."

The wizard led the party back out onto the Monarch's stage.

Vela approached the Monarch manager. "Surely there has been some mistake."

The man didn't answer. Instead he stood perfectly motionless, his eyes dilated. A strand of drool hung from the corner of his mouth.

"Hello?" said Vela.

She waved her hand in front of his face. No response.

Just then, a nova of sickly green magical energy flashed at the back of the room. The wave of swirling light spread through the crowd to the party, but the blue crackle of Albiorix's ward of protection told the wizard that the heroes had been shielded from its effects.

The others weren't so lucky. An instant after the spell was cast, everyone else in the Monarch—including the evil adventurers—fell to the ground, totally limp. Only one person remained standing.

"Mmm, mass paralysis," said Olivia Gorman, grinning. "First time I've ever tried that spell out. Pretty neat."

Vela drew her sword. "Comrades, I fear she has been possessed by the undead warlock Zazirak." The paladin turned. "Olivia, if you are in there somewhere, if you can hear me, do not lose hope. We will save—"

"Blah blah blah," said Olivia. "No, I haven't been possessed by anyone. And honestly, I resent the implication that you think I couldn't do this on my own. But that's just like you cool kids. Always underestimating us nerds."

"Couldn't do *what* on your own?" said Albiorix.

"Master the forbidden arts of necromancy and

diabolism," said Olivia. "Duh."

"Olivia, tell me this is some jest," said Thromdurr. "Tell me you haven't followed this path of darkness."

Olivia cackled. "Sorry to disappoint you, Doug. After you creeps wrecked my life last year, I was the one who happened to find the Malonomicon in the Old Mall. At first I didn't know what I had in my hands. Couldn't read it, obviously. But I knew it was important. *Somehow I just knew.* So I spent months on my laptop, using various machine-learning algorithms to try to translate it. And at last I succeeded. I was able to decipher the words of the simplest spell in the book."

"Summon smoke imp," said Albiorix.

"Ding ding ding," said Olivia. "I may not have won eighth-grade class president, but I was able to conjure forth a demon from the stygian depths of the Thirteen Hells."

"Put that on your college application," said Sorrowshade.

"Shut it," said Olivia. "So I summoned a smoke imp. And as you know, those little guys speak a crude form of Fiendish, the language of devils. I made the imp teach me. Over more long months, Smokey tutored me in the infernal tongue. Call it a language elective."

"Smokey?" said Devis.

"What? Am I *not* supposed to name the smoke imp I spent six hours a day with for eight months?" cried Olivia.

"Don't interrupt me again, worm!"

"Sorry, sorry," said Devis.

"I learned enough Fiendish to summon more . . . *things*. Horrid creatures of pain and nightmare, to teach me Shadownese and other, older languages—eldritch tongues long forgotten by all who yet live. Soon the whole of the Malonomicon was intelligible to me, Olivia Gorman. And the more I learned, the more everything just seemed to make sense."

"She's completely nuts," said June.

"Nuh-uh. *You* are, June!" said Olivia. "I can perceive the very fabric of reality now. I see it's all a game. And now I know the rules. I have become a warlock of untold power—power the likes of which Zazirak could only dream of."

"So you say, villain," said Vela. "But we found the Malonomicon. Without its evil spells, you are powerless." She held up the vile grimoire to make her point.

"Pshaw," said Olivia. "I don't need that dumb book anymore. I totally took pictures of all the spells with my phone." She held up her smartphone. Sure enough, the screen showed a photo of one of the Malonomicon's yellowed pages.

"Phone pictures," said Albiorix, shaking his head. "Should've thought of that."

"And you're wrong about something else too," said Olivia. "I'm not the villain. I'm the hero. I'm the underdog.

I'm battling injustice. Up till this moment, everything has just been handed to the Popular people, the pretty people, the people like you. But it's Nerds, Nerds like me, who deserve all the credit for doing everything useful. We're the ones who invent things! We're the ones who discover things! We write books! We cure diseases!"

"Just curious," said Sorrowshade. "Which diseases have you cured, exactly?"

"Ha ha," said Olivia. "But you prove my point for me. I have plenty of amazing accomplishments. All ignored by these shallow fools." She waved her hand at the limp crowd now lying at her feet on the floor. "Look how many people came out for this idiotic Battle of the Bands. It's an amateur pop music competition. Another popularity contest! Meanwhile, nobody cared when our team defied the odds and won the math league state championship."

"Yet we did not truly win," said Thromdurr. "I realize now that you used one of your dark enchantments to bewitch the judges into accepting your incorrect answer. For shame, Olivia. For shame."

"SILENCE!" shrieked Olivia. Thromdurr had clearly struck a nerve.

The barbarian was unfazed, though. "You know the correct solution was fourteen, nine, and five. By your sorcery, you dishonored the sacred Spirit of Mathematics."

"Enough of this!" cried Olivia. "The game is rigged. Always has been. But as I said, I know the rules. And now I'm going to change them. I'm going to fix things. *I'm going to fix people.*"

"I don't like where this is headed," said Albiorix.

"Finally I'll get the respect I deserve," said Olivia. "There is a much more interesting spell than mass paralysis in the Malonomicon. It's called mass hypnosis." Olivia glanced at her phone. *"Naz i'asuhru i'ars rusu nu i'auhsis nuhruharr."*

Another wave of greenish magical energy burst outward from Olivia's hands and washed over the room. Once again the heroes were mercifully shielded by Albiorix's ward of protection.

But the rest of the crowd started to stir. One by one, they pulled themselves to their feet, no longer paralyzed. Their eyes now showed the same dilation as the emcee's.

"Hello, classmates," asked Olivia. "How do you feel about me now?"

"We respect you, Olivia," said the crowd, in eerie unison. "We realize that we have been dumb idiots who valued the wrong things in life. We see that you are the smartest and best and coolest person in the whole entire world."

"Wow," said Olivia. "So gratifying to finally hear that."

"What should we do now, Olivia?" said the crowd. "How can we ever make it up to you?"

"Hmm," said Olivia. "I suppose you could make me class president . . . of the world. All in favor, say aye."

"Aye," said the hypnotized crowd.

"Sounds like the ayes have it," said Olivia, with a chuckle. "What an amazing honor—thank you all. You know, I guess there is one other teensy little thing you could do."

"What is it, Madame President?" said the crowd.

Olivia nodded toward the heroes. "Destroy them."

As one, the crowd slowly turned. And then they attacked.

Chapter
29

When an Advanced Homerooms & Hall Passes encounter includes too many NPCs, it can become very logistically difficult to run. If you insist on putting your players in a crowded, chaotic situation—such as a flash mob or a Black Friday sale—make sure to keep things moving and try not to get too bogged down in the details.

—Excerpt from The Advanced Hall Master's Guide

❧

*a*ND SO THE BOLD heroes braced themselves for an onslaught. Nearly all of Pine Hill High School charged toward them in a frenzy, ready to tear them limb from limb.

"What do we do?" cried June.

"Defend ourselves," said Vela. "But do not injure anyone. Remember, our classmates are victims here too."

"Fight but don't hurt anybody. Got it," said Devis. The

thief drew his daggers, then quickly sheathed them again. "Wait, no, I don't."

"Just get to Olivia," cried Albiorix. "She's the only one who can end this madness."

The first of the crowd had made it to them. Brent Sydlowski leaped onto the stage and flung himself at Vela, who blocked his attack with her shield and kicked his feet out from under him, sending the jock sprawling.

Meanwhile, Thromdurr lowered his head and bull rushed his way through Sharad Marwah, Evan Cunningham, and Caleb Greene, scattering the smaller boys like bowling pins.

As the crowd converged on them, Devis deftly slid under the legs of a wild-eyed Jenny (from Jenny and the Critters) as she tried to claw at him but came up empty-handed.

Sorrowshade quickly clambered up the scaffolding on the stage ahead of a pack of clawing classmates. At the top, she shot an arrow. But the assassin wasn't aiming for anyone. Instead the arrow hit a spot on the back wall of the club, trailing a line of thin, silken elvish rope behind it. Sorrowshade quickly looped her end through the scaffolding and then threw her bow over the rope. She zip lined across the room, over the entranced crowd.

"Get behind me!" cried Albiorix to June. *"E dekaerer ma'rn a'ph aeri!"* The wizard launched a frostbolt that froze a rampaging Hope Kaufman in her tracks. She would thaw out shortly, none the worse for wear. Albiorix pressed onward, and June followed after him.

The scene was total chaos now as the party members picked their separate ways through the wild, hostile crowd, trying their best not to do lasting injury to their peers.

Olivia laughed at their efforts. "Look at you all. Scared to hurt them because you think they're real people! Pathetic."

"Why are you doing this, Olivia?" cried Vela as she stiff armed Marc Mansour out of the way and hopped over a prone Imani Booker.

"Because," said Olivia, "I can't let you finish this scenario. If you do, everyone from Bríandalör will be transported back to your own world. But one of you is destined to remain and rule this world by my side as Nerd King."

"Despite your villainy, I am flattered," cried Thromdurr, muscling his way through the clinging crowd. "But I reject your offer, Olivia, for I—"

"Not you, dummy!" shrieked Olivia. "Morton Blanc."

A dead-eyed Brother Auros walked to Olivia's side. She smiled sweetly at him.

"Morton's the perfect match for me."

"Are you kidding me?" cried June. "He's been brain-washed!"

"You're just jealous because he's not following you

371

around like a puppy dog anymore!" shrieked Olivia. *"D'o rav gaar!"*

"Why does everybody think we're dating?" said June. "Boys and girls can be friends without—"

June's words were cut off as a vicious bolt of green energy arced from Olivia's fingertips and struck June, blasting her off her feet. Albiorix, who had just finished freezing two members of Format of Distortion with twin frostbolts turned, horrified. He saw June lying on the ground, unconscious, her chest smoking.

"Oh no," cried Albiorix. "No, no, no, no, no . . ."

The wizard knelt to check her pulse.

"Ha ha!" cried Olivia. "Nailed her."

"Nice shot, Madame President," said Brother Auros in an empty monotone. "June Westray is stupid and boring and not even that pretty. She deserved to die."

"That's exactly what I've always thought!" cried Olivia. "But of course nobody ever listened to me."

"Enough of the poor me's, you dork," hissed Sorrowshade as she melted out of the shadows behind Olivia. "I'm going to give you something to really moan about."

The gloom elf loosed a black arrow that flew straight at Olivia Gorman's back. But in a flash of sparks, the shaft was knocked aside by the axe of Skegg the Surly. The dwarf warrior stood, slack-jawed and dead eyed, ready to protect Olivia from all harm.

"Surrender now, Olivia," cried Vela, shoving George Stedman aside with her shield. "You shall not win this fight."

As the good adventurers closed in around the warlock and her so-called Nerd King, the evil party—Tristane Trouvère, Calyxia, Azheena, and Skegg—all took up positions to defend them.

"Why am I even wasting my time with this?" said Olivia. "This world and everyone in it is just an illusion—figments of a fevered imagination. None of this actually even exists." She turned to Brother Auros and stroked his face. "But once I grasped that, I knew what I had to do. I used the power of the Malonomicon to create my own world. A world that makes sense. A world where you and I can finally be happy, my love."

Olivia knelt and quickly inscribed an arcane circle on the ground. Around it she began to scribble several odd algebraic equations.

"Morton, you and I shall reign forever in the Mathematical Plane," said Olivia.

She took Brother Auros's hand. And just as the adventuring party reached them, there was a blinding flash of green light, and the two of them—as well as Tristane Trouvère, Calyxia, Azheena, and Skegg the Surly—simply vanished.

Chapter 30

So you're done with the published scenarios and you want to create your own setting for Advanced Homerooms & Hall Passes. Well aren't you a little smarty-pants? We call that world building, chief. And when you're making up a homebrew AH&H setting, the first question you should ask yourself is: What makes this an awesome place for a nonadventure?

—*Excerpt from* The Advanced Hall Master's Guide

❧

"HELP ME!" CRIED ALBIORIX.

The hostile crowd had frozen in their tracks. The heroes turned to see Albiorix crouched by June Westray's side. She wasn't moving. The wizard's face looked ashen.

"Here," said Vela. "We still have one healing potion left."

She tossed Albiorix a flask of thick red liquid. He caught it and upended it into June's mouth.

A moment later June sat up, coughing hard. "You . . . nearly . . . drowned me. . . ."

Albiorix breathed a sigh of relief. "Sorry."

"What—what just happened?" said Marc Mansour. He blinked and rubbed his head.

Others were doing the same.

"Things are a little foggy right now," said Brent Sydlowski. "Did I just, um, try to kill you?"

"Afraid so," said Vela.

"Sorry," said Brent.

With Olivia gone, her mass hypnosis spell had dropped. The crowd's initial confusion gave way to fear. Being used as an evil warlock's mystical meat puppet was an intense experience that few high schoolers could wrap their heads around. The crowd's hysteria began to build—what if she came back?—and soon they were fleeing out every exit, eager to get as far away from the place as possible.

"Everyone, try to stay calm," said the ponytailed club manager, who had retaken the mic. "The cold, alien presence that invaded our minds, that robbed us of all autonomy, seems to be gone for now, and— You know what, forget this. I'm ghooooooost!"

He dropped the mic and ran, just like the rest, his ponytail flapping behind him. For the Monarch, it was another "all-ages show" gone awry.

Soon only the adventuring party was left in the empty music club. The place was eerily quiet now. With Albiorix's help, June was sitting up and sipping a green smoothie that he'd made her with the club's now-unattended smoothie machine. The healing potion had mostly healed her injuries, but she was still in intense pain from the vile, necromantic attack.

"Well, that was quite the Battle of the Bands upset," said Sorrowshade. "Better luck next year, Jenny and the Critters."

"A legendary anticlimax!" cried Thromdurr.

"It is not the end," said Vela. "We must find Olivia and save Brother Auros." The paladin pointed toward the arcane circle Olivia had left on the floor. "Albiorix, what does it mean?"

The wizard examined it. "Hmm, yeah, it looks like a sigil of teleportation. But I can't claim to understand all the math-y stuff around it."

Thromdurr took a look. "There is much here to be deciphered. May I?" He took Albiorix's notebook of lyrics and began to jot down what Olivia had written. Things like $2x - 8y + 5z = 18$ and $a = (2, 3)$.

"Anything?" said Albiorix.

"This part, here, appears to be the scalar equation of plane," said Thromdurr. "Such an equation defines a mathematical plane in three dimensions."

"Right," said Albiorix. "She mentioned something called the Mathematical Plane in her big bad-guy speech. Might be some sort of pocket dimension she created with her magic."

Vela shook her head. "Such power. Could Olivia create a whole new world using the Malonomicon?"

Albiorix shrugged. "I mean, we created this world by playing Homerooms & Hall Passes, didn't we?"

"Don't say that," said June weakly.

"Right. Sorry," said Albiorix. "It's real here."

"So then we use the Malonomicon to find Olivia and save Brother Auros," said Sorrowshade.

"No," said Vela. "The book is evil. It corrupts those who use it. You saw what it did to Olivia Gorman!"

"Full disclosure," said Devis. "I kind of like her slightly better now."

"Regardless," said Albiorix, "aside from the stuff written in Shadownese, we can't even read the Malonomicon. In the parts of the book I understood, I didn't see any spells for creating entire worlds, and we don't have time to repeat Olivia's demonic-language tutorial."

"So the villain is well and truly gone, then?" said Thromdurr.

"And we have no way of catching her," said Sorrowshade. "I feel the sweet sting of disappointment coming on. Oh yeah, that's the stuff. . . ."

"Maybe this could help?" said Devis. The thief held up a thick tome bound in dark purple leather with bright brass corners.

"Calyxia's spellbook!" cried Albiorix.

"You're welcome, Magic Man." Devis tossed the book to the wizard.

Albiorix nearly fumbled the catch. He quickly paged through it until he found what he was looking for. "Here we go! Dimensional door. This can open a mystical portal between any two points in the multiverse, provided you know exactly where you're actually going. Thanks to the sigil Olivia left behind, I think we do." Albiorix took a deep breath. "But . . . it's a really advanced spell. I'm not even sure I've got the power to cast it. I mean, I've never pulled off anything like this before. . . ."

Vela placed a hand on his shoulder. "We believe in you, old friend. We all saw what you did during the performance."

The rest of his companions nodded.

"You . . . can do it," said June quietly.

Albiorix nodded. "Okay. But even if I successfully open the dimensional door, we have no idea what lies ahead of us on the so-called Mathematical Plane. There's no guarantee anyone who travels there will be coming back."

"As ever, I would gladly lay down my own life to save an innocent," said Vela.

The paladin stepped forward.

"Certain death?" said Sorrowshade. "That's what our parents signed us up for, the day we were born. Besides, this might be our last chance to mop the floor with Tristane Trouvère and his goons. I'm in."

The gloom elf stepped forward.

"I shall not leave my stalwart math league teammate Morton Blanc to the vile depredations of the mad warlock Olivia Gorman," said Thromdurr. "Plus, where we are going, I suspect my mathematical skill may prove critical."

The barbarian stepped forward.

"Eh, I think I'll sit this one out. I've got some bio homework to finish for Monday," said Devis. "Kidding."

The thief stepped forward.

June slowly pulled herself to her feet. As she did, she winced in pain, clutching at the place where Olivia's spell had burned her flesh.

"I'm . . . coming too," said June. "Morton . . . Brother Auros was my friend first."

"June, I understand," said Albiorix. "Nobody can say you're not brave. But you aren't fully recovered. Please, you can't risk it."

"How many times do I have to say it? I am a member of this party too," said June. She was standing now, but she looked unsteady on her feet.

Albiorix took a deep breath. "Olivia almost killed you once already today. I'm—I'm afraid you could get hurt even worse. Maybe die."

"Same," said June.

And so the two of them argued back and forth until a decision was reached.

A crackle of blue energy split a strange colorless sky. The arcane portal spread and grew until at last the party of adventurers stepped through. Five Bríandalörian heroes—a paladin, a barbarian, an assassin, a thief, and a wizard—now stood upon an equally colorless plain, utterly flat as far as the eye could see.

Vela looked around at the odd, empty space. There wasn't much to see. "Where are we?"

Thromdurr smiled. "It appears to be some sort of strange metaphorical universe purely modeled on the principles of mathematics. Very Olivia Gorman!"

"Okay, but *where* are we?" said Albiorix.

"Hmm," said Thromdurr. "I believe we are the origin of the world. Coordinates: zero, zero, zero." He stamped his boot. "Behold."

At his foot, the others now noticed, was the intersection of two perpendicular lines, labeled x and y. A third line, labeled z, extended vertically upward to infinity. Devis tried to grab the vertical axis, but his fingers slipped right through it.

"Bah! You will not be able to grasp it, friend thief," said Thromdurr. "For a line only exists in one dimension. It has neither width nor—"

"Don't you dare try to teach me math!" cried Devis, plugging his ears with his fingers.

"Education is important," said Vela. "But time is of the essence, Thromdurr. We must make haste."

"As you say." Thromdurr checked his notes. "Among the equations Olivia scrawled upon the floor was a vector: $a = (2, 3)$. In mathematical terms, a vector is an object that has both direction and magnitude. In this case, if the origin is here, then we may determine the direction by solving—"

"Thromdurr, please just tell us which way to go," said Vela.

The barbarian nodded and eyed the x and y axes at his feet. He scribbled a few quick calculations in the notebook. Then he pointed. "Follow me!"

And so the party of brave heroes ventured forth across the bizarre environs of the Mathematical Plane, as odd a place as any they had yet visited in any of their countless adventures. Under Thromdurr's guidance, they traversed a range of rolling sine-wave hills and navigated a tangled forest of variables and coefficients until at last they came to what might only be described as a mountain. Yet this mountain was steeper and taller than any mountain had a right to be. It rose at a dizzying angle to what appeared to be an infinite height. Thromdurr described its incline as "asymptotic."

"Up there," said Sorrowshade, pointing.

High upon the impossibly steep slope stood a structure composed of impossibly perfect geometric figures—cones and cylinders and polyhedrons. It looked like a fortress.

And so the heroes tied themselves together at the waist and, using their dungeoneering ropes and pitons, began to make the nigh-vertical ascent toward what Devis dubbed the Math Castle.

Olivia Gorman sat upon her throne, the god creator of the Mathematical Plane. Her Nerd King, Brother Auros, sat in silence on a (slightly shorter) throne at her right hand, his eyes fully dilated. On either side of them stood four hardened adventurers—Tristane Trouvère, Calyxia, Azheena, and Skegg the Surly—a royal guard of sorts. They were perfectly motionless, staring ahead at nothing. Their minds were still ensorcelled by the warlock's dark magic.

Olivia was finishing a long anecdote of injustice and hardship.

". . . And that's why I should've won the third-grade poetry contest," said Olivia. "Not Lucy Bennett!"

"How awful," said Brother Auros in a flat monotone. "The sheer unfairness of it all. Everyone has always treated you so poorly for no reason, Olivia. Lucy Bennett should be destroyed."

"Yeah," said Olivia. "You're probably right."

"All of humanity should be destroyed," said Brother Auros.

"I guess I could?" Olivia sighed and drummed her fingers upon the arm of the throne. "I guess I can do anything I want now. If I'm being totally honest . . . it's actually a little bit boring."

The warlock frowned.

Just then there came a mighty crash as the doors of her throne room burst open. Olivia saw an imposing sight at the opposite end of the chamber: Vela the paladin, Thromdurr the barbarian, Sorrowshade the assassin, Devis the thief, and Albiorix the wizard, standing shoulder to shoulder, ready for the final battle. Olivia smiled.

"Olivia Gorman!" cried Vela. "We have come to save Brother Auros. Relinquish him now, and we will leave you in peace."

Olivia crinkled her nose. "Brother what now? Ew, no, I really don't like that. His name is Morton Blanc. Oooh, or maybe I'll change it to something even cooler, like . . . Dax Shatter!"

"I am Dax Shatter," said Brother Auros.

"So anyway. I can't let you take Dax," said Olivia. "His destiny is to reign by my side for all eternity as an immortal Nerd god."

Thromdurr spat. "You have no right to rule over such a place. For you dishonored the sacred Spirit of Mathematics!"

Olivia's eyes narrowed. "I've had just about enough out of you, Doug. Eliminate them. Now."

At her command, the catatonic Tristane Trouvère, Calyxia, Azheena, and Skegg the Surly instantly sprang to life. The villains turned and charged the party.

"*Tyael ael e raekyntaetk ma'rn na' phsh ha'oi,*" said Calyxia, who, even in her brainwashed state, had a number of simple offensive spells committed to memory. A bolt of lightning crackled from her fingers and arced toward the heroes.

"*Ya'ois lvirr aelt'n ka'aetk na' za'sg voiddh,*" incanted Albiorix from his own spellbook. He countered the sorceress's spell, and the bolt fizzled harmlessly away into nothing.

"Raaaagh!" cried a dead-eyed Skegg the Surly. The dwarf raised his axe and charged at Thromdurr.

The barbarian took a deep breath and stood stone still. At the last possible second, Thromdurr raised his hammer, and the dwarf's axe came down with a thunderous crack against its haft. Skegg struck again, and again. Each time Thromdurr backed away, out of reach, or dodged or blocked.

The berserker was biding his time, conserving his energy, thinking it through, choosing his moment. . . .

Meanwhile, Tristane Trouvère drew his rapier and advanced toward Vela in a fencing stance. He lunged and she parried. He lunged again, and she deflected the thrust with her shield. Just then, the paladin heard a whistling sound over her shoulder. She turned to see a bolt from Azheena's crossbow flying straight for her head.

Yet, with an improbable clatter, something dark knocked the bolt off course and sent it spinning harmlessly away. Vela blinked as she realized what had happened. From across the room, Sorrowshade had somehow bull's-eyed the ranger's own flying bolt right out of the air with an arrow of her own. The gloom elf smiled. It was the shot of a lifetime.

Azheena scowled and reached for another bolt. Her eyes widened as she came up empty-handed. Her quiver was gone. She turned to see Devis, standing twenty paces away, twirling it on his finger. The thief smiled and shrugged.

Another arrow from Sorrowshade pinned Azheena's army jacket to the wall, effectively immobilizing her.

Meanwhile Albiorix countered each of Calyxia's spells, fiery bolts, and blasts of acid, as quickly as she could cast them (which was very quickly indeed). The wizard was holding his own, keeping her occupied, but if they wanted to stop Olivia Gorman, he would need to do more. He had to take Calyxia out of the fight. Albiorix discarded his own spellbook and opened Calyxia's.

Meanwhile, Skegg the Surly took swing after swing at Thromdurr, which the barbarian dodged or deflected. The dwarf reared back once more, and at last, lightning quick, Thromdurr spun and put all his might into one punishing upward blow of his war hammer. The hammer connected to Skegg's skull with a brutal *crack*, and the dwarf's head snapped back. Skegg wobbled on his feet for a moment before falling to the ground, limp and unconscious.

With a flick of her wrist, Vela used the cross guard of her longsword to disarm Tristane Trouvère of his rapier. Before the bard could react, Vela body slammed him with her shield and pinned him helplessly against the wall of the throne room.

"Wa'avl ta'z ha'oisi e yivkiya'k ha'oi da'sat," said Albiorix as he bent every atom of his will toward channeling the wild, unfathomable energies that suffuse creation into a recognizable shape. He felt sweat beading on his forehead from the effort as a swirling blue tendril of magical energy wrapped itself around Calyxia. With a bright blue flash, the sorceress seemed to wink out of existence. But she wasn't gone. Albiorix the wizard had become the tenth in history to cast instant hedgehogification.

And just like that, the evil party was defeated. The

chamber was suddenly quiet. The only sound was Azheena frantically tugging at her jacket to get free, too stupid in her hypnotized state to take it off. Olivia sat on her throne, drumming her fingers. She looked dreadfully bored by the whole thing.

"And so your minions have been defeated," cried Vela, who still held Tristane Trouvère immobilized against the wall. "Surrender now, and you will be spared!"

The other four heroes, Sorrowshade, Devis, Albiorix, and Thromdurr, began to advance toward Olivia's throne.

"Ha!" cried Olivia. "Surrender? *Surrender!* They were mere pawns. A distraction. I'm *glad* you beat them up, honestly, because they were all total jerks to me before I hypnotized them. Good riddance."

"If you will not give up, we will defeat you as well," said Vela.

The rest of the party charged the throne.

"Pshaw!" said Olivia. "You still don't get it? This whole thing was a trap, you morons." The warlock whipped out her smartphone, and almost lazily, she began to scroll through her photos of the Malonomicon's spells. She paused. "Ah, here we go."

"Albiorix, stop her!" cried Vela.

"On it!" cried Albiorix. The wizard began to cast a spell. *"Wa'avl ta'z ha'oisi e—"*

But before he could finish, Olivia launched a wicked bolt of green energy at the wizard, knocking Albiorix off his feet. Calyxia's spellbook flew from his hands and skidded across the floor to the foot of the throne.

Without looking up, Olivia scrolled through more images till she settled on a different spell. "And now this," she said. *"Nav I'g sa'rs ka tiddar aer dro vaerr."*

Instantly, the other three heroes ran headlong into an invisible wall—the same impenetrable barrier they had encountered at the math league championship. It separated them from Olivia and Brother Auros. They knew from experience that there was truly no way past. Sorrowshade cursed. Devis bent one of his daggers against the force field, searching in vain for some weak point. Thromdurr knelt to check on Albiorix. He found the wizard unconscious but, thankfully, still breathing.

The warlock Olivia Gorman stood and slowly stretched. "I left the Monarch merely to lure you here. I knew you'd decipher my clues and follow me. Thanks for doing what I wanted without being hypnotized, you idiots. Now the Mathematical Plane will be your prison until the end of time."

She nodded to Brother Auros. He stood and took her hand.

"If you'll excuse me, Dax Shatter and I have to go. We'll

leave the five of you trapped here while we return to Suburbia, where I will rule unchallenged. No more meddlesome adventurers trying to interfere. Nerds win. Olivia Gorman wins. In the end, I was smarter than all of you. I thought of every detail."

"Not *every* detail," said a disembodied voice.

Olivia froze. She looked around. "Who said that?"

June Westray removed the cap of invisibility and appeared right beside the warlock. "That'd be me."

"How did you—"

But before Olivia could finish her sentence, June attacked. Not with a weapon. Surely not with any magic spell. She attacked with a plastic cup full of green smoothie. June launched its contents at Olivia Gorman, splattering her whole left side the color of kale.

Olivia blinked. "A smoothie? You hoped to stop me, the most powerful warlock of all time, with . . . a smoothie?" Olivia began to laugh. *"A smoothie!"*

"Check your phone," said June.

Olivia stopped laughing. She looked at her phone. She used her clean sleeve to wipe off the screen. The phone was dead. Olivia gasped.

June smiled. "Oh, yeah. I know exactly what green smoothie does to a phone. And no phone, no Malonomicon, right? It's going to be pretty hard to get out of Math World here without any of your magic."

In her shock, Olivia let all of her spells—the invisible barrier, mass hypnosis—drop.

"I . . . I was just joking," said Olivia. "This was all a big joke. No hard feelings about class president or math league, or anything. I'm just . . . Things got out of hand. The transition to high school has been really tough for me. You understand, right?"

"Funny thing about math," said June. "You claim to be so good at it, but you can't even count. There aren't five members of this adventuring party. There are six."

Olivia's eyes flitted to Calyxia's spellbook at the foot of the throne. She lunged for it. But as she did, Vela the Valiant knocked her out cold with a right hook to the jaw.

Chapter 31

You've played your campaign. You've had your fun. But how do you know when it's over? A good Hall Master will see when the players have grown and changed and earned their goals. That's when you end it. Or when everyone accidentally Blows It and is eliminated from the game.

—*Excerpt from* The Advanced Hall Master's Guide

❧

"WHAT'S . . . WHERE AM I?" said Brother Auros as he looked around groggily.

"It's, like, another world, but made of, um, comically literal math stuff and . . . honestly it's kinda too hard for me to even explain," said June.

"Our minds were ensorcelled," said Tristane Trouvère, who was being held in an armlock by Sorrowshade.

"Nailed it, pretty boy," said Sorrowshade. "And since

you may not remember everything that happened, I want to be clear: we kicked your butts. Once and for all, we beat you."

"Yeah, right," said Azheena. "There's no way you—"

"Use your eyes," said Tristane. "She's right."

The situation was apparent. The villains' weapons had been taken. Skegg lay on the ground, still unconscious. Calyxia had apparently been transformed into a hedgehog. There was no question about it. The evil adventurers had been well and truly defeated.

"We surrender, then," said Tristane Trouvère, who managed to wiggle free from Sorrowshade's hold. The bard dusted his clothing and fluffed his hair. "If your party is as honorable as you claim to be, you must accept that and show us mercy."

"Did I ever once claim I was honorable?" said Sorrowshade.

"We accept your surrender," said Vela.

". . . And now you must show us mercy," repeated Tristane Trouvère. A bit of panic had crept into his voice.

Vela crossed her arms and said nothing.

"Brother Auros," said June, "I think we need your help."

Brother Auros followed June to where Thromdurr crouched by Albiorix's side. Olivia's spell had injured the wizard badly.

June blinked back tears. "Is he . . . ?"

Thromdurr shook his head. "The wizard is holding on for now, but he needs healing. Quickly."

Brother Auros nodded. "Okay. I'm not a very good acolyte, but I'll do my best." He knelt beside Albiorix and said a quiet prayer in Celaestine to the Powers of Light. As he spoke, Albiorix's body was wreathed in a gentle golden glow.

The wizard sat up, then immediately grabbed his chest. "Ow."

June smiled. "Told you this mission was too dangerous for you."

She hugged Albiorix, who winced again. But he was smiling.

"And so, once again, evil has been vanquished. Our ally rescued. The world saved," said Vela. "I increase our adventure grade to an A-plus. Well done, comrades."

"Let's blow this dorky pocket dimension," said Devis. He tossed Calyxia's spellbook to Albiorix.

Meanwhile, Sorrowshade smashed Olivia's ruined phone against the arm of the throne for good measure and pocketed what was left. The gloom elf smiled at Tristane Trouvère. "Oh, and enjoy spending the rest of your eternity in this place. Hope you like linear equations."

"I like them!" said Thromdurr.

"Wait!" cried Tristane. "You can't just *leave* us here."

"We can't?" said Sorrowshade. "Why's that?"

"Because—because you can't!" cried Tristane. "Devis, don't let them do this. We were friends once!"

Devis cocked his head. "Were we?"

Albiorix ignored the bard as he paged through Calyxia's spellbook to find dimensional door.

"C'mon, guys," cried Tristane. "Seriously?"

Sorrowshade nodded. "Interesting argument. Yet somehow I find myself unpersuaded. I thought you were a master of oratory."

The bard turned to Vela. "What about you? You're a good person! What about your code of honor?"

"Mercy has its place," said Vela. "But saving you puts many others at risk."

"But," said Tristane. "But—"

Azheena stepped forward. "If you take us with you, we swear we'll never mess with Suburbia again."

The heroes looked at each other. And once all the evil adventurers, even the hedgehog Calyxia, had sworn this same oath, Albiorix opened a dimensional door back to the Realm of Suburbia.

The silence of the empty music club was broken by a crackling sound. A mystical portal yawned, and eleven adventurers (one of them a hedgehog) passed through it. The warlock Olivia Gorman was not with them, though.

Her dark powers were deemed too dangerous. Better to exile her on the Mathematical Plane where she couldn't hurt anyone. Perhaps in time she could be rehabilitated.

"Kind of interesting how the main bad guy was beaten, yet again, by little old me," said June. "It's almost like maybe, just maybe, I'm a better adventurer than any of you."

"Agreed," said Thromdurr. "You are the best of us, June Westray!"

"Except for me," said Devis. "Obviously, I'm pretty great."

Vela looked around the dingy music club and sighed. "It is sweet sorrow to depart the Realm of Suburbia once again. I shall miss this strange world."

"Nae me," said Skegg, who seemed extra surly. "I'm tired of this dump. Tired of boring school. Tired of stealing electronic goods. Tired of shaving four times day." The dwarf scratched frantically at his neck. "I just want to hit stuff with me axe again."

"If ever we catch wind of any of you terrorizing the Realm of Suburbia, or Bríandalör either, for that matter," said Vela, "our retribution will be swift and total."

"Understood," said Calyxia, who had turned back into a human and only had her clothing thanks to the exceptional consideration of Vela the Valiant. "May I have my spellbook back?"

"Nah, I think I'll keep it," said Albiorix. "Lot of interesting stuff in here."

Calyxia sighed. Azheena whistled. A moment later, a huge, dark shape came crashing through the window of the Monarch, shattering it for the second time in as many months. Amarok shook the glass shards off his fur and licked her face.

"Yuck and aww," said Sorrowshade.

"Everyone ready?" said Albiorix. "One last dimensional door will take us home to Bríandalör."

The four villains nodded. Amarok whined.

"Wait, where is Tristane Trouvère?" said Thromdurr.

Tristane Trouvère, expert of misdirection, had managed to slip away from the group to make his escape. Sure, he'd given his word, but any actor worth his salt knew that words hardly mattered. It was the feeling behind them. And he didn't feel like giving up. He would disappear and regroup, maybe find another party of pliable dupes. He would keep running the scams that had worked so well on the simple folk of this world. And he would make a fortune doing it.

The bard leaped across the rooftops of Hibbettsfield, from the Monarch to the pharmacy next door. Once again he was alone and free of an all obligations. Probably wouldn't be the last time. He was nothing if not a survivor.

"Stop right there!"

Devis the thief had appeared in the bard's path.

Tristane Trouvère skidded to a halt. "Why, hello, Goblin-face," said the bard. "Apologies—I don't have my rapier, so a rooftop duel is out of the question. Next time." Tristane Trouvère pivoted to dash in the other direction.

Devis sighed. "I don't want to fight you."

Tristane Trouvère didn't run. Instead, he raised an eyebrow. "Come to join me at last?"

Devis nodded. "Yep. I tried being a good guy. I *really* did. But . . . there's just no money in it. Once a thief, always a thief, I guess."

Tristane Trouvère smiled and placed a hand on Devis's shoulder. The pair of them gazed out over the modest suburban landscape of Hibbettsfield. "It's your nature. It's good that you finally understand that. We are who we are. We steal. We swindle. We cheat." The bard turned. "Come, let's go, old friend. Before those fools catch up to us."

Tristane Trouvère started forward and immediately fell flat on his face. He looked down in horror to see that his shoelaces had been tied together. Devis smiled.

"We also lie, right?" said the thief. "What can I say? I learned from the best."

The thief hooked his arm through the knotted laces and began to drag the helpless bard back across the rooftop, toward his waiting companions.

Chapter 32

Without the contributions of the following people, elves, dwarves, gnomes, goblins, and extraplanar entities, *Advanced Homerooms & Hall Passes* would not have been possible. A huge thank-you to Adnon Konalt, Anarzee Valsandora, Annoloth, Arilemna Paxalim, Artin Facaryn, Awskar Brittleneck, Baerinda Oridove, Baern Grimbow, Baxir the Plaguemaster, Bellamin, Brekar Gloom, Chancellor Reinfred, Countess Heloys, Dame Adeline, Dhodeath the Chaosmaster, Dilya Uridan, Dramiloth, Erzaan, Ewrozis the Paranoid, Grand Duke Hewet, Grand Duke Steve, Gunter Belmont, Houzius the Decomposer, Huckabee Jarack, Ilmadia Yinmys, Itzen Forewatcher, Jastran, Kharszis Moonrage, Khoynea, King Marmaducus, Laamtora Sarbanise, Lord Theobaldus, Maeralya Iarna, Maerstug, Maiden Grissel, Melsoh, Mike Dexter, Monk Ranulphus, Must, Ogloraan, Podrick of the Nackle Tribe, Portia Abbot, Prince Umfrey, Ratgrum Amberbuster, Reeve Ysabel, Rogruzar, Rolf, the

King in the North, the Saint of Eternity, Salmuros, Sygg
Strongfeather, Shreeg, Strakhar the Hollow, Shrirchah
Blooddust, Squall Gantar, Strazor Shadowend, Talmed,
Thrargreat Duskrock, Thratruz Hazeblade, Thrio, Vom-
near Oakbender, Will Stutely, Xah Redwound, Xoqur
Siphon, Xorganath, Xutzan Largefoot, Yiozar the Reaper,
Yodan Void, and Zekk.

—Excerpt from the "Special Thanks" section of
The Advanced Hall Master's Guide

☙❧

FIVE ROAD-WEARY ADVENTURERS BURST through the doors of the Wyvern's Wrist tavern in the hamlet of Pighaven. They had just completed their seventh adventure in as many days: driving off the vicious hobgoblins that had overrun poor Lady Amelina's ancestral lands. She had rewarded them handsomely, and the party was flush with gold; and Thromdurr even had a cool new scar down the right side of his face. All in all, it was a very successful day in the Realm of Bríandalör.

As they entered the tavern, the heroes were surprised to find that they were the only patrons in the place.

"Can it be?" cried Thromdurr. "The common room is empty!"

Vela beamed. "I think that means we did every quest. Brother Auros, your healing magic came in very handy today."

"Thanks," said Brother Auros. "It's such a relief to be going on adventures instead of, you know, doing petty crimes and stealing credit card numbers. Sorrowshade, maybe you should compose an ode to commemorate our exploits."

"Shut up," said Sorrowshade the assassin turned bard. "But okay. I guess this is what multiclassing is all about." The gloom elf sighed and unslung her lyre. She began to strum and sing:

"We did the quests
We are the bests
We never wear vests—"

Frumhilde the innkeeper cut her off. "You lot drove off all my customers, is what ye did! Mysterious strangers hanging round with old maps account for most of my business."

"Hang on. Is *this* a quest?" said Devis. "Revamping the Wyvern's Wrist menu and coming up with some drink specials to bring in a hipper, younger non-quest-giving crowd?" Devis scanned the place and stroked his jaw. "What if we changed the name to w & w provisions, all lowercase?"

Frumhilde merely glared. She turned toward Vela.

"Parcel came for ye, miss."

Vela's eyes lit up as Frumhilde tossed her a thin envelope. It was sealed with a wax sunburst.

"It is a letter from the Order of the Golden Sun," said Vela. "I submitted an account of our victory at Battle of the Bands over Tristane Trouvère and his party. Truly a miracle if ever there was one!" She tore open the envelope. But her smile faded as she read. "'We regret to inform you that your request for promotion to Grand Seneschal of the Gleaming Sword has been denied.'"

The paladin put the letter down. She was silent for a moment.

Thromdurr put his hand on Vela's shoulder. "Worry not. You may not always get the recognition you deserve. But we were there. We know what happened."

Vela smiled and squeezed his hand.

"Maybe friendship is the real miracle?" said Sorrowshade. "Blech. I can't believe I just said that. I *really* don't like being happy."

"Next time, just tell the order you defeated the immortal vampire lord Zahd von Stranovich," said Devis. "I bet they'd eat something like that up."

The others looked at him. The thief shrugged.

Just then, two more travelers entered the Wyvern's Wrist: one, a wizard of considerable power; the other, a strange outlander from a faraway realm.

"Oh, man, have you guys even *seen* the flying castle thingie?" said June.

The heroes looked at each other, confused.

"Er, which one?" said Vela.

June put both her hands on her head. "There's more than one?"

"Of course!" said Thromdurr. "There are eight flying castles in the Realm of Bríandalör."

"And legend tells of a ninth that disappeared beyond the clouds long ago," said Albiorix.

"Dude!" cried June. "We've got to find that ninth castle. And we've got to investigate the rumors of mysterious lights and strange chanting in Goblinthicket Woods. Oh, and that tower full of skeletons we passed on the way home without going in."

"Pace yourself," said Devis.

Sorrowshade shook her head. "Imagine being impressed by a flying castle. What a hayseed."

"Not to rain on your parade, but fighting random skeletons probably isn't really the best use of anyone's time," said Brother Auros.

"You're right, you're right," said June. "I've got time." She checked her phone. "Oh no, I don't. I've got to get back. My mom's going to kill me."

"On it," said Albiorix. *"Lin di qoiln a'vit oiv e vaedlaea'ter va'a's saekyn ta'z ha'oi."*

The wizard freed his mind from the shackles of the material and focused his will to channel the mysterious arcane forces that suffuse reality to open a dimensional door back to the Realm of Suburbia. Through the shimmering hole in space, a nondescript strip mall parking lot was visible.

"Okay, later, guys," said June. She quickly hugged Vela, Devis, Thromdurr, Sorrowshade, and Brother Auros.

"Can you DVR the next episode of *Crescent City Mob* for me?" asked Brother Auros.

"Sure thing," said June. She turned to Albiorix.

"I'll see you in class, Monday morning," said Albiorix.

"Don't forget the League of Nations essay," said June. "It's due this week."

"Oh, right!" said Albiorix, slapping his forehead. He had totally forgotten the League of Nations essay.

With his ability to freely travel between the two realms, Albiorix had decided to keep attending Pine Hill High School. The others thought he was crazy.

June gave Albiorix a peck on the cheek, and she stepped through the portal, which disappeared in a flash of blue light.

"Ye mind not opening magic portals right in the middle of my tavern?" said Frumhilde.

"Sorry," said Albiorix.

Frumhilde blinked. "No, no. I'm sorry. Sometimes I think I push people away before they can get too close."

"Huh," said Albiorix, turning toward his companions. "Well, anyway, the back room is free. Who's ready to play?"

The others looked at him, aghast.

"Albiorix, you can't be serious," said Vela.

Albiorix grinned. "I am. The game is called Octagono, and I've been working on it for a while now."

And so a group of friends spent an evening playing a prototype board game that one of them had invented. On the face of it, it may not have been a particularly fun game—though it had flashes of brilliance here and there—but they tried their best to help him make it better. Or at least they tried their best to make each other laugh. And in its way, this was a sort of miracle too.